T. (Trudy) Gertler was born in 1946 ⸻ ⸻ up in Miami. She has studied playwr⸻ ⸻ ⸻ ⸻⸻ing, and has made her living by freelance copy-editing and making educational tapes.

ELBOWING THE SEDUCER (1948) is her first full-length novel and is currently being adapted for a film. She is the author of two unpublished screenplays and a short story, *In Case of Survival*, which was selected for *The Best American Short Stories 1980*.

She lives in New York where she is working on a second novel.

T. Gertler

ELBOWING THE SEDUCER

First published in Great Britain in Abacus by
Sphere Books Ltd 1986
30–32 Gray's Inn Road, London WC1X 8JL
Copyright © 1984 by T. Gertler
First published in the United States by Random House, Inc., New
York, and simultaneously in Canada by Random House of Canada
Limited, Toronto

*Grateful acknowledgement is made to the following for permission to
reprint previously published material:*

Atheneum Publishers, Inc.: Quotation from "Black Maps", in *Darker*
by Mark Strand. Copyright © 1970 by Mark Strand. Used with
permission of Atheneum Publishers.
Cherry Lane Music Publishing Co., Inc.: Lyrics from "I'm Goin'
Away", by Alan Greene. Copyright © 1964 by Clara Music Publishing
Corp. Used by permission.
Harvard University Press: Excerpts from *The Poems of Emily
Dickinson*, ed. by Thomas H. Johnson. Copyright © 1951 © 1955, 1979,
1983 by the President and Fellows of Harvard College. Reprinted by
permission of the publishers and the Trustees of Amherst College.

Printed and bound in Great Britain by
Collins, Glasgow

FOR MY MOTHER AND FATHER
AND FOR R.D., M.D., c̄ GRAVITY

You can walk
believing you cast
a light around you.
But how will you know?

—MARK STRAND

Accept the premise, you'll enjoy the bit.

—DAVID LETTERMAN

n his sleep his hands, which were small, curled into fists. In the morning he woke and found them that way. He thought he never dreamed, though some nights, turning beneath the blanket, he cried out strings of words. His wife—or, as he thought of her, the mother of his child—lay beside him, nursing a dim tickle of passion. At the sudden twist of terror on his sleeping face, her eyes startled open, searching the ceiling.

He disliked breakfast, a meal she found comforting. She contented herself with watching him scowl at his coffee, black, no sugar. Scowling made him look as dangerous as he could, which wasn't very dangerous at all. He looked, and he knew it, reassuring. In his early forties, thin, with fine sharp features and the beginnings of parenthetical lines around his mouth, he had calculating, good-humored brown eyes and an uncombed abundance of curly brown hair whitened at the temples: a professor. But no, his lean body, the spareness of his frame, the nervous abrupt movements he made with his hard slim arms stamped him as someone outside a cloistered life. His ambition, to leave a large mark on the world—a sign, not a scar—made him move restlessly. He might have been a sculptor. Still, the aura of teacher lingered about him. He was a medium for talent, not a possessor of it. His name was Howard Ritchie and he wanted to make it memorable.

Suzanne, his wife, ate toast and bright marmalade on carmine red stoneware from France. She had once been lovely in a sweet tight way. At forty she was battling the softness of middle age,

3

counting on good facial structure and a dazed girlishness to see her through. Between bites she wiped her mouth with a blue cloth napkin—he disapproved of paper ones—and watched her smart husband read the *Times*, which he did in a certain order: first the book review, then the front page, then the editorial pages, then nothing more since he was already, as usual, late for the work he did to support the two of them, their child, his second ex-wife, and his two ex-children. These last, having grown up mostly without him, followed their mother's example and hated him. Because he paid for part of their home, food, clothing, doctors, and schools, because he sent them reasonably generous checks on holidays and their birthdays, they hated him; it was as simple as that. In turn he disliked them because they weren't his any longer, could never again be his.

For his families, he worked at a university as an editor and teacher, jobs he couldn't finish during the day but continued through the spirited night, which was why he was late in the morning: he didn't get enough sleep. The perpetual weary edge this gave him attracted certain women. He recognized the effect and exploited it. Courting and chasing after and confessing to these women, he couldn't finish his work during the day because he was too busy preparing himself for it. He considered his affairs as therapeutic necessities to revitalize him for work, his calling, midwife to literature.

He told the women: Sex is one thing, my family is another; I will never lose my child, I will never allow that to happen. This child, by Suzanne, had an earnestness Howard defined as artistic temperament. Matty was seven and resembled pictures of her father at that age. She had already written two poems about God with no misspellings. She had pinched a statuette of Charlie Chaplin out of clay. It was clearly Charlie Chaplin because of the hat and the cane. Through her Howard worshiped his own hopes; she would make the world bow down. He wanted to keep her brave, he wanted to protect her memory of him.

He spent extended lunch hours in strange bedrooms, lying on, under, and beside the women who found him irresistible. Afternoon sun streaked between the slats of blinds onto parquet floors, decent Oriental rugs, the litter of his clothing around unfamiliar beds. Each time he took one of these women in his arms, he believed he was conquering death in himself. Each time he fell back exhausted in a new bed, he wondered what else he could try. A woman's long hair, black, brown, whatever, hid his wrist. A woman kissed the light-haired hollow under his arm. He thought, Who is she? What did I want to be when I was sixteen? A woman bit tenderly at his fingertip. He thought the women were as implacable as death. He kissed them, he made them murmur, he made them glad. In their arms he relished his privacy; afterward, lighting a cigarette, he inhaled the old dread. He thought, I'm tired, so tired; and he rubbed the inside corners of his eyes.

He drank much more than he should have, quantities of good Scotch that lifted him to an amber forgetfulness. He became so happy he wept. Once, after six toasts, his own, he passed out in the middle of an important dinner party, also his own, at a restaurant specializing in painless lobster killing. The guests—a sexually ambiguous novelist in rawhide; his underfed groupie deseptumized by cocaine and the sere air of vicarious success; an agent, appropriately walleyed, rumored to have been the lover of a daughter of a lover of Simone de Beauvoir, or was it Colette; another agent, a sober exquisite woman joined at either hip to the two preceding guests, having been wedged between them like an extra book on an already organized shelf; and a literary critic with severe taste and cheekbones, whose new weekly spot on a local TV news show was the reason for the celebration—all observed his right arm sinking into spinach quiche. The critic said, "Unoriginal, but not without style." The novelist challenged the critic to an arm-wrestling contest, the groupie and the exquisite agent went off to the bathroom to admire each other's breasts, and the remaining agent contemplated both the fallen editor and the dessert tray while sucking a prime rib. A waiter asked if there was anything he could do. The critic, having declined to arm-wrestle, hauled Howard through fresh snow to the dank backseat of a Checker cab and brought him home.

Another time, after eight whiskies and six pretzel rods on

5

an April afternoon, he returned to his office and worked on galleys with shivering concentration for fifteen eternal minutes before asking his secretary, Gail, to please turn on the heat, please. "It's on, Howard," she said. While two writers and an illustrator waited in the reception area down the hall, he counted seconds on his watch and tried to find his pulse. This took a long time. Finally, one of the writers, who had driven in from Massachusetts two days earlier to begin a new life in the city, knocked on the door, waited a polite beat, then went in. He saw Howard Ritchie, editor, lecturer, author of helpful goading rejection letters, clutching his neck and muttering to himself.

"You okay?" the writer asked.

"There's no pulse anywhere." This in muted panic.

The writer had delivered his former lover's setter bitch of six puppies. He didn't hesitate to place two fingers on the New York editor's neck. "There it is, see?" He was rewarded with the rare and beautiful smile Howard usually bestowed on unattainable attractive women.

"I'm Vincent Bask," the writer said, holding out his hand.

"Ah yes, a remarkable novel," Howard said, and he vomited into Bask's hand.

He walked with a slight forward tilt of his right side, lifting the shoulder, leaning into a nonexistent wind. Though strong, he could look fragile. This was effective: people forgave his insults, tardiness, forgetfulness when he offered a suddenly pale childlike face to their expected abuse. "Oh Howard," they would say and lightly slap his shoulder, "forget it." Often the problem was that he *had* forgotten—an appointment, a phone call, a birthday, a promise, a small loan. Not all those slighted were forgiving; some demanded explanations, forcing from him a mumbled charm and part of a repertoire of ethnic jokes he provided complete with accents. "So God answers, 'Listen, you t'ink you got troubles? I had a son . . .'" His wife, trying to understand him, found he eluded her; for no apparent reason except the joy of change itself, he changed from husband to child to father to monster to lover.

6

And, unfairer still, she believed he understood her completely. She told him so.

"I'm going to study French," she said.

"Good."

"Tuesday and Thursday evenings at NYU."

"Best of luck."

"Is there any reason I shouldn't?"

"None, dear heart."

She didn't study French. She knew that he knew that she didn't want to. What she wanted was to be interesting to him. She took Tuesday-night mythology instead.

One of his lovers, naked, cross-legged, peeling a tangerine on a flipout foam sofa bed, asked, "What about your wife? Does she have other men?"

"No," he said, expelling smoke. "I wish she did. It might perk up her life."

"Smug. How can you be so sure about her?"

Referring to the tangerine: "Put that down." Then, reaching between the two crossed legs: "Maybe I should introduce her to somebody."

Her hips had begun to broaden. Her belly, once a sloped landscape relieved by two prominent pelvic knobs, had softened, dropped; the image he had of it now was that of a suspension bridge strung to the high, newly padded knobs. Ah, to continue the metaphor, he thought, and dipped two fingers into the warm bay of her sex. "Wife," he whispered, and learned from the utterance that he was drunk. Her head, averted, lay on his pillow. From the middle of the bed, where he sat between her legs, he watched her. He knew that being watched embarrassed her. His fingers disappeared slowly, and he waited.

A moan triumphed over her embarrassment. She fidgeted, coughed. He kept his fingers inside her. He could do this forever, outwait her; the length of a man's patience was what determined potency. He hoped he would remember this afterward, to write it down.

7

"Do you ever think about another man?" he asked. When she didn't answer, he persisted. "Do you?"

"Howard."

"Do you?"

Pinned to the pillow, she said with a sniffle, "Of course not."

"I didn't ask if you *had* another man, I asked if you thought about it."

She twisted under his double probing. "Is that Matty calling?"

"She's asleep."

"No, her tummy hurt all day. I think she's up." She sat up, edging away from him.

"Not this time." With his free hand he gently pushed her down. Courtly dominance, he thought. He smelled a tangerine.

"Her tummy," she protested, and sat up again.

He slammed her back down on the bed. She gave a small surprised cry of "Oh!" as she landed. Like a bloodhound who has followed an escaped convict's footprints through meadow and swamp, only to lose the scent at a mud bank along a river, he lifted his head and sniffed the air, his nostrils quivering, his forehead furrowed in a houndlike droop. He saw, curved over the scent-devouring river, a gray steel bridge across which, with puffs of white steam, a train ate its way into the distance. He wanted to shout, "Come back, come back," but he knew what would emerge would be a wordless mournful howl.

He withdrew his fingers from her with an abruptness that made her cry "Oh!" again and clamp her legs together. He covered her body with his own, kicked her legs apart with his knee. "Damn it," he said as her thighs closed on his knee. He grabbed a stiff leg and yanked it up to his shoulder, a boy snapping a wishbone. He wanted her to kiss him. She pushed at his shoulders to unbalance him, and he had to release her leg to capture her hands. He pulled them to rest above her head, holding both her wrists in one of his hands while the other returned for the fugitive leg. When he finally had her accessible to him, he pressed his mouth on hers and met with lips that seemed soldered together. He could feel her clenched teeth through her lips. Grimly, silently, he tried to enter her. In high school algebra he could never make

8

the equation balance; one half, bloated, unfactored, indecipherable, always dragged the other down. Since then he believed he was forever excluded from understanding something essential. He was halted at the curled edges of a mystery as homely as an omelet. He heard the plaints of bedsprings and the deadly anger of breathing. Her resistance astonished him. Each time he drove into her and was repelled, he trusted that he must go on. He had slung her updrawn leg on his shoulder; her foot dangled at his back. She pounded his back with her heel. A great baritone, he was being pelted with flowers—whole bushes, in fact. He ignored the first blows and continued his siege of her. He would have to decide what to sing for an encore. The blows intensified, and at last one, a vital assault above his kidney, provided a passage of pain through which he glimpsed the spectacle of himself, a man raping his wife. Stunned, he let her go.

"I hate you," she whispered even before she covered herself. A long strand of reddish hair lay glued along her forehead.

He collapsed beside her. A parade of women he had never known performed splendid high kicks on a large red-curtained stage. He thought he saw flashes of brown pubic hair from one on the end, a short woman with a tear in her black fishnet stockings. He applauded, and since he was the only spectator in the large red theater, his two hands made lonely sounds like hiccups.

"Are you all right?" she asked him, and he shook his head no.

"I'm sorry, sweet Susannah," he murmured to her shoulder before he fell sadly, drunkenly asleep.

The price of infidelity, he liked to say, is eternal vigilance. He was always looking for women, and he was always looking to avoid them too. He wanted deliverance, not entrapment; salvation, not religion.

"How do you manage it?" he asked Newman Sykes, the critic with high cheekbones, whose souvenir for taking Howard home on the night of the dinner party had been a permanent spinach-green stain on his ancient prized Burberry.

"Never eat veal at a restaurant that also serves jazz," Newman said. He consigned his tortured plate to a corner of the table and studied his glass of Heineken's. "Despite its alcoholic content, beer deserves a clean glass, wouldn't you think?" he asked. The candle on the table burned in a lidless crystal inkwell.

"Waiter," Howard said as the waiter passed by without stopping.

Newman drank, and disapproval accentuated the slashed contours of his face. "Manage what?" he asked.

"How're your kids?"

"Fine. Yours?"

"Okay."

"Now what? Wives?"

"Mine's fine."

"Mine too."

"And other people's wives?"

Newman asked, "Are you taking a survey?"

"What'm I drinking?"

"Chivas."

"Waiter," Howard said to no one, "another Heineken's, another Chivas."

A thin young black woman in a red tank top and tight blue satin skirt reclaimed the microphone on a raised platform in a corner of the room. Her accompanist, a rabbity white man trying to raise a beard, refitted himself to the piano, his neck bent, track shoes yearning for the pedals. The black woman bared her teeth in song. "All I can say is, he's gone, gone, Lord, gone and gone again, sweet Lord, he's gone." Her voice glided like a gull's gray-tipped wing through the air.

"Women under forty-seven shouldn't be permitted to sing the blues," Newman said. His black eyebrows, which arched in gentle surprise away from each other toward the baby skin at his temples, gave him a look of constant bemusement. "And on no account should the blues be electronically assisted."

The mike uttered a loud whine. The singer tried to ignore it; her accompanist bent lower to the piano. The whine ascended to shrillness, an indignant screech overtaking the song, the piano, the room. The singer blushed. "Charming," Newman pronounced through the din, "to see that deepening tone on tone." When the restaurant manager rushed to the platform and silenced the mike by unplugging it, Newman alone didn't applaud. "Why is it these days that common sense has been elevated to heroism?"

Howard continued to applaud. "It *is* heroism these days." But he felt foolish. Newman intimidated him. He was ten years older than Howard, and, like a schoolboy, Howard measured seniority as power: Newman had a ten-year advantage in reading, writing, women. Slender, of medium build, he was strong; Howard remembered through shadows how easily Newman had lifted him from the snowy sidewalk and carried him home to Suzanne.

"How do I manage what?" Newman asked over the applause. Minutes had elapsed between his question and Howard's earlier one.

"Women," Howard said. The singer passed their table on her way to the bar, and candlelight or the focus of expectation flickered in his eyes. "Ass."

"Too high," Newman said.

Howard gazed after her. "Something you can get hold of."

"Honestly, I don't feel like discussing the merits of rumps. Can't we have a conversation?"

Howard ducked his head and looked sideways at Newman. "About what?"

"I don't know, something interesting. What two men who are friends can talk about. Books, art, a few minutes on tennis. Why did you ask me to have dinner with you? We don't want to fuck each other and we don't know each other well enough to have comfortable silences, so we have to talk."

Howard displayed his childlike appealing face. "Okay." The idea of a discussion with the critic terrified him. He waited for Newman to begin. But Newman, his long muscular arms folded across his chest, leaned back and waited too. Howard made his face more helpless and adorable. Newman's hazel eyes peered straight into the cavern, walls of mold and a floor of bat guano, that Howard knew was his heart. At last, out of a silence of calculation and timidity he said, "Newman, you want to meet my wife?"

"I've met her, thanks."

"When you brought me home from the dinner party?"

"Yes."

Howard's brain was fermenting; he had trouble making connections. "She likes you on TV. Did you sleep with her?"

Newman studied him with the fastidiousness of an emperor confronting a moth in the ermine. "No. She's a lovely woman. Why don't *you* sleep with her?"

Howard had no answer to this logical question. He felt offended that Newman didn't want Suzanne. "Would you let me sleep with your wife?" he asked. Since he'd never met Newman's wife, the idea had a biblical patriarchal note that promised her unquestioning submission, dampness on the floor of the tent, the sting of sand in his eyes, the strong happy smell of goats at a waterhole.

Newman gave the brief upturn of his public smile. "It's a good rule of thumb that if you have to ask, you've already earned a negative answer."

"Then who the hell can I sleep with?" The loud belligerence didn't disturb Newman, whose precisely planed face balanced light like a Buddha's. Howard grew violent at the sight of such equanimity. "Who do *you* want to sleep with?" he demanded.

Newman inspected the room. "That's *whom*, and there's no one I can point out here."

"Then make her up, describe her."

"Why?"

"Because . . ." Howard wanted a woman Newman wanted. Having her, he'd have something of Newman too. He believed the connection would bring him peace. He wanted the critic's vision, a particular dance of the irises that seemed to see the gross spinning world with amazement but acceptance, perhaps love. "I love you, Newman. You're a saint."

"I'm still not going to write a favorable review of that novel by your latest find, the backwater Balzac." Newman meant Vincent Bask.

"Excellent," Howard said, cheering up. "Now we have something to talk about: Bask." This time when he called, "Waiter," the waiter hurried to obey.

Matty, drowsy and still warm from a bath, held up her arms, and Howard bent down to kiss her. She locked her arms around his neck. "Don't go, Daddy." She released him.

He sat at the edge of the bed. In his weariness, he wanted to lie down. "Okay, I'm here."

"For how long?"

"How long do you want?"

"Till I fall asleep."

He almost whispered his laugh. "That's quite a demand."

Shy, afraid of her father's soft, sad laugh, she said, "Then stay a few minutes, please." She settled under the covers, bringing them up to her neck, and inhaled his familiar harsh scent of Scotch and cigarettes. Fearing to have her happiness taken away, she chose instead to relinquish it: she pretended to fall asleep so that her father, with light movements, could stand up and leave her room.

In the kitchen Suzanne fed detergent to the dishwasher. "She's asleep?"

Her efficiency and her blue rubber gloves distressed him. "Coffee," he muttered. In a corner of the living room his chair, his secondhand IBM Selectric, his stacks of papers and notes waited with alarming permanence. He sat down to reread a story he was considering for his magazine, *Rosemary*, which was really the university's magazine. His uncapped fountain pen accidentally stroked a black line across the title page: "Jack," by D. Reeve. He would use the pen to obliterate the author's unworthy adverbs, to weed prose and rearrange it. He'd tried to write stories of his own, but his sense of form deserted him there. Since he was quick to sense talent, he knew he had none. Able as he was to discover a ten-page story in someone else's rambling sixteen pages, he couldn't discover a story in himself. He had stopped wondering why; a sense of dignity about his failings didn't prevent him from pursuing them, though. He grunted when Suzanne brought his coffee. Safe because he was working, she kissed the back of his neck and went off to the bedroom to watch TV.

When he allowed himself a break a half-hour later, he thought of her kiss and wandered into the bedroom. She was asleep—or pretending to be asleep?—oblivious to Joanne Woodward, who was soliciting funds for the Public Broadcasting System. The actress had aged, but she still looked good enough to provoke him to fantasies of hurried oral sex with her during commercials. Then he remembered that PBS didn't have commercials. He turned off the TV and went back to his desk and counted the cigarette butts in the ashtray. He had to finish notes for a lecture on the short story, to be given at a Massachusetts women's college with notoriously chill guest facilities at a moldering country inn. The thought of two hundred earnest Lit majors without makeup appalled him. He didn't want to finish his notes. He had to decide something about Reeve's story. The night stretched out, long and narrow.

His lunchtime affairs made his life tolerable. Without them, he felt, he wouldn't survive in the structure he had built for himself. Of course, not every afternoon brought him to bed with a woman; he couldn't have survived that, either. He endured and at times enjoyed business lunches. Abandoning his midtown East Side office twenty minutes behind schedule, with papers fluttering in his wake, he took writers and agents and other editors to restaurants with good bars, uptown and downtown, upstairs and downstairs, and laid his American Express card down in wet rings on white tablecloths. But at least once and usually twice a week he lay naked, bone on bone, with one woman or another. Or with two women, because he liked playing ringmaster. Most of the women he knew laughed when he suggested a threesome, and some were shocked, and some consented. If they refused, he smiled good-naturedly and contented himself with sex for two.

Having found the women, he had to find places to take them. Some invited him to their apartments, which ranged from roach heavens to duplexes on Park Avenue, and over the years he had learned his way around Manhattan better than any cabbie. But some lived in faraway, impossible places like Sheepshead Bay and Valhalla and Rockville Centre. The married ones seldom wanted to bring him home, and the single ones often wanted the excitement of being in a stranger's bed. This was where male friendship came in. There was always an apartment at his disposal during the week. It might have belonged to a bachelor who worked all day and didn't mind strange women using his comb and leaving curled strands of hair in the bathroom sink. Or it might have belonged to a divorced writer spending a snowbound semester at Bennington as artist-in-residence and apprentice satyr. A sublet brown-walled one-bedroom on the Upper West Side; an illegal loft on Thirty-second Street, with a view of Gimbels; a Sutton Place cubby housing only a bed and an exercise bike—these were tokens of brotherhood. There had been a bleached aerie atop a Village bookstore, lent by the store owner, who withdrew permission after Howard used a signed first-edition Jack London to elevate the hips of a lover, tall Adrienne the Tarot reader. "Anyway, it hurt my tailbone," she said. For the past few years, he had been one of three people with keys to Newman Sykes's walk-up studio in a brownstone, also in the Village, on West Eleventh Street, between Fifth and Sixth. Newman used the place three days a week and spent the rest of the time at home, a converted firehouse upstate. During his absence he allowed the other two keyholders, Howard and a nymphomaniac named Maris, to devise their own schedules. Newman expected nothing for his generosity, but he did have one inflexible rule: you had to provide your sheets and towels, and you had to keep them out of his sight. That might have made two rules. "I don't want to look at your mess," he told Howard when he gave him the key. Though one of Howard's subsequent sessions left a large, bloody, ineradicable stain on the mattress, Newman merely commented a month later, "You might have turned the mattress over."

"I washed the spot. I thought it should dry first," Howard said, looking woeful and dear.

"I had a guest, and the mattress was unaesthetic, almost discouraging."

Howard brightened with curiosity. "What was she like?"

"Like a woman who wanted to make love in a clean bed. And after seeing the mattress, she suspected my sheets." Newman closed the discussion, and Howard retained his key.

It was important to him, not only for the door it opened but for its proof of Newman's friendship. That Newman also expressed friendship for a nymphomaniac didn't lessen the key's value to Howard. He enjoyed saying to a woman, "I've got a place we can go to—the apartment of a friend of mine, Newman Sykes, the critic. You've heard of him?" The woman usually had; Howard preferred literate sex. Of course, if that wasn't available, he'd take anything.

He did have two rules of his own: never sleep with a woman from the office and never sleep with a woman who knew Suzanne. He broke both rules soon after he made them, and reflected ruefully but admiringly on his own impetuousness. "There goes a *man*," he almost said to himself, avoiding the forming thought because of a distaste for parody, especially self-parody—though he wasn't above thinking of himself as a plain but honest fornicator, let me show you my testimonials, honey. What am I supposed to do, he thought, just give up and die? To celebrate Leap Year, he lay with Anne Small on the blue checkered designer mat in her guest bathroom while two rooms away Bob Small instructed his other guests, among them Suzanne, in the wonders of lepidopterology. Anne Small whispered, "I've always wanted you, always." Howard considered this reasonable, but the fine coat of talcum powder on the tile floor and the thought of Suzanne being forced to admire dead insects grieved him. He wanted to be breast-fed, held like a child. He grabbed the first part of Anne he could find and ended up licking her ankle, which tasted like hand lotion. Afterward, his arm bruised by her tennis-hardened grip, he joined the lecture group in the living room and ground to bright dust a valuable specimen from Siberia or Saint-Lô. "An accident," he muttered to Bob, who had turned ashen as the big-bodied moths thudding against screen doors in summer. Suzanne knelt and swept butterfly dust into a pile. Her round behind pushed out brown wool pants, and she kept saying, "Poor Bob,

Howard didn't mean it. Poor Bob, Howard didn't mean it." He could have kicked her for her kindness and stupidity.

He took to Newman's bed one rainy March afternoon a thin young Frenchwoman, Liliane, secretary to colleagues down the hall. Once he got over the shock of seeing her in a full slip—"I didn't know anybody still wore those things," he said, to which she answered unsmiling, "*Oui, la combinaison, le* bra, *les* panties, *le* panty'ose. *Tous sont nécessaires*"—he found her compliant but unfragrant. A nimbus of sad odors surrounded her, the acrid smell of the duplicating machine, the dark cloying of the typewriter ribbon, the burned rubber of eraser fragments, and the taste of her mouth, coffee in a cardboard cup. These odors reminded him of all he wanted to forget. In her arms he felt embraced by a symptom of his own disease, the dread of the drab.

"Are you from Paris?" he asked, hoping to heighten the interlude with the shopworn glamour of that city.

"*Non.* Guadeloupe."

She wasn't even properly French. He placed his tongue against her half-closed eyelid; obedient, she closed her eyes. He licked off iridescent mauve eye shadow and uncovered her pulsing pink lid.

"How old are you?" he asked.

"Twenty-six," she said, still keeping her eyes closed.

"You look younger."

Beneath him, she shrugged. Her small breasts briefly rubbed against him. He felt like shrugging too. Memory, not instinct, guided him on his excursion through her; a tour guide dressed like a stewardess and holding a microphone recited, "Now we will see the frescoes. Notice how the color persists, even after centuries of weathering and the shocks of wars. Notice the delicacy of line, the unusual use of perspective." High heels clicked along a marble floor while he desperately listened for the guide's voice. "In this next gallery is a minor masterpiece, often overlooked by art lovers in a hurry . . ."

Liliane cried, "*Ho! Oui! Ça!*" and soon "*Reste, reste.*" An art lover in a hurry, he raced on.

As he helped her into her raincoat, a thrifty dirt-concealing black with a label clinging by one thread to its neck, a battle of old perfumes rose from its dampness, and he thought of his daughter, Matty, and the long uneven days of love she would encounter. He settled the coat brusquely on the woman.

"We go back to the office separately, yes?" Her nude eyelid reproached him.

"Yes." Then, because he felt sorry for himself, he kissed her hand.

The next morning she passed his office several times without stopping, her eyes fixed on an open file or a ballpoint pen as compelling as a reliquary. He managed a long business lunch and returned to his desk drunk enough to ignore her. She knocked on his open door.

He glanced up too quickly; his head hurt. "Well, hello there."

" 'Ello."

"Come in." His hearty invitation sounded hollow to him.

Approaching his chair, she seemed ready to cry. She smiled. "You understand, sometimes we try and—" She shrugged. "*Pouf!* We learn something we did not *enfin* expect to learn."

Warily he nodded. "Sometimes."

"You understand. We must see each other here." She offered her hand; confused, he took it.

"So," she said, "we will think of yesterday with fondness, but we will not repeat it."

He thought, *I* was supposed to say that. He noticed, with amusement, that she was beginning to look better and better to him. He could almost desire her. He watched her walk away, checked the swing of her hips in an unfashionable pleated skirt, and relished his perversity and relief.

He forgave himself these lapses. Anne Small had become pregnant—not by Howard—and produced, as the birth announcement declared, a little Small. He wondered how he could have been attracted, even for a moment in the bathroom, to a woman who would send out gingham-bordered cards with a message like that. As for Liliane, the awkwardness of seeing her in the office proved less of a problem than he'd expected. If her presence reminded him of a damp, foolish, unhappy afternoon, it also reminded him that he was a rogue, a sexual gallant, a villain—in short, that he was alive.

And there were other women. There would always be other women. He had that afternoon attended a salon for two given by the ex-wife of an art dealer who specialized in Impressionists; through her Howard momentarily connected to Monet and a lost world of gardens and women in long dresses white as clouds. Seeing his hostess undressed, he understood why the art dealer had divorced her: tanned, thick-thighed, unashamed, with a massive, almost papal, gold neck chain jamming a Coptic cross between her breasts, she was more suitable for an Expressionist. The cross scraped his chest. Her thighs squeezed him powerfully, a boa constrictor greeting a squirrel. He maneuvered her with caution until caution gave way. She served Greek olives and Turkish figs and instant Maxwell House coffee. She showed him an original Renoir drawing in a gold-leaf frame, part of her divorce settlement. Before he left, she patted his behind and sang "What I Did for Love."

There had been no divorce settlement with his first ex-wife, Fiona, whose daddy'd had Howard annulled after a four-day marriage based on room service at the Roney Plaza in Miami Beach. "I'll always love you, Howie," she shouted as her daddy removed her to a limousine and her senior year at an all-girls' high school run by the Sisters of Perpetual Yearning for Jesus in Tallahassee or Titusville. "Me too," he shouted back from the lobby. The limousine carried her away. A twenty-four-hour jellyfish alert had ended, and he went swimming. For two years, until he was graduated *insigne cum laude* from the University of Miami with a degree in seventeenth-century English literature and assorted useless credits in prelaw, she sent him greetings at Christmas and at the Jewish New Year: "Happy Rush Hosanna. I miss your sweet thing." His mother mailed them to him at his off-campus apartment, envelopes violated, the notes ripped in pieces. He had to reconstruct Fiona's messages and, after a while, his image of her face. She might have stopped writing to him, or his mother might have stopped forwarding the letters, or he might have stopped taping them together. He moved to New York for adventures as a social worker, the Robin Hood of Avenue B. The adventures ended on a front stoop on Sixth Street when he threatened a client's common-law husband with jail: "You lay a hand on her again and you're in trouble." The man punched Howard down six steps. From a ground-floor window his client shrieked, "Ai ai ai." At the rear tire of a parked car a tiger cat gazed into Howard's open eye as he lay on the sidewalk. Fiona became a troublesome detail on job applications. Did the marriage count or didn't it? In three years the question altered. Did Fiona's unsolved murder—a bullet entering under the ear during a voter registration drive in Lamar County, Mississippi—leave him a widower? His mother wrote the news to him and enclosed a clipping from the Miami *Herald* on the dangers of New York street gangs. By then he was married again or for the first time. He had begun to examine the literal meaning of *making a living*.

In his corner with no original Renoir, he glanced again at the last page of D. Reeve's story. He hadn't used his pen at all— interesting. Reeve required another reading in a day or two, to see if he would stay as good as he seemed. Howard put the story in his bookbag, a scarred leather pouch. How old was Reeve? He lived below Canal Street, around Chinatown, according to the envelope. Was he an account exec with a loft and higher yearnings or a waiter shriven by poverty? Howard tried to imagine another's life but could imagine only his own.

To support his two families, he would go on working at a killing pace. He would come home each night to the child he loved and to Suzanne and to the pile of half-truths multiplying on his desk. He would smoke and drink and fuck too much; he would die of a heart attack in a strange bed before Matty was out of college, Radcliffe—no, Harvard—class of '94. There would be insurance for the tuition. No, he wouldn't die. He would grow old. His shirt would hang on brittle shoulders. Pink scalp would show through his white curls. He would place waxy hands on withered breasts and have to be grateful. Lipstick would bleed in creases around the women's mouths. The women's hair would smell of medicine. He would have to lie like hell to believe he enjoyed them. Matty would grow up and become famous at something and leave him, leave him alone with Suzanne, who would be old, bitter, uneasy after years of neglect. And she would still be lovely. And she would still be stupid. He wanted to name his terror and introduce it to someone. He wanted to meet a woman, an almost faceless woman with voluminous hair and eyes like resin and a foul mind riding a quiet, maidenly body, and unzip and say to her, "Here it is. Now what?"

On the worst of bad days, when the toothpaste and toilet paper both were exhausted by the time he got to them; when at breakfast there was no *Times* because of the doorman's oversight or a neighborly theft (Mrs. 9-C in crepe-soled wedgies) or a strike; when Suzanne across the table showed the suggestion of a softening in her jawline or, more frightening, looked remote and beautiful; when he discovered in his office ashtray dark beadlike objects that Reinhardt the Joycean decided were rat pellets and Michaels of Russian Studies said were beads, and that Mr. Martinez of Maintenance identified as semisucked horehound ovals favored by the night cleaning woman, Berthe from Zagreb; when his lunchtime assignation was canceled because of rain or an inconvenient husband or a stepdaughter with bronchitis and a temperature of 102.6, the red line on the thermometer speeding past degree notches to deprive him as he sat at his desk and told his lover-turned-mother on the phone that yes, he understood, but he didn't; when "Adagio Morse," a love story in code and the lead fiction for *Rosemary*'s next issue, prompted the printer to call up screaming about dots and dashes in front of his eyes, and the author, a low hum on a bad connection from Ithaca, refused to delete the offending pages, maintaining their "something something quality"—then, on the worst of these days, Howard knew to expect a visitation from Margery, his ex-wife.

It might come on the office phone, a ringing like others, but when he answered it and mumbled hello, there would be no sound, not even the static of her shallow breathing. He pictured her standing at the wall phone in her kitchen, a hymn to stainless steel, holding in one hand a gold-filled button earring with a blackened clip hinge, her other hand pressing the receiver against her chafed unadorned lobe. He couldn't remember her hands. Were the knuckles too broad? She would turn the earring over, weigh it, flicking its discolored clip open and closed, all the while staring out the window at the backyard, where a green hose lay frozen in winter, untouched in summer, had probably split along its coils, and he would have to pay for a new one to replace it, and for the call too, dead air from Mount Kisco.

"Margery," he would begin to the silence, and she would hang up the phone, not always gently.

But would call again in fifteen minutes, and an hour after that, and again, until her anger (over what?) had subsided or an errand took her away from the house. If his secretary answered the phone in his absence, Margery became an author, a lawyer, a nurse grim with lab results, an overage student in one of his classes. None of these people left a number for him to return the call, and he knew, after checking the messages on the pink While You Were Out slips, that Ms. Bliss from Con Ed was Margery playing games. "Ms. Bliss will catch you later," the slip said.

He never hung up on her, but waited her out. This was penance, social work; this was how he held her hand when she needed him. At least he didn't have to really touch her anymore. The calls, like fever blisters, erupted in clusters, then stopped for long, healing months. She would busy herself with knitting, dating, isometrics, peeling the bark from trees. Until she began to miss him again, and got angry, and called. She was angry because she missed him; he could understand that. Through the years since their parting, while he arranged for himself a new life, a gazebo built on a slag heap, but it was *his* gazebo, it was *his* slag heap, she considered him to be living in a home away from home, hers, and preserved patiently for him the dried blossomings of her hatred.

Or it might come in the office mail, an envelope of intimate

23

poison licked lovingly closed, a won ton from his wanton, he thought, a kreplach of loathing. The mailboy, a chemistry major too timorous to work his way through school by drug dealing, should have delivered it with lead gloves and a chest protector, but education had blinded him to real danger. Only nuclei and narcs could be lethal; there was no menace in correspondence unless it ticked or had a three-letter return address: FLN, PLO, IRS. Advanced Immunology II and the dreary business of infecting and then vaccinating mice prevented him from seeing the metaphorical possibilities of cancer. He was probably a mouth breather. With a glum "Here's what it is," he dumped several book mailers and large manila envelopes and two or three letter-size ones on a chair, his puffed right eye unfocused without the lens of a microscope.

One of the letters beckoned to Howard. The afternoon—in late April, with clean light—made him unwary as he grasped the envelope. Yes, the familiar handwriting, loops and whorls, his name tatted by the spider woman. Yes, no return address. As if he couldn't find the house blindfolded; as if, in the dreams he never had, he didn't go there. Disgusted, excited, he tore the envelope open.

"HOWIE DARLING" it began, printed in raucous orange capitals on the back of a torn square of wallpaper, interlocking green trefoils on a blue ground.

ACCUSTOMED THOUGH I AM TO YOUR THOUGHT-LESSNESS, I'VE GOT TO ADMIT THIS TIME YOU OUT-DID YOURSELF. ILENE DIDN'T SAY ANYTHING TO ME, SHE'S NOT A COMPLAINER, BUT I KNOW FOR A FACT SHE WAS HURT AND CRIED IN HER ROOM ON SAT-URDAY WHEN IT BECAME CLEAR YOU WEREN'T GOING TO CALL AND THE MAIL WAS ALREADY HERE WITH NOTHING IN IT FROM YOU. ONCE YEARS AGO WHEN I FORGOT YOUR BIRTHDAY YOU CARRIED ON LIKE A WILD MAN AND STARTED THROWING THINGS AROUND, BROKE A GOOD VASE I REMEMBER, AND WANTED TO START IN ON ME, BUT YOUR GREAT AND

GOOD BUDDY FELIX WAS THERE AND HELD YOU BACK UNTIL YOU FINALLY STORMED OUT OF THE HOUSE AND FELIX FOLLOWED TO MAKE SURE YOU'D BE OK WHILE I CLEANED UP THE MESS. SO MAYBE YOU CAN EMPATHIZE A LITTLE WITH ILENE, WHO WOULD HAVE LIKED YOU TO REMEMBER HER BIRTHDAY. IT'S SO PATHETICALLY SIMPLE, THEY HAVE CARDS FOR EVERYTHING. ALL YOU HAD TO DO WAS GO TO THE SECTION MARKED SWEET SIXTEEN FOR DAUGHTER AND PICK ANY ONE AND SIGN IT AND SEND IT. EVEN YOU COULD HAVE DONE THAT. I OVERHEARD PAUL TELLING HER SHE WAS DUMB, THAT WAS THE WORD, DUMB, TO EXPECT ANYTHING FROM YOU AND IT MADE ME SAD TO HEAR HIM SAY IT, BUT YOU'VE BROUGHT IT ON YOURSELF AND HE'S RIGHT. HE'S A VERY HONEST BOY, NO ILLUSIONS, VERY MUCH LIKE YOUR FRIEND FELIX BECAUSE AS MUCH AS FELIX LIKED YOU HE ALSO SAW YOU FOR WHAT YOU WERE AND DIDN'T LET IT GET TO HIM. I SHOULD HAVE TAKEN LESSONS FROM HIM.

Unsigned, as always.

She had tried to kill him: a nudge with the rear bumper of their Chevy, pinning him against the garage wall. An afternoon and a night of drinking with Felix had made him bold and hopeless. He had finished telling her to go to hell. "I'm leaving," he shouted at her, though she was the one in the car. He noticed through his tears how sooty the snow was before the car pushed him. She claimed later that she'd gone into reverse by accident. At St. Somebody's emergency room she hovered over him with a Blue Cross card while a low-browed Pakistani intern, addressing Howard as Mr. Rich, praised his x-rays and poked his injured leg before prescribing aspirin and compresses.

"Two, Mr. Rich."

"How do you mean two?"

"I mean two."

"One hot and one cold?"

"Two aspirin, Mr. Rich. Any temperature you like."

In the car on the way home, no longer home to him, she said, "You've got it wrong. He said cold compresses for the first twenty-four hours."

He felt such pain in his chest that he couldn't believe his leg wasn't broken. They had conspired against him. She must have slept with the Pakistani too. "You're a killer, Margie."

"You're a liar, Howie." Serenely delivered, with her chin uplifted as she barreled through a yellow light.

"You're a cunt."

"I should hope so."

"I can move out limping."

She glanced away from the road. Sincere brown eyes dilating. Since they both had brown eyes, how come Paul had blue eyes? "It was an *accident*."

"I don't know, you looked kind of purposeful to me."

The car halted at a red light. Her fingers stroked the steering wheel.

"I guess the accident was that I came home for lunch," he said.

"You were sent home. That's two jobs in six months. Who asked you to editorialize against codeine?"

At the pharmaceutical ad agency where he'd been assistant traffic manager, he'd also written the company newsletter, four stapled sheets passed out monthly and crammed with, he believed, ass-kissing and head-patting, and nothing in between. Instead of an interview with a VP–Production ("Let me say I get a big kick out of production") and the usual birthday and anniversary congrats, he'd typed six stencils detailing codeine abuse around the country, the countless lives ruined: "Shall we be racked by coughs or wrecked by cough medicine? We are truly between a rock and a hard place." In faint purple ink fresh from the Mimeograph, his call to action arrived in cubicles and offices. Within an hour he was summoned to another floor to meet a VP–Accounts and a VP–Personnel, both with crewcuts and both wearing black loafers. "Don't bother cleaning out your desk,"

Personnel said, dropping a filled brown paper bag in Howard's lap. "That's your stuff." The VPs escorted him into the elevator and down to the street.

"You don't want me to be happy," Margery said.

Sitting in his office, he thought he would be able to remember her hands on the wheel. He could remember her lipstick, dark red, and her coat, a gray, black, and white tweed, the collar up. The way her lips tensed, as if she were about to speak French, when she stepped on the accelerator. He could remember the weight above his diaphragm, an unexpelled scream, and the throbbing in his leg. The warmth of the car, heater on, windows rolled up, the whole goddamn car rolled up, crushed and hurtling like a spitball aimed at the back of a sixth-grader dreaming of a cigarette. He'd dreamed of a lot more than cigarettes when he was eleven.

"Kids know more than we like to think," he'd told his new boss, a VP–Juvenile, at a different ad agency. A breakfast-cereal account had commissioned an activities book of stories, poems, sports facts, projects, and puzzles. It would be free for six boxtops. Howard, a copywriter trainee, had been assigned to find suitable poems. He'd been given a box of the cereal "for inspiration." In a morning meeting he came up with a poem, Andrew Marvell's "To His Coy Mistress." How could he have known that his married boss was seeing a researcher in the legal department? A secretary in a pink shirtwaist spilled coffee on her pad.

"Okay, so Felix likes me. But I don't like him back," Margery said.

"Shut up, Margie."

"He's too analytical. And he's not smart enough to be analytical. You're much smarter."

"Shut up, Margie."

Her hands on the steering wheel. Hidden: she'd been wearing gloves, gray kid gloves he'd bought her for Christmas. With black wool lining. Cashmere? The car two-wheeled a corner.

"Felix likes Elvis *Pres*ley. Felix is ordinary."

"He's my friend."

"Some friend. He tried to go to bed with me."

Absurdly proud: "He didn't try, he succeeded."

He reread the letter vivid with lies and saluted her capacity to hurt him, even from such distance. All right, he'd forgotten Ilene's birthday, and his son probably did despise him. It made sense, and Paul might be sensible, the way Margie said. But the part about his own birthday and Felix was fiction. Did she want to remember it that way or did she want to remind him of it as revenge for Ilene's unhappiness and for her own larger, less defined sorrows? What vase had he broken?

The VP–Juvenile had moved his lips reading the poem to himself. Two bites left of a cinnamon bun fused to his palm.

"And what are the children supposed to make of the word *mistress*, Ritchie?"

"It's a great poem. And it's not copyrighted."

"It has *breast* in it. It has *Jews* and *virginity* in it. It advocates sexual license."

The VP's navy tie had a crusty spot on it. Howard imagined feeding him a mouthful of tie.

"No it doesn't, Mr. Gabriel. It's three hundred years before the Beatles and 'Love Me Do,' that's all."

"You're pushing your luck, Ritchie."

"Kids know about these things, sir. What they don't know is that people have always known about these things." Howard sang a few bars of "Love Me Do." The secretary in the stained shirtwaist stopped taking notes. A full-fledged copywriter slapped a cigarette case on his knee in time to the song. "I can do more," Howard said.

"No you can't," the VP said. "You are dehired. I kid you not."

Howard got to clean out his desk himself. He came home to the domestic sight of naked Margery astride naked Felix on the sofa. He was reading to her from a paperback. Paul was at nursery school, but the baby, Ilene, was sleeping in her playpen near them, a thumb stoppering her mouth, damp curls at her neck. The house had always been overheated. He couldn't have broken a vase because Ilene remained asleep while he was there. The scene proceeded in curt whispers. On his way out he closed the door quietly. Felix ran after him, calling, "Wait, good buddy," and he waited while Felix, in sneakers in the snow, pissed into the leafless hedge at the side of the house. Felix's shirttail hung down beneath his bomber jacket. They went off to get drunk together. What did she mean, Felix saw him for what he was? Why was *she* so angry? He was the one who'd been wronged. Felix played "Heartbreak Hotel" on the jukebox six times in a row for two quarters. "Please believe me," he said. "I just read Ferlinghetti and it blew my mind, and I came to the house to give it to you." Perfectly fine, nothing hard to believe, except that Felix knew he'd be at work, not at home, in the middle of the day. "I guess I thought it was still Christmas," Felix said, and he asked Howard for a quarter.

He filed the letter under *P*, for Proof of Insanity (Margie), a folder of evidence he was accumulating against the day she attacked him again or went to court accusing him of something less than rectitude. He wrote a hasty birthday note to Ilene— "Sweetie, I'm sorry," etc.—and stuffed it with a check, the zeros open and suppurating. "You know you're my sweet peach," he added to the note before reaching into his bookbag on the chair and pulling out a better story, D. Reeve's "Jack."

Hrubet the impresario, the director of this peripatetic nightmare, believes in justice. For the fourth time, in striped trousers and a cutaway, he is going to be married. The trousers once belonged to Marco the Monkey Boy, who retired in Orlando at the age of seventy-six and abandoned formal attire for Bermuda shorts. Now that Hrubet has had the tail hole sewn up, the trousers fit him perfectly. He sets a shining black top hat on his head.

"What makes it shine so?" I ask, pointing as best I can at his hat.

"It's silk," he says.

I am ashamed to ask him what silk is. I know he will

answer that silk is what the hat is made of, and I know that is not the answer I want....

The pack on the desk was empty. There were no cigarettes in his jacket hanging on a hook on the door, and none in his bookbag, though a frantic search of it did locate a birthday card and check for Ilene that he'd forgot to mail. Michaels smoked a pipe, and Reinhardt had no known vices, and the secretaries were at lunch. Gail, the secretary he shared with Michaels and Reinhardt, had locked her desk, but he found Liliane's available and as touchingly quaint in its tidiness as she had been in her layers of underwear two years ago. The center drawer, in addition to a built-in compartmentalized tray for paper clips and rubber bands— no chance to be creative there—showed her organizational genius: a compact, lipstick, a miniature bottle of perfume, and the key to the bathroom on a grimy ribbon were fitted into a box from a typewriter cartridge; a book called *English NOW* had a comb, teeth clenched on long hairs, for a bookmark; and tucked into a cardboard roll of masking tape dotted with lint were a pocket spray of mouthwash and an open sample pack of cigarettes, an airplane giveaway.

He took a cigarette and purposely replaced the pack wrong, a lack of stealth to assure himself he wasn't stealing. And not invading her privacy either, he thought, walking back to his office. The drawer had been unlocked. Besides, her secrets were so few and simple that— He stopped, knowing he had no justification, and admired himself for his honesty.

He settled in his chair, clicked his lighter, and resolved to dislodge from his thoughts Margery and their children and the splitting garden hose and everything else that wasn't manly and clean and suited to a high passion for literature.

Hrubet the impresario, the director of this peripatetic nightmare, believes in justice....

The cigarette was stale, the way he knew it would be. He inhaled deeply and bent over the manuscript, frowning. His fingers touched paper as shocking as skin. Alone in his office in April light, pale, angry-looking, smoking, he read. No one seeing him then would have realized how happy he was.

Howard's voice on the telephone had a guarded sound, a slow baritone growl that only people who knew him could interpret as humor. Since she didn't know Howard and since his call had awakened her, Dina Reeve heard his growl and nothing more. She squinted in the dim room. Larry had handed her the receiver; she wedged it between the pillow and her ear, and pulled the covers up over her shoulders against the room's damp chill. "Hello?" she said, warming. Through years of sleeping late she'd perfected a wide-awake hello.

A male voice demanded, "Is this *D. Reeve?*"

"Yes," she said hesitantly. She needed supporting materials, a driver's license, an expired passport. She was listed as D. Reeve in the Manhattan directory and she'd sent a story to *Rosemary* under that name. The initial was supposed to defeminize her, to prevent obscene phone calls and a reader's conscious or unconscious prejudice against writers who happened to be female through no fault of their own. After mailing the story, she'd daydreamed about the editor calling her and his surprise at her voice: female, young. Because it had been fantasy, she hadn't gone on to imagine her response.

"This is Howard Ritchie at *Rosemary*."

She put all her strength into listening. "Yes."

"Pardon?" came the growl.

"Yes. I said yes."

"I've got your story. It's flawless, brilliant. I'd like to meet you."

She rolled on her back, and the phone lurched over pages strewn across the plank between the loft bed and the wall. The Tensor lamp rocked. The clock skidded. In the bathroom Larry announced his presence by peeing a loud stream. Though he'd answered the phone, she pretended during the call that he didn't exist.

"Is that possible?" the voice asked her.

"When?" she asked it.

The flushing toilet thundered. The voice said, "How about this week?"

"When?"

"How about this afternoon? This afternoon good for you? Around three?"

"Okay." She breathed the word and sat up. Under scribbled and torn pages, crumpled tissues, a depleted tube of lip balm, there lurked a red pencil stub.

"Make that three-thirty," the voice said. "Twelfth floor."

"Excuse me?"

"See you then."

Halfway up the ladder to the bed, Larry leaned toward her. "Well?" he asked, blond mustache spread above a smile.

She wrote the time and floor in the margin of a two-paragraph essay, "How I Go Walked," by Sho, a Japanese executive exactly her height but better dressed, with a gold Cartier watch weighty as a leg iron. He was her worst pupil, trembling with distinction. His wife, in Tokyo, was expecting their first child, "Alone from me. Very morbid."

Larry's eagerness offended her. His mustache offended her. He pulled her to him. "It's the editor of *Rosemary*. He said 'flawless and brilliant,' " she told his neck. Two days of not shaving roughened it. She hid her face in his long hair. He smelled of soap and a musty tee shirt. She put her arms around him. "What time is it?" she asked, though she was closer to the clock. Movement was dangerous. Yawning, she moved. Ten after one, the face said behind a veil of dust. "Shit."

She stayed slumped in bed while he got up and turned on the fluorescent lamp suspended from chains around the heating pipe near her at the ceiling. A color like the harsh glow of gas stations on turnpikes at night glossed the room. It was their version of the day outside. Blue flowers in the sheet over her knees bruised in that light. "I'll have to say something," she said. "He might ask me questions. What it means—he might ask me that."

"Fuck him. You think Borges says what his stuff means?"

"Somehow I don't think I'm in the same position as Borges."

The water had a habit of disappearing. An apartment would spring a leak, and the super, summoned from lunch in his apartment three blocks away, on Baxter Street, would turn off the water for the whole building. That stopped the leak and kept his fried rice warm. Among other anxieties—getting cancer of the nose, losing her teeth, getting mugged, getting raped, getting pregnant—Dina worried that the water would stop in the middle of her shower. She had been worrying over this for six years. It hadn't happened yet, so the odds against her were growing. One day she would be showering, shampoo in her hair, soap at her armpits, soap inside her, and the water would stop. Or only the coid water would stop. Or the hot water. One day, she thought, and hurried through her shower.

While she was drying herself, Larry brought her a mug of coffee. She covered herself with the towel. "I heated the milk for you," he said. The mug, sending up wisps of steam, rested next to a Carb-Othello Sanguine pencil on the flat rim of the sink. He stayed to trim his mustache, thick and curved down, a music brace drawn in the wrong direction. He denied modeling it after Arshile Gorky's. ("The guy killed himself. If I wanted to be like a guy who killed himself, I'd pick Van Gogh. Gorky was brilliant, but Van Gogh knew God personally.") Rusting embroidery scissors munched through it, scattering yellow hairs over the wet pencil with a bleeding point and over the toothbrushes and the toilet seat and the floor. She couldn't step out of the tub because there was no room for them both in the narrow bathroom.

"I'd like to get out," she said.

"Wait . . . one second."

"I'm going to be late."

"Drink your coffee for a few seconds."

"I want to get out. You can do that later."

"Uh-huh, but I see these mothers now." He snipped at an outstanding hair before lowering the scissors to inspect his mustache.

She stepped quickly from the tub. She had aimed to press herself against the wall, but she bumped into him. She kept her hold on the towel. "Sorry."

"You couldn't wait." The scissors clattered in the medicine cabinet. She heard him opening a drawer in the room.

She tucked the towel around herself and took makeup from the cabinet. Closing it, she glimpsed her unprepared face in the mirror. She tapped the faucet once with each index finger, and again. The coffee didn't have any hair in it. She skimmed off the skin of milk at the surface before she drank it.

From up in bed, he watched her at the crammed closet, a doorless improvisation by a previous tenant generous with nails. It stood beside a venerable refrigerator on which was painted an almost life-sized Carmen Miranda, topped by four giant papier-mâché bananas, dusty yellow. Grease spots pocked Carmen's face and dulled her red lips. "Maybe I'll go uptown too," he said.

She yanked a pair of jeans from a hanger. The legs were wrinkled. "Damn."

"Want me to iron them?" He overemphasized the end of the question. He pronounced the words right, but the pattern was off.

"No. Thanks." She pushed aside hangers to find her silk blouse, a peach-colored one her mother had worn twenty years before. Gently wrinkled. You could always pretend to yourself that you'd started out ironed and got wrinkled along the way.

"Did you hear me?" he asked. "I'll go uptown with you."

At the bottom of the closet, under fallen boots and the buckled hose of the vacuum cleaner, she found her new shoes. They were in the back, near the baited rat trap. Her mother had bought them for her. They had unstylish square toes; she'd saved them too long. And they hurt. She hobbled to the bathroom for toilet paper to dust them. Why had she picked shoes that hurt? "I'd rather go alone."

"I'll go up to the museum. It's a free day."

"A donation day."

"You could meet me there afterward."

"But I'd like to go alone. To give me time. To think."

"Alone on the subway?"

She dumped the new shoes back in the closet, taking care not to spring the trap. She'd been traveling alone on the subway for years: uptown to a waning counterculture bulletin, rumored to be CIA-funded, where she, another woman, and a bearded psych dropout, all using the name Pilar O'Keefe, had compiled an advice column answering anguished inquiries about VD and toilet seats, the right way to steam brown rice, the advisability of using blond dye on pubic hair or, if not on pubic hair, what about on a poodle; then downtown to a registrar's office at a two-year college, where she'd shepherded financial-assistance requests from steel out-box to out-box and officially encouraged illiterate nineteen-year-olds to take Remedial Basic English I before Remedial Basic English II; and currently midtown to a private school for foreign executives, where each Saturday she taught five classes of English as a second language to Japanese men in perfect tiny suits and Russian Jewish émigrés in short sleeves with ballpoint pens clipped to their shirt pockets.

And while she rode the subway, he waited for her at home in the dampness, lulled by the boom of *Honeymooners* and *Superman* reruns on TV, with glue on his fingers and scraps of origami paper and foil on the floor and mostly sad blank sheets of watercolor paper spread on the table, over the phone (moved down from the bed for daytime use), over the lessons she was correcting (also moved down), over her typewriter and the Sunday *Times* she fought him to buy. "That's not reality. That's the *Times*'s version of reality," he would yell. "I like it better than mine," she would yell back, dancing out of his hitting range. He hadn't ever hit her, but he'd offered to.

She went to the hearth for her everyday shoes. "I'll be all right," she said.

He climbed down from the bed. "Where's your brush?" Standing behind her at the bathroom mirror, he brushed back her hair, which she had combed forward. He turned her around, wiped rouge from her cheeks with the heel of his palm, kissed her forehead. "You'll be fine. He won't believe you when he sees you." He rummaged through a pile of his clothes on a chair. "I'll walk you to the subway, little one."

"I can't wait, I'll be late." She combed her hair forward again. Black waves parted stubbornly over one ear.

"You have time." He was headless, then the neck of the faded turquoise polo shirt dilated and his head appeared, its contours readable because his long hair was pulled taut inside the shirt. He drew the hair out; honey-brown and light-streaked, it fell past his shoulders. From above a cradle of wrinkles his eyes, one blue, one green, fastened her.

"I can't wait for you," she said.

He walked her, slowly, to the subway. "You should take a cab," he said. He buttoned her jacket, black velvet balding at the cuffs. When he hugged her goodbye, she held on to the waistband of his red overalls. " 'Flawless and brilliant.' Remember," he said. She climbed down to dull mustard-tiled walls, down to eyes preying sidelong, empty hands that knew the weight of her purse hanging from her shoulder, knew how delicately her arm fit in its socket. Could she tell them when they came for her, their steps silent in stolen imitation Adidas, "Not today, please. I have to get uptown." At the bottom of the stairs she smiled up at him because she knew he expected her to.

Down another flight of stairs, she unbuttoned her jacket. On the platform a man read the *Post*, a woman hummed "O Holy Night," a girl with no mirror put on mascara. Dina saw the vast territory of the future spread out in the wash colors of maps. She would discover something she needed to know. She would be saved. The train, arriving, would roar.

She was small and occasionally pretty. She looked trusting and soft and shy, and since she examined her face frequently— in mirrors and the chrome sides of toasters and the shining blades of knives, in whatever reflecting surface was handy when the urge for confirmation struck—she wondered at her outward misrepresentation. She thought of herself as fierce and devouring, one unending demand for an unknowable benediction. She couldn't define it, she couldn't discover who would bestow it on her. She believed herself capable of any cruelty in pursuit of it. This terrifying aspect she hid so well that she felt in danger of disappearing completely. She needed to see herself in mirrors to make sure she was still there. And what she saw confused her.

Fragile-looking yet surprisingly voluptuous, she resembled a scaled-down ancient love goddess, the gilded plastic replica sold at museum shops: full breasts, a narrow waist, full hips. She looked desirable and, because of her size, manageable. Her large gray eyes, dark-lashed, and plump lower lip, somewhat chapped, were inviting. She radiated the intensity and sweetness of a young girl. Her image confused her because she felt no connection to it.

She wouldn't let Larry kiss or touch her full breasts. "They hurt." She didn't want him inside her, his hands on her full hips. "It hurts." At night after he fell asleep, she warmed her hand against her thigh, moving stealthily not to wake him.

She believed that angry thoughts, hers or anyone else's, caused harm. If during a fight she wished Larry were dead, then soon he'd end up face down, doing a cramped dead-man's float, in the ringed bathtub; or he'd slip in the unscooped sidewalk droppings of an unleashed Saint Bernard and tumble into Seventh Avenue as a beer truck doing sixty tried to make the light. To counteract her anger she tapped certain objects a certain number of times or blinked her eyes or held her breath. Some nights before she could sleep she had to climb down from the loft bed and touch the bathroom faucet twice with her index fingers, twice with her middle fingers, twice with her thumbs. Other nights required two or three pilgrimages. For her twenty-fifth birthday Larry made a purple papier-mâché faucet and cemented it to the wall near the bed. "That'll save you mileage, little one," he said. She never used it.

If a stranger passing on the street, a Portuguese woman in black contending with a toddler and a bag of dried cod, wished Dina harm, it would come true unless she protected herself. She held her breath or forcibly exhaled as the other passed. These precautions gave her a breathless quality and the tentativeness of

37

a person on the brink of oxygen deprivation. She accomplished her rituals more or less by rote, as the fulfillment of compulsions: she *had* to touch the faucet, never mind why.

She cried easily and had weak ankles, no arches, and a medley of allergies. Larry complained that they spent more money on antihistamines and tissues than on food. "It's clear you weren't breast-fed," he'd tell her when her nose itched and her throat ached and her eyes burned. It gave him another reason to hate her parents. "Any normal mother breast-feeds her child."

She had learned not to answer these provocations if she wanted to avoid a harangue about her parents, moral unfitness of. Then she would be obliged to defend them, if only for logic's sake, at key points in his oration. But sometimes she couldn't resist answering.

"Asshole, jerk, I hate you, you fucking shit," she shrieked at him. "I could almost kill for a little peace and quiet."

"Almost doesn't count," he reminded her, and twisted her arm up behind her back.

She didn't like the wild screaming person she became in her fights with him. She wondered who she would be in a room with daylight through the windows. He might be someone else there too. She could remember bright rooms she'd grown up in, a maid ironing her clothes, the endless power of her mother's checkbook at department stores. "You can't beat real estate," her mother said, and got a license to frame for the den. Dina could remember her father at the dinner table, saying that AT&T and Honeywell had gone up. She'd pictured bees ascending in a blue sky. A call from the hospital interrupted him. Until she was five or six, she didn't know the difference between *patients* and *patience*. According to her mother, somebody's daughter's ring was four carats, somebody else's daughter had been—never mind. A horn-handled carving knife slid through roast beef in a pool of red on a white oval platter edged with gold.

An upper-middle-class upbringing had convinced her that she didn't want to be an upper-middle-class wife, but it hadn't equipped her to solve poverty. Her idea of survival involved paying bills and the virtue of responsibility, which she mistook for respectability. The bills got paid sooner or later, for her pride, not honor. But poverty required more guile than she could admit to having, and less despair.

In escaping a four-carat ring and "never mind," she had hoped to unrein her imagination, to ascend with the Honeywell bees in the bluest of skies. She cashed the college graduation check from her parents and fled to New York and freedom. Her mother's weekly phone calls proposed graduate school, a white Mustang with red interior, and/or a psychiatrist. "Come home," her father said. For a hundred dollars a roommate service placed her in the East Twenty-sixth Street apartment of "a suitable young professional woman matched to your personality by computer." Carole was thirty-four and in Better Dresses at Lord & Taylor. "You want something, I'll let you in on half my employee discount." She didn't wash fruit before she ate it. Dina worked mornings as a receptionist at a furniture showroom—a forest of veneer—and spent the afternoons writing stories about working in a furniture showroom. The doctor son of a doctor friend of her father's took her out for a drink at Maxwell's Plum. He was tall and quiet and kind. She focused on despising him for his suit. When he asked to see her again, she was flattered and desolate. "I'm getting married," she told him. A mug of beer raced across the bar. Waiting for a free stool at a Chock Full O' Nuts, she met Larry, his hair in three loops tied with rawhide thongs. She knew he was a rock star with a weakness for date-nut bread. "Princess," he labeled her. "Pirate," she responded. He gave her "Guernica" at the Museum of Modern Art and ducked behind Louise Bourgeois's "Sleeping Figure." He had her blouse off at his apartment and was explaining that he couldn't sketch her if she kept her bra on when his roommate, a night clerk at the Animal Medical Center, came in early. "A marmoset bit me," he said, unlacing his sneakers. Larry and Dina splurged on a room at the Hilton, blocks away. Johnny Carson's hair was orange on the color TV. "You should take your parents up on that Mustang," Larry said. "You can always sell it. Should we spring for

39

the coffee shop in the morning?" The next day he gave her a picture of herself sleeping. He'd drawn it on a Hilton menu, under DESSERTS. They got married three weeks later and moved into a place of their own, situated in picturesque poverty that Dina believed she'd always remember fondly. They were still there. After six years Dina's fondness for it had long ago vanished. She had hoped that by holding Larry, she would be holding art. Instead she had trapped herself as wholly as a suburban matron, but with no consolations: no house, car, charge accounts, neatly stitched episiotomy.

"We can be partners," she whispered to him at the model-boat pond in Central Park one afternoon, afraid to say it louder because he might get angry. A braid coiled on his shoulder. "Just part-time jobs for both of us and enough free time to do what we want."

Two women with baby carriages went by. One of the women was wearing low-heeled brown leather boots with red cuffs. On the other side of the pond children squealed and a man shouted, "*No*, Edward, no!" A German shepherd had jumped in the water. Its head glided among miniature aircraft carriers.

Larry said, "I told you I'm not—not ever—going to work all day at some shit job so I can have a bigger apartment to fall asleep in like a fucking zombie. Where are your—"

"Just part-time, not all day—"

"Where are your fucking parents, don't they want to see you happy?"

"What about you?"

"I'm not here on earth to make you happy." His mouth puckered in satisfaction. "You want to be happy, go find a lawyer to marry."

A squirrel came to their bench, begging for food. Once, she'd liked watching squirrels, but now they reminded her of rats darting across open spaces. That morning the exterminator had left trays of poison in the cellar. She peered into a shiny black eye, round, provident, brave.

● ● ●

The train, arriving, roared. There remained the question of whether or not she'd be saved. The girl with mascara brushed against her as they entered the car. "Sorry," the girl said. Dina nodded and smiled and nodded. She couldn't speak because she was holding her breath.

R osemary was descended from the *Review*, which had established a respectable circulation among college libraries and large bookstores in college towns. The intricate woodblock *R* on its masthead had been carved by a student, Dickie N. Thornton, forty years before; thirty-five years later his widow, Lydia with plumed moles, provided a fund to perpetuate the magazine, with the provision that Dickie's *R* should also endure. Otherwise the *Review*'s budget was sheer charity from the university, a purchase of prestige, vulnerable when money was tight. If something had to be cut, it wouldn't be pipettes or textbooks on the Arapaho or "self-resilient" basketball hoops, it would be poetry. No one pretended distress or a polite hesitation, a conscience-tweaking. Howard's predecessor, Dr. Zablau, didn't protest when the alumni newsletter's funding was increased and the *Review*'s reduced. Alumni endowed libraries and locker rooms and—who knows?—Dr. Zablau's own salary; poetry's rewards, like God's, were less easily grasped. Dr. Zablau believed in God and literature, but, having fled Würzburg in 1937, had no wish to inflict his beliefs on anyone. Then too he may have worried that he'd used up his life's allotment of luck in escaping from Germany; it remained for him to nurture anonymity so one of God's bookkeepers wouldn't notice him one day and say, "Look, there's old Sam yelling about trochees, and after all we did for him." Next would come a heart attack outside a cafeteria, where he would lie twitching on the sidewalk while people passed him for a drunk and someone pretending to loosen his tie would steal his wallet. He dreaded that the last thing he'd see would be such a face, the jackal's, bending over him. As it turned out, he died inside a cafeteria, having choked on a raisin in a piece of raisin toast, though what he'd asked for was rye; noticing the mistake, he'd said nothing, thinking there are worse tragedies in the world than getting the wrong kind of bread. The last thing he saw was the face of the cashier, rouged, with very blue eyelids, and old.

Zablau's death opened a position that no one rushed to fill. Being editor of the *Review* guaranteed big headaches for practically no money. An ambitious instructor or professor of literature would do better to spend extracurricular time writing a critical study of *Madame Bovary*. The sixteen critical studies of *Madame Bovary* then circulating (among them *Emma Bovary and Louise Colet: The Distance of Art from Life* and *Flaubert and the Cost of Perfection* and *Bovary: Search for Perfection*) weren't deterrents but proof that the subject was, as the professors liked to say, viable. The existing studies made further work easier; instead of originating a theory about Flaubert, the upward-striving professor simply wrote a book attacking an already published theory. The professor now had a book of his own to wave around at evaluation time, to help him achieve tenure, and to require his students to buy during the semester they covered Flaubert. They covered too the professor's book on Flaubert and any of the sixteen other studies he may have assigned or they may have found while casing the library stacks for a private place to light up a quick joint. Some sweetly stoned students with dried chocolate milk at the corners of their mouths tried to look up Emma Bovary in the authors' catalogue. The professors moved on to critical studies of *Bleak House* or *Mansfield Park* or, for the venturesome, the works of the yet-un-Nobeled Beckett. There was no profit for anyone as editor of the *Review*.

Into this vacuum walked Howard, sober and purposeful in a borrowed suit. His eyes shone with comprehension, the whites clearer than they would ever be again. His hair wasn't yet paling with wisdom. Having tearfully and sloppily left Margery and the

43

children, he arrived in the city and through the intercession of Felix, who owed him something, achieved an interview with the chairman of the English department of the university, Felix's mother's friend's onetime Platonic lover and a specialist in Flaubert.

"Who is your favorite writer, hmm?" the chairman asked.

"Flaubert," Howard announced, "and after him Marvell, who was before him."

The chairman rode in an oak swivel chair on casters to the bright window and apologized for misplacing Howard's résumé. Howard faced a corona of glare describing a thick, shadowed presence. He hadn't sent a résumé. He knew the chairman could see him with no difficulty, but what was it the chairman saw— another body to stand yammering at kids, another mind offering itself on the grubby altar of literature, beneath a cloud of buzzing flies? Canon fodder, an unemployed homeless copywriter, a cuckold, a creep?

The shadow at the window rumbled. Had Howard ever taught?

Yes, yes, he lied. Yes.

There *was* one class in creative writing. Freshman, of course.

"Of course," Howard said. Did the chairman have a ring he should kiss? He had hemmed his borrowed pants with long stitches the night before. Bowing might loosen his needlework.

It would be in the nature of a probationary endeavor.

"Naturally," Howard said.

And there was the matter of the *Review*, a literary quarterly. He would be entrusted with its editorship—for a probationary period. He would of course receive additional compensation for those duties.

"What exactly do I do?" Howard asked.

"You read manuscripts of poetry and stories, and essays too, and you select some and get them printed."

"Writing from students?"

"Writing from people. Writers. Students are seldom either."

Howard's beautiful smile dawned. "I get *paid* to do this?" There had to be a catch. Why should he be handed this prize?

The chairman misunderstood and rolled closer. "Yes, paid. Look here, you don't have to do it, but someone has to do it, and it doesn't seem unfair to ask you, you have only one class, and that by a bit of luck, timing; the class is really not the essential matter. If you feel you don't want to—"

"Excuse me, sir. When do I start?"

He had entered the dean's office a disgraced onetime would-be copywriter and failed anthologist, and left it an editor and college teacher, still in a borrowed suit. This lesson, the limits of metamorphosis, impressed him as something worth challenging.

The energy he would have put into plotting the vivisection of Margery or at least into making her understand how much she had lost when she lost him, he now put into his work. He pitied and loathed the forty-three students in Creative Writing I for their efforts and muttered to them once in exasperation that he was renaming the course Creative Typing I. Their applause surprised him. He pitied them for trying and failing; he loathed them for trying in the first place. They interfered with his real work, a quest for love. His mistress would be literature, and he would establish her in the . . . The next word should have been *Review*, but he declined it as unacceptable, a moldy tidbit from somebody else's bygone party. He would rename the magazine, to signal its new spirit. (He'd never read the *Review*, but he knew that under him it would be different from anything it had been before.)

It seemed he had the world to choose from, short of short anatomical terms and ethnic slander. He could name the magazine *Henry* or *Tree* or *Cut Along Dotted Line*. The exhilaration was greater than when he'd tried to name his children, his lost babies, because this progeny would be solely his. But, after checking with the chairman, he saw his choice shrink to anything beginning with *R*, Dickie Thornton's hand-carved *R* that formed the logo for the *Review*; he couldn't obliterate the past, even a past he didn't know. He resigned himself, then brightened: heading a new name, the *R* would uphold continuity and acknowledge underlying values in the midst of change. He celebrated his rationale at dinner with Felix in a French restaurant serving Italian wine. After two glasses of Chianti, while Felix fired at him, "Red, robin, riff, rest, roost, rapid transit, rape, rooster, Rasputin, Raskolnikov, Rosebud, rookery, rye, Rosenberg, Rex, rattler, resource, Rhonda," he let his blurring menu scream from the translated *Poulet* section: " . . . with the Garlic and Rosemary."

"Rosemary," he said.

"Why not Rhonda?"

"Rosemary because it's a flavor *and* a woman—two women, Rose and Mary. Stein's 'I Am Rose,' Jesus's Mary, either Mary or both. The two sides of women."

Felix laughing, thrumming fingers on the table as if searching for the strings of his bass: "Okay, buddy pal, what're the two sides of women?"

Howard looked at him full-face, then inspected his glass of wine. "The front and the back. Cheers."

Months later, before sending his first issue to the printer, he added a line from Shakespeare to the masthead: "There's Rosemary, that's for remembrance." He cut it there, thinking it was enough of a nod to the magazine's academic source; drawn, overtired, living in a sublet without a roach of his own, he didn't include the next line, "Pray you, love, remember."

He sat in Sam Zablau's chair at Sam Zablau's desk, which the maintenance man, Beau, had cleaned out, packing the personal contents and three framed pictures in a carton stamped Lettuce. It remained in the office, its label a red flash at the corner of Howard's eye, until its removal to a university basement, where it waited for a year before being claimed by Rivke Bester from Fort Tryon, a third cousin of the late Sam. Beau himself would die before the year was over, stabbed at a cockfight in a two-car garage in Jamaica, Queens, far from the Jamaica of his birth. Mr. Martinez would clean out Beau's locker and store the contents in a carton stamped Eggs for two weeks until Léonie Beauvrais, widow, came to pick it up.

Howard meditated on the red word Lettuce. All his possessions—the clothes at the sublet apartment and the six books he had flung into an A&P bag as he left Margery—would have fit in the Lettuce carton, with room left over. He let this image bear down on him. His face was tranquil and grave. He took in the three beige rectangles, Cyclops-nailed, on the darker beige wall where the framed pictures had been; the filthy windows, Sam's grime, clouding light, dulling a snow-spotted park twelve floors below; and the piles of envelopes menacing him with poems and stories and essays and correspondence intended for Sam Zablau and waiting, waiting, some of them for over six months. The oak chair, movable in crab fashion on creaking casters like the chairman's chair, held his body resentfully; after twenty years or more of Sam Zablau, it didn't want him, an intruder.

"I'd like a new chair," he said.

"That is new," Beau answered. "Puffessor Zablau only had it but since last October." He set down a bucket reeking of ammonia.

"Then I'd like a different new chair."

"I'm to do the windows."

"Can I get this place painted?"

"I know you can get these windows washed." Beau opened a window to cold and the illusion of fresh air.

Howard picked up the phone and wiped the mouthpiece once with his sleeve, then wiped the earpiece. There was no dial tone.

"How do I call out?"

But Beau was already outside, strapped to the building, squeegeeing a pane of glass.

It didn't matter. Howard had nobody to call.

That Saturday morning he arrived at the office with Felix and a stepladder and two paintbrushes and two gallons of white paint and a can of turpentine and a takeout order of two cups of coffee and six doughnuts, half of them chocolate at Felix's cranky insistence.

"God *damn*," Felix said as he backed out of the room, carrying half of Sam Zablau's desk while Howard followed him, grunting, with the other half. "I got a matinee."

"Get the chair, Felix, come on."

"I need to sleep, man. I didn't sleep all night."

Howard handed him a can of Arctic White. "Open it."

Felix obeyed, cursing. "I helped you with the job, good buddy. It's your problem how to make it pretty." His long black hair covered his eyes as he bent over the can.

Howard asked, "How much gratitude would you like?"

Felix grinned, gave an unrepentant "Sorry, man," before launching into a story about how stoned they all were in the pit the night before when the leading lady raced them through her second biggest number. "We're limping in after her, man, and Dave's looking up at the stage and telling her over the music, 'Hey, mama, this piano don't have wheels,' but the bitch goes right on."

They sat on the floor and drank coffee. Felix ate five dough-nuts while Howard described the furniture he'd bought for the office, indicating with sweeps of his small hands what would go where.

"Why can't you use the stuff that's here?"

"Do you like playing on somebody else's bass?" The minute he asked the question he regretted it because a roaring rose in his ears and blotted out whatever Felix was saying.

They agreed that the paint smelled terrible. Felix decided it affected his breathing. "You're lucky I don't play a horn," he said. With the first white strokes covering beige, Howard heard himself humming. Two coats, and it would be perfect.

Preparing the first issue of *Rosemary*, he expected the chairman or another tenured professor to sneak up and stand reading over his shoulder. No one did. He thought this denoted trust and later understood it had been indifference. To others the magazine was a symbol, tired and harmless, a dribble of words. To him it was a live and burning possibility, an opportunity hammering, a door opening into a malleable future, words stretching like newsprint on Silly Putty (oh his lost kids) to a point beyond distortion. And somewhere beyond distortion but before the snapping point, before the putty fractured under stress, somewhere between the two was transfiguration, when the words meant more than them-selves, when they erupted from neat and clever patterns, when they bopped and kicked to forever surprise, when they grinned and wailed and showed their sharp shocking teeth. The chairman and others assumed aesthetic struggles were bloodless. They believed they were getting a museum. He was going to give them a zoo.

He sped through the manuscripts that had accumulated since Sam Zablau's death, scanning each submission. The word *submission* summed up the problem he faced. He didn't want writing to crawl to him, hat in hand. He wanted to be assaulted by live grenades juggled before his eyes. He wanted the stories of tightrope walkers, words from the high wire, precise and deadly, with no net. He wanted the exultation of risk; and if it meant a soundless slow-motion fall to the sawdust and a thud punctured by bone cracking and the fascinating taste of blood, his own, then he wanted that too, and the bleached immobility to follow, a steel pin through the tibia, the weight of a plaster cast and the growing filth of it, and earthbound crutches rammed against armpits.

And so, when a story began,

> Often it has been observed that the railway journey is the best method of traveling, even in this age of the airplane. It has to be remembered that speed is not necessarily progress; and that sometimes the old-fashioned ways are still the best. In the coach that had just departed Norwich and was bound for Lancaster sat a traveler who best exemplified this attitude. She was a widow named Mrs. Prescott. Nora Prescott was forty-eight years old and wore her auburn hair, which was not dyed, up in a bun. Her knowing azure eyes looked out the window. She was wearing a smart navy voile dress that her late husband, Dr. George Prescott, always liked. She liked to wear it now because it reminded her of him. She was going to visit her daughter, Jessica, in Lancaster, to try and persuade her not to become one of the Amish if she possibly could help it. Little did Mrs. Prescott know how far this journey would take her ...,

he flipped to the last page to see if there was any hope, any reason to read all nineteen pages.

"It's beautiful, Mom," Jessica whispered, "but I don't think my new religion allows earthly vanities."

Mrs. Prescott nodded sadly. "I suppose," she said, "you're right." Then she knew what she had to do. She announced, "I will sell it when I get home and send the money to you and Jim."

Looking at the beautiful pearl ring, Mrs. Prescott remembered how happy she and the Doctor had been. It was only right that she sell the ring now. The happiness did not live in the ring, but in her memory. As long as she had that, she had everything. She had come to Lancaster to rescue her daughter, but she was leaving after rescuing herself.

He packed "Earthly Vanities" into the stamped, addressed envelope accompanying it. Between the first and last pages there was nothing he could rescue with his black-ink fountain pen or a carving knife or a blowtorch. He had given more time than he owed to—he checked the envelope—Frank Driesch of Richmond, California. How old was Frank Driesch? Did he have acne or a beer belly? Did he teach botany or wash cars, and if he washed cars did he charge twice as much for a Caddy as for a Chevy? Was he a pederast or a cyclist? Did he breed chinchillas in his garage for fun and profit? Howard licked the envelope and, after speculating about a syphilitic Frank Driesch, made a note to get a moistener, a rotating china cylinder half submerged in a saucer of water, for sealing flaps.

He hastened too through stories quivering with sensitivity on onionskin sheets and stories titled "Untitled" beginning "Downdeep backward from halfheart yearning in the green and golden almostautumn of nobody's starlong youth where lion-strided Boy and blackeyed Girl befrill the crazydaisied meadow with moantossing yes yes rapture." He was equally severe with poetry.

How must this love of mine compete with tears,
Completely in your presence I do wait
To estimate the value of your fears,
The loss of which I bid you contemplate . . .

was as far as he got on a sonnet, and of the six-page single-spaced "Verdure and Ordure" he managed only

> It doesn't
> Matter
> What you tell
> The New York
> Times when
> Caliban's
> Becrapped and lost
> Beneath the furnace
> Of the smoking mouth
> That was the Camels
> Sign on
> Narrow Broad-
> Way. Synchronize
> Your watches. Here
> Comes
> Times
> Square.
> No Einstein theory...

He slogged through critiques and book reviews, the quicksand of footnotes. Who cared about symbolism in Emerson's poetry or about Jane and Rochester's sex life? What about the question of whether or not Emerson's poetry *was* poetry? What about Charlotte Brontë's sex life, a portrait to be called "Lottie Panting"? For that matter, what about the sex life of the person writing about the sex lives of fictional characters? For that matter, since he'd dreamed up "Lottie Panting," what about his own sex life?

He wanted to read words that connected to something true. He wanted to be disarmed, he wanted to be aroused. He was listening for a voice that unmistakably, stubbornly insisted on itself, couldn't be anything but itself, faithfulness as instinct or, if instinct failed, faithfulness as an act of courage.

He was searching for something beloved. It wouldn't arrive in a neat package. He expected bile and bowels, entrails of dismay, false clues, field days for maggots. He was prepared, eager even, to dirty his hands birthing it. The emergence wouldn't be pretty. He admired his own cynicism. It never occurred to him that his search for this beloved, his belief in its existence, proved his idealism. He captioned himself "Facing Facts at Last." Some nights he fell asleep on the new sofa in his office. He woke with a bruised coccyx and a rush of joy at the sight of daylight.

Among the submissions to Sam were several tolerable pieces, two derivative from Kerouac, one a fair Cheever likeness, a few decent poems by a Wallace Stevens clone, and a story about a French soldier in Saigon, which he'd seen mentioned somewhere else, in Malraux or the *Times*. He wrote an encouraging note to each of the authors, asking for more "of your best."

Next he went to the university bookstore and with his food money bought an issue of every literary review and journal it carried. That week he had a cream cheese sandwich on stale white bread for his nightly dinner. On Monday he propped an open Southern quarterly with surrealist undertones against a stack of other magazines and read about serpents laying eggs of despair while he ate. On Tuesday a California review dedicated its issue to Stephen and Ichabod Crane. By the weekend he wished he'd had enough money for a tomato. His budget, devised by Margery's lawyer, Smiling Bob McGrath of McGrath & Feinstein, had no allowance for a toaster, which in the separation agreement would have been "hereinafter to be called 'Toaster' "; and he'd already spent his "hereinafter to be called 'Household Furnishings Allowance' " on his office. If the kids needed Buster Browns and Yankee Doodles, he'd forgo a tomato. But he choked on cream cheese at the thought of keeping Margery in coral lipstick and stockings.

After reading the competition, he selected the few writers he liked and wrote to most of them in care of the magazines, inviting contributions to *Rosemary*. If the usual biographical statement accompanying a piece said the writer lived in New York City, Howard called Information for the number. The spy for literature fooled the operator. Where could he buy a decoder ring? He tugged off his wedding band and threw it out the office window before dialing.

"Hello."

"Hello, may I speak to Newman Sykes, please?"

"I'm Newman Sykes."

"Well, hello. Mr. Sykes?"

"Yes?"

"My name is Howard Ritchie. I'm the editor of a new magazine, *Rosemary*? I saw the *Continental Quarterly*. Your story? Wonderful, your story. Flawless, brilliant."

"Thank you."

". . . Like to see more of your work . . . meet . . . if you have time."

"Fine."

". . . A story of yours in *Rosemary*."

"Wonderful."

"Hope . . . not disturbing you."

"No, no. When should we meet?"

". . . Drink coffee?"

"Coffee, beer, apricot nectar."

"We could have coffee."

"Yes."

"Then let's . . . coffee."

"Fine."

"Where?"

"What's convenient for you, Mr. Ritchie?"

Nothing was convenient for him because he couldn't afford anything, but he couldn't have anyone come to the office, either. He'd been sleeping there for a week, and though his dirty socks and briefs and shaving kit were filed under *H*, for House, in his new oak filing cabinet (his new desk was a narrow slate-topped table with a single shallow drawer suitable for pencils and a dagger), he didn't feel up to conducting the business of art in what was by default—and McGrath—his bedroom. He met Newman in a bar on Hudson Street and paid for their drinks with a five-dollar bill he'd borrowed from a Creative Typing I student, a cryptorchid premed who expected to be repaid and to get an A and was, for the second and third times in his life, disappointed.

53

Rosemary's maiden issue sold the same modest number of copies as the *Review* always had. "Good work," the chairman said on line in the faculty cafeteria one morning to Howard or the stewed plums.

Howard had never seen the chairman standing. "Did you like the story about the collie puppy?" he asked.

"Yes, excellent, very enjoyable." Without casters, the chairman rolled over to the tapioca.

There wasn't any story about a collie puppy. Which explained the absence of controversy about *Rosemary*: no one had read it. Howard put a cup of fruit salad on his tray and snatched a maraschino cherry from another cup. He pocketed several cellophane-wrapped servings of crackers though he wasn't having soup. What would the chairman say about the story on orgasm, "Wrench House"?

The next issue sold better, and the next. For the fourth one, Howard increased the printing. "You'll have a ton of them left over," the printer predicted over the phone. In the background machines gnashed their teeth. With the diplomacy of a man who can't afford to pay in advance, Howard agreed while confirming the order. The issue, dedicated to Lennie and Sir David Bruce, was a runaway success, at least for a literary magazine, with all copies sold and bookstores requesting more. Newsstand suppliers in several big cities expressed interest. By then the chairman and others at the school had looked at *Rosemary* to see what the fuss was about, but by then it was too late. The magazine had done something unprecedented: it was showing a profit.

Felix said, "Money talks. Can't argue with success. A better mousetrap. The buck stops at the bottom line. In cash we trust." He was trying to cheer Howard up. "Can I have your pickle?"

Howard pushed his plate toward Felix.

"Hey, buddy pal, we're celebrating here, remember?"

Howard nodded.

"Then act, like, happy."

"Margery filed for divorce. I got the notice today."

"Well, no big shock. Can I have your tomato?"

"She's divorcing me on grounds of adultery."

"So?"

"Mine, not hers."

"Buddy, it's a technicality. You can't get divorced unless you say somebody cheated, and it's nicer to say the guy did."

"I'm getting a raise."

"Great. There's something we can celebrate."

"That means Margery gets more money."

"Spread the wealth."

"Fuck off."

"Hey, hey, hey, negativo on displays of hostility there, prince."

"You could've kept your goddamn hands off her."

"C'mon, man, she practically raped me."

"You and Ferlinghetti."

"What'd he do?"

"Sometimes I think up ways to get even with you."

"Like what?"

"Set your bass on fire."

"That's good."

"Beat you up."

"I can take you."

"I know. Hire a goon to break your fingers."

"That's sick."

"Sounds good to me."

"You can't afford it."

"I told you, I'm getting a raise."

"I love you like a brother, How."

"Lucky me."

"Hey, you'll do better than Margie, you'll see."

Oh the poor lost babies.

He moved into a one-bedroom apartment with his own name on the lease and the doorbell. He snowblinded it with Arctic White and Arctic White Enamel. On a rainy Sunday he sanded the floor twice, cleaned it up with Felix's mother's Hoover, and applied varnish. Humidity prevented the finish from drying within the four to six hours claimed on the can. His feet in old wool socks stuck to the floor. He walked to his shoes at the door with a mime's exaggerated steps and slept at the office that night, for the last time. The next day he furnished the apartment with a sleeping bag and a dying philodendron he'd found outside his sublet door a month earlier. It was still dying.

Margery divorced him, naming as co-respondent in her suit Miss Rosemary Smith. She must have thought that was hilarious. He had his lawyer, Tim Rudkin, a recent graduate of the university's law school, correct the name to Mrs. Rosemary Smith. What made Margie think Rosemary was single? "After all, Marge," he told her when he stopped by to see the kids, "we all know about some married women." Paul said, "Hi, Howard," and when Howard gently reminded the boy to call him Daddy, Paul answered, "See you, Howard," and left the room. Howard wondered if smacking his kid on visiting day, one Sunday a month, would damage their future relationship. Ilene, chubby and damp, with a new, crooked smile, settled in his lap while Margery explained how the trauma of divorce had made the baby forget her toilet training. Howard said he hoped Margery hadn't forgotten hers.

Before the final decree Tim Rudkin was arrested at a draft-card burning in Foley Square and had to remove himself from Howard's case to attend to his own. Howard signed whatever Smiling Bob McGrath gave him. The day the divorce became final he went to Sloane's and bought a sale bed, the floor sample of a plain beech style from Sweden. The idea that several hundred strangers had sat, bounced, and lain on his bed comforted him; he wasn't alone. He was sure they hadn't dragged their shoes across the mattress on purpose.

The seventh issue of *Rosemary* brought him notice from the *Times*, a paragraph in an article headed "Renaissance of the Small Presses." He didn't remember saying what the article had him saying. ("My commitment is to new writers.") What he couldn't leave uncorrected was his name, reported as Harold Ritchie. He wrote a letter to the paper on the importance of names generally and his own in particular. ("That *how* in Howard has stamped me as no *har* in Harold could do. . . .") The *Times* published it, and he had to take his office phone off the hook for a few days to get any work done.

He began to hear from established writers seeking to publish stories that their editors at *Esquire* and the *New Yorker* and *Harper's* and the *Atlantic* had rejected for being too far out or too shut in or too overtly sensual.

"What's 'overtly sensual'?" one of these writers asked Howard in exasperation.

"When you say fuck in a story."

He didn't care if they said fuck in their stories, he didn't care what they said as long as he liked the way they said it and they weren't advocating murder or unkindness to little children. For that time and with the respectability of the university behind him, his attitude surpassed arrogance: it was revolutionary.

He championed free speech for himself too. His remarks about other editors and various writers were broadcast uncensored from bars and the wine tables at literary gatherings.

"Would you like to meet the author?" a public-relations presence tending toward the female asked him at a publication party.

"No, but where's the Chivas?"

He made enemies, always a sign of ascendancy. A *New Yorker* editor lunching with an agent at the Algonquin referred to him as "a drunken boor tripping toward the sensationally obvious." The characterization enraged another *New Yorker* editor, who heard about it at a dinner party where the agent's husband's agent repeated it after the salad. In a cab stalled in traffic on the ramp around Grand Central Station, the two editors, former lovers, had a screaming fight about Howard Ritchie's integrity. The third passenger in the cab, a current lover of one or both of the editors, witnessed the fight and reenacted it from time to time, on request, during lulls in editorial meetings at the fashion magazine she supplied with breathless statements on the A-line in jet and plum.

A month later three jolly paragraphs about Howard and *Rosemary* appeared in the *New Yorker*'s "Talk of the Town." To be written about in the *Times* was certification; to be written about in the *New Yorker* was apotheosis. The university awarded him an American Express card and one-third interest in a secretary.

He went to Bloomingdale's and bought two reproduction rod-back Windsor chairs and a plain beech table for his apartment. They weren't on sale.

"My commitment is to new writers," he told the audience at a Connecticut liberal arts college where he delivered a lecture, "Brand X Literature," for a fee that could have purchased half a leather sofa. He stayed overnight at a Holiday Inn with a bidet in the bathroom, all expenses paid, and flirted solemnly with senior faculty wives at a cocktail party in his honor. A student, a blond beefy boy who was driving to New York, gave him a ride home in a VW Beetle with shearling seatcovers and made several allusions to the Movement, which Howard in his post-flirtation decline chose to ignore.

The night after his return he killed a bottle of thirty-year-old brandy with Felix, then told him to get the hell out and stay out.

"Whaddya mean, How?"

"No more How. No more buddy pal."

They were on their feet, swaying. They might have been doing a courtship dance, if they'd been birds. The beech table was a well-designed solid between them. In the harsh light of the standard ceiling fixture Howard kept meaning to replace, Felix's face greened. Why would a woman want a man like that?

"Get out." The thrill of fear as Felix passed him, close enough to touch, close enough to punch. The door closing quietly. Didn't know Felix could be so quiet.

The next morning, with a hangover and an intense stare—if he stared hard, his ears didn't hurt—Howard limped into Creative Typing I in Room 390-B. His red-threaded eyes rested on each of his female students. He'd been celibate too long, not counting a hooker (a mistake: on learning he was an editor, she

unreeled her life story in long sentences strung with *and*s and *and
so*s), a woman he'd met in a bar with Felix, a divorced friend of
divorced Margery he'd run into at a wall of hammers in a hardware
store, and a PR woman at a publication party for a cheese book,
who'd introduced herself as a hell of a lay and was. But these had
been accidental, solitary couplings generated by liquor or sadness
or boredom. He watched a thin girl with the requisite scapula-
length straight shining hair parted in the middle. She was reading
aloud her latest story drowning in menstrual symbolism. When
she finished, she turned to him, her pendulous silver and turquoise earrings, also requisite, flashing, and he nodded thought-
fully. Nice tits.

A pale, thin man came to the reception area for her. "Good God," he said, "what are you, nineteen?" The two secretaries whispered to each other. He kept glancing back at her as he led the way to his office.

"I'm twenty-eight," she said apologetically.

"Don't ever tell anybody else. It's much more . . ." The sentence finished in a mumble while he cleared a space on the sofa for her. She sat among piles of manuscripts, books, magazines. She put her purse on some magazines, picked it up again, tapped it unobtrusively on either side. His phone rang and he said, "One minute." She put her purse on the floor and looked around the room.

There were pictures everywhere, framed photographs on the walls from floor to ceiling: famous writers and obscure ones, variously inscribed to Howard Ritchie with love, respect, admiration, suspicion, hesitation, or, in a calligraphic instance, "cheerful loathing" from an infamous writer fattened on TV talk shows but bony and evasive in this early picture. And among the writers on one wall there were two photographs of a beautiful woman. She smiled on a beach, her fine-boned face aloof, a long thigh interrupting the horizon. Holding a champagne glass, she followed Howard Ritchie, hatted and one stride ahead of her, in a restaurant. His wife. His handsomeness showed more clearly in the picture than in person, as if the drama he embodied required an isolated historical moment to contain it. He said, "Margery," into the phone in a flat voice and caught Dina watching him. His eyes lowered, hers traveled upward.

On the wall behind him, between two windows, was a child's drawing. Flowers or people floated in a void created by three bold lines. Next to it was a color photograph of him with his arms around a thin blond unsmiling girl. Sheltered by his striped blue and gray shirt, the child faced the camera with measured assurance; her father, guarding her, stared down the photographer. "Margery," he said into the phone again, and Dina envied the safety and purpose of his life: his place to work, his family, the serious blond daughter and the woman on the walls who was no doubt the Margery he now politely argued with. She longed to be politely argued with. She longed to be photographed in a restaurant with a husband who was moving forward, even if he kept a pace ahead, because if it were her picture with him, he wouldn't be a pace ahead; she'd be right there keeping up, careful not to get ahead herself. "Margery." He drummed his fingers on the desk. Would he ever ask for her picture to put with the other writers' pictures? How would she inscribe it? First she had to imagine a fired and deathless friendship with him, his benevolent mentorship, her flowering, his subsequent willing eclipse in homage to her talent. She inspected the writers' gallery again, to pick her spot. All the writers were men.

"Now," he said, putting down the phone. His hungry, mournful expression stirred in her an emotion she decided was nervousness.

"It's brilliant. Flawless." He pulled a manuscript from a pile of papers.

Yes, she thought, you already said that. Her typed pages blotched with Wite-Out rested under his hands. "It's messy."

"No, it's very neat. Surprisingly neat. Tell me about yourself."

She had been found in a rush basket floating in a river. On her right shoulder she bore the sign of royalty, a pink birthmark shaped like a nuclear power plant. "What do you want to know?"

"Where'd you grow up?"

"California." Reluctantly: "La Jolla."

"That so? Do you miss it?" His questions had only a slight interrogatory inflection. He was sly or bored or tired.

61

"No."

"Your parents still there?"

"Yes." She shriveled from writer to daughter.

"You have a character here named Ritchyoffsky. That used to be my father's name. Want some coffee?"

"No, thanks. Yes, please." She called after him to the hall, "No, none for me, thanks." She needed her compact mirror. But the urge to find herself almost visible behind a film of powder didn't outweigh the risk of embarrassment if he saw her doing it. She concentrated instead on deciphering his clutter: which pile of manuscripts was favored, which was spurned.

He returned humming, slouched, with a blue mug of coffee. She puzzled over his clothes, an odd combination of casual expensive things. He looked as though he'd reached into his closet in the morning and put on whatever he grabbed first. The resulting haphazard tastefulness was disarming: tweed jacket, well-worn loose corduroy trousers, muted plaid shirt, and a bow tie, olive and navy stripes. With his air of absentmindedness and his shrewd blue eyes, the effect was one of old money, of comfort and privilege genetically obtained.

"I like your jacket," she said.

"Thanks. It's a Ralph Lauren, had it for years. Too bad he's so popular now."

His father's name had been Ritchyoffsky. Yet Howard Ritchie couldn't have grown up hearing dark melodies of guilt through the speech of parents who were immigrants or the children of immigrants. He hadn't been born with an understanding of exile. He wasn't displaced, he was at home; he couldn't be Jewish.

"You remind me of someone," he said after two silent sips. "The first girlfriend I ever had. Same eyes. Her name was Sherry Bauer. Any relation?"

She shook her head. A teacher, Rabbi Bauer, had smelled of cherry cough drops. "Learn!" he commanded the children, striking Hebrew letters on the blackboard with a rubber-tipped pointer.

"My parents were unhappy about it. I was sixteen. I'm forty-four. I remember it." His smile did nothing to cheer his eyes.

"They never said it, but I'm sure they were upset because they thought I was *shtupping* her. You never heard that? It's slang, Yiddish for screwing."

The quasi-Englishman in tweed holding her story knew Yiddish. His leanness cut into space. He was eight years older than Larry. She closed one hand to dig nails into her palm for the distraction of pain.

"Tell me about yourself, that you never heard of *shtupping*."

She had come to his office as an invited writer; since it was the only identity she had, she wanted to keep it. But, having given it to her with his phone call, he now seemed inclined to take it away. "What do you want to know?" she asked for the second time.

"School," he decided.

"Berkeley—some English, some Ed., some Psych.—and before that public school, and Hebrew school once a week till I was eleven. I know what to do if a camel falls in the marketplace on the Sabbath."

"We're both Jewish." He leaned back in his chair with enjoyment. "And what do you do now, do you work?"

"I teach English part-time to foreign executives. A semester with me, and they can say, 'I would like to see your supervisor' and 'Do you deliver?' " She wasn't a writer. She'd never believed it anyway. The story he'd called about wasn't her design, it was a freak coherent union of her terrors.

"And you do this so you're free to write?" he asked.

"I do it to eat."

"You write every day?"

"No."

"You should."

"It's hard, the apartment's small, there's no privacy, and the library's full of winos and it's closed two extra days a week to save money and I can't afford to go to a coffee shop every afternoon, even if I could get a back table in a quiet place for a couple of hours." Besides, the branch library didn't have a public bathroom, not after a librarian, the nice one with the toupee, waded through two inches of water, vomit, urine, and excrement on the bathroom floor to find the plumbing problem: someone had tried to flush down Volume 2 of the *Britannica*. The book, bloated as a corpse fished from the Hudson, was stuck in the filthy bowl while the toilet kept running. What would happen to school-children with assignments on Luther Burbank? Democracy required that since the winos had to be kept out of the bathroom, everybody else had to be kept out too.

"You should write every day. Can't your parents help you? I'm assuming they're not poor."

"They're not." It was interesting how nail-digging in both fists didn't double the pain of nail-digging in one.

"And I'm assuming they're like most parents, Jewish parents, I know I'm one, I know how it is. Why do they let you live without money?"

Parents were an idea far away. They sent the idea of concern in references to dressing warm, the idea of love in a hundred-dollar birthday check. "I moved to New York to do exactly that. I'm an adult, Mr. Ritchie."

"No, please: Howard. I've offended you."

"No, it's okay, you haven't. But we haven't talked about my story."

Half-closed eyes flickered from her to the manuscript and back to her. "I want to know about your writing. Why don't you have privacy in your apartment?"

"Because it's one small room and my husband's there." It came out with the galled relief of a confession.

"Ah, the man on the phone when I called you. I thought he was D. Reeve. In fact from your story I thought you were a middle-aged man."

"I'm not."

"I pictured you as a disheveled man in a big raincoat, probably secondhand, with tobacco stains on your fingers. That's who I expected when I called." He chuckled into his collar before asking with sudden sobriety, "Can't you work when your husband's not there?"

"He's always there."

"He works at home?"

Her head moved down for the first part of a nod but didn't come up again. His questions narrowed the present to a doorless corridor leading from shame to shame.

"He writes?" Howard prompted.

"He's a painter. Right now he's concentrating on collages."

"Any showings?"

"No."

He sat straight up. "Why can't he do something to earn money too?"

It was so constant a question in her life that a stranger could ask it. "He does sometimes. At a florist's."

"He thinks it's all right for you to support him?"

"I don't, not always and not well, either." Her father called Larry "that pimp" and didn't grasp the implication: if Larry was a pimp, what was she?

"Do *you* think it's all right?"

"He says owning stuff is a joke. He says an artist has better things to do." She was pleading with him to understand. Her nose swelled with grief.

He ignored her tears. "No wonder your parents don't help. If a healthy adult male won't work . . ."

She sniffled. She sighed. This was how she had to pay for her story. "His parents were Danish Jews. Sometime in '43 the Danes ferried Jews over to Sweden, to save them from the Nazis. He was born in Sweden. Conceived there. But his parents gave him a Danish name. They could have gone back after the war— the Danish government protected the Jews' stuff—but his father wanted to go to Palestine. He wanted to be safe. The Danes shipped their possessions to them in Sweden, someplace near Malmö. They got to Palestine in '46 and changed Larry's Danish name to a Hebrew one. All their stuff was lost in transit. His mother died a couple of years after Palestine became Israel. She was working in a kibbutz. There was a sniper. Or some tomatoes exploded. I'm not sure. His father brought Larry to Cincinnati and changed his name from the Hebrew one to an American one. The father taught music at Hebrew Union College. Larry got to be an Eagle Scout. How's that for fitting in? He was a history major at NYU. He wanted to study art and his father wanted him to be a doctor. I guess they compromised. He got his master's in history too. European history. He wrote an essay on Josephus that won a prize. He started to go for his Ph.D., but his father was killed outside a movie theater. It was a revival of *Sullivan's Travels*. Nobody's sure if he saw it. Larry says his father liked Veronica Lake a lot. Somebody mugged him and then stabbed him. Larry says his father got killed because he did other people's work. Larry says all an artist should do is his own work."

Howard Ritchie picked up his coffee mug. "But if you agree with him that artists shouldn't have to work, why are you working?" He drank coffee and watched her cry.

She had told secrets, betrayed her parents and her husband and her shame to a mumbling stranger in a bow tie; and he had given her the odd exhilaration of having no secrets. Before they'd spoken, he'd known her secrets by reading her story. If she couldn't learn to trust him, she could learn how to betray him. She watched herself cry too.

He left the building with her. He had put on a gray fedora, like the one he was wearing in the restaurant picture with his wife. Over his shoulder he carried a beat-up leather pouch stuffed with books and papers. She missed the safety of his desk between them.

After a few steps she found his rhythm and followed it. People chased after the exhaust fumes of buses, flapped hands at cabs rolling on treadless tires. People frightened her with their shopping bags and attaché cases: men in ties and trench coats, women in French blazers and dignified skirts. She envied their steadiness and pitied them for it too. Their insignificance and hers made a sorrowing kinship. What will become of me? she wondered, longing to put her hands over her eyes, as if she were sitting through an axe-wielding scene in a horror movie.

"You'll get back to me with this," he said, meaning her story, which he'd returned to her in a manila envelope with someone else's address on it.

"Yes."

"Shorter, right? More ending. You understand?"

"No, but I guess I will when I try to do it."

"And you'll bring me more stories."

He was walking close to her. His scent would be clean, with faded cologne, she thought. He smelled of liquor, his jacket was steeped in it. She moved away. "I like your hat."

He grinned sadly and placed it on her head. "There you go."

His action and her response, a shy giggle, reminded her of high school flirting. She gave the hat back and fluffed her hair out at the sides.

"I'm that way." He pointed uptown, in the direction of a pretzel wagon and a black man hawking belts: "Real leather, genyoo*ine*, check it out."

"When do you want it?"

"Whenever you're ready." He was gone.

It wouldn't be dark for another hour at least. She was alone, on her own, free to do what she wanted. She could explore a department store, spray blasts of sample perfume on her neck and wrists. She could play in a bookstore. She could walk toward home and take a bus when she got tired. The manila envelope dropped, and she picked it up without touching the pavement. Near the subway entrance she halted to dig a token from her jeans pocket. A tall man wearing a gray suit almost bumped into her, and she followed him down the subway stairs. From her height four steps above him, holding her breath, she saw how precisely he had arranged his blond hair to cover a bald spot.

The sound of the key in the lock brought no response. She turned on the table lamp; dust particles floated through the beam. There was a note from Larry taped to the bathroom mirror, where he knew she'd find it.

> Beloved, have gone to pier. Come to me with all your good news to tell. Your adoring husband who is missing you, L. Walk on left side of Canal till Varick in case I'm coming back.

• • •

An Afghan and an Irish wolfhound sniffed each other at the gate to the pier. Their owners could have been any of a dozen people sitting along the broad wood railing, reading a newspaper or a book, doing needlepoint, staring at rust patterns on a ship moored there. A man crocheting something red hooted and leaned against his companion, a man wearing ponyskin chaps over jeans. Wind carried the hoot out to the river. The wolfhound appraised Dina with yellow eyes before placing its nose in the crook of her arm, to stain silk. "Thanks," she said, "but I'm married."

Beyond the ship, at the far end of the pier, she saw Larry or a man dressed like him. He waved at her. Cold wind raised goosebumps on her skin when she left the shelter of the ship.

"Come here, hurry!" he shouted. It was a long walk toward him. His hair, unfastened, blew across his mouth. His cold hands spun her around by the shoulders so she faced the harbor. "Look."

The small and for once unmisted Statue of Liberty stood like a stripper in pink light. Blue-gray water bore facets of light streaming toward the lady, and on the other shore New Jersey in low relief had stopped smirking. A clear and beautiful evening was falling on the river, falling chilly and gentle, bringing with it a hint of contentment.

"Oh," she whispered at the sight.

"I got it for you," he said.

She told him some of what she'd told Howard Ritchie, how she'd cried. "We're out of wheat germ."

He put a jar in the cart. "What'd he say about the story?"

"He wants it shorter, with more ending."

"I thought it was flawless and brilliant the way it was."

"I guess it'll get more flawless and brilliant." She stopped at Granny Smith apples shining green, noted the price, and pushed the cart past them.

"What is he, some kind of an asshole?"

"No."

"He sounds like one. He sounds like he doesn't know what he wants." He tore the end off a loaf of French bread and tossed the loaf in the cart.

"Maybe," she said and headed for the shortest checkout line.

By the time they'd walked home, he'd eaten all the bread and described sunset on the Hudson as an extension of the reality Matisse had despaired of finding in canvases that represented it instead of evoking it. At the door to their building she reached up and kissed his forehead. He was so excited by his speech that his skin was warm in the cool evening.

That night in bed his hand traveled under her nightgown, tugging at her underpants, which she said she wore for warmth during the winter and managed not to explain during the summer. Her legs remained together—there were no banners and confetti for him, no welcoming committee—and he had to maneuver his hand through an obstacle course before he could push a finger inside her. She wriggled in discomfort. Soon his finger moved more easily and her legs relaxed somewhat, but they didn't offer him a haven. When her breathing grew shallow and quick, when she was moving with his finger, he whispered to her, "Oh little one, open your legs," which she tried to do, but her legs tightened instead. In consolation, she patted his erection, a stray dog that roused in her pity and concern about fleas. She patted him until he said, "I want to go inside you," whereupon she unhooked herself from his finger and slid down the bed and dutifully lapped at the erection. "No, *inside* you," he whispered, but made no effort to stop her. She toiled over him, with hopes perhaps of forestalling his plans; but soon with a groan of reluctance he pulled away and, hanging down from the bed, opened a bureau drawer and took out a box of lambskin condoms. She heard a foil packet tear open and raised herself to help him, a gesture made a beat too late, encountering flesh suited in other flesh, prelubricated. He rolled her over on her back and pressed himself against her, optimism born of a bad memory. She, though, could remember everything; and, stuffed with anger and long-held weariness, had no room for him. After vain and delicate approaches, he tried to be more forceful and won from her a yowled "You're *hurt*ing me!" at which he stopped and leaned on her flexed guarding knee and sighed. Trying again, he succeeded partially and might have gone further, but she cried "Wait!" so desperately that he waited while she adjusted herself to him and by the adjustment ejected him. His next try worked; he installed himself without her noticing it too much. Pleased, he smiled down at her and yanked the pillow from under her head. She smiled back at him until he pulled her nightgown up above her breasts. "Don't," she said.

"I just want to look." But he was already kissing them.

"It hurts."

"I thought it wasn't going to hurt once you were off the pill."

"I don't know, they're still sensitive."

He kissed her neck and she closed her arms around him. Her legs loosened. He began to move inside her. "Wait!" she cried again, and he stopped.

"Well, little one," he whispered, his mustache dipping in her ear, bristle on his chin sanding her cheek, "I never have to worry about you being unfaithful. When other people fuck, the woman opens her legs."

Disgrace tempered her panic; over his shoulder, her face became thoughtful. Her legs parted intentionally, experimentally, and he thrust in her with decreasing gentleness. The only time her hips lifted to meet him was when he shuddered in orgasm minutes later.

She clung to him as he withdrew. The platform creaked. He deposited the condom in a nest of tissues on the plank between the bed and the wall. Millions of his sperm were dying in dusty Kleenex near uncorrected tests on pronouns. He kissed her belly, then her dark pubic hair. "Have you been picking again?" he asked.

"No."

"It's starting to look like a supermarket chicken again."

"No, it's growing back," she said as his tongue slid down and his head pressed between her legs. She'd sat in the bathroom the night before and pulled out hairs one by one, a bit here, a bit there, a process like thinning plants. It hurt.

She admitted his tongue. Pleasure and his mustache nibbled at her. Nibbling, he swung around and knelt over her face. She freed her nightgown from under his knee. Genitals bloomed above her. He tasted faintly of semen, bitter. He'd said once, "A woman, she was Spanish, told me it was a sign of strength that it's bitter. I don't know if it's diet or what." Dina had nothing to compare it to. She thought, Tonight I'll swallow it. Soon, floating on waves of pleasure, she forgot penance, and when at last he produced more bitterness, she waited a polite few moments before, at his urging, climbing down the ladder and running to the bathroom and spitting into the sink.

While she gargled discreetly, he squatted on his heels at the refrigerator. Carmen's banana headdress made four sickles above him. The refrigerator light showed his stomach pleating into soft folds. She shut the bathroom door and sat on the cold toilet seat: though the weather was too mild for the heat to come on, the apartment, over meat lockers at the rear of a butcher shop, was chilly and damp. Spring invigorated mold colonies above the shower head and the leaking window frame. One side of the apartment met the back of another building; on the other side, a ginkgo tree's branches choked the two windows above a concrete strip where dented garbage cans sprouted in weeds. Gypsy-moth caterpillars dropped down the chimney, and centipedes bungled indoors. In recent years spring signaled the coming of rats too. They scurried up along disused heating pipes from the basement if the exterminator didn't leave enough poison there. Listening for scratching in the walls, she winced.

A neighbor, Mrs. Easton, her apartment a prize duplex, had pointed out a depression in the concrete with her glass of Southern Comfort. "They paved it over the summer the other building went up. It was a garden, dear. We had azaleas big as darning eggs." Brittle, shrunken, childless, she'd died four years ago, a month after her husband's death.

Larry opened the door. "Well?" He held out a carton of orange juice.

"No, thanks."

He took a gulp. "You almost through?"

"I can't pee if you stand there."

"A watched pot." He stepped over her legs into the narrow bathroom and grabbed the string for the ceiling bulb.

In the light she leaned forward to hide her nakedness. "Go away."

"Hurry." He stepped over her legs again on his way out.

She closed the door halfway. "Remember the Eastons? Remember how skinny he was and how drunk they got, but they were always courteous no matter what, and how the firemen came and found their armchair smoldering and put it on the sidewalk?"

"Are you picking?"

"No." She pulled out one more hair, and the skin pinkened. She concentrated on relaxing her bladder muscle. "It must've been nice here when the Eastons moved in."

"Hurry up."

"I wasn't even born then. You were already doing math."

"Where's the TV listings?"

"Behind the TV. Right?"

He answered, but she'd flushed the toilet and couldn't hear what he was saying.

3:56. The movie after Carson had been *The Search*, with Montgomery Clift, laced with commercials but a good cry. Larry turned off the TV and got into bed beside her. A central valley in the mattress united them. The room lulled itself with the hum and routine chirrs of the refrigerator. Warped floorboards swelled patiently with dampness, a molecule at a time. He cuddled to her as she read by the light of the Tensor, its thin beam swarming with dust motes. A bus braking on Canal Street echoed through a maze of walls and yards. "Why don't you read the Freud?" he asked. He'd bought a bag of cat's-eye marbles and *Civilization and Its Discontents* at a flea market.

"Mmm-hmm." Her curiosity having overcome her fear of germs, she was reading a month-old *Newsweek* she'd found on the radiator in the hall.

"Baby, you'll see. I'll make you proud of me."

She put down the magazine. "I'm proud of you."

"No, but I'm going to stop futzing around so much. I'm going to take out my files and see what I have for a series. Women, I think, maybe with fans. And gold origami paper somewhere."

"That's wonderful."

"Why do you read that? You have to nourish yourself."

"What kind of women—faces or full-length?"

"Faces. Maybe. You know, I don't want to interfere, but I don't think this guy at that magazine knows what he's talking about. You shouldn't change the story. If it's too long for him, let him take out some of his fucking ads."

"There aren't any ads in the magazine."

"So there's no problem." He kissed her and turned away from the light. "Don't read too long."

She finished an article on the intelligence of dolphins. There was a picture of one smiling in a tank in San Diego. "Betsy's vocabulary astonishes the experts." She put the magazine on the table and turned off the light.

In the dark she curved behind him, fitting her body loosely against his, her forehead at his back. She needed to touch the faucet. She would have to creep over him and down the ladder without waking him. She listened for ratlike noises above her breathing and rolled over and touched the table six times, three times with the fingertips of each hand. In the middle of worrying if six times were enough, she stumbled into the unexpected privacy of sleep.

Howard brought Vincent Bask home for dinner. Suzanne, who wasn't expecting company, stopped cranking the salad spinner when she saw Howard with the stranger. The spinner made one and a half revolutions by itself. She felt afraid that the stranger had come to deliver bad news. Later she wondered why she'd felt that. A large young man in a housepainter's white cap, the visor to the back, and a plaid flannel shirt smiled uncomfortably at her. The shirt had a history: one red button disrupted a row of white ones, and a brown corduroy patch lay like scar tissue over a top corner of the pocket, suggesting that once something—a pipe, a pen, a road map—had been yanked from there in anger or impatience. And the sleeves were too short; below the cuffs great knobby wristbones stuck out, bearing red-gold hairs caught by the kitchen light. The same color hair glittered around his projecting ears and on his brows and lashes, so that his dark brown eyes seemed to be a mistake, an incongruity as startling as the blue eyes of a Husky. His pink ugliness touched her. She forgave the misfortune of his features, an imposing freckled nose and a thin-lipped mouth. He pulled off his cap, and his face rearranged itself in harmony beneath a halo of loose russet curls. He shouldn't wear a cap, she thought, he must know how it looks.

When his large palm wrapped itself over her outstretched hand, which she had wiped dry on a Belgian dish towel as discreetly patterned as her husband's shirts, she sensed the man's power by his gentleness. He held her hand the way she imagined a retriever held a dying or dead bird in its mouth: softly, teeth barely impressing the feathers of a warm frail breastbone. This restraint reminded her of her father, who had hit her only once, though, as the punch line to several of Howard's jokes went, once was enough. She had been sixteen, out on her first real date, alone with a seventeen-year-old boy named Markie Bailey at the movies in town. She was wearing a new dress, blue, to match her eyes, with little pink and yellow flowers, and wouldn't eat any popcorn for fear of getting butter on her outfit. Markie Bailey's mouth left a buttery spot on her neck with a kiss so quick and shy that she thought a fly had lighted there and she tried to wave it away. Her finger poked Markie in the eye. He yelped and scattered the remainder of his popcorn across the row in front of them, its seats empty except for a sleeping man who was there when they arrived and who would be there for the two shows after they left. Kernels pelted his shirt and nestled in the collar. He might have been drunk or dead. Doris Day sang. "I'm *sorry*," Suzanne whispered to Markie. "It's okay," he said, squinting. "I thought you were a fly," she said. Water streamed from his injured eye. She went to the marble drinking fountain in the lobby and wet her beautiful linen handkerchief with the embroidered *S* as a compress for him. She spent her mad money to buy a giant buttered popcorn to replace the one he had dropped.

His eye, red and weepy, winked as he drove her home. When he closed it briefly, he ran his father's pickup off the road. She gave a shriek, high and abrupt as the sound from a sprung mouse-trap. The engine cleared its throat before dying. He asked, "You okay?" She cried, "I'm sorry." He flooded the engine and said, "Darn it." He switched off the ignition. "It'll have to rest a bit. Why're you crying?" She didn't know why exactly. When he finally drove up to her front yard and walked her past the porch light to the screen door, where different-colored patches shone with different density, it was forty minutes after her curfew. Moths thumped on the yellow light bulb. "Thank you very much," she said. "Thank *you*," Markie said, his wet eye streaked with scarlet. "G'night," she said and held out her hand. He kissed her cheek. His hair smelled like buttered popcorn. "See you," he called as he walked away. She went inside the house quickly, to keep the moths from getting in, and turned off the porch light.

"It's not eleven, honey," her father said. He sat at the dining-room table, his accounts book open, bills and receipts spread out like a game of solitaire. Moths danced on the burning bulbs of the crystal chandelier above him. "That's Austrian glass," her mother always announced as she carefully bathed the teardrop pendants in ammonia and water.

"We got stuck, Daddy," Suzanne said. "The truck stalled on the Merritt Road."

"That Markie behave himself?"

She blushed. "Of course."

"I mean, was he a gentleman?" Standing up, her father wasn't much taller than she was.

"Yes, Daddy. He let me go through all the doors first."

She didn't understand what in this statement provoked him, but for the first and only time in her life he hurt her. His open hand, which he scrubbed meticulously with green soap after work, his hand hilled with calluses that were clean and permanent, this hand slammed against her cheek, almost on the same spot where Markie Bailey had kissed her moments before. The Austrian tear-drops exploded in rainbows. She was too surprised to cry; she didn't immediately connect her father's open hand with the sting-ing on her face.

He pressed her against his checked shirt. "Honey, I'm sorry," he said. The tenderness she had thought natural and inevitable from him she now understood to be deliberate. It was restraint, an act of will imposed on strength, a harnessing of power. "Did you have a good time?" he asked, rocking her in his arms.

She whispered yes.

"I bet Mama's still waiting up for you."

She went into her parents' dark bedroom. "Mama?"

Her mother was sleeping on one side, the long braid a path on the pillow, legs drawn up beneath the sheet. The cool, intel-ligent hand that read foreheads for fever rested, broad-knuckled, on Suzanne's father's pillow.

In sleep her mother showed disturbing possibilities: a plain woman with a beautiful nose, she might be something more than simply a mother. Her gentleness too was chosen. The arms that reached up ballerina-like to pin sheets on the line also beat down on dough. Had struck the table once. Had pounded, Suzanne remembered, on her father's back once, a voice crying, "You can't!" Who had been speaking?

"Mama," she said again. A part of her childhood vanished. For no better reason than that loss she married Markie Bailey two years later, right after her high school graduation. The marriage didn't last. Each time he kissed her, she imagined a fly or a gnat buzzing in her hair. She had to clench her fists to keep from swatting it. She explained the problem to Markie, who had never, he swore, heard such a thing. They decided a baby would solve it. After a year of trying to have a baby and two years of trying to find a doctor who would help them to have a baby, Markie said he accepted the lab reports on the tests they'd taken. By then he was selling car and disaster insurance and had come to anticipate his two beers in the evening and his bowling night, Tuesday. Though he joked about busted pipes and low sperm counts ("No paternity suits for this old boy"), she believed he secretly blamed her for their childlessness. The fault wasn't in his body but in her rejection of it, her failure to arouse him to his natural function, fathering. *She* kept his pipes busted, *she* depressed his sperm count.

"If you'd just *want* me," he said one night after twenty minutes of bedspring-groaning lovemaking, "if you'd just *have* to have me all the way up inside, we'd get a baby, I know it." Sweating, he pried her mouth open with his tongue, and she knew he wanted to go at it again from the beginning. She wanted to take a bath with bubbles. A mosquito whined in her ear, she thought, but it was Markie kissing her ear, her neck, her breasts.

Having introduced Suzanne and Bask, Howard left them alone together. "Going . . . shower . . . you don't mind," he mumbled, whipping his back with his surah tie. She heard him open the door to Matty's room and say hello. A counter of wilted

Bibb separated her from a writer who, Howard had assured her, would soon be "fucking famous." It seemed to her that she and the writer were ingredients in a stew Howard had decided to create. Her own stew, a new recipe from the *Times*, bubbled on the stove, drooling sauce down the side of a copper pot.

"Howard says your book is wonderful."

"Can I help you?"

"No, really. Would you like something to drink?"

"I'll slice the mushrooms."

"Some wine?"

"Apple juice?"

"Wouldn't you like to relax in the living room?"

"I'm helping."

"They're supposed to stay whole."

"Sorry. Good juice."

He hummed as he quartered tomatoes for the salad and severed the tangled roots of scallions. He refused to pare the carrots. "Let me scrub 'em instead. No skin, no vitamins. Might as well eat typing paper. Which on occasion I have done." He cut alternate strips of skin along a cucumber, leaving a ridged pattern.

"Howard says you're going to be famous."

"I don't want to be famous." The large pink writer had tomato seeds drying on the back of his hand. "I wouldn't mind being rich, though. How come he doesn't say I'm going to be rich?"

She had no idea why Howard said or didn't say something, but she knew he had good taste. If he said Bask was going to be famous, then Bask would be famous. Not necessarily rich, because no one could predict popular acceptance. She knew Howard had good taste because he told her so in clear uncomplicated sentences he didn't mumble. "I have fucking good taste. I *know* good writing. I may not ever be the writer I'd like to be, but I know that too, by God, because I know what it *should* sound like. What it *has* to sound like." These declarations usually occurred thirty miles out of the city, in a rented car headed for a communion with nature devised for Matty's benefit. Matty didn't like nature;

she was suspicious of its unruliness, its lack of toilets, movies, and museums.

"You can pee in the woods, for Christ's sake," Howard told her.

"Daddy drove us all the way out here to pee," Matty told Suzanne.

"Wise guy," Howard said. "The woods are a museum and a movie too. Don't you want to draw some of this stuff?" He gestured at trees, rotting wood picnic tables and benches littered with paper bags from burger factories.

"I want to draw the guys in *Murder in Space*." This was Matty's current favorite movie. "And I want to draw the Flatiron Building." She had a postcard of the Steichen photograph "Flatiron Evening, 1905," a grimed pearl, and had gone with her parents to see the building one Saturday afternoon. As they approached it down Broadway, she held up the card and stared at it, the building, the card again.

"What you doing there?" Howard asked.

"I'm remembering it," she answered.

Dinner didn't go well. Matty asked why Suzanne hadn't peeled the cucumbers all the way. Howard sat in his terrycloth bathrobe and moved stew around on his plate and yawned irresistible gapes through what was supposed to be adult conversation.

"I guess so," Suzanne said when Bask asserted that the president lied to the country often and with relish.

"It goes with the job," he said. "They all lie. They like it. It's a skill, like hunting."

Spooning potatoes on Matty's plate, Suzanne heard silence. "Howard, you wrote—remember that essay on morality? In the *Times*?" When he said nothing, she went on, "Howard wrote an essay on morality for the *Times*."

He said, "It was on hunting. For *Boy's Life*." He assessed the table, suddenly alert. "Where's the wine? You forgot the wine."

"Not for me, thanks," Bask said.

"The hell with you," Howard muttered. "*I* want wine." He

grinned as Suzanne went to the kitchen. "And women and song," he called, reaching into his robe pocket.

"No smoking at the table," Matty said.

He brought his hand up empty. "You're too young to be self-righteous."

"You promised."

"I'm human. To be human is to be weak at times."

"A promise is a promise."

"Okay, enough. I'm not smoking, am I?"

"But you wish you could."

"Wishing doesn't count. Wishing doesn't have nicotine in it." He nodded at Bask. "How you doing?"

"Maybe I should go," Bask said. Suzanne set down a tray with three wineglasses and a carafe of red wine. "No, thank you," he told her.

"I insist," Howard said, his brown eyes expressionless.

Bask smiled. "So do I."

It was for this smile of his that Suzanne fell in love with Bask. She saw it rise like a sun over Swedish crystal and French stoneware. She was accustomed to Howard's smile, daylight breaking through clouds in a challenge, with a sense of triumph indifferently concealed. She was accustomed to her answering acquiescence, shoulders lowered, weakness at her wrists, and, beneath her compliance, pebbles of anger rattling in a rusty tin can—small stones, like calcifications in the gallbladder or the kidneys: unnoticed, potentially obstructive. In the back bedroom of her Aunt Nessa's house there had been a mason jar filled with sixty-seven brown gallstones, most the size of nailheads, and one large one, "Big as a hen's egg," Nessa said with pride, wattles trembling. In that back bedroom where nobody slept the air smelled of camphor. Aunt Nessa hefted the jar from the doily on the bureau to admire her body's handiwork and failed assassins.

"Enough," Howard said when Suzanne had filled a third of a glass. "Just a taste." He reached across the table and placed it before Bask, who shook his head.

"Never let an alcoholic drink alone," Howard said.

"I'll drink with you, dear," Suzanne said.

"Me or him?"

"You. I said *dear*."

"What is it, you a Moslem?" Howard asked Bask.

"I don't drink."

Howard took an exaggeratedly small sip. "*Ex*cellent. I bet you don't smoke, either. My daughter here likes nonsmokers. I would die for this child, who happens to be an artist, I would do anything for her, but I can't stop smoking. Isn't that right, sweetheart?"

Matty hesitated, checking her parents' faces before answering with a low yes.

"Yes, *sir*," Howard said.

"Yes, sir," Matty said, smiling, ducking her head.

Suzanne asked, "Dessert?"

Howard rolled on. "Now, my wife here, my wife, whose profile compensates for many things, my wife would also like to see me stop smoking, but unlike my daughter, she doesn't expect it. She's very tolerant of me, looks the other way, you might say, and I'm of a mind to return the favor. More wine?"

"Don't mind if I do," Bask said. He hadn't touched his glass.

Howard didn't give him more wine. "To your novel."

Bask nodded. "Thanks." Suzanne and Howard drank.

"And to your next novel," Howard said. Again Bask nodded and Suzanne and Howard drank.

"Have any ideas in that direction?" Howard asked without waiting for an answer. "Of course, there are only two subjects for fiction—love and power. The great themes of sex and money. Affairs, adultery, standing on line at the bank. Why aren't you in bed?" This last was addressed to Matty.

"I'm waiting for dessert in the first place, and in the second place it's not eight-thirty."

"There's a tone to your voice I don't especially admire."

"But it's not eight-thirty."

"Something about respect."

Suzanne cleared dishes from the table. "Help me," she said to Matty.

The girl took her father's plate of untouched food. "Okay?" she asked before carrying it out of the room.

"Coordination there," he muttered to Bask. "She'll be an athlete, maybe a dancer."

But Bask didn't seem to hear. His face was almost comic in its earnestness. He was watching Suzanne.

Months later, when he held her—when he'd loved her so well that for days afterward her thigh muscles knotted at curbs and his lower back emitted flashes of rue—she whispered to him, "I like how you talk. That's not Massachusetts, is it?"

And Bask, who'd lived in Tampa, Austin, Chicago, Denver, Missoula, L.A., Bakersfield, Stockbridge, Hendersonville, and Valdosta, answered, "No, not exactly."

The goblet set before Howard held a puddle of beige ice cream in which slivers of chocolate and almonds floated. His dessert spoon, someone else's heirloom acquired at a country auction, rested in this mire, beaming someone else's initial like a distress signal. The others had finished their ice cream, and Suzanne had already served decaf espresso in white cups. Matty had a white cup of milk with a teaspoon of coffee. Bask had plain milk. It was possible that Howard might one day disappear in the ultimate attainment of perfect thinness. He didn't eat; how much protein was there in Chivas and black coffee? He drank his espresso avidly, and the sluggishness he had worn through the evening gave way to a deliberateness bordering on animation. "Let's talk about cowboys," he said. Suzanne, with a blurred sense of alarm, refilled his cup.

"I've seen cowboys, but I don't know any," Bask said.

"I do. Did. Almost was one myself."

"What's your definition of a cowboy?"

"I don't mean a guy on Third Avenue in boots and a Stetson. I'm talking about Wyoming, South Dakota. Horses, cattle, dust so thick you think you're breathing cotton. Rolling your own cigarettes, not joints." He glanced at Matty, who was fighting sleepiness to listen, her eyes closing, cheeks flushed.

"I rolled my own cigarettes when I smoked," Bask said. "It was cheaper, that's all."

"Maybe you're a cowboy and you don't know it."

"Maybe."

"You think I'm kidding with you, Vince. I say you're a cowboy."

Suzanne wondered whether being a cowboy was good or bad. Her husband in his robe glowered at their guest, who glowered back.

"If I was a cowboy, I'd be the first to know," Bask said.

"Wrong!" Howard announced, slamming the table.

The white cups rattled. Matty woke up enough to ask, "How about an astronaut?"

"How about it?" Howard muttered.

"If Mr. Bask doesn't want to be a cowboy, he can be an astronaut. You could take turns. First he'll be the astronaut and you'll be the cowboy, then you'll switch. That's fair, isn't it, Daddy?"

"Sounds fair."

Suzanne wished she had made cappuccino. She craved cinnamon. "Which is it better to be, a cowboy or an astronaut?" she whispered to Matty while the men talked.

The girl opened an eye, brown like her father's, bloodshot like her father's, though from sleepiness, not liquor. Suzanne felt herself in the presence of an oracle; atavistic awe placed her, chilled, on a mountain slope where marble columns fronted uncomposed truths gnarled as olive trees (the mythology class had met only three times). She waited expectantly, but Matty closed her eye.

"It's a compliment," Howard was saying to Bask.

"When were you in Wyoming?"

"Montana too. I worked there. Played Autoharp in a marching band. And Colorado."

He was lying. She recognized the wild, dangerous note he tried to swallow every time he hit it, as though ingesting revelation. His mumbled lies dropped into the neckline of his robe.

"A cowboy's just a guy with a sore butt," Bask said. "A guy whose hat gives new meaning to the word *sweatband*. A guy who spends most of his time risking sunstroke or frostbite in order to be with other cowboys and crushes of cattle you can hardly see for the flies."

"You're knocking our American hero."

"Jesus, Howard, I'm a Catholic from New England and you're a Jew from Miami Beach—"

"Coral Gables."

"Coral Gables, and we're neither of us cowboys and that's not our hero."

"Course it is. We're the ones who need him most."

Bask smiled at Howard admiringly. "You ever been on a horse?"

"Yes." The word trumpeted truthfully. "Didn't you ever hear of Durango Chaim?"

"Sure, he went partners with Longhorn Nate Loyola."

"Exactly."

"Over in Sioux City."

"Fargo."

"Okay. Two mean guys."

"But not to each other."

"No, partners."

"Everything the same."

Bask laughed. "Not exactly. Longhorn Nate wouldn't get himself circumcised."

"Durango Chaim wouldn't rustle on Saturday. But otherwise they shared everything. Loot and women."

"What'd the women think of that arrangement?"

"They were grateful, Vince, really grateful." Howard allowed himself a small sorrowing smile. "I wish you hadn't mentioned the part about my being a Jew in front of my wife. I haven't told her yet."

Bask raised the glass of wine that had been waiting for him. "Howard, you know you're devious."

"I'm a peach," Howard said, raising his own glass.

Suzanne left her glass on the table. She watched Bask with dismay and a guilty fascination. Wine shone on his thin lips before he licked it away.

"Can't stand the stuff," he said. His prominent ears, poking through curls, seemed primed for flight.

Howard kept a grave bloodless face. "To you, Nate, and to your long horn." Then he smiled triumphantly and Suzanne knew why: for his own reasons, which were never easy, he had just seduced Vincent Bask.

There was blood on the space bar. The outer corner of her right thumb had a cut. She was bleeding at the typewriter because of procrastination, not industry. She'd fled the unaccustomed quiet of the apartment soon after a phone call from the florist, Ralph Cohen, stopped Larry in the middle of a tirade on Van Gogh's sanity.

"The old fart thinks he can call me anytime and I go."

"He said it's an emergency."

"It's always an emergency. Now it's his heart. He's all alone and bored."

"I guess the money—"

"Fuck the money, fuck all the money there ever was." He gathered his hair in a green rubber band at the nape of his neck. He put on yellow socks and Mexican huaraches with soles made of tire treads. He'd bought the shoes on Canal Street, after switching them from the five-dollar bin to the three-dollar one. "Goodbye, little one. I go forth to the cold world to earn."

He rolled paper into her portable typewriter, next to a Russian student's essay, "From Smolensk to NYC, Life in the Quick Lane."

"There. You have a good time and write."

She heard the door to the building close downstairs. She stood alone in the room, waiting. The fluorescent fixture droned. She picked up the pages of the story Howard Ritchie wanted improved. Staring at it didn't improve it.

Five minutes later she was outside, hurrying to the market

for apple juice because there was very little at home and she didn't want to run out of it in the middle of writing, which she wasn't doing because she was hurrying to the market. She walked around the block, squinting into the sun, hands in her jeans pockets. The day clarified each brick of each wall she passed. She came home. Green bumps on the tree outside the building had turned into leaves. She cut her thumb tapping the bark. Brave as a lion tamer, she went inside to the dark room.

There was blood on the page too. A thin streak of red in the upper right margin lent significance to the paragraph she'd managed to complete. She covered the blood with Wite-Out and, while that dried, anointed her thumb with antibiotic cream. Her thumb seemed the only real part of her. It throbbed against the space bar. It left bloody proof of its presence. Despite monthly cramps and bleeding, she remained insubstantial. If *Rosemary* published her story, then she'd be better than real, she'd be justified.

She was dreaming of bridges, he was dreaming of tunnels. He woke to find her back nestled against his chest, her hair tickling his nose. He had his arms around her. He wanted comfort, the spare oblivion of fucking. He was dying in a flower store, surrounded by carnations. His parents had died for history. Van Gogh, with a pistol, outstripped time. Picasso lived too long and time outran his talent. For saints and artists, it was a race. Van Gogh won by losing. Picasso won by winning. Morally superior to murderers, his parents lost by winning. What this foursquare theorem demanded was for him to lose by losing. He could do that. He didn't have Van Gogh's or Picasso's talent. He didn't have his parents' opportunities for martyrdom. As usual, he was overqualified for a job.

Her small hands, twisting fingers on the knees of her jeans, distracted Howard.

"It's good," he said, "you did good work here."

"But?"

Her eyes heated him. Wonderful obscene visions lurched toward him: behind his desk, those small hands on him, those gray eyes lifted to his. He would pull up her tee shirt advertising THE GRATEFUL DEAD. He would make her cry yes. His mouth, which he imagined clamped around her breast, proceeded to speak. "You write almost too well. It's too beautiful, the surface is shining, like a mirror. It can repel the reader, this perfection. It doesn't give him any place to get in, it's too smooth, too unyielding. You should open it up in places, make it jagged, leave room for the reader to enter the story."

"You're not going to publish it, are you?"

"I'm going to get better ones from you."

"What's wrong with this one? You called me about it."

"It's good, but it's not what I want from you."

"And what's that?"

Amazed at his own sincerity, he didn't hesitate. "I want to hear your voice completely. I want you to tell me in a story the most important thing you know."

Her downcast, chastised face stirred him. "There was a writer," he said, "a young woman like you. She wrote a wonderful story and I published it. Now all she can write are imitations of the story she already wrote. She sends them to me, and I send them back. She hasn't found her voice except for that one story. She keeps trying to recapture what she never had. I'm not going to make that mistake with you."

He couldn't remember if the young woman actually existed. The episode rang true, he heard such conviction in his voice. He might have made it all up. "As for my calling you, yes, the story excited me, and I wanted to know something about the writer. But you should know I'm a terrible liar. I lie all the time. I hinted to you about publishing the story because I wanted to see if you could change it so maybe I *would* publish it. But it hasn't worked out this time. I'm telling you, you're going to write better and I'm going to publish you. Now, you're not unhappy, are you?"

Her head bent to her tee shirt. He would have liked to slip

his hand along each groove in her rib cage. His other hand would be kneading a nipple between the E and the A in DEAD.

"Let me keep the story," he said. "I'd like an agent I know to see it."

"Okay."

"You *are* unhappy. Someday you're going to thank me. Meanwhile I want you happy as a clam." He gave her three addressed, stamped manila envelopes sent by other writers for the return of their manuscripts, a black felt-tip pen, and a qua-drille-ruled memo book with a blue cover. "You soak the stamps off and glue them on other envelopes," he said. "Now tell me you're as happy as a clam."

"I'm as happy as a clam," she said.

Larry consoled her. "He's crazy." The regret on his face was real and so was the relief. "Little one, you're good." His arms around her prevented escape. "Those assholes don't know what they're doing. You're good, you don't need them."

"I wanted the story to be published."

"You don't need to be published. We know you're good."

His consolation shut her into a dark box. It was hard to breathe. "He says he's going to get better stories from me. He says he's going to get me to tell him the most important thing I know."

"Fuck him."

"I don't have any better stories to write."

She sank with new density through thick, waste-clogged water, brown like the Hudson, toward litter at the bottom, eels and the rusting upraised sharpness of tin, clouded spines of glass. She settled through layers of ruin, bubbles at her mouth. Her eyes would rot; the sockets, water-rubbed, would be satin bone.

He shouted, "It's one fucking room, damn it. You can't sit here and sulk. I don't want to live with that fucked-up face."

Her fear goaded him. The way she shrank back in her chair enraged him.

"What *is* it?" he hissed in her ear. He dug his fingers into her arm.

"You're hurting me."

He shoved her back. She rubbed her arm, crying.

He was losing her. He saw it every day, she was slipping away; but he didn't know where she was going. Her attention, the light of her concern, had deserted him. She looked at him without love. His testicles withdrew upward in the scrotum. His penis, unloved anyway, retreated.

He yanked her from the chair and in his fury didn't notice the blue memo book on the table. He had come home and found her sitting there, her expression distant. He could claw under the mattress for a stranger's socks.

"Stop it!" Her scream, caught on an indrawn breath, was a warning. He slapped it away with an open hand. Four red finger marks and a palm appeared on her cheek: Matisse cutouts. Lapis lazuli cost twenty-six dollars a tube. Vermilion cost eighteen. She screamed again and he slapped her again. He was creating an art form. In the last two months he'd earned one hundred and forty-three dollars. He could talk about brushstrokes, but he had no paint; he didn't want paint because he didn't know what he would do with it if he had it. His vision of himself as an artist had diminished to the urge for acclaim; or that was all it had ever been. The work itself was an obstacle to acclaim.

Her body swung forward and heat exploded at his knee. She tried to wrench free. Gasping, he held on to her. She swung forward for a second kick, and he grabbed her by the hair and pushed her off balance. "You kick my balls and I don't know what I'll do to you," he whispered. She stumbled, shrieking, as he pulled her hair. "Coward, bastard, asshole," she cried at him. She dragged on his hair as if it were a bus signal-cord and she wanted off at the next stop.

"Let go," he said.

She held on.

He tightened his grip on her hair. "I said let go."

She tugged harder on his. "You let go."

He had the advantages of height and weight and strength; and he was pulling her hair from the top up, while all she could do was tug at his from below. He forced her head back.

Water ran from her eyes, down her cheeks, along her neck. Water ran from her nose. Her mouth was open because she couldn't breathe through her nose. From underwater she stared at him without love.

Her stare unnerved him into laughing. "If I let you go now, promise not to kick or hit?"

Since he was holding her head immobile, she couldn't nod. She wouldn't speak. Her eyes lowered, and he took that for assent. He let her go.

He wanted to kiss her. He wanted to find her again. "Baby."

She went back to the chair and sat. "Coward. Going to hit me some more?"

"Baby."

"I wish I could leave you."

"What stops you?"

"I don't have any money. I don't have any place to go."

"Go to your fucking parents."

"Go to hell."

Angry at the devastation in her face, he slammed the door on his way out.

The bathroom mirror showed her ugly and red. She washed her face. Cleanliness might be an escape. She wanted to die. She opened the medicine cabinet and took out Larry's bottle of Valium. She broke a pill in half and swallowed it with water.

She picked up the blue memo book and wrote.

Valium 10 grows octopuses in my brain. I'm past the stage for suicide. Since I've no self to kill, I'm ripe for murder.

And since I was a writer, I wrote the word *gun* on a piece of paper, I held up the paper, and I shot him.

• • •

In the morning when she woke up, he was sleeping beside her in their bed. His honey-brown hair fanned out over the pillow. Terrible things had happened while she slept, perfectly ordinary things had happened terribly. A man had come home and undressed and gone to bed. The network of veins at his nostrils stopped her breath. She wanted to find a bed he wouldn't be in.

They were polite with each other. She worked on students' essays. He pretended to read Kandinsky's *Concerning the Spiritual in Art*. ("The impossibility of a red horse demands an unreal world.") At the market he let her wheel the cart alone to Canned Vegetables, but soon she heard him calling her. He was searching for her in the wrong aisle, Cereals and Rice. He'd abandoned their cart near Frozen Foods. On the way home he urged her to buy an ice cream cone and promised he wouldn't taste it. They shared it, vanilla fudge, one of her favorites, instead of cherry vanilla, one of his. After dinner he dried the dishes for her.

That night as he slept in shadow beyond her reading light, she wondered if she were viewing history. It made his nose eloquent. Hoots came from the leather bar a block away. In the hall two voices climbed the stairs.

He had told her once about Jeannie, his great love at eighteen, years before he'd met Dina. He lay down on a sofa with Jeannie one afternoon, his head resting on her arm, and fell asleep. When he woke, it was night. The room was dark. And she was there beside him. She hadn't slept but had stayed with him, unmoving.

"Her arm must've hurt," Dina said.

"She didn't want to wake me."

"She could've slipped it out from under."

"She didn't want to risk waking me."

"She just lay there with a crushed arm for hours to avoid interrupting your nap?"

"Yes. That's love, that's tenderness."

"That's crippling."

"That's the mother in a woman's love. You wouldn't understand."

"Was she on the inside of the sofa, between you and the back?"

"Yes."

"So she couldn't get out. She was stuck there."

"It's beyond you, isn't it? The idea that she could want to stay like that?"

"It's not real. What'd she do for hours? She didn't even have a book to read while her arm was risking gangrene."

"Love and comfort are not the same thing."

"Not with you they're not."

"Not with anybody, little asshole."

June 6, 1980

Dear Howard,

Out of a balancing act under a full moon last night, a contemplation of the long fall below. Rope burns on the insoles of my archless feet. Buses and the luck of poets wheezed outside the room where I wasn't sleeping. Off-duty cops were shooting real bullets.

I turn the points of scissors and knives away from me. Rats gnaw at the wall behind the radiator. Traffic hurts my ears when I step outside the freshly painted bile-green door. The Puerto Rican exterminator says someone could throw a bomb—or maybe that was palm—into the unlocked basement. The past, which is always changing, waits to be invented.

Here are the two most important things I know:

1. Things are themselves, not symbols of themselves.
2. It is natural to eat; it is not natural to be eaten.

(The concept of nature presiding over the predator-victim cycle is a lie, worse even than religion.)

Dina

6-9-80

Dear Dina,

You write a hell of a letter. When do I get another story? Or are you angry? You shouldn't be, you know. Call me—we can always talk.

Friendship,
Howard

His office window had a green view of a park where muggers and rapists and rats big as alley cats watched benched gothic readers and nannies with prams. She hadn't noticed it the other times she'd been there. Katharine sat with them. She was young and pretty and had tanned oily skin. She wore a thin white dress with a full skirt and gold sandals. Her toenails were painted gold.

"I studied writing with Howard," she said, flashing a gap between her front teeth.

"I'm a wonderful teacher," he muttered. "It's the thing I do best. Katharine here is very talented. Wants to rethink the paragraph."

When Dina had called him, he'd asked her to come for lunch, to discuss writing, but he seemed to have forgotten it. He did say that Updike was one hell of a writer, she should read Updike. Katharine said she didn't read contemporary writers. "They haven't been purified by time." She left reluctantly after an hour.

He said, "I didn't expect her to stay. I don't know what she wanted."

"She looked as if she wanted you."

"She's lonely. Bad marriage." He stared at Dina's breasts as if he could see them through her camisole. She moved in the chair so that her breasts moved. He said, "Loneliness. You don't know about it. You've got your husband—Larry, right? Most people are lonely."

She had bathed carefully that morning, soaping herself as if she were polishing intricate repoussé silver. She had put on the blue camisole she'd been too shy to wear before. She had applied perfume to the back of her neck and her inner thighs. She had been able to do these things because Larry, cursing, had gone off to the flower shop to work.

Howard consulted his watch. "It's too late. There's an apartment, a place we could have gone. But it's too late. I shouldn't have let her stay, I should've taken you there." Low, his head to one side, eyes averted: "Would you have gone?"

The salt and pepper shakers, the white china bowl containing packets of sugar and Sweet'n Low, her glass of white wine, the waiter's black-sleeved arm reaching across the table to serve her something she could eat daintily while discussing with Howard how to rethink the sentence, never mind the paragraph—all disappeared. The restaurant crumbled and from its ruins—here a melted fork, there butter soup—an apartment grew, with sunlight and beige sofas and a view of the East River from twenty stories up. He would hike across the living room to the sofa where she reposed against a scarlet cushion and waited for her life to begin. His kiss would break the spell she'd been under; without morning mouth or sand in her eyes, she would at last awaken.

Yes, she nodded, and astonished herself.

He took her to a bar down the block for a quick drink. He had to get home, he said. They sat side by side in a red vinyl booth. He ordered Chivas Regal. Because she was hungry, she ordered a glass of milk.

"What if we're no good together?" she asked.

His sad smile, fumed with liquor, touched her. "It's just something else to find out. Finish your milk."

Larry brought her a rose. "The bastard charged me for it."

Sitting on wood railing on the pier, she let him hold her hand. A ship pulled on rope thicker than her leg. A dog flew past with a frisbee. She said the word *divorce*.

"I'll make a deal with you. We try to fix things up." Soon his stricken look would turn to fury. He kissed her hand. "I'm going to be making money. I'm running the store. Ralph's going into St. Vincent's for tests."

"What's wrong with him?"

"Heart. He doesn't have one."

"Is he in pain?"

"He'll live forever. Baby, it's a real job, every day. And you'll write."

That night he whispered oversweet love, struggled to get inside her. "Open a little more."

"I can't."

"Try."

"I can't."

The cab crept uptown through midday traffic, but she felt the thrill of speeding. She had her ten-dollar bill ready. Tucked behind her social security card in her wallet, it was her life savings. Larry didn't know about it. In six years of living with him, she had managed to provide for a puny emergency. She preserved her fund against puny pseudo-emergencies. Once, for four days before Larry got a temporary job helping movers pack sculptures on White Street, they had only a head of iceberg lettuce, a quarter of a loaf of French bread, and a half-quart of low-fat milk for food. She didn't use her money to rescue them; hunger wasn't an emergency.

The meter clicked. She was purchasing with her safety net the chance to leap from nowhere to another place.

Howard sat hunched over at his desk and searched among papers for something he said he had to take care of. The secretary with the French accent stopped at the open door: " 'Oward," then left. He typed a note to someone. He mumbled on the phone to someone else. She had spent six-forty to experience this. Her perfume was fading, her cotton gauze blouse wilting. Water beaded on her nose and upper lip. She pressed a tissue to her face.

At last he presented his mournful hungry expression. "Should we go for a drink?"

In the elevator he hummed what he said was the theme song of the Cossacks. At the door to the street, he placed a hand against her back, to urge her through first. His hand stayed there, and her own moved around his back, to rest at his waist. He felt less solid than Larry. She lengthened her stride to match his as they walked to the corner.

"That apartment," he began.

"Yes," she said.

He seemed to have made a random gesture with his free

hand, but a cab stopped. He mentioned an address in the Village to the male driver's ponytail, long hair that could have been Larry's. They were going to be blocks away from Ralph's flower store, on a street Larry might pass. She had rushed uptown in order to be rushed downtown.

He put two fingers on her inner wrist. He was taking her pulse. Next he would produce a blood-pressure cuff. She struggled against her response: a feeling of dissolving, a feeling that her wrist had become part of his touch, dependent on it. He circled her wrist lightly with his fingers. She wanted to learn to be defenseless.

The cab stopped at a row of brownstones. He gave the ponytail money. Waiting on the sidewalk, she became the sidewalk, planted in it. Someone she knew might see her. To the west were the top stories of St. Vincent's main building. Later Larry would tell her how he'd taken Ralph to the hospital in the afternoon, and she would discover the charm of parallel lines. The sun defaced a No Parking sign. Flies with bottle-green wings convened on a turd at the metal base of a tree with a trunk guard. Nothing in the day indicated that she was about to do something momentous on Eleventh Street.

She followed him up pink stairs to a glass door reinforced with wire mesh. It opened on a wood door with a lock protected by an angle iron. He pressed the bell marked Sykes; when there was no response, he fitted a key in the lock. It fought briefly with his key. Inside the hall, an airless smell of old wool rose from the carpet. Darkness closed out the street. She followed him up more stairs, past a landing with a Steinberg poster, to another with no poster. At a door, one of two on the landing, he fiddled with locks. He wasn't good with keys. The door relented.

Three sunny windows, books and books, two frayed Oriental rugs, a bed, a small kitchen. He turned on an ancient disgruntled air conditioner. He took an almost empty bottle of white wine from the refrigerator. "Want some?"

She stood on a blue rug and clutched her purse. He uncorked the bottle and drank from it. When he kissed her, he tasted like

97

white wine. He put her purse on a table. Her hands, helpless, hung at her sides. His tongue in her mouth swayed her on the rug.

He was unbuttoning her blouse. It dropped to the floor. Cool air at her back, the pressure of his mouth on her breast. He was taking off his clothes, tossing them anywhere: his jacket on the floor, his tie on a stack of books. His shirt caught on a lamp. One of his socks hit the telephone. She took off her shoes. She undid her skirt. It fell around her ankles, and he pulled her blue underpants, the best pair she owned, down to her ankles before lifting her out of a pool of cloth. His pants landed on her skirt. He didn't have on underpants.

He was tearing off the bedcover. From a drawer that stuck halfway open he extricated an orange sheet, whipped it over the mattress: light housekeeping performed with an erection. She kept her eye on it, awed, and considered worshiping it as a delaying tactic. It yearned for her, stretching away from his leanness. In her purse she found a foil packet which she held up like an amulet.

He lowered her to orange. She wondered if the sheet was clean. A vegetable-stand scale, she registered the difference between his weight and the one she was reluctantly accustomed to. She couldn't cry no to him as she did with Larry; it wasn't in these rules. A hard thigh knocked against her thigh. Her legs parted, her hips lifted. He moved inside her. She fitted around him. This was what people did all the time.

"Howard." Their noses brushed. She blinked, showed him the foil packet.

"And what's this?"

"Birth control."

"Timely." He peeled away foil and examined the small white rocketlike object. "A silver bullet."

"It goes inside me, then we wait for fifteen minutes while it melts."

He slid out of her, provoking her to sigh, and inserted the suppository for her. She enjoyed her bold open legs. Yes, anything, do anything, she thought. He told her a joke about a Jewish policeman and God. His face, as he told it, grew sorrowful. While she was laughing, he kissed her stomach, lower and lower.

"Maybe I'll taste like spermicide. Oh!" The exclamation of pleasure ended that worry. Instead she worried she would take too long. She drifted into a precise understanding of something or other. She was sprouting branches. Wordless, her body traveled.

She cried out oh and oh and oh. She was hurtling away. She sat up to find him. His eyes floated above dark springs of her hair like a crocodile's eyes floating above water. She saw an intelligence see her. Strong hands grabbed hers, pinned them down. He would keep her from traveling too far. She lay back, her body arched while he held her down. He was sending her out and holding her down. Held, she sped outward or inward or both. She couldn't name things. She climbed, she fell, she climbed. She came, crying.

There was nowhere else to go. But he didn't stop. Her legs didn't dare close. She wiggled her pinned hands. He shook his head no and kept on tonguing her. All right, she thought, here. She stretched for him, pushed against his mouth. Pleasure surprised her again. Her legs, pushing upward, trembled. Again he spun her out; again he guided her return. With an occasional time-out—a pit stop?—she was prepared to continue for the afternoon. The sun could set on them. This was the meaning of forever: again.

She glided on currents of air conditioning. He was gone. Her legs stretched out.

"I'd say that's a good fifteen minutes," he whispered. She tasted herself in his mouth. They'd already rehearsed this part.

But no, he was turning her over. No, Larry had once tried entering her from behind. She'd been too clenched together to admit him. It had ended in a fight: Why-can't-you-I-can't-You-mean-you-won't-I-mean-I-can't-You-didn't-even-try. She remembered his instructions, "Lift your ass, damn it." She remembered the humiliation of failure, and the relief.

Her forehead met the orange sheet; head up, she saw a yellow pillow through the tossed veil of her hair. She was kneeling in a loud field. It was the obeisance of a pilgrim at the gates to a shrine. It was a grave courtesy. She lifted for him and, as he entered her, she cried out as much in pleasure as in fear.

"Do you believe in God?" he whispered. They lay facing each other.

"No."

"I do." He leaned on his elbow, resting his head against his palm. "I've led a very strange and marvelous and sad life, but I believe in God."

She hoped he hadn't said that. She wasn't sure he had because he swallowed his words and he had a cigarette in his mouth.

"Did you know I herded cattle in Montana? I sang with a dance band in college. I was married to an heiress. Spice importers. Could've been opium. I have two children by another wife, who's insane, and a daughter with my present wife. She's the only thing that matters to me, my daughter. My wife's a wonderful girl, good-hearted. Collects copper pots. When it comes to sex, she lies there waiting for an act of God to prevent it. She believes in God too. I'll never leave her—because of my daughter. You don't have a child, right? You should, it makes all the difference. Do you want a child?"

"I don't know. Not with my husband."

"Pick someone to be the father. That's happened to me. A woman told me—afterward—she'd gone to bed with me to conceive. I have another kid somewhere, a couple of years old. Maybe a few others I don't know about."

If she did want a baby, she'd pick him to be the father. She loved him for his curly brown hair, white curls at the temples, his leanness, his mumbling. She admired his solemnity. The cigarette smoke made her eyes water and her nose itch. He had disclosed her female nature. Smoke drifted against her breasts. What else could he teach her?

Growing Pain

by Newman Sykes

Bandaged Moments
by Vincent Bask
Linnaeus Press
257 pages
$11.95

A first novel, like first love, usually is more sentimental than wise. Its charm, when it is charming, lies in its celebration of adolescence. Even if that time of transition is not overtly the novel's subject, it remains the underlying theme, the secret structure, for a first novel is the coming of age of its author—that is, in the author's view.

Vincent Bask's *Bandaged Moments* is one such write-of-passage: a story about a family in which there is, you may be sure, an adolescent boy, Lulu, a nickname for Leon. You may be sure too that Lulu is going to share his growing pains—bandaged moments—with us, in a lulu of teen turmoil. Unfortunately, this first novel suffers from juvenility without youth's redeeming energy. A clue to its confusions may

be found in the title, extracted from a poem by that problematic genius Emily Dickinson.

The Soul has Bandaged moments—
When too appalled to stir—
She feels some ghastly Fright come up
And stop to look at her . . .

The poem's intent has nothing to do with Mr. Bask's book, but he took the words he liked out of context to use for his title. This is emblematic of his other muddled choices throughout the novel. (His only previously published writing, a story called "Eating Peaches," appeared in *Rosemary* last year with an epigraph from Eliot's "Prufrock," which seems to prove that his taste in poetry is degenerating. The story, by the way, was included in the *1979 Maupassant Prize Stories* collection and is worth reading to see the potential Mr. Bask has not yet fulfilled.)

What has gone wrong here? Well, Lulu, mainly. At first the author commendably regards the boy with humor not untempered by compassion. Caught in the perfervid squeeze between a Unitarian mother and a Catholic father, Lulu finds himself "mumbling through a responsive reading from Gibran with the taste of the communion wafer still in his mouth." He declaims a Latin prayer at his mother's church and confesses to the wrong clergyman. "Reverend Bob clapped him on the shoulder and said to forget it. Father Boisvert was not so forgiving; the assigned Hail Marys would stretch into Monday." While clasping his father's mother's rosary in "wet working-class hands with two long nails for guitar picking," Lulu falls into sexual reveries, one for each bead. His mother, observing his rapture, thinks it religious and weeps bitterly that she has lost her son to "Mother Church, stony and omnivorous, lusting for children and the sightless obedience of the unborn." Lulu's father, hearing her rant, demurs. "Let me urge specificity," he says, and she refuses to pair his socks any more. This is genuinely funny domestic warfare, set in a small Massachusetts town with "long memories, long winters, long johns, a few years before yellow scum plated the river and sent the local fishermen off to the shooting range to become hunters."

Soon Lulu, understandably weary of his parents' tug of war, falls in with what used to be called a bad crowd, boys who go beyond boyish pranks but stop short of big-city delinquency. There are no guns or hard drugs, but through a haze of marijuana and beery bravado Lulu manages to effect a semirape upon the over-described and undermotivated high school homecoming queen and neophyte virago, who is—could it be otherwise?—blond. I would like to plead for blonds as one of our time's few maligned minorities without a spokesperson or mimeo machine or proposed constitutional amendment. Years ago, all the princesses in fairy tales were golden-haired; now there are no more fairy tales, and blonds, like immigrant Russian countesses of the thirties, have been reduced to selling gloves at Macy's. Unfair!

But even if Mr. Bask had made Lulu's victim a brunette, the novel would still be mortally wounded by its leap from comedy to melodrama. Lulu's sudden transformation from small-town boy to Little Caesar and the novel's shift in tone are bewildering. For the remaining three-quarters of the book, Mr. Bask struggles with material that overwhelms him. His prose thrashes like a drowning man: "Always at the back of his mind was the idea that if nothing else ever happened, if nothing else in this incredibly evil damn town ever shook up the locals so that they really listened to what their children were saying, this day would remind them of their deafness and the vastness between what they preached and what they did."

Vincent Bask is not without talent, but to realize it he will have to work harder than he did in this book. *Bandaged Moments* is swaddled in problems.

• • •

Maybe the pound cake was a mistake. She shifted the bag of groceries in her arms, and a staff of celery shook dirty green leaves under her nose. Howard sometimes found cake annoying. "I don't think we should have this," he'd say, declining a slice of marble cake or carrot cake or nut cake as if she'd offered him a poison mushroom or a small dead animal scraped off the highway. She looked down at the white cardboard box Matty was carrying, one short finger looped under red and white bakery string. With her free hand Matty reached back to check the knapsack holding her library books and final report card. "Is it closed?" she asked, patting the zippered pocket. The straps cut into her shoulders. Suzanne said, "Yup," determined not to wonder what inside the pocket made the girl so anxious. In the shadow of their tall, old, expensive building, sixteen blocks north of the office where Howard worked hard to keep them in their apartment, she wanted to drop her groceries and kiss her daughter, but Frank, the day doorman, was walking toward them.

She was at least four inches taller than Frank and twenty years younger. Reluctantly she allowed him to disburden her. She didn't want to humiliate him by noticing his age, but her packages, groceries, suitcases, Howard's starched shirts wrapped in brown paper, all were speeding him into disability and early retirement. "His face gets so red," she told Howard. "That's Four Roses, not exertion," he answered. Howard had gaps in empathy. He was overworked from empathizing with writers and critics and other exalted souls.

Frank heaved her groceries to his gut. "Somebody's waiting for you in the lobby."

"Hey, Frank," Matty said.

"Hey, honey."

Armed with grit and the day's heated staleness, wind pushed the three of them toward the building.

It was Bask. He rose from the worn velvet chair beneath the three-armed sconce with one blind bulb.

"Hello." She recognized her young-matron sound, delivered with a mix of warmth for spontaneity and of coolness to correct any misimpression the warmth might evoke. She tried to remember why she loved him. She hadn't seen him since April, when Howard brought him home for dinner; for the second time Bask surprised her.

"Hello." He was pink and glum.

"Matty, do you remember Mr. Bask?"

They exchanged reserved *his*. Bask's rust-colored hair, longer and unrulier than before, covered his forehead and ears, and sprang down along the sides of his neck. He needed a shave; in the dim lobby she saw shadings of red-gold contouring his cheeks and the stubborn jawline. That stubble would scrape against her face. She blushed.

He said, "I called Howard at his office and he said to meet him here. But he's not here." Gripping the navy web straps of a dirty white canvas bag, he reminded her of Matty with the knapsack. She would give both of them cookies and milk.

"Please," she said, "please come up and wait."

Frank handed Bask the bag of groceries. She blushed again. "I can take that," she said to Bask.

"So can I."

In the elevator she held Matty's hand, which wriggled with impatience. Celery leaves brushed Bask's Adam's apple. It wasn't four yet, and Howard never got home until five-thirty or six. The door opened on low-wattage hallway and green print wallpaper. Matty scuffed the toes of her sneakers on the waxed floor for sound effects, squeaks Howard wouldn't have permitted. Otherwise the walk to the apartment was silent.

Suzanne and Bask sat in the living room, alone with apple juice and a wedge of Caprice des Dieux and English sesame crackers Howard bought but wouldn't eat. "They cost too much to eat," he said. They tasted good, but no different from local brands. If he ever tasted one, she thought, he'd find out. From Matty's room came low radio noise. It sounded as if the door was closed. She looked into Bask's dark brown eyes and asked if he'd prefer Brie.

In his eyes she saw her daring reflected, deepened with a stranger's resonance. Everything she didn't know about him attracted her. His green tee shirt was wonderful. She expected him to do something: pull her toward him, cover her mouth with his so that before she closed her eyes she would see a flash of green and his brave, troubled face.

He took two folded pages from his canvas bag. They'd been torn out of a magazine; pictures squeezed blocks of print. "Newman Sykes reviewed my book."

If he'd grabbed for her instead, she would have felt more comfortable. She would have had precedents—advice columns, TV, novels, movies—to consult. The Married Woman Who Is Come On To by a Friend or Colleague of Her Husband's was a clear and standard situation with clear and standard options: power steering, disc brakes. The Married Woman encouraged or discouraged. Morally there were no options. At a party some years earlier she'd told Bob Small under her breath but very distinctly that if he brushed her breast with his arm one more time she'd dump her sherry on his alpaca weskit and not even consider paying for the dry cleaning. She'd been mildly drunk or she wouldn't have had the nerve to be so direct, but as she spoke she'd heard a chorus of approval from Dear Abby and Dear Ann Landers and Dr. Welby and Perry Mason and Doris Day and Terry Moore (no, seriously, whatever happened to Terry Moore?) and Debbie Reynolds and, yes, Sandra Dee and Tolstoy too (the Constance Garnett translation, unabridged, the summer in the Hamptons before Matty was born, Vronsky and morning sickness; she'd been nervous on subway platforms ever since) and certainly her Sunday-school teacher, Mrs. Baugh (rhymes with caw), wife of the Reverend, who later married her to Markie. The chorus hallelujahed her at the Smalls breakfront. She had known what to do then. If Bask had told her, "I'm crazy for you, run away with me," she would have groped her way to the right response, whatever it was. But when he said, eyes hurt and angry, "Newman Sykes reviewed my book," he was asking for something too large from her, initiative and not response.

She said, "Oh yes, congratulations about your book."

"Thanks."

"The cover is really wonderful. On the jacket."

"Thanks."

"Howard says that's important for selling it." Howard might have said that.

"*This* is important for selling it." He flapped the two torn pages. "And after this, nobody's going to buy it."

"He didn't like it?"

"On his list of things to do, reading it comes after cleaning out your neighbor's cesspool, which comes after cleaning out your own."

"No." She laughed at the description, and he grinned at her. "He says my prose thrashes like a drowning man."

She could touch his shoulder to console him. His shoulders were powerful, hunched in despair. "Really, Howard should be here soon."

Brown sorrowing eyes questioned her. "I'm sorry, I'm keeping you from something." He reached for his canvas bag and stood up.

She was surprised to find no leaves, no branches lodging birds' nests, no sun shining through the crown of his hair. "No, no, you're not, really you're not. Howard'll be very angry if you don't stay."

"I can get him at his office tomorrow." But the canvas bag again settled its soft bulk on a kilim which Howard claimed had been woven fifty years earlier by a twelve-year-old girl, hymenless and on the way to being toothless, in a desert within commuting distance of the Khyber Pass.

"Is Newman Sykes so important?" she asked.

"It's all relative, right? The pope's important if you're Catholic."

"I've met him—Newman Sykes, I mean. He seems like a nice man."

"Traitor. I bet you watch him on TV."

"He *did* seem nice. He brought Howard home when he was . . . sick. He carried Howard into the apartment." She wondered if she'd betrayed Howard by admitting that another man had carried him home. "Besides, it's only one opinion. It's not the *Times* or *Time* or *Newsweek*. And it's not one of his TV reviews. There'll be other reviews."

Bask slugged down apple juice. "I've got stuff to read. This way I won't disturb you." He took a paperback from his canvas bag.

"You're not disturbing me."

"You must have things to do." He had the book open to a dog-eared page.

Dismissed, she went into the kitchen. Boil water. Pare. Chop. She was noticing how her hands under the faucet stream resembled her mother's, except for the wedding ring—Howard had better taste than her father—when Bask said, "Suzanne?"

He hesitated at the entrance to the kitchen, as if it were her bedroom. He hadn't spoken her name before. "Let me help," he said.

When Howard came home at six-thirty, he found them in the kitchen, the three of them, laughing. There was an odor of burned carrots. Matty was reciting the Gettysburg Address between giggles. She had cake crumbs around her mouth.

Suzanne never asked him why he was late. He never told her not to ask him why he was late, but she couldn't. If she asked, "What did you have for lunch today?" he shrugged and mumbled a rambling, epic joke about a Jewish tailor and God. His Jewish tailor's accent was singsong and plaintive; his God earnest and cruel and whimsical. There were low wails of *oy vay* and inventories of horn buttons and bolts of gabardine. She didn't get the punch line, but she laughed. Since she couldn't make him tell her what, if anything, he'd had for lunch, how could she expect him to tell her why he was late?

Howard didn't answer questions for one principled reason: if you answered questions you didn't mind answering and could answer, then sooner or later someone would ask you a question you did mind answering. Or couldn't answer. But if no one expected answers from you, you were safe. Being specific wasn't a good disguise. Vague waves of the hand and rambling, epic jokes kept things nice and unclear. The way used-car dealers stress their honesty, he cultivated his unreliability. He was steady about it.

She simply said, "Hello?" when he walked into the kitchen, and he could ignore the question in her greeting.

Matty licked at the corner of her mouth, where a vanilla crumb had lodged, and finished quickly, " '. . . By the people, for the people, shall not perish from the earth.' "

"Amen," Howard said.

Bask stood up.

With the water running and the dinner dishes clinking in the sink, she couldn't hear the men's conversation in the living room. Grasping a plate between blue rubber fingers, she listened for the voice of the man she loved, but she couldn't tell who that was. The plate almost slipped from her hand.

"It just seems meaner than necessary."

"He's a strange guy, Vince."

"He's a putz."

"Where'd you learn to say that?"

"He *is* a putz. I tried to break into TV. Wrote a sitcom pilot. It's the second sentence you learn at Berlitz in L.A.: 'This is a producer. He, she, or it is a putz.' "

"He liked the writing, he commented on the writing, did you notice?"

"Come on, Howard, he hated it."

"Once we were talking about you, and he compared you to Balzac."

"This is depressing."

"Want a drink? It'll take your mind off Newman Sykes."

"No, thanks, I don't drink. Besides, what happens when my mind gets back on Newman Sykes—I take another drink?"

"No, you do what you can. You write."

"I don't feel like writing. Look, I'm sorry, I shouldn't be here whining at you. You've been great to me. If you hadn't published my story, I never would've gotten a publisher for the book. I guess I'm lucky he reviewed it at all. How many first novels get reviewed? Or published?"

"Vince, you have to get your mind off this. It's one review."

"Maybe I should consider myself lucky and be grateful for any attention. Maybe I should hope he'll crucify me on TV between deodorant ads. But the guy panned Dickinson too."

"Visit with a friend."

"I am—you."

"I mean a woman friend."

"I was living with someone in Massachusetts, but we split up."

"There's no one?"

"Not now."

"You need a woman, Vince."

"What am I supposed to do—head over to Forty-second Street for a pavement princess?"

"Find a woman. After splitting up and being anxious about the book, you should have a little something in between real events. You're upset. What you need is a strong feeling of temporary security. A woman who won't cling when it's over. And it will be over."

"Jesus, Howard, you're fine."

"You need a woman who's mature, a couple of years older. And married. With a woman like that, when it's over, it's over."

"Can she be gorgeous too?"

"There's no point if she isn't."

"Okay, where do I find her?"

"Now, Vince, that is up to you. Look around. But I would say . . ."

"Yes?"

"If you see what you like—no matter where you see it—go for it."

"People can get hurt that way, Howard."

"People can get hurt no matter what."

"What about 'Do unto others'?"

"That's what I'm saying, Vince. Do unto others."

He sat on the sofa, reading a manuscript with a red cover. He had an empty glass in his hand.

"Where's Vincent?" she asked.

Without expression, his face was pure. He gave her an abstraction of himself; what she could have, always and forever, would be his denial. "In Matty's room, with a puzzle." He set the glass down and took an English sesame cracker from the plate she'd brought out for Bask that afternoon. "Matty likes him." He bit into the cracker, and alarm spread across his face as he swallowed.

"Is something wrong?"

"This is awful." He put back the remaining piece of cracker.

She sat down beside him. After a desperate silence in which she searched for something to say and could think only of her blue blouse at the cleaner's, she sighed. He closed the manuscript and left it on his lap. "I hope it's not boring for Vincent, doing a puzzle with Matty," she said in a low voice.

"Vince can take care of himself." Equally low.

"Maybe he's too polite."

"Nothing much I can do about that." He leaned back and closed his eyes. "What do you think of him?"

"Vincent?" She stared at his profile, unyielding as a statue's. "I think he's very nice. Very quiet." She could hear Mrs. Baugh, the Sunday-school teacher, saying, "Suzanne's a good girl. Nice and quiet."

He said, "I think he has a crush on you."

"No."

"Yes." His eyes were still closed.

"That's ridiculous."

"Why? Why shouldn't he have a crush on you?"

"Because it doesn't make any sense. Because I'm married."

He opened his eyes. "What does that have to do with any-thing?" He seemed mildly curious to know her answer, as if it wouldn't affect him, as if he'd peered over a splotched menu in a coffee shop at lunch and asked her what she was going to have even though he thought he knew what she would have. Maybe he expected her to say, "Tuna salad on white bread, please, and no mayonnaise." Maybe his question was a formality, to give her the illusion of decision. What would he say if she ordered a bacon burger with a side of fries?

Bask bent down and kissed Matty high on the forehead, at the hairline. "Good night," he told her as she arranged her pillow.

"Night, Vince."

Howard said "Mr. Bask" to her and sat on the bed.

The girl's eyes, his own but alive, widened. "Mr. Bask said I could call him Vince." A sharp white baby tooth pulled her lower lip.

"Yes, I did," Bask said politely, acknowledging that Howard, as father, would have to decide the case.

"Well," Howard said. "If Vince says it's all right with him, then it's all right with me. I think 'Uncle Vince' might be better."

"Howard, I'm not anybody's uncle."

"Fine." He deferred to Bask's deference.

The writer's jaw jutted fiery stubble in the lamp light. "I'd better go. Thanks for listening to me complain."

"Don't worry, Vince."

"And thanks for the advice."

"I meant it."

With a wave to Matty: "Good night."

And again her voice, less sure this time: "Night, Vince."

As he left the room, she giggled. He turned around and saw Howard whispering to her.

Alone with him at the door, she confronted the texture of his green tee shirt. "Yes," she answered to a question about whether she was usually home in the morning. He took her hand, he took her hand, he took her hand. He kissed the side of her mouth because she didn't keep still. Her face burned from red bristle; her hand in his died from fear and was reborn a pulsing starfish, holding on. Behind her an imaginary Howard emerged from Matty's room and watched her treachery.

Closing the door, hearing Bask's footsteps retreating, she wondered if Howard would be so kind as to perform a husbandly ritual and behead her. The neat prospect of annihilation as safety had its appeal. They could buy a secondhand sword with faded crimson tassels. He called to her from Matty's room and she went.

"But why can't we see each other on Mondays or Tuesdays or Wednesdays?" Her teeth pressed his shoulder, her hand closed on his thumb.

"I can't get the apartment then. That hurts."

"What about another place?"

"Yours?"

"No." She bit him again.

"This is what we've got. Stop it."

The next Tuesday, at eleven, when the temperature had already reached eighty-nine and was still climbing, she arrived at his office wearing a halter top and a full skirt and sat with her back to the open door.

"And how are you?" he asked, bent over a note he was scribbling. A blue oxford-cloth shirt made him studious.

"I want you," she whispered.

He glanced at the hall and said in a voice that carried, "You're certainly looking well."

"I *want* you." Hissed.

"I'm afraid that's impossible today." His voice fairly boomed.

"I need you."

His eyes narrowed and his features assembled into a mask. A wooden sound emerged. "Sometimes, you see, there's an unfortunate confluence of events. Right now I have a lot of work and there's no place for us to go anyway. So though I appreciate your coming up here—I think it's very dear of you, very touching—I can't."

She loved him because, with his back to the wall, he still used a word like *confluence* in his lies. She needed to identify her rivals: gap-toothed Katharine or his wife or someone unknown to her. If his work was the competition, she could try to engage him in a discussion of *Heart of Darkness*.

She put the heels of her sandals on the seat and lifted her skirt to her parted knees. She was naked underneath the skirt.

"Yes, you're looking well," he said.

Crumbs and a slick of marmalade littered the carmine red stoneware plate. The two cups had coffee stains inside. Bask placed a plaid elbow where Howard's blue oxford-cloth one had rested a half-hour earlier.

"Please, let me clear—I didn't expect—it's not clean." Suzanne hovered over the table, a butterfly in an eyelet robe.

He liked her confusion. It colored her delicate face and eased his own confusion. She was about ten years older than he was, she was married, her husband was his unofficial mentor. Despite or because of these facts, he wanted her.

He thought about her when he was supposed to be doing other things. In the cluttered room he was temporarily subletting in the apartment of a friend of a friend, he put down the *Times* apartment listings and remembered how her eyes had lifted to his. On a blank piece of paper he drew lines and crosshatchings. He had to write a proposal for his next novel in order to get money from his publisher, but each time he settled down to work, her image teased him into daydreams, doodles, despair. He couldn't concentrate without her. He assumed this because he was without her *and* he couldn't concentrate. As an observation, it lacked scientific control. He forged questionable connections between unrelated phenomena. Being with her, he believed, would solve all his problems: love, reciprocated, would not only be his muse and show him what to write, it would also find him an affordable apartment in a seller's market in New York City and help him to forget Bonnie, the woman he'd left in Massachusetts. He needed to believe in something ennobling, even if he had to invent it. Suzanne's hair, fired with morning sun, echoed flashes of his own red hair. Her breasts rode in wrappings of eyelet. Her bottom rounded out eyelet. Giving him a plate of toast, she managed a cunning smile. His adoration cracked, regathered. Hopeless, he watched her drink coffee. He loved her the way any creator loves the thing created: with intensity and suspicion.

The toast wasn't whole wheat. The marmalade had refined sugar in it. Daylight burned through his plans for her. He ate breakfast, listened to mythology-class tales of Hecate, bemoaned his apartment troubles, and said thank you. He didn't kiss her goodbye; but, waiting for the elevator, he waved to her before she closed her door, and she waved back.

Dina heard someone passing in the hall behind her. "I thought we could go to lunch." She parted her knees further.

"Today, I'm sorry, it's impossible, deadline," he muttered, eyes going from her to the hall to her.

"A short lunch." She touched her exposed flesh in a gesture of presentation, as actors did with products in commercials. Try this.

Anger or fear pulled along his face. "Let's go." He hustled her ungently from the office, his hand firm around her upper arm. In the elevator he stared straight ahead and whispered, though they were alone. "Don't you dare do this again. I have a family and I have a job, and I intend to keep both."

The floor numbers lighted up in descent. She felt carsick. Her teeth chattered. She'd already failed at being a writer; now she was failing at being a lover.

Outside he dragged her toward the street and pushed her into a cab. Her arm was free. He climbed in after her and slammed the door. He spoke an address. His hand slid up under her skirt. Her legs parted in triumphant submission.

They got out on a street in the East Village, far from the apartment on Eleventh Street. A movie house down the block had CHAPLIN FEST on the marquee. They were going to see *Gold Rush*. He hurried her into a bookstore. They were going to read.

It was cool and dim, a cavernous room rising two stories. The walls were books. Wood stairs led up to a balcony that ran along three walls. The balcony rested on books. Beneath it wood ladders leaned against high shelves where gold leaf on old book spines glinted. Metal stacks in the shadows created more shadows overlapping on the floor, uncoated wood dull as clay. Through a doorway she saw concrete stairs painted battleship gray and leading down. Wood tables before her overspilled with paperbacks; piles of paperbacks on the floor narrowed the aisles. In shadows under ladders and at tables solitary people gathered books or read them or ran fingers over torn covers. She inhaled dust or a fine powder of disintegrated old paper: she was breathing sonnets and treatises. Visiting the scene of a disaster that hadn't happened yet, she saw firemen's hatchets eating the tables, stacks crashing, books tumbling down, pages turning or returning to pulp in a flood of water. She sniffed for the acridity of wet smoked wood. In an emergency, she would be sorry she wasn't wearing underpants.

He deposited her in the PSYCHOLOGY, NEW AND USED aisle with the admonition "Stay here." She peered around a shelf ending with the title *The Survival of Thanatos* and watched him talking to a man behind a register. The man—slight, brown, bald, bearded—shook his head. Howard said something more. The man nodded, straightened a yellow sign: SELL YOUR USED BOOKS HERE. He glanced at her appraisingly as Howard returned for her.

She was always following him up stairs. At least they weren't going down the concrete stairs to the basement, where the dead bodies were. On the balcony she looked down at the man behind the register. He was still looking at her.

"This way," Howard whispered.

The floor sounded beneath them. Light from below defined the spaces between the floorboards. He pushed a door open—it must have been swollen from humidity—and they entered a room that was another place.

It hurt her eyes. Day poured down through a skylight gridded with wire. Light reflected from the ceiling, walls, and floor, all painted with white enamel. The only pieces of furniture were a floor lamp and a wood platform bed, both white. The bed had white sheets and a turned-down white woven bedspread. A small white ceramic bowl on the floor contained the greenest jade plant she'd ever seen. It should have been white too. A white woman should have been lying naked on the bed and eating white chocolate.

"Whose place is this?" she asked.

It needed red. The room's denial of red threatened her with red. It needed a red pillow or a picture of a ripe tomato. It needed blood spattered on the walls.

"C'mere," he said. He sat her down on the bed and walked away from her. Leaning against a white wall across the room, he shimmered. "Okay, let's see what was so urgent."

Flushed—some red for the room—she pulled up her skirt. His grave, observant face confirmed her modesty; a spotlight of sky released her. In his face she saw, unconcealed, her progress.

From the middle of the block Suzanne saw Howard hurrying along the cross street. He was coming from his office. She had given him that blue bow tie. The young woman he was guiding by the arm flew with him, her halter miraculously in place, her skirt flaring. They got into a cab. It had to wait through a red light before it could take off. Suzanne waited too. Pedestrian traffic streamed around her. Frozen like a trapped chameleon, she wished her pink flowered dress would change to pavement dun. The light turned green.

The woman with Howard might have been a new secretary or a new professor. They were going off together to attend a conference on halters. She was a student with an emergency writing problem. He was going to parse a troubled sentence for her.

Suzanne had decided to surprise Howard because that morning Bask had surprised her. He showed up at the apartment and didn't touch her. Every weekday morning for two weeks she'd been hoping he would show up. With Matty on the day-camp bus and Howard waiting for the elevator in the hall, his bookbag slung over his shoulder, her blue bow tie at his throat, she studied herself in the bathroom mirror while brushing her teeth. She powdered her nose and forehead and chin, patted faint rouge on her cheeks. When the house phone buzzed later, she knew it was Bask. She undid the top button of her robe, then closed it.

Serving him in Howard's place at the head of the table, she wanted to kiss his red-gold curls. She hoped he would take her and leave her no decision. But he'd gone away, eyes yearning, ears pink. She was left with the need to decide. She put his plate on top of hers in the sink.

She dressed slowly and spent a long time on her makeup. Seeing Howard would affirm her fidelity. She would go to his office right away. She changed belts before leaving. She could have called to tell him she was coming over, but she didn't. She wanted to experience contingency. On the sidewalk outside the administration building, she saw exactly what she had come to see.

Crouching naked over his jacket on the white floor, he took a pack of cigarettes and a matchbook from a pocket. He stepped over a skirt and set the white ceramic bowl with the jade plant near the bed, to use as an ashtray. A pale body on white sheets curled toward him. He admired what his lovemaking had done to her. A trail of wetness along her belly shone under the skylight. Her nipples had reddened from his mouth and the play of his teeth. Her mouth had reddened too, been rubbed and stretched to accommodate him. The thought lifted him for a second. He still felt the draw of her mouth, the slide of the inner sides of her teeth. "Ah yes," he said, stretching out next to her. A match scraped, burned. She settled her head against his chest, but the room was warm and soon she moved away, to rest on the sheet.

Idly running a hand along her breast, he told her stories about himself, two cigarettes' worth of sad true stories about wives and women and children and writing.

"I'm not good at it, you see, not the way I need to be good. The best thing I do is teach, I'm a very good teacher. What do you want for yourself?"

"Don't know."

"Are you happy with your husband?"

"I don't know. No."

"You should be writing. Nobody's happy. You have no right to expect to be happy. It's a mistake that happens sometimes and gets corrected."

She kissed above his navel and below it, along a line of hair. She kissed from the root of his cock to the head, her tongue busy as an anteater's. With little complaining noises of pleasure, she licked at his scrotum gently, roughly, gently, her forehead against him. She pushed at his thighs, mouth closing on him. Desire traveled in him to her mouth; he was erect. Applause. He crushed a cigarette in soil and observed his engagement.

She asked for her husband, knowing he wasn't there. Liliane, with a shrug, dismissed him. " 'E is gone to lunch, Mrs. Ritchie."

"I was supposed to meet him here." It was easy to lie; she'd given Howard more credit for it than he deserved. "I was supposed to have lunch with him and a friend of mine—a young woman."

Liliane tapped a pencil at the opening to the electric sharpener. "I did not see 'im leave." Gail, Howard's secretary, typed diligently.

"But did the young woman—my friend—meet him here?" A high note vibrated through Suzanne's question.

"There was . . . no one that I saw."

"I see. May I use the phone in his office?"

"Of course. I am so sorry not to be more—"

"Yes, thank you."

The pencil jabbed into the sharpener. Whining followed her to his office.

She sat in his chair at his desk. On the wall younger Suzanne at a beach posed foolishly and gladly. The window behind her projected her shadow on the desk. This was how the world appeared to him. A chair facing her might have held the haltered woman she'd seen rushing away with him. She flipped through the *B*s in his address wheel. A typed address in Massachusetts had been crossed out on Bask's card and a Manhattan one, midtown on the West Side, with a phone number, penciled in. Using Howard's pen and a sheet from one of his memo pads, she wrote down the information.

Sooner or later the pants have to get pulled on again. He balanced on one leg, then the other: the dance of the pants. A button entered a buttonhole. He grasped his zipper and abruptly stopped it from grinning. His life consisted of dressing and undressing and dressing and undressing between jousts with literature. Or it was jousts with literature between cycles of dressing and undressing. He sat on the bed, defeated by the prospect of having to put on his socks. Part of an old song hummed in his head:

> Oh who will tie your shoes
> And who will glove your hand
> And who will kiss your ruby lips when I am gone. . . .

She was kissing the back of his neck. Her teeth grazed it. "Stop it," he said. Kneeling behind him on the bed, she rested her hands lightly on his shoulders. Her hair tickled his skin. Her breasts brushed his back. He tried to understand what it must be like to be a woman. Waiting for the courage to put on his socks, he couldn't understand how a woman, yielding to entry, reclaimed herself. Women must be half-persons, part of them never reclaimed. Which explained Suzanne's reluctance for sex:

a sensible precaution against loss. He knew *he* wasn't the reason. The limp argyles on the floor reproached him. He had his own fears of loss; but except for Matty, he had nothing to be afraid of. He reached around to squeeze the girl's thigh—what was her name? Contrite, he kissed her tenderly.

When he was dressed, he muttered, "Bathroom's next door." It was possibly the only bathroom in New York with both a rare private edition of a Pinter play and a baited mousetrap. He relieved himself in an exalted and defended place. On the balcony, hearing a familiar voice, he looked down and saw Newman Sykes selling a shopping bag of books. He descended the stairs whistling.

"Hello." Newman's black brows lifted. "Dan here, as usual, is offering a magnificent sum for all these."

Dan, the brown man behind the register, punched a key and handed Newman thirty dollars.

"I could probably get forty at the Strand, but I come here for Dan's conversation." Newman folded the money into his wallet. Dan stacked books on a cart.

"Wait a minute." Howard picked up a copy of *Bandaged Moments.*

"Your protégé's effort," Newman said.

"Why are you selling it?"

"It's hardly for my permanent collection."

"You haven't read it."

"Didn't you see my review?"

"Yes. That's why I know you haven't read it."

Newman threw back his head and laughed, a brief exuberant *ha* cut off in his open mouth. "It's not a very good book."

"It's better than you said."

"Allow me to present it to you with my compliments."

"Thanks, but I have it."

"I'd like you to have *my* copy. Maybe you'll read it my way. Dan, how much do I owe you for this?"

Dan shook his head.

Howard opened the book and checked the price on the front flap. "It's eleven ninety-five new, so you owe Dan six plus tax."

"I don't think I should pay the store price. I want to repay Dan what he paid me for the book."

"The transaction's been accomplished. It's Dan's book now. And he sells review copies for half-price."

"That isn't what he paid me for it."

"It's the American way."

Dan placed the book in a bag and gave it to Howard. Then he wheeled the book-laden cart into the stacks.

"Dan's un-American," Howard said.

"Maybe he'll charge you double for whatever you buy."

"I'm waiting for a lady."

Newman inspected an emaciated blond wearing a large NUKE THE PREZ button at a nearby table. She was reading a paperback by Jung. "Anyone in particular?"

"Upstairs."

"The famous upstairs. I thought Dan had put a stop to that."

"The lady insisted." Howard lowered his eyes modestly.

On the balcony a door opened, flooding light across dimness. Light shaped a small silhouette before the door closed. Watching with Newman, Howard made out a figure disappearing inside the bathroom.

"Another protégée?" Newman asked. "Enjoy the book."

Howard produced one of his iridescent smiles. "I'll treasure it."

There were too many things to hide. She walked home carrying a book, *Bandaged Moments*, which he'd picked up for her while waiting downstairs.

"It's a good book, very talented writer, very."

"Thank you."

Larry would want to know where she got it. On the back cover flap the author's face in black and white contemplated a private distance. Crossing Broadway, she felt sperm and spermicide seeping from inside her. A taste of Howard lingered in her mouth. Everywhere he'd touched her had been impressed. She inhabited her body.

In the bookstore bathroom she'd taken her underpants from her purse and put them on. Larry might already be home. Though he worked at the shop all day because Ralph was in the hospital, he made surprise visits for lunch or "just to say hello," a casual explanation for a trip of three subway stops and several blocks. He was trying to catch her at something. Infidelity, for him, meant her brief conversation with the boy who weighed produce at the market. If she imagined Larry's reaction to her real unfaithfulness, she became afraid. But she also was afraid to stop seeing Howard. He'd given her life a purpose: him. On Tenth and Broadway she started from the curb against the light to catch a bus, and her inhabited body had to run to keep whole.

A fly crawled over a tree in the mural of a Mexican village at the Athena Coffee Shop.

"Coffee, please," Suzanne said.

"The souvlaki is real good today," the waiter said. His accent wasn't Mexican.

"You got fresh orange juice?" Bask asked.

"Fresh only in the morning."

"You mean it's been sitting for a few hours or it's canned?"

"Not fresh now."

He ordered club soda. The waiter, printing, strolled toward the kitchen.

He grinned. "Breakfast and coffee together in one day. Want to try for dinner?" When she didn't answer, he fiddled with the sugar dispenser. "You sounded upset."

"I was. But after I hung up, I felt better. I guess because I knew I was going to see you." She waved a fly away. "If I ask you something, will you tell me the truth, even if you think I won't like it?"

He nodded red-gold, his brown eyes promising.

She asked, "Do you ever think of going to bed with me?"

"Yes."

"Do you want to now?"

"Yes."

"I would like you to."

"Now?"

"Yes."

He wondered if the friend of his friend would be in the apartment when he brought Suzanne back with him. He began to slide out of the booth.

"*Bon appétit*," the waiter said, serving their drinks. He dropped a straw and two paper napkins on a wet spot on the table.

She asked him, "Do you have pie?"

"Apple, cherry, blueberry, chocolate cream."

The waiter slouched toward Bethlehem. Bask hadn't heard her choice.

She said apologetically, "I'm hungry."

Blueberry pie, girded with cornstarch or blue putty, arrived. A fork slid across the table. She offered him a taste, which he declined. By a well-timed question between forkfuls she started him on the limitless topic of his writings.

"Mostly it's hard work, paying attention to what you're doing, noticing what you're not doing, always asking yourself how one part relates to another and to the whole. You can be obsessed by form if you're not careful. If you *are* careful. I mean, somewhere between confessional stream of consciousness and the over-restricted well-made tale, there's a blessed ground. That's where the story counts and the form it takes builds from it. The form is the support that has to be there without showing. It's invisible, like gravity, and inescapable."

"The astronauts escaped gravity. Remember those wonderful pictures of them floating around on the ceiling of the spaceship?" Behind a loaded fork her teeth were blue.

"Yes, like a re-creation of uterine existence, floating in amniotic fluid."

"I never thought of it like that." She drank coffee. His heart expanded. Again he prepared to pay and leave. The waiter reached for the empty plate.

"Tell me," she said, "what other pies did you say you have?"

"Apple, cherry, blueberry, chocolate cream."

The crust on the apple pie had ruptured. Steam rose from the filling, an ooze surrounding the crust like a moat around a besieged castle. This she ate desperately, he thought; and she talked about growing up on a farm in either Iowa or Idaho, he couldn't be sure and he knew it made a difference, Iowa or Idaho; and though he wanted to ask, he didn't. She swallowed decorous mouthfuls. He could remember the pattern of acne on the back of his first girlfriend, Danielle Boisvert, whose last name he'd given to the priest in *Bandaged Moments*, but he couldn't remember what Suzanne had just said. Later he remembered the dress she wore that afternoon, pink flowers; whether he remembered it correctly or as he preferred to remember it, he didn't know. A young and fairly simple girl would wear it in one of his stories, which would be rejected by eight magazines, including *Rosemary*, before being accepted by a ninth, a southern quarterly. The story would win a Maupassant Prize, his second.

She was saying, ". . . And Markie agreed. No alimony, no fuss. We divided up our things. There was a cheval glass I wish I still had."

"He got it?"

"It was his mother's. She took it back."

The split-up with Bonnie had been simple. The house, the car, the setter bitch and one remaining puppy, the turntable and metal-capable tape system were hers. He took some of his clothes and books to New York, leaving the rest with her in Massachusetts until he could find a place of his own. She had storage space; he'd built it, and bookshelves and kitchen cabinets and one-third of a redwood deck. The deck halted in midair, without a guardrail, giving the house a bombed-out look he considered European. Responding to his ad on the bulletin board at Grove's Market— "Literate Carpenter, Construction and Term Papers, Roofs, Odd Jobs, None Too Small, Irate Letters, Love Letters, Letters of Introduction, Latticework"—she'd hired him to build two closets. Three days after he started work, a morning blizzard closed the road; two days of being snowed in together altered their relationship. She stopped paying him. By the time the snowplow got through, they were planning a summer house. After two and a half years, he was somewhere else, but he also was where he'd started, looking to move in.

"Would you like something else?" he asked her as the waiter approached.

"No, thank you. I've had more than I should have."

She seemed to have acquired an attitude of resolution. He had hoped for anticipation or at least curiosity. But not resolution—not that set of the jaw, that forced line of the mouth—as if he were medicine she didn't want but had to take.

"Are you in a hurry?" He allowed a dangerous pause. "Because I'm getting hungry." He enjoyed her surprise. "Okay," he said to the waiter, "what's the grilled cheese?"

Outside the restaurant she tried to repay him. He closed her hand around her five-dollar bill. They came to his building debating the uses of money; and, passing the storefront apartment of Mrs. Lotta, Adviser and Reader, whose forested underarm sprouted from a taxed French-cut tee shirt as she waved prospective clients closer, they entered the small, chairless lobby. The digit roll showed the elevator at six, the top floor. He pressed the Up button. She said, "Oh, the poor thing," and stepped back. A cat wearing a dirty blue felt collar with rusting bells cried, scratched gray tiger fur, jingling.

"That's Mickey. Mrs. Lotta feeds him goulash and Häagen-Dazs."

"It needs a new collar," she said, but the elevator had opened and Bask was already inside.

In the friend of a friend's apartment the air maintained an odor of insecticide. A gray-green sofa, collected on the street, buckled in resignation, a tail of yellowed batting between carved legs.

Bask said, "Jonathan?" No one answered.

In the kitchen he offered her orange juice. A dying cockroach weaved across the counter. She shuddered and he killed it with a rolled-up copy of *Gourmet* magazine.

Four cartons of *Bandaged Moments* defended his room. He kicked one listlessly. "I got carried away. Want a book?"

"Thank you, but you already gave one to Howard."

"I guess two of them is excessive. *One* of them is excessive. I've got about eighty."

"Do your parents have one?" she asked helpfully.

Beneath plaid shirts he found a chair for her. "Yes. But I don't think they've read it." He grabbed two white athletic socks from the chair before she sat down. He piled the shirts and socks on yellow typing paper next to his typewriter, a green portable manual that he said had previously been owned by Gutenberg. He kissed her, stepped over a carton, and sat on the Science section of the *Times* on the bed. "Come here," he said politely, sweeping the newspaper away. Sections fell on a carton and the floor. She stepped over another carton and sat beside him. They sipped each other.

The fabric of her dress seemed weightless in his hands. An imago, she emerged from it or it fell away, and after it the bra with ribbon straps slipping from her shoulders. He pared away the inessentials, close work like diamond-cutting. He had aimed at exposing another facet when she fled. Her back bare, fabric gathered at her waist, she clambered over a carton. An arrangement of ribbon and net, her bra, stayed in his hands.

At the closed bathroom door he heard feeble retching. He slung the bra over his shoulder and knocked before opening the door. "Go away," she said hoarsely, huddled at the toilet.

"Stick your finger down your throat. And leave it there till the action starts."

Soon she was vomiting splendidly. He admired the dance of her shoulder blades and the tension of her slender spine down to its prominent bumped coccyx. Her back straightened. A sweep of hair resettled on her shoulders. She flushed the toilet and went to the sink. She washed her face and drank water from her cupped hand. He touched her damp back.

"Feeling better?"

She nodded. Her eyes and cheeks burned in the mirror.

"You look like Ray Milland in *The Man with the X-ray Eyes*."

She dabbed toothpaste onto her forefinger and licked it. She gargled delicately, the song of a baby swamp bird. "I'm sorry. This isn't the way it should be."

"How should it be?"

She said over her shoulder, "Easy."

She might not ever turn around because she was naked. "I'll bet you'd like some privacy," he said, "so you can finish undressing."

That made her laugh. He glimpsed breasts and an outstretched arm. He gave her the bra and left.

Two glasses of seltzer gone flat topped a carton he used as a night table. He was undoing her bra. Scene one, Take two. In the movies, when the jet pilot keels over at the controls, his heart having attacked him, the young stewardess—okay, it's sexist, but go on—the stew who doesn't know how to administer CPR, much less how to fly, panics. The copilot and navigator have checked out too, a first instance of a contagious high-cholesterol count. After screaming and crying and flaring her nostrils, the stew hears this voice on the radio. It's the chief control-tower guy or maybe the head of the FAA or FTC or FBI. He says with calm authority, "Forget you're scared. Forget there are three hundred and forty-six hysterical passengers in Tourist and sixteen bombed out of their skulls in First Class. Forget everything. There's just you and me, there's just the sound of my voice. I'm going to tell you how to land this plane, step by step. And I'll be with you every step of the way. You're going to land this baby, baby." He talks her down. Bask had been talking Suzanne down. Epaulets grew on his bare shoulders. Her bra dropped to the sheet. He refrained from calling her "baby."

Her mouth tasted of toothpaste. Her neck gave off perfume. A horizon revealed itself to him; all things were possible. A breeze swept under the drawn window shade tapping the sill. Bonnie receded; he was waving goodbye when Suzanne said, "Oh no."

"What?" He knew, but he asked anyway, suffering a sharp blend of embarrassment and pride.

"How can it fit?"

He thought of it as the curse of the superlative. His standard answer appealed to womanliness. "If a baby can fit coming out of you, I figure I can fit getting inside." Even Bonnie, who was an antitrust lawyer, hadn't debated the point.

He was right. They fit together neatly and she beamed at him as if they'd accomplished something extraordinary.

A folder of twenty sestinas on Platonism, written by an economist and submitted to *Rosemary* with prefatory remarks about publishing ("Experimentalism is an exercise in antiliterature and an endorsement of anarchy, in which no coherent communication can occur. By preferring experimentalism over classicism, the literary magazine thus effects its own demise. I wish to be in the forefront of the return to classicism. The new avant-garde must lead us backward."), rested on Howard's navy cotton pajama top with white piping, which rested on his chest and beating heart. The best and most expensive room air conditioner ever made in the history of the world vanquished a summer night. After a depressed peek at the first stanza of the eleventh sestina he dropped the folder on the floor beside the bed and opened a book, *Anxiety in the Narrator*. He propped it up on his chest and started at page 27. There were footnotes. He coughed, skipped to page 98. Inches away, Suzanne was reading too; instead of that week's mythology-class assignment, *Bandaged Moments* weighed on the satin bodice of her nightgown.

"How do you like it?" he asked.

She viewed a scene beyond where he lay. He felt superfluous. "Yes," she said and returned to the book.

A knot of excitement formed in his stomach. "He's not bad, huh?"

"Mmm?"

"You're enjoying it."

"Mmm."

She had retreated into the terminally bovine. She might be

contented. He said, "It's not fair. I've got this anxious narrator while you're in bed with Vincent Bask."

Now he had her attention. Io had no place to hide. He went on, "He's pretty funny."

She said solemnly, "Yes."

He slid over and kissed her, sniffing for Eau de Bask. Even after her evening bath, even with his sense of smell dulled by cigarettes, he tried to detect traces of another man. "Allow life to impose on literature," he said, and tugged at the book. She held on to it. He pulled harder and performed a bookectomy.

"Give it back."

"Later."

"I don't want to make love." She'd never come right out and said it before.

"But I do."

"I think you must have had enough."

Enough? They hadn't made love in almost two weeks. "It's been a while, in case you haven't noticed."

"I've noticed."

"Well, then, let's try it, dearest."

"No." She grabbed her book and reopened it on her bodice.

With the craft of a man building a model schooner from unused toothpicks, he had guided Bask to her; stressing husbandly indifference, he had primed her for Bask. If they'd consummated their flirtation, it was because of his well-placed words, his un-spontaneous urging. And they had consummated it, he would bet his life (but not Matty's) they had, and only that afternoon too. He knew it as he knew good writing; his gift was to recognize the inevitable. They had united under his direction. He couldn't write a satisfactory story, yet he'd created a real-life one. He wanted to explore her character further.

"You're not entirely pleasant. What happened today?"

"What *is* it?"

"Something must have happened to make you so snappish."

"Something must have happened to *you* today to make you so curious." Her voice had jutting corners he could bark his shins on.

"No." He had gone to work; been kidnaped for a double matinee by a small, sexually excited woman; discussed modern literature with Newman Sykes in the sphinxlike presence of a bookstore owner with a spare bedroom; taught remedial Jorge Amado to sun-crisped college juniors spending the summer semester in cutoffs; returned to his office for phone calls and R and R; and, when there was nothing else he could do to divert himself, gone home. "Nothing happened." His hand expressed enthrallment with her nightgowned thigh.

She said with ominous tranquillity, "If you touch me again, I'm going to call the police."

No, she'd read this. Three sentences into a paragraph about Father Boisvert, she came upon an unknown arrangement of words and settled into them. After she read the sentence twice, she abandoned it to brood on Howard's disgusting nature. He had run off with the girl in the halter that afternoon. They went to the girl's apartment and made love on a peach satin chaise longue. His bare foot pushed against cool black and white marble floor. Or they went to a hotel, where he signed the register V. and V. Nabokov. He had signed like that once with her at a Holiday Inn outside Baltimore. He never took *her* to a hotel. The Holiday Inn didn't count; it was a business trip. Now he wanted to make love. Her own unfaithfulness to him that afternoon didn't temper her resentment. She had acted in self-defense; he had acted—and clearly had been acting for a long time—out of sheer selfishness. A movement of the bed. She persisted in staring at the page. His lighter clicked. He exhaled. What if by accident she called him Vincent? "The burning bush," Vincent had dubbed his red-gold pubic hair. They'd found a jock strap and a crumpled piece of typing paper in the folds of the sheet. She wished she hadn't gone to bed with him and she wished she was still there. She moved on to the next sentence.

A copy of *Bandaged Moments* lay between them on the bed. The Tensor lighted an airless night. "I don't like this guy," he said. His hair hung in damp strands to his shoulders. His tee shirt stuck to his chest. "What are you doing in his office?"

"We talk about writing." She wiped a collection of moisture from her forehead.

"What's there to talk about?"

"Same way as you go on about Matisse or Gorky, only we talk about writing."

"This book looks like shit."

"You haven't read it. He says it's good."

"How come you're running uptown to talk about writing? Why don't you stay home and write?"

"It's not so easy. I don't see you painting."

"I'm working."

"What about six years you didn't work? What was the reason then?" She thought she saw his fist, and she raised her pillow against it.

"You have an ugliness in you, you know that? You don't know how to build a man up." He kicked the sheet off and lay still.

She cried, "Why is it my fault if you don't do what you want—what you say you want? Should I blame you if I don't write?"

He immobilized her with the blue and green hatred in his eyes. "This must be a philosophy you learned from your good friend Ritchie." He hurled *Bandaged Moments* down into the fire-place. The book landed hard against brick, falling into the winter's unswept ashes, which exploded from the impact. A section of pages popped out like a slice of toast from a toaster.

He occupied the outer side of the bed. She crawled over his feet to the ladder, tripping over her nightgown.

The spine was cracked, along with the ineffectual glue binding. The jacket had slid forward in flight and was crushed against brick. Beneath ashes and dust the author smiled with a closed mouth. She exhumed the book and refitted the ejected pages to the spine.

Gray water flowed from her hands. Her fingers tapped the

faucet once, twice, three times on each side. In the mirror she saw a woman's face streaked with gray and tears. The marks might have signified caste or crime. She washed them away.

She climbed back up to bed with the book, careful to keep its loose pages from slipping out. She cleared one of his legs, knocked the other, said, "Sorry."

"Your fucking light is in my eyes," he said.

She adjusted the reading lamp, twice tapped the table.

"Turn it off," he said.

"I want to read."

"I want to sleep. Turn it off."

She turned it off, turned it on.

He sat up. "You playing games?"

"Let me fix it so—"

He reached past her and turned it off. "You want to read, go somewhere else." And lay down, his back to her.

There was nowhere else to go. She climbed over his legs again and down the ladder, clutching the book. She closed the bathroom door behind her before fumbling for the light string. She put down the toilet-seat lid to sit on. This was happening to someone else, not her. Only the burning was real, a burning almost painful and almost pleasureful. She connected it to Howard. She burned for him. She slumped forward, leaning her elbows on his stand-in, the book in her lap.

The Carb-Othello Sanguine pencil was gone. A wet charcoal stick lay on the sink rim. She took a gray eyeliner pencil from the medicine cabinet and opened the book to the dedication "For my parents . . . ," an almost blank page. She began to write.

I am working on the theory (unproved) that I love you. You make me laugh because you keep dropping your keys. Your hair grows commas along the back of your neck. And there's a question mark too. Soon my diligence will lead to a new problem, the corollary theory that you love me. . . .

Sealing in light, the closed bathroom door also sealed in heat. Sweat spread at the nape of her neck and under her breasts. She wiped her face with toilet paper. After writing on both sides of the dedication page, she went back to the title page for more space and finished that on both sides too. She wrote in the top margin of the first page, stopping at the bold CHAPTER ONE, wondering if the book would interest her. She skipped down to the bottom margin, then proceeded to the second page. Sweating, burning, stopping only to drink water or sharpen the eyeliner, which gave way to a blue one toward the end, she wrote.

No breeze moved the window shade. Surrounded by cartons of *Bandaged Moments*, he lay alone in bed, naked, in the dark. A vision of Suzanne moving beneath him caused Code Red, erectility. A hand, not his, entered the vision and caressed her. It was Howard's hand. She was in bed with Howard now. Cancel Code Red.

From the living room came the staccato of Jonathan switching channels. The TV insisted, "Heeee-ere's Johnny!" He thought, There's Bonnie. Johnny started in on a presidential candidate, Ronnie. He would never sleep again. When the first Alpo commercial boasted about real beef, his eyes were shut and rolling with dreams.

A life-size four-color plastic replica of the female uri-nogenital organs sat on the desk, next to a bronze plaque engraved HAVE A NICE DAY. Dina read the exhortation and despaired of fulfilling it. Dr. Scarcella, white-smocked, degloved, his chubby cheeks glowing from hypertension, wrote in her chart. "You have had intercourse in a position you're not accustomed to," he said. "Penetration from behind, I would think."

"How'd you know that?" Pigeons would soon be flying from his white sleeves. His accent added to the mystery: How did Chico Marx get through med school?

He lined up the July issue of *Vaginal Digest* with the corner of his desk. *His* doctor had put him on a low-sodium diet, refusing to debate the quality of life without parmesan cheese. "The burning you complain of is traumatic cystitis, a mild bladder infection caused by the penis pounding against the bladder before slipping fully into the vaginal sheath. Pounding." With an enthusiastic smile he disassembled the red, blue, pink, and cream plastic reproductive system, pointing out a passageway here, a blind alley there. He brushed dust from the isthmus of a Fallopian tube. An ovary snapped. "You may have had such intercourse without problems, but most recently the angle of entry was wrong for you. When your husband enters you from behind—"

She amended *husband* to *Howard* and had to gallop to catch up with the doctor, who had arrived at ". . . slowly until he is in place. Then he may move as aggressively as he wishes." He sounded wistful. The lecture ended with a prescription and "No intercourse for the next week."

She doubted Howard would like that. He'd never mentioned if he played chess. "*No* intercourse?"

While a woman with a tipped uterus sat in a closureless pink examination gown near stirrups in the next room, he folded his hands beside a silver letter opener inscribed with a pharmaceutical company's name. "Your husband will have to understand."

The doctor's pills turned her pee a luminous orange. The one advantage of cystitis was that it gave medical backing to her refusals of Larry. She worried how she would refuse Howard during her week of abstinence, but he didn't call. She could have called him, but her justification, sex, was gone.

In an iced room nicknamed Siberia at the Babel Language Institute, fifteen Russian students of English persecuted the comma. "Necessary, yes," Vova said, "but no so important." He stuffed toilet tissue into the central air conditioning vents. He was nineteen and a future computer programmer.

With stiff fingers Dina wrote on the green blackboard.

> Yes, he is Mr. Gogol.
> Yes, he is, Mr. Gogol.

"The same words, but a comma makes the second sentence mean something different from the first sentence," she said. Her nose was running. She sneezed. "Can anyone explain the sentences?"

Vova wrote on the board. His shirt pocket gaped with a plastic penholder.

> Is googol Mr. Gogol.
> Is googol, Mr. Gogol.

"I think your first sentence needs a question mark," she said, wiping her nose.

"Possible," he said.

After class he asked her to go out for coffee, "to talk over these commas." The collar of his short-sleeved shirt was opened to a white undershirt trimmed in brown chest hairs. He had on black trousers and a wide belt with a buckle of metal flowers spelling out PEACE.

"Thank you, but I think we've done enough commas for one day," she said. "See you next week."

"My heart crashes for you." The row of pens in his penholder hid the crash. "Dina, you are Jewish also, yes?"

"Yes."

"Gogol wrote the *Dead Souls*, yes, but he also wrote the *Taras Bulba*. You understand me?"

"Yes."

"We must take our opportunities."

"See you next week, Vova."

"School is named for Babel, Isaac, yes?"

"I don't know."

"Possible," he said.

At home she corrected lessons and in daydreams shuttled between the shower and the Eleventh Street apartment or the shower and the East Village bookstore. It was a damp time. She begrudged Larry the space he took up with his body and thoughts and endearments like "little one." Knowing she couldn't will him to disappear—she'd tried to, on and off, for years—she intensified her own efforts to disappear, grew fiercely quiet. He brought her a bird-of-paradise flower. He brought her a thin gold neck chain. He brought her a bottle of Chanel No. 5 cologne. The flower, resembling an alert bird, browned. She would wear the gold chain and the cologne to her next meeting with Howard, if only he would call. Sho, the Japanese student, called to tell her that his wife had given birth to a boy. "Already in Tokyo, but tomorrow here. Or yesterday. I am most excited to know which."

She swam through hopelessness, surrendered to panic. Panic hardened to anger. She collected her paycheck early at the Babel Language Institute and quit. "I didn't think you were unhappy here," the president, Demetrios Papadopoulos, said.

"Not here," she answered. "Thanks, Jimmy."

Because Larry was working, they had a novelty of riches. After paying rent and phone and Con Ed bills, they could pay this debt, that doctor, including Scarcella; they could buy new jeans for Larry, pain-free new shoes for her. They could buy Granny Smith apples and a jar of marinated artichoke hearts. She took *Bandaged Moments* from her underwear drawer and typed a copy of her writing from the bathroom palimpsest. She brought the manuscript to a bargain copy shop. The Xeroxed pages, still warm from the machine, she put in an envelope and mailed to Howard.

On the seventh night she threw out the empty pill bottle and applied demanding kisses to Larry's mouth. He received her far-open legs with the fortitude of a lottery winner and asked no questions lest fate withdraw what it had so freakishly bestowed. "Little one," he whispered in happy perplexity, his hair falling in her eyes.

His weight wasn't Howard's. His body bound her differently from Howard's. His hands on her breasts clung more heavily, with less authority. His mouth lacked the heat of cigarettes and white wine.

She made love to him for an idea of a hint of a fossil; memory shaped tenderness. Without anger, she had room for him, and sorrow for his past privations (Nazis and painters) and future ones (too terrible to surmise). Tangled in his hair, she stretched. His back rounded under her embrace. Six years of intimacy with the ceiling above the bed had left no souvenir. She followed him to pleasure, she led him to another loss.

An Affair, I Guess

by D. Reeve

I am working on the theory (unproved) that I love you. You make me laugh because you keep dropping your keys. Your hair grows commas along the back of your neck. And there's a question mark too. Soon my diligence will lead to a new problem, the corollary theory that you love me. When I don't see you, I forget many things.

There you are, licking my breast. How small the world is growing, to cunt-size. Come, unfold your prick. You're pushing my thighs apart. I could do that myself, but it's so much nicer when you do it. Take charge. Charge.

Not yet. First you will turn me over. This is the way doggies and horsies do it, boys and girls. And houseflies and camels and gnus. Dinosaurs did it this way when they were doing it. You nip at the back of my neck, you enter me, you withdraw. I'm trembling and sighing. Now you're turning me over again. Maybe I'm being barbecued, I'm burning for sure. You grapple with my clitoris, make my cunt contract. Your tongue declares itself and, as it does, you swing your body round and offer your prick my mouth. On this exotic matter I chew without teeth, I am so happy I could die, let me die now. You take the prize away, put mouth on mouth to pour my cunt juice into me again, wrong end on purpose. Please, I've lost my body, I'm all cunt, come inside.

You stab at me, slick road, you've missed the opening, I grab your prick and show it where to go. You slide in me up to your nonexistent hips, I exhale loudly. But no, you pull away, uncork me. I'm hissing like an old radiator. One of your hands holds my wrists together on pillows above my head. Unassisted, your prick sniffs out my cunt. You'll have it your way, on your own, and so you do. This entry makes me gasp. My dance card's full. You're moving in and out, I'm wrists and cunt you've pinned. Your fingers buff my clitoris, I ring and wring your prick with muscles I've acquired for that purpose. You're riding now, I'm being ridden, my toes are pointing east and west, spread-eagle ballerina. You're in no hurry, you detour here and there, I think I'm going crazy. We ride for miles, desert and oasis, an arching bridge, the West Side highway. I'm dreaming that I'm talking. I see your eyes see mine. We climb a hill, we're over treetops, there's a star or circling satellite. There's no more place to go. One of us is moaning, I can't tell which.

We're lying side by side. You want to know if I believe in God.

You're telling me your wife's name, which isn't Carmen

or Mary Sue. I'll have to memorize it. You want to see a picture of my husband; I show you what I've got, my driver's license and a Band-Aid. You suck my teeth. You say you have to be going. You do, by the way, believe in God, even if I don't.

*

How We Met

I was looking for someone to pay attention and you did. I reminded you of a girl from your childhood, late adolescence, or so you said. You held me closer to the light, inspected me. Your gaze was wonderful, the rest of you was odd. I didn't know you were torturing me, bestowing your attention in order to withhold it later. You recommended coffee. Sex waited everywhere, even in your patience, but I didn't see it. I asked, How can I ever thank you? You said, looking up seriously from a depressed chair, You can go to bed with me. I laughed and stammered something, tried to make a joke of it. Your eyes, which can sometimes seem small as the eyes of a bear, bared nothing.

Weeks later I came back to see you. I think I know what I'm doing now, I said. You mentioned you had to find someone to reverse your shirt collars. He's strange, I thought. You said, My wife is charming but passionless, she just lies there. Exit cue for me, and I went out waving.

More time. I worked with the unreasoning endurance of an animal, which is why they're called dumb. My husband was kind, cruel, all-encompassing. He struggled with his life, I shook my head. He bent my arm, I cried. He went to work. In the new silence of the apartment, I saw that all I had was my own destruction.

Frightened, I called you up. Frightened, I came to see you. I thought I wanted order, honor, help. You offered me a fuck.

Now you're curled up naked on the white bed, talking, lighting a cigarette. I miss every third word because you whisper. Sometimes when I whisper to you, I can tell by your answer that you haven't understood me, either.

*

140

Why You're Sad

Because you're spent, you're overspent, life is seeping out of you, not from the prick, that miracle, but from your pores, your eyes, the dead cells of your fingernails. You have had and still have too many women. You long for sleep. Ghosts lie down with us in bed. Transparent naked women, some of them the same woman at different times, at different ages, observe our passion. There are too many women and you are keeping them all. The collection owns the collector. They weigh you down, they drag you down, they kill you with your children. The women are your ballast; without them, you fear, you'd drift away from earth. Wanting to stay, wanting to keep alive, you add me now, a plummet to an anchor. You're sad because you're getting the uncomfortable feeling that I love you.

*

Your Wife

She has dinner set out, porcelain and blood, and greets you in the kitchen with a chaste kiss. Your children have already met you at the door, crying. The youngest holds your hand as you kiss your wife. What's wrong, you ask, what's all this crying? They will tell you stories, they will let you be the judge. Your wife bending to open a low cabinet displays a great ass in jeans. You'd like to reach for it, but the children are explaining Occam's razor. What tragedies they deliver you try to measure. Your wife stands up, the ass that was so pretty tucks away. You send the children off to wash their hands—With lots of soap, you call—then stealthily, a cartoon wolf, you stalk her jeans. You hug her from behind, place unwashed hands on breasts, your stirring prick against the backside groove. She says, The children. You say, They're washing. She says, That doesn't take forever. You let her go. Half in apology, she kisses your mouth. Can she smell me there? Not over the tobacco and the Scotch. Why don't you take a quick shower, she suggests, and I'll keep dinner warm. Keep me warm, you say. You don't want to shower, you want to fuck her with your body still wearing our fuck. You want to link the women through yourself. This idea compels you to pursue her. She runs, hands full of salad, to the dinner table, where the children play with salt. Don't do that, you say; and the children, thinking you mean them, stop playing.

You eat, you drink, you hold your children as if your love could keep them young. You kiss their foreheads when you say good night, a reed of parent over their breathing beds. You shower—I go down the drain—then stroll naked to the living room, where your wife untangles yarn for needlepoint. Or paints. Or sculpts. Or weaves hair baskets from your brush's gleanings. You ask her, Do you love me? Yes, she says, I do. Take off your clothes, you say. Not here, she says. Then where? you want to know. Let me bathe, she says. Don't bathe, you say. You're angry, she says.

Naked, you sit at your desk and stare at paper. She drapes your bathrobe over you. She kisses you the way you kiss the children.

She thinks in colors: the sofa will be blue, she'll have persimmon streaks across a pillow, the walls are beige, the walls of colors make her home. Your sex needs decorating.

I imagine this woman smaller than life. She is older than I am. So are you, so is my husband. Everybody is older than I am, though this won't always be true. Against that day I stroke clear cream into my pained expression.

*

My Husband

Has seen me crouching, ratlike, in our room. Has told me, Don't panic; sensing I'm about to run, and run blindly. I don't trust him anymore, he talks so well, he does so little. Refinement's costly. I need a winter coat. With you things are easier, I have never trusted you, not from the beginning.

My husband lives to waver, watches from the sidelines while others scramble, thinks being on the side is being up above and looking down. It's not. His eyes are beautiful and unmatched, his soul is flawless as a baby's. He blames me for his terrors. I'm drowning, I don't want him on top of me, it hurts too much. One breath, another.

He understands the concepts of rent and health insurance. He understands the word *please*. He thinks I'm hang-

ing him, I think he's strangling me. The truth is not electric.
Manners are better than nothing at all.

*

Fears

Your wife will take sex lessons. My husband will read
what I'm writing. You'll die. You won't want to see me. I'll
discover you aren't the one thing that's keeping me sane,
you're the one thing that's driving me crazy.

*

Facts

I never wanted to have a baby. Bring life into despair?
I knew my husband wouldn't be the father of my child. I
swallowed pills, dammed up the cervix. I spat out sperm.

The first time you entered me, I wanted to have a baby
with you. My husband needs a different woman, I need a
different man.

*

Solutions

Your wife will conveniently develop terminal movie-
star disease and die peacefully in two days. She'll feel no
pain, only a flicker of surprise before the lights go out. My
husband will die instantaneously in a plane crash, boom
against a mountain, so I won't have to hurt him with my
departure. He'll be pleasantly stoned at the time. You'll need
someone to care for your children. Interview me. I'll learn
to cook if you insist. We'll all live happily somehow.

*

And After That

You'll have other women. I'll meet you for illicit fucks
even though we live together. You'll never know what I'm
thinking. I'll never believe what you're saying. We'll be alive,
we'll be alive.

*

Then let's continue as we have until we stop. Put your prick in my mouth. I have to find an apartment because I'm leaving my husband. You have one finger in my cunt, one up my ass. I'm scored, I'm skewered, I'm screwed.

* * *

"I worry about their future," she hissed.

"Don't I pay?"

"Yes, but you could stop any time and then where would I be?"

"In court, sending me to the Bastille."

"You've got another kid. You don't care about Paul and Ilene."

"I care, Margie."

"You're a shit, Howie. You don't love your kids."

"I don't *know* my kids."

"Exactly. And whose fault is that?"

He hated her when she was right more than he hated her normally. "It's my fault. I should be smeared in the *National Enquirer*. What do you want?"

"Your head on a pike," she said and hung up.

Suzanne didn't answer at home. He decided to call Bask and cheer him up about critics, but there was no answer there, either. Howard beat a pencil against a mug. He'd manipulated his wife and a moderately talented novelist into an affair for his own comfort, not theirs. Fine, he found young love agreeable, he hoped the two of them trembled with the exaltation of mutual irrationality, he wished sensuality to confound Suzanne as it did most people, including himself. But her affair shouldn't interfere with any of *his* needs; it should enhance her observance of his needs, whether through guilt or wisdom, he didn't care. Now she wasn't home when he called; and when she *was* home, she regarded him sullenly as an enemy and not a benefactor. She hadn't spoken to him for a week, nothing more than hello, yes, no, and then in a civil tone only in Matty's presence. Adultery hadn't changed Suzanne for the better. She had become a reader. Dinners tasted sour. The sensuality he wished for her hadn't erupted, or if it had, she kept it from him.

His choice of Bask for her lover might have been the problem. He'd settled on a moderate talent because a lesser one would be too sentimental to desist at the right time—before the affair could threaten the marriage—and a greater talent would be too austere to desist. But, now that he thought about it, a moderate talent might lack the catalytic power to transform her.

Or the fault might be hers. She might be impervious to desire, passionproof: a likely explanation. Given the splendid opportunity of his marriage bed, she hadn't ignited. And all Bask had managed to produce in her was anger. Perhaps, knowing her own coldness, she'd imagined an affair would release her; now, having failed, she was forced to face her nature, unloving. And it made her angry.

The anger piqued him. For her to reject him without apology showed a new side of her. He wanted to enter her and drive down into that solid sphere of anger, split it with a well-placed thrust, and see what emerged. Suzanne as piñata. All week, scourged by her anger, he had been unable to concentrate on any other woman, had ceased admiring lasciviously on the street expanses of tanned bosom in elegant linen dresses, had repudiated the high cheap joy of girls in slit skirts. The forever rising and forever ruptured mystery of lovemaking with a stranger now resided in the unwilling body of his wife. If in bed with a strange woman he could for a brief trajectory blast himself away and become another Howard, a stranger to himself, then who could he become in bed with a stranger who was his wife?

The mailboy's summer replacement, a theater majorette on roller skates, zipped in with a stack of envelopes. Baby fat quivered along her bare arms. She had the misfortune to be chewing gum or he might have said hello with real interest. Unaware of her loss—and just as well, he realized, checking her departing bottom rippling in prewashed, presoftened, preworn, prepatched, presoiled, pretinged-with-vaginal-discharge Levis—she skated out, popping a bubble.

He needed Suzanne; and recoiled from the thought. It wasn't the way he'd arranged his life, to need her. Two phone calls researched an antidote to need, a lunch-hour frolic for three at Newman's place. The two ladies didn't mind last-minute invitations. He'd been celibate for over a week, long enough. In a few hours he'd be too busy to worry about Suzanne.

He dialed home and, listening to the ringing, glanced at the mail. Dina Reeve's name on a manila envelope made him mutter "Damn" with a start of what in another man would have been guilt. He hadn't thought of her in a while. He hung up the phone. The envelope seemed thick with reproaches. He opened it carefully, quietly, as if he were reading mail at a funeral. He saw the manuscript, "An Affair, I Guess," and gladdened. Good girl. She'd sent him fiction, not reproaches. He established a cigarette in his mouth and began to read.

When Gail buzzed to say that Dina Reeve was outside asking to see him, he'd typed the following on a *Rosemary* memo sheet:

Dear Dina,
   Yes now, this is one hell of a story. A screed more than a story, but fiction nonetheless. Congratulations, sweetie, you've amazed me. I'd like to run it as my lead next issue. You can

He rolled it out of the typewriter as she entered his office.

She looked thinner than he'd remembered her, and more encumbered. She carried a suitcase; or the suitcase by its weight impelled her forward to counterbalance it. She dropped it in order to stop moving. An overstuffed canvas sack populated by industrial zippers, it thudded to the floor, near a pile of old galleys. She put down a portable-typewriter case.

"Well, there you are," he said. "I've read your story."

She slumped on the sofa. A tower of manuscripts beside her inclined toward her shoulder. Her expression, sullenness or exhaustion, seemed to have been penciled on and then imperfectly erased. An essay called "Borges Through the Prism of Barthes" landed in her lap. She removed the pages, swiped at her damp chin with the back of her hand. "I left Larry."

This scene was his favorite waking nightmare, to be run through and rerun on insomniac nights. A woman would love him so much that she would ruin him. He was, he assumed, capable of inspiring such love, though the idea of ruin wore old-fashioned charm; it befell nineteenth-century unmarried girls with bodice-popping pregnancies.

Suzanne stood at their apartment door and threw him out into a snowy night. Her arm pointed, unrelenting: leave. It was July, but the scene needed snow. He took a last look at Matty weeping silently in a Kiss tee shirt. The door closed and he shivered in a moonless cold night. The hall, the elevators, and the lobby had disappeared, along with the uniformed attendants smelling of egg salad and red wine; the city had disappeared too. The place he found himself was bitterly familiar: in Mount Kisco, at the bare hedge outside the house he had lost to Margery. He couldn't imagine any other exile than the one he already knew, but this loss included Matty.

He prepared to audition the woman in his office, prepared to humor her, prepared to squeeze ten fingers in unkind emphasis around her neck. He would not lose Matty. "I'm sorry to hear that. You two had a fight?"

She shook her head. She had been small in bed, compact, easily moved. Now she grew larger and more fixed, a monument to folly, an obelisk aimed not at the sky but at his foul and uncertain heart.

"I need a favor," she said. "I need a place to stay for a while."

Disillusioned wives were supposed to go home to mothers in Winnetka, Illinois, or to recently widowed aunts in cavernous rent-controlled apartments on Central Park West. What responsibility did a casual lover owe? He said, "I hope this had nothing to do with—I don't believe I had anything to do with your breakup. I have a family, I want to keep my family."

"I didn't leave him because of you." Crying, she spoke carefully, as if he were a lip-reader. She had cried in his office before. "You had nothing to do with it."

He marveled at her obtuseness. She didn't understand that she was his victim. Her reddened nose and eyes, her tear-streaked face, her unresisting body stormed by sobs—these awakened in him an unwelcome desire. "That's not what your story says."

"It's a story."

"You write about leaving your husband and here you are."

Her tears gave way to dry thoughtfulness. "What did you think of it?"

"It's very good."

"Flawless?"

"No, but I'd like to buy it."

"You're going to publish it?"

"Yes."

"You?"

"You said it's a story. But I don't have a place for *you*."

"The apartment we went to—"

"No, no, that was borrowed. You know that."

"Can't you borrow it again?"

"I don't see how—"

"You borrowed it so we could fuck there. Why can't you borrow it so I can sleep there?"

Leaning back in his chair, his fingers interlaced in a meditative pose, he stuffed her into a giant black plastic trash bag, slung her over his shoulder, and carried her to the river. He added his office typewriter and the supply closet's gross of medium ballpoint pens to the bag for weight. A jukebox played "Heartbreak Hotel." The pens had blue caps. "Let me think," he said.

2

Newman Sykes was chopping wood. He liked how the muscles of his arms worked, liked to feel the axe swinging up and down, liked the way his arms and the axe became one force stroking in one rhythm. It merged with the rhythm of the afternoon: July sun heating through the back of his shirt, a warm breeze shaking the heads of daisies and black-eyed Susans at the edge of the field, where tall grass parted and closed, wounded and healed by the path of the breeze. Crazed yellow butterflies rose in the air like confetti and fell again, fluttering. On a brown bank of earth along a neighboring meadow, dark spots marked the burrows of woodchucks, who kept poking their heads out in of movements as rigid and regular as the peg pistons of a toddler's pull-toy, the wood kind drawn by a dirty string attached to a yellow wood ball graspable by small splayed fingers. Across the meadow a red tractor droned through nettles and grass.

Stripped of its thin uprising shoots, the branch at his feet lay solid and mysterious. No longer part of a tree, not yet a fireplace log, it seemed in its present purposelessness as remote and unyielding as a god or an autistic child. He noticed he was thinking about children. The axe bit into rough gray-brown bark, bounced back, bit again. Splinters exploded at each attack; the sound of the blade deepened. His arms rose and fell, rose and fell, in welcome monotony. He stopped thinking, except for the thought *I've stopped thinking*, a last, fleet glimpse of himself before he submerged in an ocean of contentment; and with the exhilaration of emptiness, a keen sense of absence, he watched his hands and the axe and the branch, and saw them and not himself seeing them. His face, harsh, set, grooved as a walnut, took on tenderness. He was chopping wood for this moment when thought abandoned him. Sometimes he said he did it for the exercise, sometimes to save money. In cords near the garage and in others under tarp near the back door to his house, he had stacked more than enough wood for his two fireplaces for the coming winter. He had more than enough for a cold summer too. Passing the cords, he would wonder at their wry significance.

He halved the branch. With creamy yellow centers wrapped in bark, the halves were enormous pieces of candy. He upended one on a tree stump and split it. Sweat dampened his hair, which was straight and glossy black relieved by coarse strands of white. A bee whined near his ear, and the breeze, sweeping in a new direction, brought him the clean smell of cut grass. He lifted his head to inhale it and saw the blue station wagon turn off the highway, bump along the dirt road to his house, and disappear behind trees. He heard it stop, heard the engine cut off. This took a while: she was always fumbling with her purse and packages, with doors and windows, because she dreaded moving from one place to another. ("Look," she'd once called to him as she walked away on Madison Avenue, "no net!" And she'd held up her arms and laughed.) The car door slammed. He'd been standing, sweating, waiting for that sound. He turned back to his wood and brought the axe down.

Biscuit, an old springer spaniel lying in the sun, thumped his tail against the ground in greeting. Slowly, with the laziness and arthritis of his twelve years, he got up, stretched, shook himself and his incorrigible fleas and vet-certified kidney stones. "Hello, boy," Newman said, putting down the logs and axe, and going over to him to save him the walk. Biscuit licked the back of Newman's hand, stared through cataracts at him as he patted the contours, bone and silk, of the dog's forehead. Satisfied, Biscuit lay down again, tongue out, and Newman said, "Don't you look handsome."

He stacked the logs with others at the back of the house, wiped his feet on the mildewed hemp mat before entering the back door. He placed the axe in the orderly arrangement of the tool closet near the pantry. No sounds reached him from the kitchen, though he expected a cabinet creaking open or the complaint of a faucet. The new water heater stayed mute. In the downstairs bathroom, the one for guests, he washed his hands and face with yellow soap shaped like a lemon and dried himself with a green velour hand towel. He spread the towel neatly on an empty rack to dry.

She was sitting at the kitchen table, which held an assortment of groceries: canned goods, boxes of pasta and beans and cold cereal, a gallon of milk in a white plastic jug, perspiring cans of frozen orange juice, a squashed bar of sweet butter, a cup of sour cream, bottles of Heineken's, a cellophane package of chocolate-chip cookies. A cash-register tape wetly embraced a box of frozen Chinese vegetables. On the floor empty brown paper bags were open-mouthed, like beached fish.

He said, "Don't you look pretty."

And she did look pretty, blond hair pushed back with combs and falling, limp and shining, to her shoulders. Her ears were charming—he'd always thought so—lying snug against her head, flaring out only at the small lobes pierced by minute gold stud earrings. What he had particularly liked when he met her was the fact that such a big-boned woman, a strong, athletic woman, chose to call attention to her delicate ears with equally fine earrings out of all proportion to the rest of her. Remembering their meeting, he approached her in the kitchen, past screens of longing. But, closer to her, he saw blue shadows beneath her dark eyes and spun spider lines there and between her eyebrows, nights of the floor creaking under her feet, back and forth, back and forth, to impress those lines, and the downward pull at the corners of her mouth. He felt the same pull at his own mouth. Her hairdo seemed girlish, wrong; he wished she'd worn it up as she usually did.

"We'll have to make these," he said, leaving aside two cans of juice. He handed her the box of Chinese vegetables. "What do you think—freeze or not?"

"I got you your beer."

"Yes, I see. Thank you."

The box dented under her thumb. "It's nice of you not to point out that I let all this food spoil." Coiled around a slippery center, her courtesy wasn't as sure as his; despair at controlling it threaded through her voice.

"Nothing spoiled." He put the thawed vegetables in the freezer.

"I sat here and *watched* them." Head against her arms on the table, she cried.

"Clare," he said quietly. He didn't go to her.

"What?"

"Go upstairs and lie down. I'll be there in a few minutes."

With her long blond hair on defeated shoulders, with her wrinkled denim skirt and grass-stained sandals, she was a tall chastised child being sent off to bed without any supper. The stairs announced each footfall; in the kitchen, holding the cans of juice, he heard the echo of her passage.

Will said, "Disgusting!"

Newman said, "Why don't you try it?"

"Is there something else?"

"Salmon mousse, steak poivre, and four thousand apple popovers."

Will checked his plate again. "What is it?"

"According to the package, 'an Oriental vegetable fantasy.' With eggs."

Leslie said, "It's not bad."

"A testimonial. Thank you." At the head of the dining-room table, Newman swallowed a hard mouthful. The two black-haired boys watched him.

Will's tee shirt rode up over his belt. His chair teetered on its back legs. "Dad, can I make myself a sandwich?"

"Be my guest."

"That's the trouble," Leslie said. "He thinks he's a guest."

"Shut up," Will told him without enthusiasm from the kitchen. "It was your turn to cook tonight, not Dad's. If you don't like dinner, it's your own fault."

Will came stomping back with a jar of mayonnaise. "It was *your* turn. I cooked last time."

"No you didn't."

"Yes I did. Chili—remember? Two Saturdays ago when Mom started crying at Stop-'n'-Shop."

"Uh-uh. *I* cooked. Tuna casserole—remember?"

"Who could forget it? But that was when Dr. Linker came over."

"He didn't come over. Dad drove Mom to his office. And I made the casserole."

"You made the casserole when Mom was upset after the museum. I made the chili when she cried at Stop-'n'-Shop. And that was the last time. So it was Dad's turn, so bug off."

Leslie struggled with indignation. "He always walks away before I can answer him," he told Newman. "He's immature."

"And you're an idiot," Will shouted from the kitchen.

"Lower or you'll wake your mother." Newman peppered his Oriental fantasy.

"He's immature and inconsiderate," Leslie said.

Will arrived in the doorway to deliver his answer quietly. "And you're an asshole."

Leslie gasped, "Daddy!" Will waited for his father's reaction. Newman kept on eating.

"Dad, did you hear him?"

"It's better not to comment on boorish behavior, especially when it comes from someone in your family."

"He called me a name."

"Name-calling is a sign of an impoverished vocabulary. Perhaps Will should consult a thesaurus."

"He's always butting in. He pisses me off," Will said.

Standing, Newman offered the laser of his serene gaze. "There will always be people who'll make you angry. And if you call them names, then you'll lose friends and jobs and other assorted necessities." He went into the kitchen.

"Hey, Dad?" Will had followed him.

"Yes?" Newman poured beer into a glass and gave Will a ritual sip.

"There's a kid at school," Will said, "who says he can drink a whole six-pack and not get drunk. He's a senior."

From the dining room Leslie called, "I'm all deserted."

Newman told Will, "Make that sandwich and come back," and he went out to face Leslie's dark, reproving eyes.

He woke and found her turned toward him, her eyes closed, lips parted. Shadows and the blue light before sunrise lapped the bedroom; he swam in thought through unbuoyant air as beautiful as water. Her breathing was slower, shallower than his. Her sealed dreamless sleep, chemically induced, affronted him: she preferred it to any comfort he could present. It was an extended time-out for her. Playing stickball in a weedy lot in Camden years ago, he'd scraped his knee and seen his blood outside his body, where it didn't belong. He'd started to walk away, and one of the older boys, a McBride or a Sullivan, had grabbed him and said, "You can't leave without we call time-out."

"So call it," he'd said.

"Can't. There's only three time-outs allowed and we ain't wasting one of them on you. Get back." The press of fingers on the nape of his neck.

He got back.

The sense of fairness—no, not fairness: rules—the sense of rules the bigger boy had laid on Newman's neck stayed with him. He grew up to love books and women, in no special order, though he believed women were the more predictable. He stopped going to church. He attended World War II as a propagandist's aide in Washington, D.C. Three blocks east of the White House he yanked an undersecretary from the path of an oncoming car. He fell in love with a pregnant technical translator who lived with her mother in Bethesda and was engaged to a staff sergeant she hadn't seen in fifteen months. Newman drove her to a closed restaurant in Silver Springs for an abortion and straightened fork tines on the bar while inside the kitchen she cried, "Oh God, *oh* God, oh *God*!" He had an affair with a typist, Gillian, from the FCC. At a party he saw Mrs. Roosevelt carrying a teacup. After two promotions and a peacetime offer of the good life in intelligence, he came to New York convinced of the need for balance. Suffering the polar pulls of reason and passion, fearful of losing himself to either, he indulged in both. He would master each from the center, a kind of access by excess. He rutted through college and years of glad bohemianism beneath overpainted tin ceilings in Greenwich Village studios. He peeled off dancers' black tights, exposing white, sometimes defiantly unshaved legs. The women gave their bodies freely, but saved their souls for Rilke or Marx. He prepared underdiluted Campbell's tomato soup on his hot plate. The women brought packages of bread and sliced cheese with tough rinds. Alone, he opened with knightly reverence the bound wisdom of books and surrendered himself to naked and voluptuous language. If his choice of women remained random, his affairs with writers didn't. Study sharpened his taste; kings were deposed, some beheaded, as new masters loomed. E. E. Cummings, who lived several blocks away, may one night have heard the thud of his reputation on an enamel-blackened wood floor; Newman had discovered Yeats.

Soon literary magazines discovered Newman. He erected fiction. For stipends barely covering his coffeehouse bills, he grasped the privilege of seeing his words, and the typos they engendered, endure in print. With the double edge of fixity, his well-chosen paragraphs would live, but so would the bad ones, monstrous as taxidermy, dead-eyed in glass. He wrote skillfully, searching for greatness, uncertain of the results. Awe for great writers burdened his stories, and his contempt for the second rate turned inward. He confronted his relative value: a minor-league hopeful. He took pride in renunciation: he would serve art in a humbler way. The real issue, his fear of the uncontrollable and shapeless substance of creation, he didn't admit. He withdrew from competition with himself. Having reasoned with his passion, he bent his tender nature toward criticism, which brought him the rapped-knuckle attention of writers he admired. An idealist, he was perpetually disappointed by the actuality of most prose. If he had renounced art because of his high standards, then writers who pursued it would have to vindicate his standards. If he wasn't worthy, then they had better be. In essays and reviews he lashed out at the writers; and they, in print or face to face in bars, cried to him, "No! But tell us more." Much as his comments stung, he was, after all, a fascinating voice, the conscience. "Art is a toenail clipping in your salad," a former surrealist said, yellow-spattered fingers around his glass. "Pompous fart," a poet answered. "Art is a pompous fart after the salad," the former surrealist went on. "I wish I had the money for a salad," the poet said. Further down the bar an Abstract Expressionist teethed on his mistress. Newman passed them and chose a stool next to a plum-nosed bisexual poet from out of town. "You know what your problem is?" Plum Nose asked.

Years of attacking the literary establishment made him part of it. He had regular columns in two journals. At the Ninety-second Street Y he enlivened symposiums on the death of the novel, the future of the novel, the religion of T. S. Eliot, the need for exegesis of Kafka's "Metamorphosis." "No need," he said, confounding his fellow panelists, whose dissertations and sabbaticals and hard-won grants assumed that need. Honorariums and tomatoes stuffed with chicken salad and celery inspired him to lecture on Oscar Wilde at banquet halls, Pearl Buck at women's clubs, Ralph Waldo Emerson at prep school graduation ceremonies. He moved to a sunny brownstone apartment with an even white ceiling and an unpainted oak floor; the cheerful ascetic, he furnished it with a bed, a table, a chair, and books, wall-to-wall books. He loved, in his bed and a few times on the table and once on the floor, a variety of women, among them a painter, three writers, innumerable students and disaffected wives, a saleswoman from Abercrombie & Fitch, a gymnast, a Communist (she was the one who'd insisted on the floor), a photographer, and several dancers with fertile opinions on Martha Graham. Clare was the photographer. She carried forty pounds of camera equipment and talked about epiphanies of light. He thought, It's about time. He was thirty-five, she was twenty-four. He rolled down her nylons and married her. While he discussed Hans Castorp at a radiologists' convention and tried once more to write fiction, she took pictures of benches in Central Park. "It'll be a photo essay called 'Four Winters,' " she said. His stories appeared in literary magazines, including *Rosemary*; five winters' boxes of her pictures commandeered the sweater shelves in the closet. She complained of headaches. He framed one snowy bench and hung it in their living room. Before moving upstate, they had Leslie and began Will. Newman packed his books. Clare bought dimity curtains for the new bedroom windows, "for diffusion."

They settled into their house in a rainy spring. He built bookshelves, nail-less marvels to fortify the walls of the upstairs room he'd picked for his study. Lavishly pregnant, she followed him slowly, as if underwater, holding Leslie and trailing a tangled measuring tape.

"How about this for a darkroom?" he asked her. He indicated half the large pantry. "I'll put walls here." His gesture excluded their small store, cans of cling peaches and tuna, a sack of flour.

He thought he remembered her whispered "Okay." He had built walls and a lightproof darkroom. Crying, she had given birth to Will; and hadn't stopped crying. Yellow light overwhelming the blue. Morning again, through windows without dimity; something in a flowered print there now. He had fed the babies, bathed them, changed them. Had held them on nights when Clare, sobbing her outrage, demanded to know where he'd hidden her talent. Leslie had come home from second grade with a note from his teacher about his gold-starred story beginning "Momy wants lite but Dady says no."

Inches away, her dazed warmth drew him. Her white breasts wore the ghost of a bathing suit. He pulled the blanket higher around her because it was cold. He thought, I have responsibilities. He had made his life tidy. He had compressed his feelings into a space narrow enough to fit between two lines on a printed page.

For years he reviewed books and scrutinized the state of literature in a respected monthly meekly celebrating the arts. A conglomerate on a pretax spending spree bought the magazine, along with an aglet factory and a third-world film distribution company. The new editor, fresh from streamlining a newspaper chain, said, "Let's break up all that print." A design consultant created a look and brought in his stable of artists to maintain it. Truncated columns of text supported dazzles of illustrations. The editor directed any remaining text toward upward mobility. She had "There's Room at the Top for Our Readers" professionally needlepointed and mounted on a knife-edge pillow for a high-tech chair in her office. She hired editors for fashion, sports, pop music, science, and psychology. She fired the language columnist and the gently humorous essayist. "We need Richard Pryor, not Will Rogers," she said. She didn't interfere with Newman's freedom to write as he pleased—"Polysyllables Spoken Here" backed with burgundy velvet was on order at a needlepoint atelier selling do-it-yourself petit-point canvas for *Unicorn in Captivity* pillows and "Home of the Whopper" jockstrap covers—but she did encourage his pessimism. "Take 'em on, take on all the sacred bulls. If it's shit, say so, no matter who made it." She pyramided her third prelunch can of Tab, with its lipsticked straw, on the other two empties, and swung back in her chair. Red running shoes thudded down on computer printouts on her desk. Linen pants cuffs rolled back over a fading tan. "I'm not afraid of controversy, Newman. I'm afraid of low circulation."

He straddled her rowing machine. "If I like something, I like it, Julie. I can't say I don't."

"You don't have to. Just keep doing what you've always been doing. Be cantankerous. Don't be soft, Newman."

"I never am," he answered. Row one, breathe; two, breathe; three. "How about a drink later?"

"No, thanks, but now that the obligatory nod to my gender is out of the way, we'll be fine."

Besides reviews, he conducted an inquisition of a writer, a tape recorder the instrument of torture. It lay near the steak sauce on the writer's dinner table. While Newman speared a roast potato, the writer changed cassettes because the first ninety-minute tape had run out. "Don't want you to miss a single word," he said. Reading the published article changed his mind. "Not so much an interview as a vivisection," he complained in a letter to the editor among several such outraged responses Julie printed. The writer canceled his niceness campaign for a Pulitzer and his tutorial at a midwestern writing conference. Abandoning wife, children, mistress, and therapeutic dominatrix, he checked into a fat farm for megadoses of B-6. Newman had asked him if clit lit was his chosen specialty or simply his horizon.

Julie declared the article to be the start of a series, "Newman Sykes Talks to . . ." She told him, "Keep filling in the blank."

He filled it in with a zest for lethal impudence that made each interview a suspense story and an exposé. When, during the subject's rumblings about himself and Faulkner and the American tradition, would Newman remind him of charges he'd plagiarized parts of his last book from Artaud's essays and ask about his first wife's claim that she'd written the parts Artaud hadn't? See the famous writer recalling how his first wife, the poor frigid bitch, was a pathological liar who went down on busboys and whose silicone-enhanced breasts had hardened to concrete jugs you could break your teeth on. Some interviewees thanked Newman; the dialogues were benign, dulled with Newman's sincere respect. Most of the writers, with livelier exchanges, threatened to sue him or beat him up; they called him a John Bircher, a Communist, a fascist, a wimp, a queen, a homophobe, an illiterate, an old lady, a male chauvinist, a piranha. "It's like being on *60 Minutes*," a poet said, digging at her cuticle. "You start out nice and polite, and by the end you're cornered and you're itching to punch out Mike or Morley." But the need for publicity to sell books, coupled with essential authorial narcissism, created willing subjects.

"How about me?" a short-story writer of undeniable shining talent asked him at a party after a bilingual poetry reading to benefit Appalachian hunger. "You can trot out your clit lit line again with a different slant. Slit lit. We can chat about my lesbian tendencies. I'll tell you my latest poem: 'Girls who are Sapphic / Seldom stop traffic.' I'm also an anarchist and I sew all my own clothes. You make me sick to my stomach." She moved aside to join a pleasanter conversation. Across the room a woman seemed to be kneading Howard Ritchie's shirt label.

Someone pumped his hand. "Mr. Sykes. Pleased to meet you, Newman. I'm a fan." A gray blow-dried edifice and snub-nosed pasty face bobbed at Newman's chin. A business card slapped his palm. "Have to run. Call me," the man said. The card was from a local TV station. A low herringbone tweed jacket hurried away.

The short-story writer read the card over Newman's shoulder. "Goody," she said, "maybe soon I can turn you off on a regular basis."

She was right: for three to five minutes once a week on the evening news Newman gave the tristate area what the female anchor introduced as "the book roundup. It's culture time and we don't mean yogurt." He reviewed books and commented on trends in publishing. He interviewed authors plugging books. "The women in your book all find your hero irresistible, Jack. Would you say your fiction is revenge against life?" He learned to smile at the camera with the red light. He learned which colors not to wear on camera. His dentist's receptionist asked him if he knew Judith Krantz personally. He asked the makeup man to tone down the base. He got letters requesting autographed pictures and/or advice about breaking into the book biz. He got death threats, marriage proposals, unsolicited manuscripts, and six handknit scarves. TV critics reviewed his reviews: "the poor man's Dick Cavett," "a welcome relief from Dick Cavett," "the electronic Edmund Wilson." His dentist's receptionist asked him if Ann Beattie was Warren Beatty's other sister.

Besides the magazine and TV work, he gave a series of lectures—funded by a federal program a United States senator denounced as "a viper in our fiscal bosom"—on Eastern thought in Western literature. The jobs required his presence in the city for two days each week; he arranged to spend three days and two nights a week in the city, in an apartment he'd rented when he started at the magazine. He sent Leslie and Will to good private schools. He bought Clare a new enlarger and the solicitous hairy ear of Dr. Max Linker, psychiatrist. He had his own psychiatrist, Steve, and from time to time a lover. Ex-lovers and potential lovers crowded his lectures, watched his lithe body on the podium, their bracelets clinking; he was grateful Steve was male. Steve collected rare books, which gave them something to talk about. Newman's first editions were less valuable but better loved. All this took money. He wrote articles for magazines, persuaded publishers to hire him to anthologize *Underground Writing Today* or to introduce *The Complete Skelton, Unexpurgated*. He rented a summer house for two weeks on Block Island and wondered why. In her sleep Clare turned away from him.

He got out of bed, shivered because the windows were open and he was naked. Alert with anger, he padded down the brightening hallway to the bathroom.

The landscape chugging past greasy windows belonged above a calendar, with the blue legend "Savings Banks Are PEOPLE Banks." He unwillingly beheld perfection: sunlight flooding, through one convenient cloud, over a lunate brook and stands of unblighted green trees. If he looked away from the window, he would encounter Sheila Dunne, gilded and dressed for the city.

"Well, hello," she said.

The car was almost empty, since the 1:09 was too late for the matinee and shopping ladies, and too early for the evening crowd. He smiled at her, a handsome made-up woman with real pearls, and shifted his heavy bookbag from the seat to the floor. She sat down and gave his arm a brief squeeze. "How are you doing?"

She exuded a new fashionable scent he'd been hating for weeks. It lingered in elevators at the magazine, assaulted him from the ranks of his high-minded lecture audiences. One of the reporters had sprayed the studio with it. "I'm fine," he said. "You?"

"The usual. A hundred things to do and no time." With a manicured hand she signed *no time* as an ideogram. She seemed dangerously close to a giggle.

"How's Harry?"

The question produced the desired result. "Fine, thank you." Now she was getting the hang of it: formality. "How's Clare?"

"Not too good." He'd topped her. After formality came such indifference that a straitened intimacy was possible.

"I'm sorry to hear that. If there's anything I can do . . ."

"There's nothing to do."

"Newman."

"Yes?" he asked deliberately. An overweight conductor with unshining buttons caromed along the aisle.

"I think about you. I worry about you."

"I'm all right." He felt glad he wasn't a conductor or even an engineer.

"If you have problems, you can call me."

"Why?" That should have stopped her.

"Because we're neighbors. And because we're . . . friends. At least I like to think we're friends. I never know what you're thinking. I never did know what you were thinking."

Her courage touched him. "Of course we're friends." Then, seeing an hour of reading time vanish, he yielded to the sound of her voice.

Women's voices, a keening, breath, an echo of sorrow falling away—he heard these repeated in the train's progress toward the city, where turrets and cupolas, beautiful with verdigris, risked eyes, the terrible power of the beholder. I am a witness, he thought as the woman talked and he answered her. He saw the spread of his fingertips, dark on a woman's pale behind; he grasped, he took. The women. Time stirred, measured by women. Calendar girls weren't decorations; they were time itself, everything revealed and, by that openness, everything shrouded. Here it is. What is it? Come, bite my ass, three-quarters of an apple. The other quarter, the one not there—where is it? "And have you been reassessed?" she asked, adding, "It's outrageous, money and more money and the sewage system is still prehistoric." The other quarter skimmed over green trees, that slice, the triangle rounded and with dimension, shape given flesh. Weary of women, he still yearned for something beyond himself. The train carried him, with Sheila Dunne and the enormity of his longing, to New York.

The first thing he saw when he opened the door was a man's ass, the last thing he wanted to see, but there it was, hovering over hair streaming from a woman's head. Another woman's head shot up from somewhere else in the orange sheet. A magician's illusion? He smelled burning leaves. Howard Ritchie could pull women's heads out of a top hat. The lamp on the night table had been moved aside. In its place were a hand mirror, a razor blade, a rolled-up dollar bill, and a saucer with a lumpy joint that had gone out. "Hi, Howard."

Three faces whipped toward him.

"Hi, Maris. And hello to you too," he told the stranger.

He hung his jacket in the closet. The hanger scraped against the rod. He put his bookbag near the desk. "Anyone for a beer?"

Howard stumbled over clothes on the floor and, hopping on one leg, thrust a foot into khaki pants. His penis lolled against his thigh, the tongue of a panting dog. The strange woman said, "Hey, those are mine." He recovered other khakis.

"Sorry," he mumbled to Newman at the refrigerator.

"You don't wear shorts." Newman sipped beer and watched the women dress.

"Nah, more trouble than they're worth. That's Katharine."

More nipple than breast, Katharine hurried a tank top down over ribs, hips. Maris halfheartedly held a blouse against herself. "Sorry," she said.

"This isn't part of the contract," Newman answered.

"But you're early," Howard said.

"It's my day, not yours. But it's nice to see two of my friends have met each other."

Maris buttoned her blouse up to her throat, where the skin sagged. "Shit," she whispered, "I didn't even get off."

"Do you?" Howard asked in a low voice. He slumped into his jacket. A pair of green bikini underpants clung under the back of the collar.

"*There* they are." Katharine peeled her underpants from twill.

"I mean, you do, huh?" Howard pursued Maris to the bathroom.

"How about privacy?" was all she said before the door closed on the two of them.

Katharine buttoned her khaki pants. Something familiar there. She sat at the edge of the bed, a stewed sheet, to put on her sandals. She had gold toenails. She reminded Newman of a woman he'd known, and of another. And another. And the way she bent her head—another. There are only so many ways of bending the head. He thought, How sad she is, she's like so many people that she's no one at all. Tin cans strung to the tail of the thought clamored at him: The sadness is yours, the fault—defective observation, obsession—is yours.

Before she spoke he wondered if possibly he could desire her. She asked in a pleasant voice, "Weren't you on Johnny Carson last week?"

"Yes."

"You're . . . you're . . ." She screwed up her face. "You're, you know, *him*, the guy with—" She laughed. "Help me."

He shook his head.

She came toward him, laid hands lightly against his shoulders. "I know who you are, it's on the tip of my tongue."

"Show me."

The tip of her tongue parted chafed lips. He closed his mouth around it. Her mouth opened. Not an offering, he thought, but a reflex. He tested it anyway, probed it with his tongue, searching tongue, teeth, gum, ridged upper palate, tongue again, the slick insides of lips, the bubbles below the tongue, searching for something familiar, for home. It was familiar. It wasn't home. Her tongue flicked his. She tasted like whisky—what else would Howard's women taste like? He pushed his tongue toward the back of her mouth, then reeled it in. Out. She whispered "Cold." He drew in breath. "The beer," she said. "Cold mouth."

The sound of running water came from the bathroom. She said, "You're a painter, right?"

"Right."

Her face in muted daylight—for the curtains had been drawn, one of Howard's few discretions—showed solemn and greedy as a child's. She wasn't much older than a child, early twenties, large face, with shiny skin, no makeup, not even powder, which she could have used, light blue eyes, and long hair, her pride, untidy. An oiled Madonna, a piglet, a bit of both. "You did that stuff, those sports pictures. Hockey and stuff. Right?"

"Right."

Her two front teeth, separated by a wedge of gum, had no sign on them saying, "Here passed the tongue of Newman Sykes." He wondered if she ever closed her mouth. She did, only to open it again.

"You don't look like a painter."

"What does a painter look like?" Out of politeness he didn't yawn.

"During the commercials does Carson talk to you?"

"I don't remember."

"God, I'd remember." She tapped his belt buckle, stroked the fabric of his fly. He stood still, listening. She said, "You don't want me." She was puzzled.

He took her hand, a warm live thing he'd have preferred not to touch, like a squirrel or a woodchuck, a wild animal that might bite or transmit disease or parasites. "I'm knocked out. Painting, California, jet lag." He performed Sheila Dunne's no-time gesture.

Twining a strand of hair between two fingers, she stared at the rug, a small worn Oriental, its random fraying almost a pattern on the pattern. She smiled—out of embarrassment, he thought. He reached for his beer. Empty.

"You shaved off your mustache," she said.

"Never had one." He hesitated between another beer and righteous indignation, chose the second as safer. He banged on the bathroom door. "Hey!" No answer. Again "Hey!" with anger at the water running, anger at the sounds it must be covering, anger at his exclusion. No whispering secrets in company—didn't anybody know that rule? "Hey!"

He opened the door—it was his bathroom—and steam rushed toward him. The shower pounded. It wasn't his bathroom anymore. Transformed by fog, it breathed, a place inspirited. Should he remove his shoes? He had wandered onto holy ground. Mist rolled past him toward the open door. He pushed it shut. Through the green-tinted translucent shower curtain from Woolworth's he saw spectral dancers, Howard and Maris, slow and eternal. A plant, a flower bending, she stood on one leg, stemmed, swaying. Her other leg lifted to crook around Howard's thigh, which dipped to receive it. Now her fixed leg moved, she uprooted herself, twined around him. A new form showed through green plastic, a humped unwieldy form on two legs dancing. Water beat down on it, tattooed the cries that came from it. He waited for something to call his name. Vapor condensed on his face in saltless sweat and tears. He saw his past filtered in green. The deft monster in his shower arched, limbs extended. A starfish. It contracted. Began pulsing. There was nowhere to go. Here was verdurous obscenity; outside, Katharine waited. From clothes on the floor he picked up Maris's blouse to wipe his face. He could have used the towel on the rack, but he didn't know who had used it before him and for what. Too late he realized the same uncertainties applied to the blouse at his forehead.

He took off his shoes, socks, pants, underpants. The monster moaned. He unbuttoned his shirt, dropped it on the floor with the other clothes. Glanced at his unimpressed penis, slack in dark hair. He pulled aside the curtain. Water spattered his face and chest. He saw a breast, a spare muscled arm, a prominent tendon;

tried to identify the tangle. Howard looked tired but determined: Maris had weight to her, a surprising generosity. With her hair flat on her scalp, though, she didn't show to advantage. Water ran from the corners of her open mouth. Gray streaks of mascara had settled in the lines under her eyes, which were startled and excited and sad. Water hit the floor. It trickled down his legs, steel beams.

"Come in or stay out, but close the . . . curtain." Suspicious, flattered, Howard must have wanted to say "goddamn curtain," but respect and his nakedness had made him amend it. Maris ushered flurries of kisses across his neck, yellow butterflies hovering over tall grass.

Newman hesitated, heavy with indifference. "This isn't going to work," Howard said. Newman stepped into the bathtub and drew the curtain closed.

He jostled Maris, whose mouth was exploring Howard's neck. Howard said, "This is like the BMT," and she told him, "Your Adam's apple tickles."

Newman bent down and bit into her behind. She shrieked, laughed, shrieked. He didn't let go. Her shrieks grew louder. He held on calmly. His teeth imprinted flesh. He had no intention of tearing flesh, but he had no intention of releasing it. If she kept on wriggling, she'd cut herself. He steadied her with his hands on her buttocks, projecting marvels that Howard balanced. "Jesus," she wailed, and Howard grunted. It must be a struggle to keep her aloft, Newman thought. Bent in an attitude of prayer, he had captured something. Ass on the wing. He dreamed of blue and a harpsichord's voice spiraling. Led by his teeth, his head followed each squirm of her body. Sometimes he made her wriggle, sometimes Howard did, sometimes she wriggled on her own, chirruping. He and Howard were joined in that fragile spirit of sharing common to audiences, travelers, castaways. Should he regard Maris as a lifeboat? Her anal sphincter winked at him. He touched a wet finger to it, pushed. "Ahhhhhh," someone said. "Ahhhhhh." The shower went on.

• • •

Katharine was gone when he and Howard and Maris emerged from the bathroom. Howard didn't seem to notice. Maris said, "Jesus, look at the time." The expression made Newman want to smile.

He sat in a blue upholstered armchair and mentally connected the mildew spots on the title page. He produced a picture of a cow's udder or a man with a beard. The book, a first English edition of Tolstoy's *What I Believe*, had a dejected brown binding. "Where'd you get it?" he asked.

"The Strand," Steve, his psychiatrist, answered from another blue armchair.

"There was a dreadful song years ago, late fifties, called 'I Believe.' "

"I remember." Steve was decent; he made Newman feel they were having a conversation.

"A credo by the unimaginative for the unimaginable. Yet we remember it. Will sings ad jingles, Burger King, Coke. Why'd you buy this?"

"Why do you ask?"

"Sometimes, you know, I'd be sitting in my study, reading, and up it would come. I wouldn't be reading anything arousing, but there it was, pressing up, so I'd unzip and let it stretch, all very friendly, very . . . reassuring. I miss that. I suppose I got in the shower with Howard and Maris because I hoped something different would have an effect. But it wasn't the sort of thing a decent man does. I'm glad it didn't work." He replaced the book on a shelf near his chair. "How forbearing of you. Don't you want to ask me my definition of a decent man?"

"You'll get to it."

"A decent man takes pride in his responsibilities, a decent man accepts them, welcomes them."

"Responsibilities?"

"Work. Wife, children. Aging parents."

"Duties."

"If you like."

"Imposed by . . . ?"

"Self-imposed."

"I'd like to know where joy and love fit in."

"Perhaps you're suffering from overlarge expectations."

"I don't pay for this. You do. That's my definition of who's suffering here."

"Is that what's called being cocksure?" There was a long, not entirely uncomfortable pause before Newman said, "I can't stand it when you're imperturbable."

"Maybe you're getting an idea of how some people may respond to you."

"I know how I am. How I seem. I haven't done so badly with it."

"Then stay that way."

"Maybe it's all physical. Arterial blockage."

"Have you gone for the tests yet?"

"No. What if it turns out there's no physical cause?"

"You'd have to confront the problems you've merely acknowledged by coming here."

"I *am* confronting them."

"By getting in the shower with Howard and, um—"

"Maris. No, that was an excursion. An experiment."

"What did you find out?"

For the first time in the session, Newman's voice faltered. "That I'm sad."

The room smelled of furniture polish. Steve swiped at cigarette ash on his gray polo shirt, ample-bellied. They both were fifty-four, but he was in rotten shape. Maybe Steve couldn't get it up either. "I'm not unaware of the homosexual implications," Newman said.

Steve stretched the ashy spot on his shirt.

"Burned?" Newman asked.

"I don't think so. My wife would have a fit." Steve patted his belly. "Biting the behind of a woman who's having intercourse with another man doesn't qualify as a gay experience."

"The woman could be an excuse, a cover-up. She could be a metaphor for a connection between the two men."

"A woman isn't a metaphor, a woman is a woman."

"Shouldn't I be stumbling onto these timeless truths myself, not have them lectured at me?"

"A direct or indirect homosexual encounter doesn't mean you're gay; it means you're curious or adventurous or drunk or a number of other things. We can talk about bisexuality for months. If you want us to spend time and your money speculating on what gender you prefer at what hour of the day with what brand of beer, it's fine with me."

"You're rushing me."

"You have problems. Wouldn't you like to discover what to do about them?"

"I'd like to find . . . grace in whatever I'm doing."

"Therapy isn't graceful. Analysis is. You want to lie down and talk for eight years?"

He piled the books on the counter. Dan went through them, punching prices on a pocket calculator. A young girl beside Dan watched what he did. Her eyes seemed enormous in her small face. She reminded Newman of pictures of children in wartime. She was lost and she was a survivor. He wanted to offer her a loaf of bread. In return she might offer him something. She didn't need delousing.

"I see you've got new help, Dan."

Dan nodded. "This is Dina. Dina, this is Mr. Sykes."

"Are you the critic?" she asked.

"Yes."

Her lips disappeared between her teeth. She put his books on a cart and wheeled them away.

The cash register sang. Dan said, "Thirty-eight."

On his way out, a richer Newman told the girl goodbye. Arranging his books on a sale table, she ignored him.

• • •

He called her to say good night when he was away in the city. He sat on the closed toilet seat, the phone in his lap, and dialed. The bathroom door couldn't shut completely because of the telephone cord reaching from the room. He heard the air conditioner barking and someone moving in the room, a drawer opening, a sheet slapping the air before settling over the mattress.

"Hello?" Her voice had a hoarseness he liked.

"Hi."

"You're home early."

"I'm tired. Lots of running around. Got to get enough sleep. Can't disappoint my public tomorrow. I saw Steve, then took some books to sell. Are you okay?"

"Don't you want to hear how it went today?"

"I was getting to that."

"I was nervous. Naturally. The photographer—her name's Bea—she's tough but okay. She's teaching me what to do."

"What about the doctor?"

"He wasn't there except for an hour. There are four doctors altogether, with a lot of patients, lots of face-lifts and nose jobs. There are clinic patients too—people with terrible things wrong with them, but they don't have any money, so the doctors operate on them for nothing—"

"So you enjoyed yourself. You did well."

"Newman, there was this man who came in. He had no face. He was shot in the face, and he had no—"

"Was he a clinic patient?"

"I don't know. His wife was crying and holding on to him. I felt so sorry for—"

"If this upsets you, maybe you shouldn't—"

"I'm not upset. It's just you're not letting me—"

"I'm not stopping you."

"If you'll just listen."

"Now, Clare, don't I listen to you?" He listened to silence. "Clare?" A sigh from upstate reached him. Silence again. "Clare." He heard crying. "You're not all right," he said.

A sobbed "I *am*" came through.

173

"Clare, I know how important a job is to you, but not if it's going to—"

"I'm *fine*." Still crying.

"—upset you. We don't need the money, it's not much money. Is it too late to call Linker?"

"I don't need Dr. Linker."

"Is Leslie there?"

"Yes. They're both home."

"Maybe he'll play gin rummy with you." He heard sniffling. Her voice arrived steadied by anger.

"I don't need a fifteen-year-old boy as a baby-sitter."

"I'm concerned about you. And I'm not there to take care of you."

"No, you're not."

"I can't be. Let's calm down. You've had a strenuous day."

"It was mostly good, except for that man—"

"Yes, the one with no face."

"And his wife. Bea told me—"

"Who's Bea?"

"The medical photographer. She told me the wife was the one who shot him."

"Why isn't she in jail?"

"He wouldn't press charges."

"You know, we're going to end up with a phone bill like last month's. Why did she shoot him?"

"Bea said it was in all the papers. He stabbed her and she shot him."

"I wonder what papers Bea reads." He heard her give a small giggle. "There, that's what I wanted to hear. You can call me anytime."

"I know."

"Sleep well, darling."

"You too. Good night, Newman."

"Good night."

He carried the phone back into the room. His ear felt red. "Sorry to be so long," he said. "Clare was a bit upset."

"Is she okay now?" Sheila Dunne asked. She was lying on the made bed, flipping through a book he had to review, *Anxiety in the Narrator*.

"Yes." He bent down and kissed her.

As he was taking off his shirt, she said, "I don't see how you can read this. Every other word is 'semiotics.'"

"It's actually a quite provocative book."

"There's no sex in it. I don't like books that don't have sex."

He hung up his shirt. "Then you wouldn't like this one."

Steering Sheila's heavily perfumed body through acts of precipitation, he imagined himself at home with Clare. He sat on the chintz sofa in his living room, with Biscuit's head resting on his knee. The gray muzzle left a wet imprint on his chinos. Adored by the dog's large mournful eyes, he stroked the silky head, scratched behind unalert ears. In the ladderback chair, Clare sewed a white button on red fabric. She was using black thread. *Clare*, he said, *stop it*. The sewing had turned into a shotgun, the same one Harry Dunne displayed on a wall in his den. Harry had made it himself, producing a stock of exotic and well-rubbed glossy wood better attended to than Sheila and perhaps more dangerous. *Clare*, *stop it*, Newman said calmly. *I'd like to*, she answered, *but I don't know how*. Also calm. She must have taken a pill earlier. The gun pointed at him, and he worried that Biscuit might get hurt, but Biscuit had turned into an axe. It should be a knife, for stabbing, he thought, but it was already an axe, his wood axe, in his hands, resting across his knees. He didn't know where to cut her, nobody had told him where. He understood she'd be shooting him in the face as soon as he hacked at her. He was holding up the event. *I don't know where this goes, I need more information*, he said. She said, *You should have listened when you had the chance. Now you'll have to improvise*. Slowly he got up and went to her and raised the axe. Where? Should he slice into her shoulder, against her chestbone, or into the blond hair piled on her head? Should he shut his eyes against flying bone chips? *Hurry*, she said, *because it's my turn next*.

Sheila trilled a note of pleasure. Her thighs closed on his hand. Her grip on his unemphatic sex tightened; he hoped she'd removed her engagement solitaire. The day had started in bed with Clare and was ending in bed with Sheila. It wasn't improving.

Squatting, she opened the canvas bag on the white floor. She had packed a cotton skirt, a pair of jeans, a belt, the silk blouse, the camisole, three cotton blouses, four tee shirts, a cardigan, underwear and socks, a nightgown, a pair of winter boots, her rolled-up winter coat, a plastic sandwich bag each of toiletries and cosmetics, a box of tissues, several story manuscripts, *Bandaged Moments*, a notebook, an address book, two pens, two hard-boiled eggs and two pieces of French bread wrapped in cellophane, a picture of a dog she'd had that died, Howard's letter, a love letter from Larry, and four paperbacks: *Farewell, My Lovely*, the *Selected Poems of George Herbert*, a dictionary, and *Pride and Prejudice*.

She unwrapped the eggs and sat on the floor to peel one. She had left behind a glass paperweight, a shoebox of snapshots, her velvet jacket and other clothes, the unwearable new shoes, the rainbow afghan she'd crocheted one winter when she'd given up writing, her red pencils, the *Fannie Farmer Cookbook*, and, because he'd written his name in it, *Lolita*. It was her book, but his name was in it and she didn't want to take his name with her. She checked the George Herbert book to make sure his name wasn't there. She took off her wedding ring and dropped it into the bag.

"Is that dinner?" Dan stood in the doorway, holding money.

"I'm not very hungry."

"May I come in?"

She nodded. In the white room, his slightness and brownness

intensified; he shriveled into a smaller, darker man. He might have been her age or twice it. The short beard had gray in it.

"This is for today," he said and gave her twenty dollars. "That's five hours at four each."

"I was working to pay you back for letting me stay here."

"A separate issue. When you work here, you get paid. Not much, but the fringe benefits are incredible." His voice, soft and unaccented, lulled her. "First, you can take any book to read at night after we close. You have to put it back in the morning. If you're not finished with it and somebody buys it, you're out of luck. You learn to read fast. I still don't know what happened to Little Eva. Second, you can stay until somebody else needs the room."

The bleached haven, warmed by evening sun through the skylight, receded. The white walls lifted away like stage scenery, and she sat in the lightless blank of the future. "You mean if somebody needs it tomorrow, I have to go?"

"Not tomorrow."

"Then when?"

"There's no point in worrying about it now."

She disagreed, but how could he know that worrying about things was her hobby? "Is this your room?"

"No. My apartment's down the hall. This room and the bathroom next door are yours."

"What did Howard tell you about me?"

Without pausing, he said, "That you need a place to stay."

"I was here before with him."

"A few times, yes. But who counts?"

"You're a good friend to him, letting me stay here."

"He isn't my friend. There are keys downstairs on a shelf under the register. Use both locks if you go out. There's a laundromat on Ninth Street. And there's a deli that stays open till twelve. Sometimes the heroes are stale. Good night."

She hurried to stand up and follow him. Down the dim hall she saw his faded blue work shirt before she saw him. The peeled egg in her hand felt clammy and alive. "Then why are you letting me stay here?" she asked. "If he's not your friend?"

"I have the room. You need it. Sometimes the bagels are stale too." He opened a door to a flood of light.

"Thank you," she called before the door closed.

"Hello?"

"I have a collect call to anyone from Dina. Will you accept the charges?"

"Yes."

"Go ahead, New York."

"Mother? Hi."

"Dina?"

"How are you?"

"Well, it's raining here. How are you, darling?"

"I'm at a pay phone. I left Larry today."

"Where are you?"

"At a pay—"

"Where are you *staying*?"

"I thought you might try to reach me at the apartment or Larry might decide to frighten you by saying I'd disappeared, so I want you to know I'm okay."

"But where—"

"I'll call you again soon."

"What's your number?"

"I'm moving around for now. I don't have one."

"Don't be ridiculous. We can help you. Daddy and I can help you. I'll send you money."

"I have money."

"Come home. I'll send you money to come home."

"I don't want to go to California now. But thanks."

"There's nothing to keep you in New York. Hold on a minute."

Leaning against a scratched acrylic divider, she held on. Cars bolted under the yellow light. A maroon van with mirrored windows pulled up at the corner and parked. Twilight silvered the mirrors. The driver, a shirtless, barefoot man about twenty-five, got out and with a scowl indicated that he was waiting for the phone. Through the divider she saw the other phone. Its receiver had been torn off. Wire hung down, carrying phantom sounds from the amputated mouthpiece. The man had tanned arms and a reddened torso. The elastic of his underpants showed above his unbelted jeans.

A male voice asked, "Dina?"

"Dad," she said, turning back to the acrylic divider for privacy. "Hi."

"Your mother just told me and all I can say is, Right on. You should have left that bastard—"

"Dad—"

"—that pimp—"

"Dad—"

"Aaah, what the hell. Come home."

"There's somebody waiting to use the phone."

"Let them wait."

"I'll call again soon, I promise."

"Are you in some kind of trouble?"

"No. I have to go now."

"Tell us where you are."

"Goodbye."

She hung up the phone. The barefoot, shirtless man advanced toward it. "You take your sweet time," he said. He had a purple bruise under one eye. Without breathing, she walked away.

The nun in the elevator said "Excuse me" when he bumped into her. She was old enough to be his mother, if his mother had survived. On the third floor he bumped into a black woman with a clipboard. Stethoscope tubing trembled above her jacket pocket. If she had a beeper, she was a doctor. If she didn't, she was a nurse. Without stopping to frisk her, he went to Ralph Cohen's room.

It smelled of cigar smoke. But the other bed was empty.

He leaned on the guardrail at the old man's bed. Gray skin draped over bones. The head had the soft look of an overripe pear, brown-splotched. Gnarled veins could have been bruises. Tufts of sparse white hair could have been mold. He recognized a clouded eye and a keen one. He and the old man were freaks, he thought, each with unmatching eyes.

"What's the matter, artist? You couldn't find no flowers to bring me?"

"You're always screaming how the flowers are for paying customers only."

"You want dinner?"

On a wheeled tray at the foot of the bed was St. Vincent's version of dinner: string beans and mashed potatoes shored up a beefy fabric.

"You're supposed to eat it and get better."

"I don't want. I had the roll with the butter. Since the plumber left, I got no appetite." The plumber had been the patient in the other bed.

The potatoes needed salt. So did the string beans. The meat evaporated in his mouth like cotton candy. He hadn't eaten all day, not since he'd come home for lunch and found her note. She was gone. He touched the note in his pocket.

"Sit down, you'll get sick that you eat standing up."

"What's this stuff?"

"Apple betty, the nurse says. You'll be crazy about it."

It tasted like the meat. "What happened to the plumber?"

"He got better or he got worse."

He took the paper place mat from underneath the dishes and smoothed it out on the bureau. He scraped a blob of potato from it. His black felt-tip pen bled a little, but the place mat wasn't Arches paper, after all. With the first line he remembered his father's desk and the cloisonné jar with a hinged cover. Standing on tiptoe, he'd reached up for it and heard laughter. With the second line he saw his mother holding a bouquet impossibly high above her white-aproned stomach.

"Here." He held up the place mat. He had drawn on it a large open rose. "It's a red one. You like the red ones, right?" He propped it up against the water pitcher on the night stand.

The old man fixed his good eye on it. His hand, banded with a plastic ID bracelet, clawed a bar. Yellow-brown needle marks stained the inner wrist. "Sign it. It's worth more if you sign it."

He signed it with his Hebrew name, Eliezer, and below that his un-Americanized name, Laurits Rabuchin.

Dear Larry,

    I'm going, I'm gone. I'm taking what I can carry of what I'm sure is mine. I took out half of the bank account ($150) and left the book in your drawer. I'm going to lock the door and push my keys under it so you'll have them all. I paid Con Ed and telephone. Your blue shirt's fixed. Just wash it. I changed the sheets. The towels are clean too. One of us will have to start divorce stuff. I'll do it as soon as I can if you don't do it first. The towels are clean. Hope you'll be okay. And me too.

Dina

Yes, the towels were clean. On the steps of St. Vincent's he tore her note in half. A woman carrying a crying baby hurried past him toward the hospital. She murmured in Spanish, and a small fist struck air. The baby wore gold earrings with red stones. On the corner of Seventh and Greenwich a dirt-encrusted man browsing through the trash basket found a beer bottle and wiped the neck with a filthy hand before draining it. Larry put the pieces of paper back in his pocket and walked in the other direction, east along Eleventh Street. His lengthening shadow preceded him.

He crossed Sixth Avenue and considered stopping at Balducci's for an apple or a bag of raisins and nuts. They cost the same there as at a supermarket. A block down, people with full shopping bags hurried out of the store, going home. He didn't envy them; he was an artist. He was alone, he had been abandoned by all the world, but he was an artist. Someone laughed. A couple laden with Balducci's shopping bags came toward him. They were young, both about Dina's age. "You put the cassis in first," the woman was saying.

He continued east on Eleventh Street. Two lhasa apsos barked at him from the corner. A radio on roller skates sang. He thought he saw her. She was standing in the middle of the block, staring up at a brownstone. It might have been shadows making a stranger look like her, but he knew the tilt of her head, black silky baby hair parting over her ear, the short arms like sticks growing from pockets hiding her small hands, the particular jutting angle of her hips in loose jeans. In one day he had lost her and found her again. "Dina," he called. "Dina."

From the distance her face might have seemed welcoming. He ran toward her.

"No!" she shouted, and she ran away.

He heard the "No!" when the buildings were already rushing past him. He couldn't stop. The sight of her receding, instead of growing larger, drove him on. She had never been an athlete, not with her small flat feet and her fears of falling. He could overtake her. He saw her turn right on Fifth Avenue, but when he got to the corner, she was gone.

Panting, he stared down Fifth, to Eighth Street, thick with summer strollers and dope peddlers and ice cream vendors. She couldn't have reached Eighth Street that quickly. He saw the cab at the corner of Tenth Street.

"Dina!" he shouted.

She was looking at him, yes, she was. He chased across Fifth after the cab. By the time he reached the corner of Tenth, the cab had sped the long block to University Place and was waiting at a red light. He leaned against a lamp pole to catch his breath. Joggers in tee shirts and shorts bounded past him on their way to the park. He'd have to start jogging every day. That way, the next time he'd catch her. The cab drove off. Working to push air through the pain in his chest, he began to cry.

She peered through the rear window to make sure he wasn't following her. "I'll get off at the next corner."

"You okay, hon?" The driver, a gray-haired man with a neck mole exactly like a pencil eraser, lurched the cab to the curb. She gave him two dollars. "If some guy's bothering you, you should go to the cops," he said.

She wondered if his wife ever bit his mole in a moment of passion. She felt ashamed for wondering that. If Howard had a neck mole, what would she do? When he bent down naked to pick up his clothes from the floor around the bed, any bed, his vertebrae stood out because he was thin. The bumps formed a keyboard, each bony projection a note in a tapering human xylophone. With two small wooden hammers and six years of lessons, she could play "Danny Boy" along his spine. The next time they made love, she'd ask him what he thought about the raised dark brown freckle on her right arm. There would be a next time. At his office that morning he'd been angry with her—but he'd found a place for her to stay. He would love her again, pinning her arms down on orange sheets and telling her a joke about God trying to buy a cameo on Forty-seventh Street. Something about a discount for cash. Minutes before, outside the house where he'd first made love to her, she'd wanted one of those afternoons back, fucking in the critic's apartment. Seeing Newman Sykes selling his books, she'd hated him because he was cold-eyed and clear-eyed and he wasn't Howard. She wanted to lie in Newman Sykes's bed again and have Howard hold her. On the sidewalk where she'd waited for him to pay the ponytailed cab driver weeks ago, she saw herself as she'd been then and as she was now, shoulder to shoulder with herself: time squared. She'd traveled a hard distance to get from one place to an adjacent one. And Larry had found her and frightened her into doubting she'd traveled anywhere at all.

What did husbands and wives do together—real husbands and wives? Larry hated her family and had driven away her few friends. Janice Wrightson, a neighbor upstairs, used to visit despite his comments about her father, whom he'd never met. She was finishing her dissertation on the probability of altruism in times of disaster and worked as a bartender. "The industrialist fattening on my blood," Larry called Mr. Wrightson, a grocer in South Dakota. "Come over to my place for a while," she told Dina. Larry said, "We'll see." Dina went once by herself. There were squares of sunlight on a green tablecloth and a feeling of space. Air. There was a green china sugar bowl with red flowers painted on it. Janice asked, "How are you doing?" She might or might not have been condescending. She had on purple cutoffs and a pink tee shirt. A pink plastic band gripped her blond hair, exposing a smooth, high forehead. Dina drank a cup of coffee fast and left. Larry didn't speak to her when she came home. "Poor Janice," she said, "she's all alone." "Boring," he said. Janice stopped visiting them.

So did Nicola, a teacher, with Dina, at the Babel Language Institute. The one time Nicola came to dinner—a chicken stew Dina had labored over all day, cutting onions and potatoes with dreamy diligence—Larry accused their guest of being overweight and a nihilist. She'd brought a copy of *Ms.* magazine in her brief-case. Her ruffled yellow blouse might have been snug, but the full black skirt fit her fine. She left a coral lip mark on her water glass. After that night, whenever Dina saw her at work, Nicola asked, "How *are* you?" Dina would say, "Okay, thanks. How are *you*?"

"They don't care about you, little one. I'm the only one who cares," Larry said. "And that includes your parents, the happy misers." Afraid to contradict him, afraid that what he said was true, she'd allowed him to reduce their world to a thirteen-by-sixteen room. By the light of the TV, she'd crocheted intricate pillow shams for their prison, pineapple motifs hooked during late-night reruns of *The Twilight Zone*. He wanted her to have nothing and to be nothing without him. She'd wanted that too. Now, since she intended to be without him, he would have to inflict nothingness on her.

"He wants to kill me," she said matter-of-factly.

"You better go to the cops," the cab driver said.

"No, it's something between him and me." When she realized he wasn't going to give her change, she got out of the cab.

Any one of the books at any time might hold a meaning, a sign especially for her. In the hundreds of thousands of books around her, she would have to find that one at the right moment and open it to the right page. She ruled out the foreign-language and chemistry sections; whatever meaning was there she couldn't decipher, and if the special meaning intended for her was there, then it would be her fate never to find it and never to know she couldn't find it.

Surrounded by possibilities, she stood in her nightgown in the dark store, enjoying her fear of the dark. No matter what else might be in the cavernous room with her, Larry wasn't.

She ran her fingers across book spines on a shelf above her head and stopped at a book she believed would be bound in blue and would tell her something essential. She pulled it out and inclined it toward the window to catch light from the street. Though the book was green, she opened it in the middle and struck a finger on a page. By low light she read,

> . . . a diamond is explained as a person, a turtle, the navel, a mountain, a lake, a star, an eye. The setting of the design does not by any means explain sufficiently why these varying interpretations should be used.

She flipped to the title page: *Primitive Art*, by Franz Boas.

On her first try, she might have found the special meaning intended for her—or she might not. It hadn't occurred to her before that she might not recognize it when she found it. She put the book back and went to a table of paperbacks for something to take upstairs with her to the white room.

Ten minutes later, having picked up and discarded Mailer's *The Deer Park*, which was missing the first three pages, a *Middlemarch* that smelled funny, *Knowing Your Sun Sign Can Save Your Life*, *The Canterbury Tales Coloring Book*, and a book of poems called *Why I Don't Like Japanese Prints*, which began

> Utamaro Utamaro Utamaro
> Creeps in this petty pace from day to day,
> To the last syllable of recorded time . . .

and was written and illustrated in two colors by M. "Hokusai" Donnelly and dedicated to Shiva the Destroyer, she climbed upstairs, holding a copy of the *1979 Maupassant Prize Stories* collection. Her story was going to be published in *Rosemary*, and she wanted to look over the competition.

When she was a little girl in California, a story appeared in the L.A. *Times* about a little boy, a tourist, who'd been standing in shallow water in the ocean, up to his waist, and a shark came along and bit off his leg. She wondered if the shark ate it on the spot or swam away with it. The story confirmed her suspicions about the dangers of submersion. From the age of eleven on, she swam only in pools. Some years later she saw a James Bond movie in which the villain released sharks into a pool through a secret underwater passageway. By then she was living with Larry in New York. She stopped taking baths and began showering.

She thought of writing as a kind of submersion: dangerous and contrary to natural buoyancy. Still, something about that risk tempted her and, struggling between fears of being devoured by work and fears of being lost in silence, she had managed over the years of her marriage to produce several stories and fragments of stories—messages smuggled out, notes in amber seltzer bottles bobbing in blue-green waves patrolled by fins, or shreds of paper bearing the hastily scrawled "Help, I am being held prisoner in a fortune-cookie factory."

In her white solitude in the white bed, she became accustomed to writing in a notebook. It kept loneliness away. She wrote about what she didn't have, in order to possess it: love. She wrote about an idea of love embodied in a man she imagined was very much like Howard. She made him look different from Howard, she gave him a different family and a different job. He was part her, part her mother, part her father, part the boys she'd known in school, part the clamorous voices of the rabbis, part Larry, part Howard. He had her mother's desire to shine in the eyes of the world. He wore her father's anger more stylishly and felt it more acutely. He suffered frantically and with appetite. He was, this imagined man, most nearly the person she feared she was, a spectator, though with a good seat, at the literary circus. Her fictional maleness had a sideshow logic: determined to seem as lost as a hoop-skirted southern belle in a mud-wrestling contest, she believed unhappily that talent and ambition made her masculine, and being masculine made her a freak. For her imagined man she created a world, occasionally hospitable, in which to live.

Though Dan had warned her that she could stay only until someone else needed the room, no one showed up to claim it. Every day she expected to lose it, every night brought a reprieve—and disappointment: she was waiting for Howard to show up and claim *her*. At night she worked very hard not to think about what she was writing, cryptography against abandonment, and in the morning she typed a clean copy of her writing while more or less ignoring it. She aggressively ignored how the number of typed pages grew from three to several to twenty to forty and more. Forty-six. As Dan said, who counts? Fifty-one. She was swimming into the mouth of the shark, and she didn't want to see where she was going.

On clear nights, after she put her notebook and pen on the floor and turned out the light, the skylight above her framed stars. She wondered if Howard was sleeping. His beautiful wife yawned in his arms. Dina tried to find Orion's Belt, the only cluster of stars she knew. Once she thought she'd found it when a cloud rolled out of the way, but the three stars were irregularly placed and she remembered dimly from a sixth-grade science class that Orion belonged in the winter sky. She could feel Howard's terror at being trapped in sleep, without lies to protect himself. If he loved her, she would protect him. If he didn't love her, then all she had was a notebook of embroidered fears. She fell asleep searching for something—a dipper or a bear—she could recognize. The next morning she woke up afraid that Larry was going to find her.

He didn't find her that day; and Howard didn't call, either. She sat down on a pile of three unabridged dictionaries and wiped dust from her face. She hadn't seen or heard from him in the two weeks since he'd sent her to stay with Dan. If he didn't want her anymore, she would die. She would fall away from life with less than a sigh, a browned leaf riddled to lace by insects (cutters, borers, or juicy green caterpillars, the better to symbolize with) and dropping unnoticed, three months ahead of autumn, to a sidewalk littered with Good Humor popsicle sticks. If he didn't want her anymore, she would kill herself. A few days earlier she'd read about a spy in World War I or II—it didn't matter which—who'd committed suicide by eating the contents of a tube of toothpaste. The tubes might have been lead-lined in those days. It might have been during the Korean War. She'd read only up to page 26, and somebody bought the book the next day. "It's a rat race in here," Dan said. She would eat two tubes of toothpaste, one mint and one regular flavor, both with fluoride. For lead, she would add ground pencil from a pencil sharpener. *There* was symbolism. No, she would nick her wrists. No, she would gnaw rat poison. Then he'd be sorry and have to publish her story posthumously, with a black-bordered note about the author. He would confess his love for her publicly and too late. She inhaled dust from her hand. If he didn't want her anymore, he might not publish her story. She sneezed.

"Bless you," Dan said. He had a ledger book open at the register. Two slender brown fingers trailed a column of figures. The set of his shoulders seemed easy yet prepared, as if he could with no effort begin a mime or a karate lunge.

"Thanks. Would it be okay if I stopped in a few minutes? I have to go see somebody."

"Sure. Leave me here all alone with no help and no company."

"Can I ask you something?" she asked shyly.

"You just did." He smiled at the ledger.

"What did you do before you had the store?"

"I had another store."

"What'd you sell?"

"Books. It was a Marxist and health bookstore."

Staying with him might have put her on an FBI list. "Why'd you stop?"

"It went bankrupt."

"I'm sorry. I mean, I'm sorry for your sake, not about the store." There might be a microphone hidden in a hollowed-out *Golden Bough*. "That whole subject confuses me."

"Health?"

"Marxism. I'm glad you have this store now." She stood, lifting one of the dictionaries. "Which name do you like better— Reeve or Leitman?"

"Reeve. Why?"

"That's my ex-husband-to-be's name. Leitman was my name before I got married."

"Which one do you prefer?"

"Bob Dylan. He named himself."

"Lenin."

"Picasso."

"Stalin."

"Colette." She tottered toward the front of the store, resting the dictionary low against her pelvic bones. She had to hurry to get out of the way of a tall man who entered the store carrying two cartons of books. His face was red, his hair was red, and he was wearing an orange tee shirt. He blazed past her. The cartons slammed down on the counter. When she returned for another dictionary, at least thirty copies of *Bandaged Moments* had grown on the counter. The man—a thief? a wholesaler?—took more copies from a carton, and something white dropped silently to the floor. It was a sock.

"Shit." He picked it up and stuffed it in his back pocket up to the grayish heel. "I've got another couple of cartons. You want them?"

Dan nodded, dispensing money.

"I'll bring them by. Thanks." The money, uncounted, joined the sock. The man frowned with embarrassment. His thin lips were familiar.

On his way out he stopped at a sale table: seventy-nine cents each or three for two dollars. He bought a copy of *No, But I Read the Book*, a collection of reviews by Newman Sykes. He glanced at her as he paid Dan. His face surprised her, as if she'd come upon a faded photograph of a childhood friend. Determined not to be surprised, she fled up the stairs.

She washed her face quickly and reapplied liner to her eyes. She put on a clean blouse, dabbed cologne at the back of her neck. She dropped a packaged contraceptive suppository and a subway token in her purse. A second token went in her jeans pocket. She couldn't think of what she was going to say to Howard. She took a second suppository with her. She unzipped her jeans and patted cologne on her underpants. By the time she got downstairs again, the red-haired man was gone. On her way to the subway she tried to remember where she'd seen him before.

Newman had seen the girl somewhere before. Her arrival interrupted Howard's monologue on the new fiction, whatever that was.

She seemed stuck in the doorway to Howard's office, seemed to be tugged both away from the room and toward it. A heavy hand had drawn dark lines around her eyes; the rest of her had been better sketched. "I'm sorry, I didn't mean—nobody's outside."

"They're having coffee," Howard said. "Come in." He was improbably jovial. A browning apple core and an open bottle of red wine rested on manuscripts on his desk. Both men were drinking from mugs. "Dina Reeve, Newman Sykes."

"Hello." She blushed.

He liked to see a girl blushing. At his lectures he encountered few who blushed. "Please join us. Howard was pontificating about writing."

"Dina here has a wonderful story that's my lead for *Rose-*

mary." From under a stack of manuscripts Howard unearthed three long printed sheets. "Your galleys."

She received them cautiously, and a slow half-smile, a secretive glee, becalmed her face. "You're really doing it."

Newman smiled too, trying to remember how it had felt to see his writing in print for the first time. "You must be a very good writer if Howard publishes you."

"She is," Howard mumbled. "Sit down, sit down," he told her.

"And you'll have to be a very patient writer until Howard pays you."

"I have her check right here." A storm of papers followed his efforts to locate the check.

"There's one thing," she said, sitting next to Newman on the sofa. "The name. Can it be changed?"

"It's a good title," Howard told his mug of wine.

"No, *my* name. It's not Reeve, it's Leitman."

"It was Reeve on all your manuscripts."

"I'm going to get a divorce."

"You don't look old enough to be married," Newman said.

Howard said, "You should think it over."

"I'm getting a divorce," she insisted. "The name is Leitman."

"You're being hasty, you're not thinking this through." Howard's face had whitened and thinned. Seams along his forehead deepened. His eyes moved from paper to paper on his desk.

"How can you say that?" she asked with such exasperation that Newman patted her shoulder.

"He's an editor, not a marriage counselor."

Howard muttered, "How do you spell Leitman?"

While she spelled it, Newman read a few lines of a galley over her shoulder. He could have read more, but he glanced down her blouse instead. "May I see this?" he asked.

"He can buy it at the newsstand," Howard said.

"I have a subscription," Newman answered.

"Then let him wait for the mail. He'll have something to look forward to."

"Why don't you give this young lady her check? And some wine. I think we should toast her." Newman leaned toward Dina and asked in a low voice, "This is your first publication?"

"Yes, sir."

He wanted to brush her hair out of her eyes and request less politeness. She had a beautiful long neck, and a brown freckle perched on her right breast. "You have every right to get a divorce," he said. "Aren't you at the Karatasi bookstore?"

"Yes. We'll toast her." Howard refilled his mug and gave it to Dina. "It's clean, it's clean, the alcohol kills any germs." He emptied a square plastic cup of paper clips and rubber bands, blew dust out, and poured wine for himself.

"It could be worse. He could have used the envelope-moistener dish," Newman said.

Howard lifted his cup. "To your story."

"And to many more," Newman added.

She drank, and the three galleys slid from her lap. Newman had taken them.

Without its night-table carton, the phone sat on the floor, near the bed. Reaching from the bed, she pushed aside a pair of jeans to uncover it. One-handed, she laid the receiver on the floor and dialed. The fingertips of her other hand were being nibbled. The nibbling stopped.

"Don't," he said.

"I have to."

"Just stay." He rolled away from her, and the bed, on retired springs, shuddered. With the receiver ringing in her ear, she examined the expanse of his back, freckles at his shoulders, the spine like the shaft of an arrow leading to a red-blond arrowhead patch of hair above his buttocks. White against his tan, rounded against the rest of his angular body, they had an innocent look. She thought of patting baby powder on their unsmiling cleft.

"Hello?" came the voice on the phone.

"Hi, it's me." A monotone suppressed her anger. Hearing

him speak—even the one word—outraged her. "I can't—I won't be home until around twelve."

"Oh?"

"I called the camp. The bus is dropping Matty off at your office."

"Why twelve?" His calm inquiry invited anger.

"Because that's when I'm coming home."

"Suzanne, I think you should think this over."

"I think it's none of your business what I think." She slammed the receiver down on the jeans, fumbled for it, and dropped it in place in the cradle. "There," she said to the unmoving arrow, "now we can have dinner like a real couple."

The critic definitely had looked down her blouse again. She laughed, then covered her mouth because Howard was on the phone. She tried to organize finishing the mug of wine while her hand stayed plastered over her mouth. He'd said the alcohol would kill any germs. He hadn't worried about germs when they fucked. Beside her, the critic chuckled.

"I like this," he said quietly, not to disturb Howard's conversation. "Of course some of it, no: 'My dance card's full.' I don't like the flip attitude there."

"It's not flip—"

"You could find something better."

She discovered wine in her mouth and heard Howard say "Suzanne" into the phone. A curious pain traveled between her breasts, a stabbing. From high above the room she watched the three of them in it: the critic, cold as a dead star, his unhappiness so powerful that it drew her toward him; Howard, lost and nobly foolish, a liar, a circuit rider, a lover of complications; herself, grotesque to have felt less pain in leaving a husband of six years than in losing a lover of a few weeks, with time out for cystitis. Help me, she thought when Howard hung up the phone. If he didn't save her, she would have to go with the critic. The severe presence at her side, reading her story, threatened to excite her.

Unless there was someone to see her, she didn't exist. Assisted by wine, she sped toward whatever solution would present itself.

Howard refilled his square cup. "To *Rosemary*, the constant woman," he muttered.

She lifted the empty mug. She wanted to kneel at his chair and unzip his pants and take him into her mouth. Let the critic review that. She wanted to be obliterated by servitude to love. Who would she be if Howard didn't want her?

"We have to talk," she told him. "I have to see you to talk."

"Shall I leave you two?" Newman asked.

"No, no," Howard said. "We can't . . . talking now . . . not now."

"What about my story?" she asked.

"I'm enjoying it," Newman said.

Howard picked up a pencil and examined it as if he'd never seen one before. "Yes, a story, a fine story." The phone rang again, and he grabbed the receiver ardently. "Yes?" he asked it.

The critic whispered to Dina, "More wine?"

"Yes, please. A lot."

"Margery, you've caught me at a very bad time," Howard explained to the phone. ". . . No, it's worse than that . . . That's nice, Margie . . . I could suggest something." He winced and hung up. His hand opened, palm to the ceiling, as if he were appealing to God, and tipped over the square cup. Manuscripts absorbed wine. A handwritten note across the top of a cover page dissolved in blue. He blotted it with the dry side of another manuscript.

"I'd like to know what else can happen," he said.

"Hi, Daddy." A little girl holding a birdcage and a few wilting daisies walked slowly to his desk.

In the elevator the critic said, "If you're going downtown, I can give you a ride."

"Yes, thank you," she said. "I've seen you on TV."

On the street he said, "I have some ideas about your story. Why don't we discuss it over dinner?"

"Yes, thank you," she said.

In front of the restaurant, before he opened the door, he asked, "How well do you know Howard?"

"Not very well at all," she said.

"I don't care what its alias is, it's a rodent." The manuscripts had stiffened as they dried; he arranged mummies on his desk.

"It's a gerbil," she said. "It's clean. His name is Mork."

"It's unappetizing and it can't go out to dinner."

"Mommy said it was okay. It's my turn to keep him overnight. It's not his fault we're not going straight home."

"Whose fault is it?"

"I don't know." Wisely she said nothing more, but retreated to the sofa and held the cage on her lap. Her feet in miniature running shoes jutted straight out in front of her. She made soft kissing sounds to the rat in the birdcage and stuck a small finger between the bars.

Her wilting daisies stayed on his desk, a bonus for Berthe the night cleaning woman. He didn't need dead flowers to underscore the absurdity: bringing a rat to a New York City restaurant.

He muttered at the papers, careful to keep damp ones away from his *Rosemary* galleys. When Gail buzzed him, he heard "Larry Reeve to see you" and, preoccupied with rodents and wives, said, "Fine, fine," before realizing who the visitor was. In the few seconds it took Larry Reeve to reach his office, Howard had time to repent of a thousand sins of commission and omission. Not to mention emission, he thought, saluting his gallows humor. At the sight of his visitor, all humor vanished.

The man could have been an eccentric billionaire disguised as a bum. He could have been an artist or a mass murderer. His green overalls were grimy and wrinkled. The collar of his Hawaiian shirt was torn. His hair hung in yellow-brown strings past his shoulders, which seemed drawn up to brace his neck. A mustache smothered his upper lip. His eyes searched the room, resting on nothing. They glittered, dulled, flashed light again, the inner lids red and swollen. One eye wept a colorless fluid.

"Matty," Howard said, "go ask Gail for the key to the bathroom. You have to wash your hands before dinner."

It might have been the fact that he pronounced every syllable distinctly, with no muttering, that made Matty look up in alarm.

Reeve took a folded piece of paper from his pocket. "You're Ritchie?"

"Yes."

"Where is she?"

"Who?"

Reeve glanced at Matty and the birdcage in her lap. He asked Howard, "You think because *she's* here you have an easy out?" The delivery belonged to a spy or a scientist: unaccented but alien.

"What exactly do you want, Mr. Reeve?"

"The name is Rabuchin."

"You told my secretary it was Reeve."

"That's so you'd know who you're talking to."

Everybody was changing names in his office. He could change his name too—he liked the sound of Rex Adamson—and live alone in tequilaed anonymity in Mexico, in a hammock in one of those dusty outlaw towns no bigger than Orson Welles in a white tropical suit. There would be no women, no wives, no children. He would bring with him a lifetime supply of deodorant and a subscription to the *Times* Book Review. "What are we talking about?"

"You know." Reeve—Rabuchin—waved the piece of paper. "You gave her ideas. You poisoned her against me. Some professor. How about if I show you some of *my* writing? Want to see a letter to the college president about what you did to my wife?"

"You write fiction, Mr. Rabuchin?"

"I write the truth. Tell me where she is or I mail this."

Howard measured the awfulness of the threat. He had spent

almost fifteen years at the school without meeting any of a succession of presidents, and he wanted to keep it that way. If he told Rabuchin where Dina was, he'd be admitting to an involvement. And Rabuchin might still send the letter, whatever it contained. And he might hurt Dina. That, Howard reflected, wasn't *his* problem, it was Rabuchin's—and hers. He thought of her litany of oh-oh-oh-no-no-yes-oh croaked into his ear at Newman's place. She had bitten him gently on the shoulder. Or was that someone else? He hadn't seduced her, no; and she hadn't trapped him. The clear voice of her writing accused him. He turned his copy of her story galleys face down on his desk.

"I don't like being threatened, Mr. Rabuchin. I can see you're upset and I'm sorry you're having domestic problems, but that has nothing to do with me."

"I'm in pain, you shit. Someone I love has disappeared from my life. How would you like it if someone you love disappeared?"

Howard said to Matty, "Leave the room now," but the girl stayed.

"Daddy?" she asked, crying.

"Leave," he said coldly. She scrambled off the sofa, struggling with the birdcage. "Leave that," he said. "Go."

She left the cage on the sofa and ran to him, past Rabuchin. She climbed into Howard's lap and sobbed against his shirt. He put his arms around her.

"Now that you've terrified my child," he said to Rabuchin, "maybe you'd like to pull the wings off a couple of flies."

The man put his hands on the desk, bending papers. His weeping eye swam in glare. "You think you have everything on your side. You play at art and make money from lies and now you think having your kid cry makes you honest. You're a parasite. You live on the blood of artists. If you really love your daughter, you should stay far away from her so you don't poison her too."

A stranger asked, "Everything all right here?"

In the doorway Liliane and Gail stood behind a campus cop, a stocky black man outmuscling his gray uniform.

"He was saying goodbye," Howard said.

The cop beckoned to Rabuchin. "Okay, bro, let me help you."

Rabuchin laid his paper on Howard's desk, on top of Dina's overturned galleys. "I have more," he said.

It was a Xerox copy of neat and dark hand-printing that slanted downward.

Dear Sir,
    The ones who believe they possess the truth, are dangerous. They corrupt the ones who are young and impressive. Kierkegaard writes about the seducer, that he perverted the others not outwardly but in their inward natures. It is a double crime when the victim is an artist because, then the world loses, not just the individual person.
    There is a man who seduces under the name of literature. He is one of your teachers Howard Ritchie. He has taken a sweet and loving woman and turned her frightened and angry. He stole her happiness because he cannot steal her talent. But he has hidden her from her family. She is my wife. I need to find her and deprogram her. She cannot survive in a world made up by Ritchie to suit Ritchie. He should not be a teacher or allowed to infect others. I know you must do something about this.

Sincerely,
Laurits Rabuchin

P.S. I am a citizen.

Howard put it in a drawer. "All better?" he asked Matty, who had returned with Liliane.

"We wash the face and it is much better," Liliane answered.

"I hope Mork didn't get too upset," Matty said.

In her favorite daydream they were together, with Matty, in a farmhouse in Massachusetts, near where he was born. He was writing at the kitchen table, golden oak with four lions' heads at the pedestal base. There were apples and pears—little Seckel pears—heaped in a blue and white bowl. She was baking butterscotch-chip cookies—no, she was making veal ragout—no, a vegetable stew. Matty was doing something in another room. The problem of Howard had disappeared. She didn't know if he was dead or if they'd divorced. He had simply ceased to exist for her, except as an immensely satisfying absence.

The daydream tranquilized her when Howard was home. Thin as he was, he filled the apartment and she needed something to defend herself against him. "Any mail, dear heart?" he'd ask and, blurring him across the room, she'd launch into her farmhouse.

He had on a plaid flannel shirt, and his red curls covered the back of his collar. "For Suzanne, for all that is and all that will be," he wrote at the front of his manuscript. She went on stirring her vegetable stew.

"Dear heart, the mail—is there any?"

At a Chaplin double bill in an old movie house downtown, she and Matty had watched Charlie walking away from the camera. The screen had gone black except for a narrowing circle around him. He got smaller and smaller, his twirling cane an asterisk, and the circle around him got smaller and smaller until it finally closed and the screen went completely black. "That's called irising out," Matty said later. For two years at school—a private school selected by Howard despite or because of its cost— she'd been taught Film Appreciation. Once at dinner he'd asked her if she knew who Lewis Carroll was, and she'd answered he was a character actor in MGM movies and later played in the TV series *Topper* and *The Man from U.N.C.L.E.* "Lots of the old movies had that between scenes. You go: 'Iris out on Charlie.' I'm going to use it in all my movies." They were passing the Karatasi bookstore on their way to University Place to catch an uptown bus. Sometimes Howard bought books there. "It's a wonderful old place, there's always something there I want to have," she'd heard him say to somebody at a party in a Tribeca loft with a picket-fence quilt on a wall and a boa constrictor in a tank with an understandably agitated white mouse. Poor mouse. She could have stopped at the bookstore to buy him a present, but she didn't know what it was he wanted to have. She decided to give up mythology and take a film course for the fall semester.

"Suzanne, give me the courtesy of a response."

On the way to the farmhouse, iris out on Howard. Trapped, without knowing it, in the tightening circle of her anger, he made his first aesthetic error that she had ever witnessed: he walked toward her when he should have been walking away.

She began to need the daydream not only with Howard but with Vincent. Lying in his bed with him, she imagined herself lying in bed with him at the farmhouse. When they made love, she imagined he was making love to her in the farmhouse. Sometimes they were in the master bedroom, sometimes the guest room. She preferred the color scheme in the master bedroom, blue, white, and soft peach. The guest room, on the other hand, had a canopy bed draped with yards of crewelwork. Once they made love on the kitchen table, but she worried that Matty would come home and see them, and besides, it was uncomfortable lying over his papers, a pencil at her back. She returned their love-making to the master bedroom. After a while, whatever happened with him happened better in the imagined farmhouse.

"You okay?" he asked. "You're quiet."

She buttoned her blouse clumsily with her mother's arthritic hands. "Like a mouse."

"Faraway." He finished buttoning the blouse for her.

"If anyone's faraway, you are."

"I'm right here."

"Only in the strictest sense." Behind the window shade New York honked. The room had grown larger since he'd removed two of the cartons of books. It seemed too large, impossible to cross.

"Sorry. I keep thinking about what to write and there's nothing to write about. If I don't write, what do I do?"

"You could always be a carpenter again." He could strengthen the canopy bed in the guest room and repair a splitting lion's head under the table.

"Thanks."

"You can make money that way." She would wash his carpenter's shirts and mend pockets pierced by nails. "It's honest. How would I make money if I had to?"

"You could be a carpenter's assistant."

"I don't want to be anybody's assistant." In the farmhouse, she dumped the pot of vegetable stew on the floor. Hot gravy spattered her ankles and burned. He didn't turn around from the kitchen table to see what she had done.

"Okay, you be the carpenter, I'll be the assistant."

Because he took her hand, she walked easily to the door.

The singer wasn't good, the piano player wasn't good, the food wasn't good. All the tables had candles stuck in ink bottles. It wasn't a place he would have picked, but he didn't mind the expense; he still had two more cartons of *Bandaged Moments* to sell. And he could get an advance from his publisher if only he could manage to write a few pages describing what his next novel would be about. He didn't know what his next novel would be about. He didn't want to write another novel, he wanted to lie naked in bed all day and feel sorry for himself.

She insisted it was her treat, and he said, "Nope."

"Why not?"

"It's like the line in the Ring Lardner story: 'Shut up he explained.' I'm paying."

"You don't want me to pay because you think it's Howard paying."

"An interesting theory."

"What if he does pay? He should pay, and pay and pay."

When she lifted the napkin to her lips, he hoped it would wipe away the bitter lines there. He reviewed the eggplant on his plate for overlooked chunks of cheese. "We shouldn't be here," he said. "Howard eats here, doesn't he?"

"He has Matty to take care of. Besides, what if he does show up?"

"You don't want us to have dinner together. You want to stick it to Howard." He stated this while buttering a broken-off curlicue from a seeded crescent roll. The red-gold hair at his wrists glittered in candlelight.

"That's not true."

The black woman at the microphone said, "And now we're going to give you our rendition of a little Willie Nelson."

"And now," Bask said, "having decimated Billie Holiday and Rodgers and Hart, she's going to screw up 'Night Life.' "

"Let's go."

"And it's not 'a little Willie Nelson.' Willie Nelson's a giant."

"Vincent, let's go."

"We haven't had dessert—you know, like a regular couple."

"It's clear you don't like the place. And someone just came in that I'm sure you don't want to see."

"Howard's here?" He wondered if he'd have to hit Howard or if he should let Howard hit him.

"No, Newman Sykes."

He followed her gaze and saw a slender black-haired man escorting a woman to a table. She had black hair too. "I thought he was older." He recognized the woman: all eyes and shyness behind the Karatasi cash register. She probably needed transfusions after a brisk three-block walk. He wondered how it would feel to hit Sykes. "What if he sees you?" he asked. "You want that?"

Suzanne stared at the woman. "She's given up wearing halters." Her voice was thin and tremulous, a cassette played on a recorder with failing batteries.

"You know her?" He watched the woman smile at Sykes.

Suzanne put a cold hand on his wrist. "Do *you*?"

"She works at the Karatasi bookstore." Sykes seemed to be reading the menu to her. "You'd think somebody who works in a bookstore could read for herself."

"Let's go." Suzanne stood up. "Please."

He held on to the crescent roll and didn't get up. "Maybe Sykes'll tell Howard he saw us. Isn't that what you want?"

"I'll be outside." Panic, like a glaze on porcelain, crazed her face.

He should have smoothed her skin with long thumb strokes.

He meant to ask, What's the matter, babe? Across the room the woman from the bookstore would be listening to Newman Sykes condemn the menu for lack of character development.

Bask turned back to Suzanne, to tell her not to be upset, but she was already beyond the bar, on her way out. He signaled the waiter for the check—at least *that* was his—and fed bread crumbs to the candle flame.

He gave the waiter her order: a glass of white wine, a baked potato with butter and sour cream, and a small green salad. She wondered why she wasn't supposed to talk to the waiter. She wanted to say to him, This wasn't my idea. The wine she'd had at Howard's made her almost brave enough to do it.

A black woman sang, "And listen to what the blues are saying." Dina would have listened, but, looking up from a relish tray eyed with olives, she saw the red-haired man, without cartons, walking toward her.

He stopped at their table. His hair in loose curls seemed about to explode. "Mr. Sykes?"

"Yes?" Newman said with aggrieved reasonableness.

Before the red-haired man spoke again, she recognized him: saw his face under ashes in the fireplace, where Larry had thrown *Bandaged Moments*. In the store that morning the man, embarrassed, had been selling copies of his own book; now she flushed with embarrassment. The book, which she still hadn't read, had given her story its first home, print crowding script in smudged eyeliner. She'd read his story "Eating Peaches" in the *Maupassant Prize* volume and admired it. Awe and gratitude welled up inside her; the olive in her mouth kept her silent. If she concentrated on his nose, he didn't have three eyes. Freckles shimmied on his nose. Remembering the fifty-dollar check from *Rosemary* in her purse—Howard had found the check in an envelope marked IMP. and given it to her—she told herself that she was like Bask: a writer. The tablecloth hid her hands as they moved up under the table to tap once, twice, a third time. She studied the red-haired man's nose for clues about how writers behave.

He bent toward Newman and said, "My name is Vincent Bask and I think you're a putz."

A smile cut into Newman's face. His black brows stretched above his light eyes. He delivered his answer with puzzling enjoyment. "You'll pardon me then if I don't get up."

It was eight, not twelve, when she got home. Slumped at his desk in his work corner of the living room, he didn't turn to greet her. The manuscript before him said, ". . . but though the Jungian view of the dragon presupposes this conflict, we cannot resist questioning why it . . ." He heard her open the door to Matty's room, close it, and return to the living room.

"The prom let out early?" he asked.

"I will never forgive you." Her statement, hissed across the room, made him turn around.

She was sitting in an armchair. She looked clean and thoughtful and only a bit edgy, as if she were a housewife trying to decide on camera which pile of diapers was cleaner, the Tide pile or the other. She crossed her legs with finality. She had made her decision. The off-camera voice, inevitably male, prompted, *Now let's see what's under that pile you've chosen, Suzanne.* Howard knew what was under any pile of diapers. *What does the card say, Suzanne?*

No ice cubes rattled comfortingly in his glass. It was empty except for a puddle of water. He took it to the kitchen. She followed him there.

One loose ice cube remained in the freezer. Gouging ice from the trays was her job. He dropped the lone cube in his glass and floated it in Scotch. He had left the freezer door open, expecting her to close it. Though she stood beside it, she didn't move. He went back and slammed it shut. He was close enough to strangle her if he put down his glass. He shambled back to the living room. She was right behind him.

"I'm not used to all this sudden togetherness," he said.

"If you don't like it, you can move out," she said.

"Where were you?"

"I had dinner with a friend."

"You're supposed to have dinner with your family."

"I didn't realize you were such a family man."

"I had dinner at McDonald's with Matty and a rat in a shopping bag. If one of the girls at the office hadn't given me the shopping bag, I couldn't have had dinner even at McDonald's. Did you ever eat there? Everything's in paper. And Matty *likes* it."

"I saw a friend of yours in the restaurant."

"What restaurant?"

"A woman. Small, with black hair. Young."

"I don't have any friends."

"She was with Newman Sykes. He's married, isn't he?"

"Everybody's married. You're married."

"Who is she?"

"Who'd you have dinner with?"

"Who do you think?"

"You're supposed to be home for dinner. I always am."

"That's because you're not home for lunch. I saw you on one of your business lunches. You were running for a cab with that woman. You were holding her hand."

"She's Newman's friend."

"I thought you didn't know her."

"I don't. You just told me she was with Newman."

She picked up a small lopsided bronze rectangle he'd bought at a gallery in SoHo. She seemed to be considering throwing it at him. *And now let's see what's under this bloody pile, Suzanne.* When she put it down, he thought she'd remembered that it cost over three hundred dollars.

"Sweet Susannah," he murmured from a safe distance.

She sank into a chair and began to cry. He edged toward her. She hunched over, her head to her knees. He stroked her hair. A few white ones trailed through the auburn.

"It'll be all right, sweet Susannah."

"No it won't," she cried.

• • •

At the top of the stairs she glanced over her shoulder at the sidewalk. The front door sailed open. He didn't have any trouble with locks. The familiar smell of unventilated carpet greeted her. She followed him up more stairs.

Everything in the apartment was the same except for him. She worried that she'd call him by the wrong name. Howard's mug of wine at the office had made her giddy; the first glass at dinner, instead of making her sleepy, had heightened the giddiness. She might have been drunk because Newman fed her roast beef from his fork. She noticed it was his fork. "Taste," he said. Speaking about Bellow, he touched her arm. "The causality of geography. Does it inflame talent? Who celebrates pithily Bucyrus, Ohio?" Speaking about Roth—"Fearless. A toreador waving a tallis."—he touched her hand and interrupted himself. "Very small," he said. She said, "I have to buy knitted winter gloves in the children's department at Lamston's." He held her hand and explained that her story was very good despite several lapses in language. "Examine Didion." Stung, she was about to wish for Vincent Bask to return when he said, "We haven't properly toasted your publication yet." She requested—and he ordered—a second glass of wine, but it wasn't for a toast and she wasn't much of a drinker.

The air conditioner complained starting up. "Wine? Beer? I think there's ice cream." He opened the refrigerator. "There seems to be a dying sandwich." He poured a glass of beer. "I never know what I'm going to find. Once there was a urine specimen in a baby-food jar."

"Isn't this your place?" she asked with well-inflected surprise. He might be testing her.

"Yes, but I let certain people use it during the week when I'm not here. Sometimes Howard uses it. Once he left a bloodstain on the mattress." Lamp light deepened harsh grooves in his face.

"Doesn't he have his own apartment?" It *was* a test.

"He can't bring women home to his wife."

"Is that why you keep this place?"

"My work's in the city and my family's in the country and

I don't like daily commuting and, yes, that used to be why I kept it, for women. But now it's more for me."

He scanned her as he sipped beer. "I once carried a fairly large woman up and down and back up the stairs here simply because she asked me to. That's about six steep flights. Once I ran out of here at two in the morning to get a strawberry milk shake because the woman in my bed—I think she was a tree surgeon—wanted it. She had calluses on her elbows."

"Did you get the milk shake?"

"No. I brought back an Oh Henry! bar that I bought from a cop who wanted to know what I was doing running on Sixth Avenue at two in the morning. It was winter. There were Christmas decorations in all the closed stores. She was asleep when I got back. In the morning she told me she was allergic to chocolate. I don't like it, myself."

She had known the apartment in afternoon, north light filtered through curtains. In the low, yellower light of two lamps, with the curtains backed by darkness, with colors warmed and softened, it detached from the surrounding rooms and buildings and, traveling alone through night, took on the spun mystery and menace of a spun cocoon.

His kiss tasted of beer. Where was Howard's white wine? He took off his plaid shirt. His arms, she thought, were beautiful: lean, muscled, smooth as polished wood. She kissed the round hardness at his upper arm. She wished she were alone in her white bed, sleeping. He smelled faintly of soap and wood shavings. She kissed cool skin and with her tongue traced a roped vein down along his inner forearm.

He undid her blouse, bra, belt. He didn't touch her breasts. She started to unzip her jeans, but he whispered, "No," shaking his head, black hair falling across his forehead. She let her hands drop. He unbuckled her sandals, pulled her jeans down as if he were opening a package and didn't want to tear the wrapping. She wished he would kiss her again or touch her breasts. Slowly he pulled down her underpants and slid them over her feet.

"There," he said.

Where? she thought.

He stepped back and looked at her before bringing her close. She waited for the blue government seal of quality to be stamped on her rump. His tongue quizzed her teeth. His hand skimmed along her stomach. Fingers approached between her legs. She parted them in a kind of first position for ballet.

"You're wet," he said.

Hooked on his finger, she danced and wondered at his surprise. "Please," she whispered.

His finger withdrew. He kicked off his shoes, took off his socks, jeans, and underpants. He was all polished wood. His cock nested in black hair. She knelt and kissed it, trying to coax it out. What was his name? Her fingers circled it at the base and squeezed gently. It lifted briefly but didn't grow. She rested a hand against his thigh and continued coaxing.

He guided the top of her head back and forth. She tugged and caressed him.

"Come up here to me," he said.

She stayed fixed to him, working, until he insisted, "No, come up here."

He hugged her tight, his chest pressed hard against her cheek. "It's been like this, you see, for a while now," he said. The ceiling lowered. He was carrying her.

His blue sheets weren't orange. She'd managed to get back to this bed, anyway. On blue he spread and fingered her. She strained for pleasure.

"Let me inside you."

In a spirit of scientific cooperation, she wet him with her tongue. He managed, after some maneuvering, to enter her. They moved in a stately minuet. He semiprobed and semiplumbed her. She felt a distant neighborly interest in his efforts, which didn't affect her, until she realized they might affect her after all.

She said, "I have to get something."

"Birth control?"

"Yes. Suppository."

"No, no, I can't stand that stuff. No, I've never made a mistake."

"I think I should."

He pulled out suddenly and easily. "No."

His leaving made a small new emptiness inside her. "But then you can come inside me."

"It's all right. It felt good being there for a while."

She closed her mouth around a huddled pulsing humming-bird. Soon with a sigh he came. That urge to fulfillment, no matter what the difficulties, amazed her, like the sight of green leaves sprouted through cracks in the sidewalk, or tree roots having broken through concrete to expand.

He kissed her nose. His black hair or her own covered her eyes. "Well," he said. He blew on her nose as if it were a kazoo.

"Ugh." She scratched her nose.

"Let's lie together." He rolled her to his side. "I'm going to hold you very tight."

She glimpsed his Buddha smile before her ear fitted against his chest.

"You looked quite angry at the Karatasi bookstore." His speech resonated from his chest to her ear. "I'm glad you were happier at Howard's office today, or how would I have been able to ask you to dinner?"

An ironic tone drove his voice and made what he said sound important. On his voice went, and on, talking about his youth, his women, the books he had made his by ferocious admiration. She listened carefully, taking each disclosure for a gift.

She couldn't hear what he was saying to his wife because he was in the bathroom for privacy. "She's been through a bad time and she needs my support," he'd explained, trailing the phone cord. Low reassuring murmurs issued from behind the almost-closed door. She got out of bed and turned off the lights. At the window, she peered between the curtains. Two stories down, nobody was on the sidewalk or across the street or, as far as she could see, on the street in either direction. She put the lights on and went back to bed, arranging the sheet up to her neck. The bathroom door opened. "Butter almond?" he asked.

He brought two filled bowls with spoons and sat on the bed,

a naked doctor examining a covered patient. His carved body resisted her. "Can you stay tonight? I'd like you to."

She sat up, the sheet around her, and nodded. The bowl was cold. She was never going to go away.

"I have to finish writing a review in the morning, a half-hour or so, and then we'll go for breakfast. Is that all right with you?"

It was. It also was all right when he took away the ice cream and drew her from the sheet to his lap. Now it was her turn. The room sprang upside down. Her mouth arrived at his knee, his calf, his ankle. A hard finger bumped her cervix. Something unpleasant continued there. She concentrated on his high-arched instep. At last she produced a yelp.

"Did I hurt you?" the voice came from above.

"Yes," she called.

He gathered her up in his arms. "You have to tell me. I don't want to hurt you."

Safe in his arms, safe in his unchallenging lap, she whispered, "Okay."

The page had more crossouts than text. In light from the lamp set on one of his two remaining cartons, the yellow typing paper looked jaundiced. He punched a *c* by mistake. From the next room came a hiccuping of voices as Jonathan changed channels. "Well, let me say this—" a campaigner said. The *e* was so filthy its eye was closed. The simple, the reasonable thing would have been to get drunk. Or stoned. He had to rethink his purity.

He would have gone to sleep, but he didn't want to dream about her, not as she'd been in his bed and not as she'd looked later in the restaurant. "It doesn't matter," she said when he showed up outside the restaurant after paying the bill and guaranteeing himself future excoriating reviews from Putz Sykes. "What doesn't?" he asked, but she'd already hailed a predatory Checker. "You're not the only one, you're just the first," she said before the cab removed her, and he thought she might have been addressing the driver.

He filled two lines by typing *SuzanneSuzanneSuzanne* over and over. Maybe the publisher would buy *that*. On the third line he typed,

The first time he saw her, she was peeling carrots.

Surprised, he went on:

He immediately explained to her that carrots must be washed, not peeled. She seemed worried by the information.

Curious to find out what was happening, he kept typing.

"There are at least fifty thousand of them in readiness right now," the beautiful woman said. Howard admired her fluency with facts.

"And the policy is, let's have more. We could characterize this as a state of global insanity," she went on. She had the kind of beauty useful for a crusade: strong, classic, riveting enough to gain attention, but not so demanding that it detracted from her subject. He approved of her high-necked white blouse. Passionate natures often covered up. He tried to think of an example.

"I'm not disagreeing with you, Lorraine," a man said, "but I don't think you're going to get an organization going here." With his forefinger and thumb he fondled a nonexistent beard; it had been there on the jacket of his last book.

"Doctors did. Look at Physicians for Social Responsibility."

"Yes, fine, but how many writers do you know who are social and responsible?"

This provoked laughter around the large, crowded living room, even at the back, where several plotless novelists had knotted symbolically behind a Mission chair. A Sullivanian and frequent contributor to the *New York Review* occupied the chair in obvious discomfort, perhaps because among those sitting on the Navajo rug at his sneakered feet was a former movie actress and recent memoirist whose newspaper picture he'd taken into the bathroom for masturbating sessions when he was eleven.

The beautiful crusader laughed too, to show she was human, then began describing what Manhattan would be like one minute after the air explosion of a one-megaton bomb. "The equivalent of about eighty Hiroshima bombs," she said pleasantly.

"Let's get out of here," Howard muttered to Newman.

"I have to stay to sign the petition."

They were on a red leather sofa in the middle of the room. A needlepoint pillow scratched Howard's back. The apartment's owner, the son of a publisher of erotic art books, sat on Newman's other side. Howard's other neighbor was a woman who'd written a novel in which the heroine had a mastectomy. He scrutinized her chest for a clue.

". . . immediately for more than one million people," the crusader was saying.

"Mail them your signature. Let's get a drink."

"She's interesting, isn't she?"

"She's blowing up my apartment building and melting my family."

"I hear she got two hundred thousand for the film rights to her book—what was it called?—and the first thing she did was have her teeth capped."

They'd looked natural enough when she laughed. Newman proceeded to analyze her overuse of the passive voice. "Other than that, her prose is oddly muscular, as if she'd been lifting weights."

The man who'd spoken before said to the crusader, "If you dropped a bomb in this room now, there'd be a lot of deadly literary fallout." He grinned, expecting laughter. When none came, he rubbed his minimal nose, the result, it was rumored, of a Pinocchio complex. Howard had started the rumor in '78 in a station wagon going downtown to a fund raiser for what he'd dubbed the Kurds and Ways Committee.

"Amazing, isn't it?" Newman whispered. "A man can be so meticulous in his work and so boorish in person. It's enough to make you believe in divine evenhandedness."

"Speaking of which, how's Dina?"

"Fine."

"You've been seeing her?"

"Yes."

Howard lapsed into silence until a description of burn victims. He refused to think of Matty that way. Suzanne might already be lost to him, but not Matty. "Our Dina likes to bite, have you noticed? She used to chew my shoulder." He caught the flash of disappointment on Newman's face and wished emotions could be bronzed like baby shoes; he would keep that one on his desk for a paperweight. The next minute he regretted his meanness, and the minute after that he was wondering if he should sign the upcoming petition as Captain Marvel or Barbara Cartland.

Aug. 13, 1980

Dear Mother & Dad,

Hope you're both well. I'm okay. There's still no place you can reach me. I'm moving around a lot. I've sold a story, and it's going to be published. I don't know if I want you to read it. It's not as hot here as it could be. The evenings are pretty cool if you don't move too fast.

Love,
Dina

The man's eyes were close-set and a wolflike yellow-brown. His several chins hadn't been shaved, but the hair was too sparse to constitute a beard. It looked like a map of areas of population density in Utah. He breathed a cloud of herring and onions when he requested timidly, in a southern accent, a life of Einstein.

She found several books for him. "No, no, no," he whined, "Einstein."

"I don't think he knows what he wants," she whispered to Dan. Two aisles away, the man, a squat hulk in a short-sleeved plaid shirt, with green suspenders holding up baggy gray pants, wrestled a three-page foldout of the human skeleton back into a medical dictionary.

"Don't you know who that is?" Dan asked.

"No."

He shook his head and spoke a name she'd never heard before. "Probably one of the greatest writers alive."

"He wants stuff on Einstein, but when I bring it, he doesn't want it."

"Not Einstein—Eisenstein."

"He says Einstein."

"He means Eisenstein."

"How am I supposed to know that?"

"The references are in his last book."

"I haven't read it."

"Excuses, excuses. There's more to life than Paul Newman." A sweet, expectant smile overcame Dan. "I'll help him. There's mail for you."

"I *like* Paul Newman," she called after him.

Near the register, a thick manila envelope addressed to D. Leitman produced two copies of *Rosemary* with her story. Her name in type on the contents page seemed to be somebody else's. There was a listing for contributors on page 242. Howard hadn't mentioned that. On page 242 she found herself between Blaine Jason and Sandra Olivieri. For all she knew, they were the second and third greatest writers alive.

This is D. LEITMAN's first published story.

Blaine and Sandra each had a paragraph detailing their recent books and grants and awards and degrees and hobbies and marriages and children. Between them, the brief sentence about her seemed miserly and inflexible. It bristled like somebody being pressed in a crowded subway. She could hear her father saying, "As long as they spell your name right, kiddo."

It was spelled right in the byline for the story. She couldn't read any more than that. What if there was a mistake in it? What if her writing embarrassed her? She felt carsick.

"Watch out," a man said. Two cartons slammed down beside her on the counter.

Queasy, she glanced up at Vincent Bask.

"Something wrong?" he asked.

She shook her head.

He picked up the second copy of *Rosemary*.

"That's mine," she said. She closed the copy she was holding.

"Can I look at it for a minute?"

"Why?" If he flipped through the magazine, he might notice her story or he might not notice it.

"Did I do something to upset you? Is it because I said something to your friend last week at that restaurant? Or is that your father?"

"He's not my father."

Bask put the magazine back on the counter and opened the cartons.

Dan had a special formula for buying books; he gave people he liked more money than others. She didn't know if he liked Vincent Bask. "Dan's busy right now." She pointed out the plaid hulk. "Do you know who that is?"

"I think he used to be on TV." Bask went to a table to search through coverless paperbacks.

She reopened *Rosemary* to the contributors' page. Bask's name was there, in a four-line paragraph.

With his third story for *Rosemary* in two years, VINCENT BASK extends . . .

She said to his broad back, "Excuse me."

"What'd I do now?" he asked, large and undangerous.

"Your story's inside." She gave him a copy of *Rosemary*.

"Oh. Yeah. Right." He scratched his head, and a pink ear poked out from russet curls.

"I guess you'll get copies in the mail too." There was no way to ask him not to look at it too hard and wear it out.

"You have something in here?" he asked.

"I read your story 'Eating Peaches' in the *Maupassant Prize* book. I liked it—"

"Thanks. What's your name?"

"I have a copy of *Bandaged Moments* and I'm going to read it."

"What'll your friend Mr. Sykes say about that?"

"He's a very nice man."

"What's your name?"

"Dina."

"You have a story in here?"

She didn't nod, but she didn't shake her head, either.

"Can I read it?"

He succeeded in making her smile. "How could I stop you from reading it?" she asked.

"If you don't want me to, I won't. Not even at home with my own copy."

"I didn't ask your permission to read 'Eating Peaches.' "

"You didn't know me then."

"Can I read *Bandaged Moments*?"

"Sure. The question is, should you? Can I read your story?"

"Yes." She would have preferred to say no, but *no* would have taken too long; Dan and one of the greatest writers alive were heading toward the register and she wanted to grab her other *Rosemary* before they got there.

The blue leather album was half-price. It had overlapping plastic sleeves, one for each snapshot. The saleswoman shot the sleeves up and down with long, curved nails. "It makes it easy to locate the one you want." Light bounced from frosted polish on her nails, from plastic sleeves, from chrome-trimmed mirrored display cases, from windowless mirrored walls, from silver belt buckles and hammered silver bracelets, from glass stoppers in perfume bottles. An atomizer released a cloud of jasmine. The saleswoman looked across the aisle, past Suzanne. At the next counter a silver compact, shaped like a rose, winked.

The first picture would be of Matty in a white cotton dress with blue smocking. There wasn't much smocking done anymore.

And Matty preferred wearing pants or shorts. She tolerated a red gauze tent dress with tie straps. "As long as I don't have to wear tights with it," she said.

Suzanne flipped up an album sleeve. The second picture would be of Howard and her laughing, arms around each other. It would be a little out of focus because Matty would have been giggling when she took it. She needs me, Suzanne thought.

Over brandy after a dinner of paella with saffron rice and ecstatic murmurs from the guests ("How do you *do* it?"), she would set down on the coffee table a white bowl of perfect strawberries and a red bowl of unsweetened fresh whipped cream. She would see Howard's crossed beige trouser legs. "Howard," one of the men would say, "you lucky man."

"And what's this?" the man's wife would ask, opening the blue leather album to divert attention from Suzanne. "Oh, marvelous."

"Please, don't bore yourself with family pictures," Suzanne would say. Then: "Yes, that's in Connecticut. Howard insisted we get away for a weekend and relax. Yes, that's Washington. The National Gallery. Howard took it. That's the Pont Neuf. We had a long weekend there. Howard surprised me." Lovingly, eyes adoring the crossed beige trouser legs: "He always surprises me."

"Do you want it?" the saleswoman asked. She had on a white blouse. Her eyes were the pure blue of tinted contact lenses. She could have been a nurse except for her long nails. She was too young and beautiful to be anything but an actress.

"No. May I see that wallet? The red one."

Before the saleswoman returned with the wallet, Suzanne picked up a pink snakeskin billfold from the REDUCED MERCHANDISE tray and dropped it in her purse.

She examined the red wallet quickly. "No. Thanks for all your help." She almost added, Break a leg; but she didn't know if the actress had a part in a new play.

On the escalator going up to Lingerie, she saw herself in a blue satin nightgown, brushing her hair with a silver-backed brush.

• • • •

Aug. 17, 1980

Dear Howard,

   Thank you for the copies. Thank you for publishing my story. Thank you for telling me not to write beautifully. I'm writing now and it's not beautiful at all.

                                                                    Dina

The second time she read the story, she noticed the typo: ". . . so I won't have to hurt him with my depature."

"Depature," she said. "Newm."

He folded the tip of his index finger into a thick hardcover novel about six generations of an American midwestern family. He'd been skimming it, making notes and sighing or laughing now and then. His reading glasses had slipped down his nose; above tortoiseshell his hazel eyes were serene.

"Perhaps the typesetter is from Boston." He adjusted the pillow at his back and the mattress dipped briefly. "Think of it as a found object: 'depature,' the act of depatching—to depie the Harlequin, to retear, or to make whole. You can use it somewhere else."

"Are you this calm about typos in your own stuff?"

"My writing has been cut, garnished, rearranged—without my permission. Patched and depatched. It happens to everybody. Except, unfortunately, him." He opened the midwestern saga. "It's not even a good beach book, except to hold down the corner of a towel."

"Do you know him?"

"No."

"What if you did? Would it matter?"

"If he were my friend?"

"Yes—in a review."

"I suppose I'd try to be kind."

"What if you liked the book but hated the author?"

He pushed his glasses up along his nose. "I don't particularly hate anybody."

"What about Vincent Bask?"

"If he has another book, I'll read it and review it, not him." He resumed paging through the Midwest.

"What if I write a book?"

"You should."

"Maybe you'd be nice to me because we're lovers, but what if we weren't anymore?"

"That'll have nothing to do with your book." Again he looked at her over his glasses. "An affair runs its course, like a fever or a mass delusion. We're having a mutual delusion."

She slid down in the bed and lay her head against his thigh. *Rosemary* fell between the bed and the wall. She was always lying on the inside half of a bed, unless she slept alone. "I'm writing something. I don't know if it's a book."

"You can show it to me if you like."

She didn't know if she'd like that. Since she'd met him, a second man had entered her writing, a character who was critical, analytical, and remote, a severe man who drank beer. "Maybe," she said.

He patted her breast briefly before turning a page. When his hand moved away, she thought, *That's* depature. But she didn't say it out loud.

8-25-80

Dear Dina,

Of course you're welcome, sweetie. I'm glad you're writing, but all advice I give should be cherished only after strenuous examination. And if I'm one hell of a teacher, you're one hell of a writer. Let me see it when you're done.

Friendship,
Howard

She hadn't expected to feel horny. If she were a serious writer, she wouldn't be feeling horny. But Ned, staggering under the burden of his adventure, had impaled a woman in the shower, and Steven was watching them.

She clamped her legs together and kept writing. Ned, the character who wasn't Howard, and Steven, the character who wasn't Newman, were both married men who fooled around. Ned's bed-hopping had a feverish glee; Steven's adulteries were narrower, more sober. Using his apartment for their respective affairs gave the two men an uneasy friendship. The woman in the shower with Ned moaned.

The pressure of her legs started a slight, rhythmic rocking. She scribbled Steven into the shower with Ned and the woman. The rocking quickened. She hurried the wet threesome toward a triple climax, but before she could arrange it, her breathing became irregular, her body stiffened and arched, her voice whispered, "Oh oh oh." She lay unmoving on the white bed, a notebook over her breasts, an uncapped felt-tip pen drying out in her open hand.

MORRISSE AND PINCHANSKY
LITERARY AGENCY

Sept. 3

Dear D. Leitman,

Howard Ritchie showed me your story "An Affair, I Guess" in galleys and gave me a copy of an unpublished one. They're both quite fine. If you'd like to come in and talk, please call me for an appointment. We represent, among others . . .

Most of the names were familiar to her—older writers with good reputations and famous prizes; younger writers, including Vincent Bask, with one or two books to their credit—and among those that weren't familiar, she assumed, was a genius like the plaid hulk requesting Einstein. Eisenstein.

She called the agent and agreed to mail a copy of her latest writing before she came in to talk. She gathered up her seventy-eight and a half typed pages about Ned and Steven. The weight and thickness of the accumulated pages satisfied her. Reluctantly she choked them with a rubber band. She took enough money with her to make two copies. The second one, she decided, might as well go to Newman.

Humming, the machines ate pages and spat them out. Behind her the line had grown. "Forty-nine," a boy yoked in gold jewelry called. She put her ticket on the counter. Beside her a woman with a cartoon panel demanded of the boy, "But will it reduce *well*?"

A copier the size of a restaurant stove swallowed her pages. If she watched carefully, the operator, a tiny girl with fuchsia-streaked hair, wouldn't be able to run off an extra copy to keep.

"Long time no see." The accented voice promised old terrors, the fear of disappearing, the lure of disappearing.

He'd trapped her again. If she ran now, she would have to leave her manuscript behind.

He was old. His skin, his tangled hair, his eyes, even the green one, had grayed. His untrimmed mustache aged him further.

"Aren't you going to run away screaming?" he asked. His smile frightened her.

"No. How are you?"

"Fine, fine. And how are you? It's so nice to see you again. We really have to stop meeting like this. We should get together sometime, don't you think? Coffee or a light intimate dinner for two. We do have so much to talk about."

The boy behind the counter called, "Fifty."

"Excuse me," a woman said, poking Larry with an attaché case. "I'm next."

"So you are, madam," he answered with exaggerated deference. "Everybody is next but me." He didn't move, and the woman had to go around him.

"Tell me," he whispered to Dina, "how long until you're like her, one pushy bitch looking to trample the world?"

Pages shot out of the copier eating her manuscript. "What are you doing here?"

He checked his ticket. "I'm sixty-one. Cheap copies do attract a select clientele." He took a folded piece of paper from his pocket. "You may be the writer in the family, but I'm going to publish something. How about two thousand copies of this? Want to see it?"

"No." She concentrated on her reproducing pages.

"It concerns you and your good friend Ritchie. I visited him a while back, did he tell you that?"

She shook her head.

"And yesterday I saw your story in his garbage magazine. I was in the library, just so you know I wouldn't pay to read that *Rosencrantz*."

"*Rosemary*."

"Now I think I should get published too. This is a democracy, right? Equal time for opposing views."

The fuchsia-haired girl brought Dina her manuscript and copies. She turned the top page over and asked the girl for a bag.

"You're certainly busy," he said. "But instead of making copies of writing, why don't you write?"

"An agent asked to see a copy." She wondered how she'd pay for that burst of pride.

He followed her out of the store. "Agents, you realize, are parasites on society. They produce nothing."

"You'll miss your turn," she said.

In daylight he seemed more faded. "Listen," he said in a suddenly gentle voice, "maybe you haven't really thought about it. After a while, you won't be able to come back, even if we both want it. We'll have hardened into our positions. Don't you want to come back?"

She hugged the manuscript and tried to speak gently too. "No."

"Don't you miss me, don't you crave my body?" An edge of mockery sharpened the questions.

She said quietly, "I don't miss you."

"Little one," he said so tenderly that she couldn't object. His blue eye pleaded with her. "I'll have to do terrible things to forget you. I'll have to go with other women." Their faces were close together. They exchanged breath. If he cried, she'd cry too. He whispered, "Your friend Ritchie's a fag. And you're a whore."

She started walking away.

"Wait," he said. "Aren't you going to ask me how Ralph is?"

"How is he?"

"He's dead. The doctors and a nun named Sister Anne killed him."

"I'm sorry."

"He left me the store. I've got property. I'm a businessman. Come back and I'll knock you up and we'll move to a nice apartment. Maybe if you work very hard with me at the store, we'll get to move to the suburbs and have wall-to-wall carpets before the Nazis come back and take it all away again. Isn't that what you want?"

"For the Nazis to come back?"

"No, a baby and carpets."

She put up a hand in a parting gesture. "Bye." She got a few steps away before he grabbed her and wedged her against the window of a shoe store. In her terror, she noticed a pair of red high heels she wouldn't be able to walk in. "Let go."

He tightened his grip on her shoulders. An old man passing glanced at her without interest. The store window was warm against her back.

"I'll scream," she said.

"I'll break your face," he said. He yanked the bag with her manuscript from her.

"Give it back."

He took out a page.

"I don't want you to touch it," she said.

He crumpled the page and threw it in the street, between two parked cars. A puddle of water or urine received it. "It's garbage, see?"

She lunged at him, trying to pull the bag away. He laughed. "Easy, easy. I'll give it back. First listen to one thing."

"Give it back."

"Listen. You see your paper? That's what happens when you put anything out in the world. People use it for garbage. What do you think people do with magazines and books? They drop them in garbage cans, they use them to pick up dog shit on the street, they roll them up and kill cockroaches and spiders with them. Keep it safe, away from everybody, because otherwise it's going to be garbage. All these years I protected you from that and you think I'm the monster. You don't know who the monster really is."

He gave her the bag and sauntered toward the copy store. She could tell by the stiffness of his shoulders that he was determined to look strong.

She picked up her crumpled, soggy page by a dry corner. She could type another one. She carried it back to the bookstore, to throw it in the garbage there. On the way, she turned around a few times to make sure he wasn't following her.

The brown tee shirt was torn in front. He threw it across the room. It landed over his typewriter and the mail. A letter from his agent confirmed, with a bold black signature, that soon the publisher would be sending a contract and a check as "advance against royalties for a novel in the English language of approximately 60–100,000 words in length, to be delivered by Sept. 30, 1981. Working title: *Paula*." Part of a letter from Bonnie in Massachusetts, blue-inked ". . . yours if you want it till then," escaped from under the agent's letter. He put on a faded green Celtics tee shirt and, for the first time in three weeks, dialed Suzanne's number.

She sounded angry, but she agreed to meet him. He waited for her downstairs, near Mrs. Lotta's storefront. The bells on Mickey's collar made a tinny jingle as the cat vigorously licked itself. He envied that ability; it kept things simple. In sun on the sidewalk the cat's fur was glossy. From inside the store Mrs. Lotta paused in her crocheting to wave at him, and he nodded.

He was looking in the wrong direction when Suzanne said a cool hello. She pulled away when he tried to kiss her.

"Want to go somewhere for pie?" he asked.

"No."

"Want to go upstairs?"

"No."

"Well. How've you been?" he asked.

She resembled Paula in his book. Maybe Paula should be shorter, he thought. Maybe Paula should have black hair. She had on a dress he'd once told her he liked because it was thin and scoop-necked with a few bits of crucial lace.

"You want to fight in the street?" he asked.

"Let's go in there," she said, pointing at Mrs. Lotta's.

"Let's talk," he said, but she was already in the doorway. Against his quickly reviving beliefs in Unitarianism, Catholicism, and isolationism, he followed her.

In the crosswinds of two electric fans blowing from opposite sides of the room, her hair lifted from her shoulders. She was admiring Mrs. Lotta's crocheting.

"Five bucks any color, six for two color," Mrs. Lotta said.

"What is it?"

The reader-adviser spread the needlework on the table and folded her hands across her stomach. "This is the body for the poodle. After the body, you make the head. Then you cover the extra toilet paper with it."

"I know what I'm going to give you and Howard for Christmas," Bask told Suzanne.

Ignoring him, she placed a finger lightly on the green yarn. "How much is it for a reading?"

"Jesus, Mary, and Joseph," Bask said.

"The short one or the long one?" Mrs. Lotta asked.

She didn't use a crystal ball. She didn't ask about birth time. She took Suzanne's hands and turned them palm up on the crocheting and glanced at them. Then she closed her eyes.

The fan behind Suzanne parted her hair and blew it forward while the fan facing her blew it back. Her hair billowed at the sides. A red bandanna hid Mrs. Lotta's hair. Standing over the women, Bask felt directed air rush over his neck. His forehead stayed warm. With her hands outstretched on the table, Suzanne seemed to be appealing to Mrs. Lotta for something, but Mrs. Lotta was blind, Justice with a crochet hook instead of scales. The smell of cumin wafted in from a back room.

She opened her eyes. "You are feeling lost and confused. You seek guidance," she told Suzanne.

"Bravo," Bask said.

The women ignored him.

"You need to know that your man love you," Mrs. Lotta said. "He must sacrifice for you. For love he must go even into hell to rescue you."

"Give the world a break," Bask said.

"You must pray he is strong enough for this."

"I can't pray, not really," Suzanne said.

"In your way," Mrs. Lotta said.

"God's green earth," Bask said.

The edge of the reader-adviser's bandanna darkened along her forehead. "It is necessary to pray. It is not necessary to believe."

"You ever teach at St. Agnes?" Bask asked.

"Hush," Suzanne told him. To Mrs. Lotta she said, "Tell me how to make it right." She opened her purse and took out more money.

Dan said, "Wear jeans. You look anxious in a skirt."

"I *am* anxious. And my jeans are dirty."

"Wear dirty jeans."

"This isn't a Marxist agent."

"You're a writer, you're not going on a job interview. You should look reliable, but not predictable."

Dina leaned against the counter, her head in her child-size hands. "Do you have any Dramamine?"

The coupled windows overlooking Fifth Avenue needed cleaning. Four buses nudged each other from stop to stop. If she waited long enough, she'd be able to watch them travel from midtown to Twenty-third Street. Cautiously, the receptionist, a boy in a polka dot shirt, typed a label.

"Dina?"

The woman who'd entered the room was tall and once must

have been athletic. Passing time had settled her hips, had blurred the sharpness of her face. It was a face Dina liked: mobile, quick, strong. The eyes were bright between puffed lids, the nose thin and elegant, the mouth wide and wry. The woman extended her hand, square-cut unpolished nails, a thick gold band on the middle finger. "Hi, I'm Maris."

Her office had a blue fishnet draped from the ceiling, a small wood African fertility goddess with memorable buttocks, and books and manuscripts and boxes of manuscripts and towers of manuscripts. A path between books and manuscripts led to her desk and two chairs for visitors. Dina sat in the strongest-looking visitor's chair and held on to the sides of the seat.

"I like the pages you sent me," Maris said. "I feel as if I know these two men." Her wide wry mouth might have been smiling.

"Ned and Steven?"

"Yes. That's some shower scene. I sent the pages to Cal Thomas at B&G. He's very good with young writers, that whole house is good for a young writer. You wouldn't get lost there."

"A publisher?" Dina jammed both forefingers on the underside of the chair once, twice, three times.

"You understand, it could go on for a couple of years, from one publisher to another, before someone buys it, if anyone ever does."

"Buys it?" The tip of a gray-brown dorsal fin cut through waveless, unnaturally still ocean.

"You'd get an advance on your novel."

Dina's fingers stayed glued to wood. Maris asked if she wanted coffee, and she shook her head before whispering, "No, thanks."

"Cal likes what you've done. He wants to meet you. He said he's got time around two today. I think he wants to buy the book." Maris twisted the gold band around and around her middle finger. "You're the sixth writer Howard's sent to me, and every one is wonderful. He's got an incredible eye for talent. He should be locked up somewhere and prevented from doing anything else but that, looking for talent. Did you hear what he did at a party for Francine Gray?"

"No." Croaked. She was concentrating on Cal Thomas, who had her pages and was an editor like Howard and might be like him in other ways too. She laughed at what seemed to be the end of Maris's story about Howard.

Maris joined in with deep laughter. "He's a character," she said. "There's nobody else like him. Thank God."

He was sixteen, and she was afraid of him, an editor in a red bow tie. He might have been twenty-six. She expected a combination of Howard and Newman: a man who would flirt with her and then analyze her response. Her Xeroxed pages and a copy of *Rosemary* lay spread out before him. She crossed her legs and wrapped one foot around the other calf. Sunk in an upholstered beige chair in Cal Thomas's large, light office, she felt like a laborer summoned from the fields into the boss's house for a lecture.

"I like it a lot. Where do you think it's going?" he asked. A gargle tossed the words. Light glanced off his red-framed glasses.

"I'm not sure. I'd like to write about these two men."

"What do you think happens to them?"

"I don't know. They meet a woman, I guess. They both meet the same woman." She hadn't known that would happen until she'd said it. She glared at him because he'd tricked her.

"What I'd like is for you to give me an idea of the direction of the book."

At the word *book* the shark's mouth opened larger than the desk between them. She swam inside to explore for molars. "What if I say something's going to happen and later I change my mind?"

"Of course you can change your mind."

He might have been twenty-eight—or the interview was aging him. Clearly he accepted her as a writer, even though she was female. And clearly he wasn't flirting with her. He spoke to her gently and with respect. His courtesy alarmed her; his lack of flirting annoyed her. Something was wrong with him. His game might be to not have a game. Sooner or later his mask would slip and she would see what it was he really wanted.

"What happens after we talk?" She continued glaring at him, her toes curled up in her sandals.

"You start to work on that book, I hope." He leaned back in his chair. At that angle his eyes showed through his glasses: blue, inquiring, reserved. He had light brown hair with a cowlick. His red bow tie bobbed when he swallowed.

Her leg loosened around the other leg. Her toes uncurled. She watched them. The two big toes tapped the innersoles three times. She would leap up on his desk and spring over him to burst through the closed window twenty-two floors above the street. Smiling, triumphant, bleeding, she would enter the air. Around her a corona of broken glass would flash like diamonds in the sun. Her blood would shine. Behind her the broken window would bear the silhouette of her leap, a cutout of a hurtled figure with arms upraised. Wherever the window wasn't glass, there would be emptiness shaped into Dina. Through that cutout Cal Thomas would call "No!" too late. Thinning, the word would follow her down. She would be speeding at last in a precise direction.

It was hard to pull air past the block in her chest. She'd been holding her breath. Her lungs, which she imagined as two deflated purple balloons, expanded. The balloons scraped her rib cage, squeaking. "Okay." She must have said that. Besides the window, talking to him was another way out of the room. She began, "The two men meet this woman. She's running away from her husband." She glanced at Cal Thomas.

He nodded encouragement. The room sighed. "Go on," he said.

Twenty-two floors down from Cal Thomas's office, the elevator door opened on the lobby and, queasy from motion sickness, the novelist-to-be got out. An elevator opposite hers opened too, and the plaid hulk from the bookstore, Dan's "one of the greatest writers alive," got out, carrying a torn Macy's shopping bag. He was wearing a black shirt and a navy blue tie and yards of green pants shepherded by yellow suspenders.

She asked a woman with a blond ponytail and a packed briefcase, "Excuse me, do you know who that is?"

The woman sighted the plaid hulk crossing the lobby. Her earrings were silver arrows. "Doesn't he work at the cigar stand here?" she asked.

There she was, uninvited again, on his sofa. He'd had the chance, after Gail announced her, to say he was too busy to see her. By not doing that, he had in a sense invited her. Honest to a fault, he thought, and muttered, "Honored by your presence."

Something fired her small face: a breathless, hopeful look. He wondered if she intended to repeat her bare-bottom display. He should have closed the door.

"It's been a while," she said.

He checked to see if it was a reproach. Her eyes burned above her smile. She'd grown thinner. Or longer. Could people her age grow? She had no right to reproach him. He asked, "And how's our friend Newman?"

"Fine."

He liked the hesitation in her voice. Yes, Captain Marvel was in command of the situation. He folded back the cuffs of his green pima cotton shirt.

"I have something to tell you," she said.

She needed another place to stay. She wanted to move into his apartment disguised as an au pair girl. She wanted him. "Good news, I hope." Let her ask.

"Very. I was a few blocks away, at B&G. I'm getting a book contract." She smiled at him so openly, with so many of her small familiar nibbling teeth, that he smiled back.

"Congratulations. A novel?"

"Yes. And I have you to thank for it."

"Hardly."

234

"You sent me to Maris, and Maris sent me to Cal Thomas."

"Maris is a peach. Have I seen any of this novel?"

"No, I have to write most of it."

"You're getting a good advance?"

"I don't know."

"Cal Thomas'll get you something decent. He's pretty good. I could've steered you to someone better."

"I like him."

"He has excellent taste, but he's not all that experienced."

"He's got a big office. It's bigger than yours."

"By that standard, any dentist is a better editor than I am."

She seemed to be tapping her fingers on an invisible piano in her lap. Her voice was low. "I thought you'd be happy for me."

The invisible piano played a sad song. Suzanne, beautiful in a blue nightgown, had told him at breakfast that she'd go to bed with him if he bought her a silver-backed brush. "Favor for favor," she'd said. "More coffee?" Humming, she'd buttered toast. He'd read a marmalade label; somebody'd stolen his *Times* from the doormat. He could still hear her tuneless humming.

"I am," he said. "Maybe we could get together to celebrate. Lift a glass or two. Lift other things. I could call you tomorrow."

She nodded, lowered her head, came up grinning. "What took you so long?"

"I can't believe you believe that shit." Through the store window he saw Mrs. Lotta pick up her crocheting.

"It's not shit. And I don't, not really." She walked past the door to his building.

"You paid for it." He followed her with his accusation.

"People pay *you* for stories and nobody believes they're true."

"They *are* true."

"They're fiction."

"Yeah, but they connect to something real. They're not toilet-paper covers."

They were stalled in front of a dry cleaner's. An old tailor at his sewing machine watched them through the window, his lips pursed around pins. Bask swore to himself that he would never have any clothes altered there, even if he had to wear unhemmed pants and short-cuffed jackets for the rest of his life.

"Let's go somewhere," he said. "Let's go on the Staten Island ferry." If they were saying goodbye, they could do it moving. She wasn't his Paula, she wasn't his Suzanne. They would free each other at the harbor. "We can eat stale potato chips, as many as you want."

"That's not what I want," she cried so angrily that he put his arms around her to comfort her. She punched his shoulder hard enough to make him grunt.

Behind grimed glass the tailor took a pin from his mouth and stuck it through houndstooth check.

Bask rubbed his shoulder. "What do you want?"

"Not you," she answered.

"Babe, let me take you home—"

"No!"

"*Your* home, let me—"

"Go away. I want Howard."

The tailor might have heard her whisper, he thought. "Fine."

"Go to hell," she said.

"No way," he answered, and he started walking.

After he walked away—after she sent him away—she waited. 1. He would return. 2. She would call to him and he would return. 3. She would run after him. None of these things happened. He kept walking. He was going somewhere. He must have caused the fight to get rid of her. He must have known all along that he would leave her like this. Seeing him disappear down the block was like seeing Howard running along the street with the halter woman from the bookstore: the shock of spying on him. She had told Vincent to go away, but he had actually gone. What remained for her was the superiority of the observer tracking the observed, the target, the prey.

Tall, with his red curls beckoning over the heads of strangers, he was easy to follow. The hard part was matching his pace. Her high-heeled sandals wobbled in potholes and stabbed subway gratings. After eight blocks she was carrying her shoes, a barefoot country girl, far from the country, cultivating urban fungus in pursuit of love. By Fortieth Street she'd lost one of the sandals. She looked back to see if it was lying behind her. Strangers' feet stamped toward her. Before the light changed, she hurried after Bask. The shoes had cost ninety-five dollars on sale. She kept the surviving one. Her feet hurt. "Our Father which art in heaven," she whispered. At the corner she stopped and watched him walk downtown, toward Thirty-ninth Street. The red curls flared among strangers. A man who'd been running to make the light bumped into her and kept running. The back of his jacket had a wet stain. She couldn't see Vincent anymore. "Hallowed be thy name," she whispered, and deposited her shoe in a mailbox. NOT FOR METERED MAIL, a sign said. USE ZIP CODES. She changed direction.

She walked east along Thirty-ninth Street and at Madison headed uptown. One foot was bleeding. Empty cabs cruised past, but she persisted with her penance. She had stolen. God helps those who help themselves. She had committed adultery. God helps those who help themselves.

Further east she hobbled past Howard's office building, but she didn't stop there. She had to make things right one at a time. Minutes after she passed, Dina came out the lobby door, smiling, and ran to the downtown subway.

Bask walked past bodegas and delis and Chock Full O' Nuts, past arcades whining with electronic kills and home runs promising ballpoint pens free for six coupons. Two blond women, one of them black, offered him blow jobs. He parted a pack of yellow cabs honking. He followed Broadway downtown, through the theater district, past Times Square and peep shows, through the garment district. Bales of gingham trussed with wire dollied beside him. Winter coats wheeled by. Howard had told him to have something between real events. A thin man in an army shirt tried to sell him a gold Omega quartz watch for fourteen bucks cash. Bask couldn't read what was stenciled on the man's shirt pocket. On Twenty-third Street a bus aimed at him, and a cop yelled, "Hey, Red, watch it." That was a real event.

He stopped at a hot-dog vendor's wagon and asked to buy a can of salt-free seltzer. "I got Tab, I got Coke, I got Seven-Up," the vendor said. He was Greek, no more than twenty-five, and wore a gold medallion around his neck. The medallion nestled in curly dark hair. Bask moved on to a pink and white striped wagon selling watermelon ices. Yes, the tanned young woman in a tank top and shorts informed him, the ices were made with refined sugar. She seemed genuinely sorry before going back to her book, a paperback on Noh plays. It would have been nice for *Bandaged Moments* to be out in paperback and for her to be reading it. At a falafel stand run by a tall, healthy-looking black woman he discussed ingredients. He ordered falafel on whole-wheat pita without sauce because he wasn't sure about the sauce, and ate it on a shaded bench at Madison Square Park. A girl in a white sundress went by. Thongs from her shoes laced halfway up around her legs. She wore a brass collar. Her mouth was the pearly purple of the inside of conch shells. When their eyes met, he nodded and kept chewing. He tore off a few pieces of pita and threw them to an audience of pigeons.

After eating, he folded his arms across his chest and stretched his legs out in front of him and closed his eyes. The city disappeared in explosions of purples, reds, yellows. He spent several happy minutes following a stream along a meadow behind Bonnie's house in Massachusetts. Then he was in the kitchen with her, arguing. Butter bubbled in a frypan. She chopped parsley on an antique breadboard. He admired her long, elegant fingers flecked with green.

"Just once," she said, "you might think about what you want to be doing when you're sixty."

"I have. I'd like to be writing."

"Let's establish goals."

"Let's not."

"You have to prioritize, Vince. You can't let things happen, you have to make them happen."

Paula, the title character of the book he was writing, entered the kitchen. She didn't look like Suzanne. She did look angry. Before she could say anything, he opened his eyes and stood up.

He followed Broadway across Fifth Avenue, down past rug stores and furniture stores and discount drugstores, to Union Square, where a temporary greenmarket of farmers selling produce at the north end of the park abutted a permanent drug market, illegal but unquiet, in the park.

He picked an apple from a crate and asked the farmer, meaty in overalls, "How much?"

The farmer had an enormous mottled nose and not terribly kind eyes. "That's a Molly Delicious. You try it."

"But how much?"

"You'll come back for more if you like it." The farmer dropped somebody's plastic bag of peppers on a swinging scale. Their colors, bright red with grass-green stems, hurt Bask as profoundly as a sunset. He bit into sweet and crisp Molly. "Ludes?" a man asked him. He ate the apple to the core and, after Fourteenth Street, the seeds in their hard-skinned chambers. The stem reminded him of the twiglike stub of umbilical cord on each of the Irish setter puppies he'd watched being born. He tossed it on pizza crusts in a garbage can guarded by flies. An auction gallery and an antiques store had three seatless gilded chairs and a standing birdcage on the sidewalk. If he wanted to, he could build better chairs than those. He turned off Broadway and walked quickly until he came to the Karatasi bookstore.

He knocked on the door but didn't wait for an answer before opening it. Wearing a red blouse and underpants, she was sitting at the foot of a white bed and toweling her hair.

"Dan said you were up here," he said.

She pulled a white sheet over her thighs. Her wet hair made black ink lines on her forehead.

"I thought this was an office. You live here?" he asked.

She nodded.

"You and Dan?" he asked.

"He lives down the hall. Anything else you want to know?" The towel covered her ears against him.

"I was in the neighborhood. I thought I'd say hello."

"Hello." She smiled before the towel hid her face.

"I liked your story," he said.

Now he had her attention. Even her hair seemed alert: drying, it curved.

"I liked yours too," she said. "And that's not in return for your liking mine."

"Want to go get some juice or milk?"

"I have to go somewhere."

"Okay." He had to get back to his own place and write. Being with her would have taken up too much time. He wanted sympathy because he and Suzanne were through, he wanted to celebrate because he had a new book contract. But writers shouldn't go with other writers, they should go with normal people, for balance. He decided to fall in love with an architect or a telephone repairwoman.

"We could walk part of the way together," she said from the folds of the towel.

"Great." He stood grinning at her.

"I have to get dressed," she said.

"Right." He backed out the door. Before he closed it, he thought he saw her tap the mattress.

By the second block she was saying, "It's good, but it'll be better when you take more care with it. I take too much care. I have to loosen up the language, you have to condense."

He resented her enthusiasm. "Your friend Sykes's criticism is catching."

"They're my own thoughts, thank you."

"Touchy."

"So are you."

"I just split up with somebody."

"Did you want it to happen?"

That wasn't sympathy. "No. Yes."

"Well then?" She shrugged as if she'd proved something.

He bent down to smell her hair. "Want to go to the movies tomorrow?"

"I'm seeing someone."

"Every minute?"

"I'm not looking for anybody else."

"I didn't say let's get married, I said let's go to a movie. It'll give you something new to criticize."

Walking beside Bask, she felt peaceful. He had a quiet, unimposing voice, his words a blend of regional sounds, unstressed, unhurried. Compared to Howard or Newman, he was a boy— or a Great Dane puppy, with large feet and at times ungainly movements. He was a sweet boy who happened to be a good writer despite a marked absence of suffering and brooding.

She didn't worry about whether or not he liked her. She had

blundered into a radiant calm. Soon Howard would love her again. Soon she would have a book contract to prove she was a writer. Cal Thomas in his high beige office that afternoon had been an annunciating angel kneeling to greet her. Howard would complete her transformation. The warm evening molded itself around her body. She could imagine the next day. She felt almost real.

At the corner of Eleventh Street and Fifth Avenue he tried to set a time for them to meet. "Friends, nothing else," he said, holding up his hands as if surrendering, and she would have smiled, but Larry was walking toward her, carrying a large potted palm tree tied with red ribbon.

She stayed rooted to the sidewalk as the palm tree passed. From behind fronds Larry sneered at her, at Bask, at her again. He didn't say anything.

"You know him?" Bask asked, watching the departing tree.

"My husband," she answered.

He punched his fist into his open hand. "Why do I keep ending up with married women?"

"First of all, I'm not going to be married much longer, and second, you're not going to end up with me."

"I know that. I'm going back to Massachusetts. Day after tomorrow." He hadn't known he was going until he said it. "A friend of mine's in Washington to play with the FTC for a while and I'm going to stay in her house. I half built it. You'd probably say it's too loosely constructed."

"Probably," she snapped at him, and he wondered what he'd said to offend her. She walked to the middle of the block, climbed the pink stairs of a brownstone, and went inside.

The long-haired man held the tree between them while he spoke. "Were you bothering her?" A muscle at the side of his face might have been working in and out, or it might have been the shadow of a palm frond.

Bask squinted down at him. "Who wants to know?"

They stood on the sidewalk three houses away from the house Dina was in.

"I have a right to know."

A blue eye and a green eye regarded Bask spitefully. Even a son of a bitch could feel hurt. He knew that from personal experience. He'd betrayed his friend Howard to sleep with Suzanne. Whatever this man might have done to Dina—or she to him—he could still want to protect her too.

"I wasn't bothering her," Bask said.

The man must have thought he intimidated Bask. "All *right*," he said with unearned triumph. Then, pushing his luck, he demanded, "You live around here?"

"No. Do you have a lot more questions?"

"You leave her alone." Fear made the command unconvincing. "Are you a friend of that shit Ritchie?" He didn't let fear stop him.

Bask admired the man's audacity. "Let's say goodbye now, before you get carried away."

"I'm going to make that shit Ritchie pay for what he did to her," the man confided.

Bask went closer to the palm. "What'd he do to her?"

"You'll see." The man walked his palm away slowly, for the second time.

Bask kicked a No Parking signpole to see it shudder. Being a writer, he should have been able to imagine the man as Dina's husband, but he couldn't. He continued west, to go home.

There were baby-blue canvas espadrilles, red patent leather flats with navy grosgrain bows, white and brown spectators, white sandals with bronze-studded heels, green mules with matching feather trim, purple tennis shoes with yellow laces. They were all on sale. Spotlighted recesses in a wall displayed fall merchandise: brown suede boots, black calf boots, fleece-lined waterproof khaki rubber boots. Suzanne paused at a pair of maroon half-boots with tassels.

"Nice, aren't they?" The salesman balanced four shoeboxes. His eyebrows sent out black and white antennae. "Italian."

"No, thank you," she said, and moved on toward the cosmetics counters. One of her bare feet left small bloodstains on the gray carpet in the shoe salon. A model handing out free samples of cleansing grains didn't give her any.

She went through a bower of silk roses. The air smelled of roses. She searched past crystal bottles and silver compacts until she came to a counter with wallets heaped in a bushel basket on a platform draped in green wool. A rake lay beside the basket. The actress saleswoman was there in a black and red striped dress: the nurse on her day off.

"Hello," Suzanne said.

"Hello." The saleswoman was still beautiful. Her improbably blue eyes gazed past Suzanne again.

"Do you remember me?"

"Can I help you?"

"I was here before. A few weeks ago. You showed me a photo album. It was blue? On sale?"

"I'm sorry, but the sale's—"

"You also showed me a red wallet. Like that one, only red. There was a tray here of sale things."

"I'm sorry, but the sale's—"

"I took a billfold."

"Sale merchandise isn't usually returnable."

"I didn't buy it, I took it."

Fascinated by events at other counters, the saleswoman combed five long, frosted nails through her platinum bangs. "If you don't have a receipt for it, you might get a credit."

"I stole it."

The blue contact lenses blinked at Suzanne at last.

"A pink lizard thing. Or snakeskin," Suzanne added.

"Well, give it back." The saleswoman would have used the same tone in directing a transvestite in a ballgown to the ladies' lounge.

"I can't. It's at home. And I cut off the price tag."

The saleswoman's hands caressed her slender red and black striped hips. "What do you want me to do?"

"What's the store policy on shoplifting?"

"I don't think we're for it."

"I stole a billfold."

"You have to have it with you or it doesn't count. I can't help you. If you like, go see a floor manager or somebody in Security."

In the glare of a lamp trained on her in an otherwise darkened room, Suzanne would weep while two retired policemen in short sleeves questioned her. "Why'd you do it?" Bad Cop would ask. Good Cop would ask, "Cigarette?" Though up till that moment she'd had two cigarettes in her whole life and hadn't inhaled either time, she would blow smoke rings through the lamp beam.

"Where's Security?" she asked. "Can you call them?"

The store detective said her name was Jo. She offered Suzanne iced tea with lemon. Suzanne said she preferred it plain, thank you. Jo told her she could lie down on any sofa she wanted.

"I'd rather sit, thank you."

"Where's your shoes, hon?" Jo was stocky and had short brown hair brushed back from her face. She looked like a professional bowler. Suzanne remembered the women bowlers from the tournaments Markie Bailey had played.

"I don't know." Suzanne sat at the edge of a brown corduroy sofa. One of the cushions had a big burn in it.

There were about fifteen other sofas in the room. A camel-back convertible must have been knifed: slashes of pin-dot velvet hung down with clumps of erupted foam. Near her a yellow ottoman had suffered something orange. She was in a way station for derelict furniture. A smoke-veined oval mirror with a cracked wood frame rested against a gouged green lacquered Parsons table. A Queen Anne chair had a taped ankle.

"This isn't Security," she said.

"Sure it is," Jo said.

"It said Employees Only on the door."

Jo showed her a plastic ID card. It had a color picture of Jo looking unhappy. "See? No kidding." She was about forty-five, not much older than Suzanne, but she acted in a motherly way. She was playing Good Cop.

When the door opened, Suzanne thought it might be the detective to play Bad Cop, but it was a boy who delivered a glass of iced tea and left.

"I shouldn't have this," she said, and drank greedily. The tea cleared the sad afternoon from her throat and washed it further down, somewhere else.

"Better?" Jo asked.

"Yes." Suzanne used her good-girl voice.

"Wouldn't you like to go home now?"

"No." The hell with the good-girl voice. "I stole something."

"The merchandise isn't in your purse. It's not in your pockets."

"Maybe I put it up inside me."

"Then I guess it wasn't a microwave oven. Ahhnngg." Jo gave a satisfied snort, as if she'd made a spare.

"It was a billfold."

"Tell you what," Jo said, wiping her eyes—she was still enjoying her joke. "How about you take the money this billfold was supposed to cost—"

"*Did* cost."

"Fine. And how about you give this money to charity?"

"Why can't I give it to the store?"

"Because the store can't take money unless it's for merchandise."

"But it *is* for merchandise."

Jo sat in the Queen Anne chair and rocked it dangerously. She shook her head. Her brown hair didn't move. "Hon, I can help you call home if you like, I can help you pick out a pair of shoes to wear, but after that I'm going to have to ask you to leave."

Suzanne held the empty iced-tea glass as if it were a scepter. Jo couldn't help her pick out shoes because Jo had no taste: she was wearing navy Oxfords with repulsive rusted grommets. Suzanne smiled at Jo with generous pity. "You can't make me leave. I have a gold-card charge account here."

- - -

shots & certificates
blue looseleaf binder (not green)
2 felt-tip pens (blue)
2 no. 2 pencils with erasers
blue schoolbag—canvas
blue corduroy jeans
cotton socks
shoelaces (not with hearts)
index cards

"What about a fountain pen? There's no fountain pen," he said.

"It says pens," she said.

"Have you ever used a fountain pen?"

"No."

"It has a good feeling to it. Something solid. Try it."

She wrote her name on the list, underneath "index cards," with his pen. Her name looked sober in black ink.

"Do you like it?" he asked.

"It's nice," she said politely.

He took it back. "If you'd like one, I'll get it for you."

"Thanks, Daddy, but I like the regular kind better. Can I have the fried rice, please?"

" '*May* I have the fried rice, please?' " He opened the cardboard container. It was the same kind Woolworth's used to give, when he was a boy, to carry home a pet turtle or a goldfish swimming in three inches of greenish water. His turtle had died because he'd forgotten to feed it. His hunger surfaced through a sea of guilt. "How about the lemon chicken?"

"No. Thank you."

He spooned more Buddha's delight on his plate.

"Did Mommy call the doctor for me to get vaccinated?"

"You'll have to ask her."

"What if I'm not up when she gets home?"

"Then I'll ask her. Wipe your mouth."

The blue cloth napkin removed a grain of rice from the corner of her mouth. She spread the napkin over her lap again and cleared her throat.

The actress who had once been a model was talking to the actress who had always been an actress. "But I love him," she said. Her eyelashes must have been twenty feet long. In the vast, almost empty theater her declaration squeaked.

Newman had insisted on going to Radio City Music Hall because he wanted to see a movie there even though he hated movies. "It's supposed to take place in North Africa at the turn of the century. At least you get to see another country and some costumes. In color. And big."

The screen filled with the face of the actress who had once been a model. "And I know that's not enough for him," she squeaked on.

"I hope there's a sandstorm," Newman whispered. He put his hand in Dina's blouse. The seats around them were empty.

Howard had liked it when she didn't wear underwear. Thinking Newman might like it too, she'd taken off her bra and underpants in the enormous ladies' lounge at the theater. A mirror in a gilded frame caught her as she left the bathroom, closing her purse. She was pale against red flocked wallpaper. Tonight she would do this for Newman. Tomorrow for Howard? Practice.

Newman moved his hand up under her skirt. "Nice and accessible," he said. She wondered if that would apply to her writing. She slid down in the seat and opened her legs for him.

She had to learn perfect obedience: to be available when her man wanted her. It would balance out her anger at Larry, all the years she'd withheld herself from him. It would balance out her fear and her ambition. She'd be able to see herself at last as a woman. She'd have to work very hard at it because she was also trying to see herself as a writer. She'd have to discover her will in order to write, and she'd have to relinquish it in order to be properly female.

The actress who had once been a model enlarged that ideal. "Wherever you go, My Lord," she squeaked to the sandals of her lord, "let me go with you. And if this cannot be, permit me to be here to await your return."

More than Newman's fondling, this speech stirred Dina. She wondered if a man or a woman had written it. The screen dimly lighted her nakedness. Practice. She sighed, her skirt up across her belly, her blouse open at her breasts, and willed herself to know only Newman's will.

She came home barefoot. There were cuts on her feet. She rested a foot on the bathroom sink and poured peroxide over it. The cuts bubbled with white foam. Peroxide dribbled paths through the dirt on her foot.

"Where are your shoes?" Matty asked her.

"I lost one, and the other one needed stamps."

"What kind of stamps?" Matty asked.

He waited to hear the answer, but she said nothing. A gray puddle collected on the tile floor at her peroxided foot as she washed the other one.

"Your mother has a knack for loss," he said. "She once lost her dinner on the Connecticut Turnpike."

"I never did," she said.

"It must have been someone else," he said.

"We had snow peas for dinner," Matty said. "There's some fried dumplings left."

She kissed Matty's forehead. "I'm too tired to eat."

"How about explaining? You too tired for that?" he asked.

"I'm too tired to shower." Leaving gray footprints on the bathroom tiles, she passed him in the doorway and went to the bedroom. He and Matty followed her there.

She pulled off her dress and let it drop to the floor. She undid her bra, dropping it too. Wearing only underpants, she lay down on his side of the bed she hadn't made that morning and pulled the covers up to her shoulders. "G'night," she said.

After he kissed Matty good night and dumped the dinner dishes on top of the breakfast dishes in the sink and had a juice glass of J&B and a cigarette and a long, hot shower, and checked the front-door locks and the gas range, and rechecked them, and turned off the lights, he climbed into bed on the available, wrong side. Suzanne's lips were slightly parted; her deep, even breathing lulled him. He felt peaceful enough to cry. He brought his mouth close to her ear. His nose plunged into her reddish hair. He whispered, "Tell me, bitch, tell me everything." Her eyebrows moved toward each other above closed eyes. Her mouth closed. He considered torturing her with a thumb rack. He would fuck a stranger in their bed, in front of her. He fell asleep, plotting, on her pillow on her side of the bed.

He looked down at her over his glasses. She had burrowed between his left arm and shoulder. Her head lay on his shoulder. The sheet covered her to the waist. Above it was pearled pale nakedness, small and thin. He tried to see through the top of her head, black hair like his, into her skull, into her brain, the left or right side—he couldn't remember which side supposedly controlled thought processes. There he would find her thoughts, some neatly folded and wrapped with tissue paper, some tangled as fine gold chains which, left alone in jewel cases handpainted with willows in Taiwan, spontaneously knotted. At times, usually when they were late for a party, he'd seen Clare, still undressed, sit among rejected outfits on the bed, in the angora and silk litter of her indecision, and drive a straight pin into a gold knot and unpick it, loop by loop. He would have liked to see the bright strands of Dina's thoughts, even the knotted ones. He wanted to know what produced her writing, how she, with her pliancy and hesitation, with her inexperience, her deference to him, her floating, large-eyed helplessness—how did she manage to arrange mostly uncluttered language into sentences that lured him along from one to the next. If the pull faltered at awkward phrasing, lumpy with undigested thought, like a snake that has swallowed a rabbit whole, then the next sentence, clean and recklessly accomplished, retook him.

Split the Lark—and you'll find the Music—
Bulb after Bulb, in Silver rolled . . .

He dismissed the lines. Emily Dickinson was a problem, not a poet. Over the years her words came to him unbidden, despite his best efforts to ignore them. He was like his son, singing ad jingles.

He closed Dina's manuscript. "It's very good. You've certainly caught those men. Especially Ned. It's marvelous how you've captured Howard."

"That's not Howard." She sat up abruptly. Her breasts flashed into view.

Barebreasted women huddled in a tent during the first sandstorm the movie had provided a few hours earlier. He'd gotten his money's worth of sandstorms. "I think you've been a bit overkind to Steven, perhaps because you knew you were going to show it to me. I don't mind being portrayed, you know, as long as it's done with underlying compassion. I think you've done that."

"I wasn't writing about you."

"I said I didn't mind."

"I made it all up."

"Your characters have a lot in common with Howard and me. Ned, for instance. His past, his preoccupations, they're all Howard's. In fact, it seems to me now that you lied to me." He said this quizzically, as if, having pulled a car up to a curb, he'd fished a map from beneath a roll of quarters and a waterproof flashlight in the glove compartment and learned he was in Pittsburgh when all along he'd thought it was Philadelphia. "I asked you how well you knew Howard, and you said you didn't know him well."

"I don't."

"He does imitations of you threatening to bite his shoulder." He took a breath to enjoy her hurt expression. "And it's clear from what you've written here that you've been lovers."

"What I did with Howard is nobody's business, just as what I do with you is nobody's business." A flush had spread across her breasts and up to her neck. She crossed her arms over her breasts. "You had no right to ask me about him. I wouldn't tell you about him, and I won't tell anybody about you."

"You wouldn't have to," he said mildly. "All someone has to do is read this. Howard and I are both quite recognizable among book people. But that's minor. The point is, it's good. You might think of making it into a novel."

"I'm going to. I saw an editor at B&G today. He's giving me a contract. And money."

She was smiling at him, expecting congratulations or, worse, a display of enthusiasm. Under the stamped-tin ceiling of his first Village apartment, designs deepened by lamplight, he had written brief literary stories that he believed then were pure and alive. "You'll have to change this. You can't publish it this way. Howard has a family and a job to keep. And so do I."

"He says he's happy for me."

"You've seen him?"

"Yes."

"Has he read it?"

"No."

Newman savored an unexpected pride and said with what he thought was patience, "You'll have to change it so people aren't recognizable. Otherwise they'll get hurt. Clare has worked very hard to deal with her problems. You could make Steven's wife something besides a photographer."

"But it's not you—"

"All I'm saying is, don't hurt people. Steven doesn't have to live upstate. He could live somewhere else."

"Yes, I can do that."

"It's not for myself I mind so much as it is for Clare. I don't mind being portrayed."

"I'll do it. I don't want to hurt anybody. I made it all up. I want to write, that's all."

"You should." He kissed her lightly, with regret. "It'll be an odd first novel—there's not too much sentimentality about it so far." Because she blinked at him unhappily, he added, "And that's good." The young man under the stamped-tin ceiling had written from ten at night until dawn. The words had marched out like soldiers. Eight cups of coffee through the night had jolted him to what he believed then was artistic frenzy and now knew was a caffeine kick. He'd greeted the morning expecting glory. The words hadn't brought him that.

She was kissing his hand. He tossed her manuscript down to his slippers on the frayed Oriental rug. She was kissing his stomach. His thigh. He fell into desire. He crept inside her, hoping there would be an exit sign or he'd never find his way out again. He fiddled her with an artless impatient finger and after a while knew from her continuing high-pitched whispered *oh*s that she hadn't come. It was his cock failing him again. He stopped and allowed her to please him instead. She did this gratefully, ardently. Across the room the table lamp blinked. He swelled with power and finally said in a conversational tone, "Oh. Yes."

Again her head lay on his chest and she snuggled against him. They drifted to drowsiness. "I'd like to be with you on a ship," he said, "a cruise on the Nile. On a houseboat. Imagine stepping out on land in the morning to go see the pyramids."

She burrowed deeper into his protecting arm. "Newm, if the Nazis come back, will you hide me?"

The young man under the stamped-tin ceiling tore up four stories and cried in a secondhand butterfly canvas chair. A booted foot, impeccably polished, banged at the door to his house upstate and menaced his wife and sons. Upstairs, the study, lined with books, had room for only one writer.

"The Nazis can't come back, because they've never been here." In the same extravagantly deliberate voice, he'd once explained away a son's fear of lightning. "But if they did come, then, no, I couldn't hide you because I might get into trouble myself."

She didn't move. Her breathing seemed to have stopped, the way a sleeping baby's breath sometimes suspended, the shadow of a crib bar across the baby's head. He returned to the pyramids. She sat up, and the space she had occupied against him became available and hollow, filled with possibilities.

The bed bounced as she left it. Watching bulrushes go by along the riverbank, he listened for the sound of peeing in the bathroom. He heard the closet door open. The bulrushes shriveled. He sat up and saw her getting dressed. Her breasts disappeared behind cloth. He'd seen that happen somewhere before.

"What is it?" he asked.

Her hair needed combing. Her small pale face seemed to concentrate its whiteness. Smudges of makeup ringed her gray eyes. In the beam of his waterproof flashlight he'd caught the startled face of a raccoon beneath an apple tree at night.

"You're being foolish," he said.

She took underpants from her purse and put them on under her skirt. She fastened her brown unswift sandals.

He got out of bed and went to the desk for his wallet. "Take a cab," he said, handing her a five-dollar bill.

She shook her head no. She picked up her manuscript from the rug.

"This isn't reasonable behavior," he said.

She left without combing her hair.

It was cool. At the top of the stairs she checked the dark street in both directions. A mugger with a dull carving knife might be waiting. A palm wrapped with red ribbon might follow her. The ginkgo trees she saw remained earthbound. If there were Nazis behind the ginkgos, she was on her own.

She darted down the stairs and ran the half-block to Fifth Avenue. There she stopped and looked behind her and to the sides. Four blocks down, floodlit Washington Square Arch curved over tourists and homeless natives and people scoring insecticide-sprayed oregano laced with grass. Uptown, Fifth Avenue unreeled light after light.

She held on to her manuscript as if it were a safety jacket on the *Titanic*. Nobody would be able to take it from her, not Larry or Newman or Howard. The Nazis could. She breathed in cool air, her heart a kettle drum struck during the Labor Day parade. She began to run. She was going home, wherever that was.

• • •

He heard the trap spring shut. Three daisies leaned in a water glass. Before them on the table a sketch pad lay opened to a blank page. He'd been sitting and holding a pen in readiness for almost half an hour. Now the closet held two problems: her clothes and a dead or dying rat. He wrote on the page,

Throw out her stuff.

He drew a line that coiled at the end. A rat's tail. He yawned. His mouth felt dry. He went to the fireplace, where he'd left the manuscript boxes from the copy store.

The two thousand pages were different pastel colors: yellow, pink, blue, green. He would have preferred deeper tones, but the printing wouldn't have shown up as well. He stacked the pages neatly in two rainbow piles and put each in a supermarket shopping bag. He carried the shopping bags to the door and left them there so he wouldn't forget them in the morning.

The window-shade pull tapped the sill. A cool gust surprised the room. He stopped typing because he couldn't decide what to call her. Should she be Mary or Linda? Sally, he thought. He would have to go back through the previous pages and change her name from Paula. Sally was close to Suzanne, but not dead center. He would have to do better about the husband: Harold was too close to Howard, and Glen was too far away.

The TV in the living room subsided. Barbra Streisand sang, toying with syllables. If Jonathan had given up TV for a record, the regular programs must have been preempted by political ones. Or by another hostage special, Islamic radicals strolling through the American embassy in Iran.

The song was about falling in love. Walking with him, Dina had explained what was wrong with his writing. Lowering sun colored her face, blued the black hair. A single straight hair jutted from one of her eyebrows. If he saw her that clearly, could he also see her seeing him clearly?

He pulled two large suitcases from under the bed and dusted them off.

"Hello."

"Clare?"

"Hi. You're early."

"Everything okay?"

"Better than okay. I'm going to have a show."

"Of what?"

"Pictures."

"Your benches?"

"No, the photographs of the patients. Mine and Bea's. Before and after. Unretouched."

"A medical show?"

"No. In a gallery in SoHo. A dealer came in with her daughter for a nose job and got this great idea."

"Whose nose job—the dealer's or the daughter's?"

"She wants us to blow them up to life-size. The doctors say it's okay if the patients say it's okay. She wants to do it all before Thanksgiving."

"Don't we all."

"Newman, are you glad for me?"

"I'm glad for you, Clare."

"Are you okay?"

"I'm very happy for you, Clare."

He hung up the phone and lay back in bed—the luxury of a call that didn't take place in the bathroom. That afternoon in therapy Steve had mentioned confronting solitude. It meant: no Dina, no distractions from unhappiness. "The idea doesn't excite me," he'd answered. He smelled her on his finger.

He took a pencil and pad from the night table and began to list, in no particular order, women he'd fucked. He tried to remember something special about each one, a grace note to place beside the name, if he remembered the name.

1. Alice—brsts
2. Georgianna—blnd pbc hr
3. ?—brsts
4. Dina—eyes
5. Alice (diff.)—Wolfgang
6. Maris—lion
7. Sheila—prls
8. Barbara—Freud
9. Jane—baths?

Women he hadn't thought of in years came back to him, their hair rising and falling like wings, their breasts giving refuge.

10. Marilee—bckwrds
11. Rhea—Szechuan
12. Gillian—frère Jacques
13. Noriko—gum
14. Amy—wrkrs of the wrld
15. Sylvia—loosestrife
16. Clare—

He thought a moment before writing beside her name:

exposures

Because he couldn't allow himself to end it there, he went on listing.

The doctor's office put him on hold before he could say anything. "Hello?" he shouted into a void. The woman from C.E.W.—the Committee for Endangered Writers—leafed through a back issue of *Rosemary* on the sofa. The receptionist's voice, West Indian, returned to demand "Yes?" as if he'd kept her waiting.

"My daughter needs shots for school," he said.

"Doctor has an opening in . . . two weeks."

"No, she needs it for next week."

"I'm sorry, if it's not an emergen—"

"They won't let her in school without the shots."

"I'm sorry, Doctor doesn't have—"

"It's an emergency. My wife's sick and I'm here at the office and my daughter needs shots and Dr. Grossman has to give them to her, he doesn't have to see her."

"What's your daughter's name?"

"Martha Ritchie."

"Uh-huh. Next Tuesday at nine."

"I can't—"

"I'm sorry, that's the only—"

"Okay. Next Tuesday at nine."

He replaced the receiver gently to prove he was still in control. Suzanne at a beach ten years ago smiled from a picture on the wall. To wipe that smile from her face, he dialed the Karatasi bookstore, imagining Dina beneath him in the white bed. He got a busy signal. Tried again. Busy.

The woman from C.E.W. said, "I'm sorry to hear your wife's

sick." She was in her late twenties and wore silver arrow earrings.

"It's nothing. She cut her foot. It might be a virus." He worked on a charming smile.

"There's a lot of that going around." Without a preamble, she named areas in the world where writers suffered censorship or imprisonment or worse. South Africa. Argentina. Russia. Her long blond ponytail shivered with emphasis. If her eyes hadn't been close together, two planets about to collide, she would have been pretty. Instead she was momentarily interesting.

She described the scars on the back of a South African poet imprisoned for four years with no charge ever brought and no trial. He finally got out of his country through the international efforts of various groups, a burst of acronyms that reminded Howard of comic-book sound effects: ZIP, ZAM, BIFF, ARGH, UMPHGH. "He's teaching literature in Utah now," she said.

That sounded worse than imprisonment.

A Russian writer had been committed to a psychiatric prison for six years because of his unpublished novel satirizing the Revolution.

"You all got him out?" Howard asked. The Russian would be teaching Pushkin in Fairbanks.

"No, he died there from an overdose of a tranquilizer. There's no way of knowing if it was an accident or murder or suicide. His wife, who's a biogeneticist, hasn't been able to get a job since he was imprisoned. Now that he's dead, they may let her leave. She has a fourteen-year-old son, a math genius of some kind. They may not let *him* leave. But you've heard about cases like these, Mr. Ritchie."

"Howard. Howard."

"Melanie." She wanted to give him an assortment of manuscripts from endangered writers. "If there are any you see fit to publish in *Rosemary*, great. It would be a great help in publicizing our work."

"I'm all for endangered writers," he said. "But I publish only what I think belongs in the magazine."

"Sure. If you don't find anything you can use to help us, I hope we can still send you more." She patted a foot-high stack of manuscripts, tied with twine, on the floor. "There are always more. I'm sure in all of these you can find one—"

"I didn't find one in all of those," he said, indicating three stacks of submissions against the wall. They were from unendangered writers. "But you can give me whatever you like."

"If you could find room for a poem, with an accompanying note."

"There's always room for a poem if it's good."

The blond ponytail bounced fervently. "Sometimes, Mr. Ritchie, there's a need to look beyond literary merits."

"Not in a literary magazine. I could publish a note, unaccompanied by a poem—unless it's a good one. Otherwise, you should try a newspaper."

"You can't ignore politics, Mr. Ritchie, and pursue some pure literary goal as if there were no real world with repressive governments bearing down on dissent."

"Why not? That's what the endangered writers do." He gave himself a point, reconsidered, and added another. "How about lunch? I'm supposed to meet the critic Newman Sykes a couple of blocks away. Maybe he can help you."

He called Dina one more time. Still busy. He slammed down the phone.

She was taller than he was, and her stride was longer. Hands in his pockets, he struggled to keep up with her. She ignored traffic lights. All the way to the restaurant she rattled off the names of the missing and the wounded and the dead. Before he saw Newman's serene face in the crowded back room, he grabbed a waiter's sleeve and demanded Chivas on the spot. "My stars," the would-be actor said, smoothing his sleeve.

"This is Ellen," Howard told Newman. "She's a liaison."

"Melanie," she said.

"She wants to make the world safe for writers."

"How about making it safe *from* writers?" Newman lifted his empty glass. He wasn't serene. He was unobtrusively, critically drunk.

"Have another," Howard said. "What is it?"

"Vodka."

"I'll have Perrier," Melanie said.

"She's writing a book about you," Newman told Howard.

"No I'm not," Melanie said.

"She's got me in it too, but you're the center of it, and anybody who knows you or knows about you, everybody who counts, is going to know it's you."

"I'm not," Melanie said again.

"It's not about me," Howard said. "It's a novel."

"It is," Newman answered. "All about you."

The waiter proffered Chivas and a leading man's smile beneath his leading man's mustache. Howard snatched up the drink.

"Perrier with lime," Melanie told the waiter. "And vodka for him." She pointed at Newman. "And hurry." The waiter hurried.

"I told her to change things, I told her to disguise things," Newman said. "She thinks I'm a Nazi. Maybe that's why I'm not more prominent in the book. I said people could get hurt."

"*She* could get hurt," Howard said mournfully, lifting his face from the glass. A woman had once taken a Polaroid of him in her bed. He'd lunged for the camera and ended up cutting his chin on the lens rim. He shredded the picture—a headless, very thin nude man holding a cigarette on a tartan blanket—and carried the pieces back to his office, where he threw them away after turning his pocket inside out to make sure they were all gone. "I'm not losing Matty. And not *Rosemary*. Never." He underlined *never* by banging his glass on the table. Chivas Regal sloshed over his hand.

"Waiter," Melanie called.

"We can see that it dies. People owe us. I can see that it doesn't get reviewed anywhere important. You can see that it doesn't get talked about. What are you going to do?" Newman asked Howard.

"I'm going to have another drink. And then I'm going to kill her." He licked his hand.

"Should I get us menus or what?" Melanie asked.

・ ・ ・

He left the blond ponytail with Newman and walked to his office, smoldering. He would call Dina. He would call a lawyer. He would call a hit man.

It was snowing around the building. Pink and green and yellow and blue sheets of paper drifted down. From across the street he saw a man standing on the roof and scattering papers as if he were sowing seed.

Papers floated over the campus. Reinhardt the Joycean leaned out his office window and grabbed a green page. Other hands from other windows did the same. Students and teachers were picking up pages from the ground and reading them. Cars ran over pages in the street. Two grim campus cops with fistfuls of pages entered the building.

He picked up a few pages that had fallen near him. They all were the same—copies of a letter addressed to the president of the university.

Dear Sir,
    The ones who believe they possess the truth, are dangerous. They corrupt the ones who . . .

It was Rabuchin's letter, the same one he'd personally delivered to the office. Matty had cried. The only change was an addition at the bottom. Under "P.S. I am a citizen" he'd typed:

LAURITS'S FLORALITY on Horatio Street.
Formerly Ralph's Florist.

On the roof the two campus cops grabbed Rabuchin. He kicked a shopping bag over the edge. Hundreds more pages spilled out, a poisonous rainbow riding a breeze. Pigeons flapped to get out of the way.

Howard stuffed pages in the ample pockets of his cotton cardigan. He didn't have enough room, though, to hide all the copies. Accusations spread around him, bared him to ungenerous judgment. He couldn't face Reinhardt or Gail or Liliane at the office. He couldn't face Suzanne at home. He waved frantically at a cab, leaped inside it, shouting the address of the Karatasi bookstore, and expected to hear a satisfying screech as the cab took off. It lumbered up to a red light instead, and he sat digging his fist into a split in the vinyl upholstery.

Near revolving doors a few buildings away, she watched him gather up pages. This time she had the pink snakeskin billfold with her. She could prove everything. There were bandages and flat shoes on her feet. Her dress was the same one from the day before, and she had no makeup on. She'd gotten up too late for niceties and missed following him at lunch. She wouldn't let that happen again. If she was good, very good, he would lead her, she knew, to the end of all her unhappiness. On separate beaten sofas they would have iced tea with Jo at the store. "My wife doesn't lie," he'd say. "Not this sweetie."

She picked up several pages from the ground and folded them into her purse. Green and blue corners of pages poked through the shut frame like tongues.

She got into a cab behind him. "Go wherever that cab's going," she said. The seat was warm.

"It all depends," the driver said, hitting the accelerator.

A halfhearted breeze came through the window. She took a blue page from her purse and began reading. . . . *They corrupt the ones who are young and impressive.* Howard's cab was two cars away in the next lane. *It is a double crime when the victim is an artist.* . . . The lights were green for blocks. *There is a man who seduces under the name of literature. He is one of your teachers Howard Ritchie.* A mockingbird flew out of her dress. The white markings on its wings were a code. *He has taken a sweet and loving woman.* . . . Howard's cab ran a yellow light and sped away. She slid forward and back as her cab halted at the light.

"It doesn't matter," she said, and she gave the driver the address of the Karatasi bookstore.

I know you must do something about this.

She arrived in time to see her husband throw a cigarette on the sidewalk and go into the store.

The door simply opened. Nobody knocked. She thought it was Vincent, though she didn't know why he'd show up again. Howard said, "I want to talk to you."

She sat cross-legged in the white bed, holding her notebook and pen. In his thin colorless face and narrowed eyes she verified her portrait of Ned. Tenderness for him—Howard or Ned, she couldn't tell which—swelled in her. "Hi. I thought you were going to call," she said.

"I'll sue you. I'll get you," he said more clearly than he'd ever said anything to her before. "You can't write a book about me."

Tenderness vanished. "It's fiction." She put the notebook under her. The spiral metal spine pressed against her jeans. "And you can't tell me what to write."

"If you're going to steal my entire life and screw it up, yes, I can."

"It's not your life." Was it his life? If someone used something of hers, a pen or a sweater, or had a piece of paper she'd written on, she worried that she'd lost a part of herself. Someone wearing her sweater might absorb part of her soul. There was spirit, too, in her handwriting; and when she'd lived with Larry and paid bills, she hated signing the blue checks because one of them might get lost and never come back canceled from the bank. It would pass undefended through abuse at the hands of strangers before fluttering into a mass grave for checks in a triple-locked basement on Wall Street, where her signature would lie against a chartreuse check that had a picture of a daisy on it and was signed by a schizophrenic with leprosy who picked his/her nose. "You haven't read it. What makes you think it's about you?"

"Newman told me. He's my friend."

"Great. He thinks it's about him too."

"No, he says it's mostly about me. All about me. I'll lose

my family. I'll lose my job. As a teacher I'm supposed to give the illusion of conforming to the community's illusions of its morals."

When his hand moved toward her, she flinched. He held out a crumpled green page. "After this," he said, "I may not have a job to lose anyway."

Reading the page, she heard the creak of floorboards under his feet. *She is my wife. I need to find her and deprogram her.* "Larry sent this to you?" she asked.

"No, he was on a roof, dropping hundreds of them over the campus just now. It was like a ticker-tape parade, with no parade. The cops stopped him."

"Is he all right?"

"I don't care."

"Did they arrest him?"

"They probably threw him off campus. They should've flayed him. Or flogged him. Or whatever." He sat on the edge of the bed and slumped over. "And here you are, the literary gossip columnist."

She tucked her feet closer to her body so they wouldn't touch him. "Are you drunk?"

His head down, he nodded. "I know what I'm saying."

She could have put her hand on his shoulder, he was that near. He wasn't going to hold her ever again. The idea of *never* fattened between them. She remembered who she'd been when they were fucking. He wasn't her character Ned because she loved Ned and she didn't love him. She touched his shoulder.

"Howard, I'm not doing anything to hurt you."

He presented his woeful pinched face. "I can understand that you're writing about me." His beautiful smile began. "We had some interesting afternoons here. And here we are."

"No." She shook her head and laughed. He watched her for a moment before he joined in her laughter. She took his hand and kissed it quickly. "You're too dangerous for me."

His brown eyes widened. "I'm afraid it's the other way around."

• • •

Her reddish hair grew above a poster for *The Great Dictator*. She'd hidden behind the Coming Attractions easel of the theater as Howard came out of the bookstore. When he turned the corner, she went to the bookstore.

The halter woman wasn't there, but a bald brown man was. She could tell he was gay. She knew the secrets in all the books on the shelves without reading them. She opened one to a poem in Italian and stared at it. It was shaped like a house with a mansard roof.

"I want to buy something. For my husband." She went close to the brown man because he was kind.

"Poetry?"

"Yes." She waited for him to give her a book for Howard.

"Any particular poet?"

"I'll take this." She hugged the book with the Italian poem in it. "And do you have *Bandaged Moments*?"

He went to get it behind high shelves. The only other customer, a white-haired man at the Judaica section, had his back to her. She leaned across the counter and took a pen and a set of keys from a shelf below the cash register. They were souvenirs, like ashtrays from hotels. She dropped them in her purse. She'd hoped to find a clue to the halter woman's name. The white-haired man sneezed mightily. She didn't have the right to say bless you. The brown man returned with Vincent's book. She'd read it in bed with Howard, the pages heavy on her midriff. The brown man put it and the Italian poetry book in a blue and white plastic shopping bag that said KARATASI. She had counted out eleven dollars when she saw Vincent.

He told her she looked fine, and she answered that not much could have happened to change her since yesterday. Her dress was dirty across the front. Lace at the low neckline wilted. He offered to take her home. She said no, dignified as a nun. She might have whipped out a ruler and smacked his hands. He told her he was sorry, she asked what he was sorry for. When she saw Dina coming down the stairs, she whispered to him, "Please. Introduce us."

"I'm in a hurry," Dina told him. She didn't say hello. Seeing her, small and intent, made him forget what he was supposed to say. She nodded at Suzanne.

"Don't you work here?" Suzanne asked.

Dina smiled politely. "Dan'll help you." She seemed to be trying to place the other woman. "Were you here yesterday?"

Bask said, "This is a friend. You two should know each other. Dina Leitman, Suzanne Ritchie."

Dina's polite smile petrified. It had been painted on by somebody with a palsy.

He got the idea that he'd made the introduction wrong. "See, Suzanne's married to Howard, who knows all about books, and Dina's a writer who lives in a bookstore. And Howard published one of Dina's stories."

"It must be a very good story." Suzanne's mouth tightened around the words. "What issue is it in?"

"Howard's a very good editor," Dina said.

A gross unease had settled, like ashes from a volcano, over the women. They would be preserved in this moment for thousands of years, the way the bodies had been at Pompeii. Bask was glad he wasn't the future archeologist who would discover them.

Dina blushed. "I should've recognized you. Howard has beautiful pictures of you in his office."

"I'll have to give him a more current one," Suzanne said.

Dina glanced at the white-haired man at the Judaica section. "Is Howard still here?"

"No, he's gone. Gone," Dan said from behind the counter. "We didn't have the book he wanted. Nice to meet you, Mrs. Ritchie."

"And what book was that?" Suzanne asked.

"I'm sorry I missed him," Bask said.

"Me too," Suzanne said.

"Why no Chagall?" the white-haired man asked.

"Under Art," Dan answered.

"I must apologize, but I'm in a hurry." Dina edged toward the door.

"You can't help that," Suzanne said.

Bask squeezed her hand. It was cold. "I'm rushing too."

"One minute, Mrs. Ritchie," Dan said. "Let's see if we can't order that book for Howard. Let's see."

The book she agreed to order was about the Dead Sea scrolls or the life of Elinor Wylie. "What about Pissarro?" the white-haired man asked. "Under France," Dan answered.

She left the bookstore and walked until she came to a drug-store on University Place. She held the door open for a woman with a baby in a stroller. There was a special on ear syringes. She bought a bottle of aspirin, a toothbrush with a black and white striped handle, a pack of cigarettes—Howard's brand—with matches, two cans of lighter fluid, and a can of powdered infant formula. On the street she threw the aspirin and cigarettes and formula in a garbage can. She put the toothbrush in her purse. It was getting full. She put the cans of lighter fluid and the matches in the Karatasi shopping bag. If you added water to powdered infant formula, did you get an infant? She went across the street to a Greek coffee shop, decided on a tuna salad sandwich on white, no extra mayo, with a glass of milk, and took out Vincent's book to read again.

He loped beside her for a block. She worked hard to keep running and he worked hard not to pass her.

At the corner, waiting for the light, he asked, "Where are we going?"

She wiped her forearm across her face and managed to say, "I didn't invite you."

"I came to say goodbye," he said. She was too short, too thin. You could snap her in two at the waist. She wouldn't be able to carry a backpack in mountain country. They walked west along Tenth Street, a block down from the house she'd visited the night before. "I think we should sit at a table together and do our writing. It's nice to write with somebody there."

"I don't know about that." She walked as fast as she could, and he sauntered along beside her. On Sixth Avenue he stopped at a deli and bought a bag of salt-free pretzels. He had no trouble catching up with her on Greenwich Avenue. "You just broke up with somebody," she said. "So did I—with three people."

"You think I'm lonely and that's all?"

"I think I'm going to write and that's all. I'm going to try and write."

"Backtracking so soon? Have some," he said.

She still had a few pretzels in her hand when they got to a flower shop on Horatio Street. The wooden sign was cut in the shape of a tulip and painted orange with green lettering: LAURITS'S FLORALITY. There were no lights on. The door was locked. He wondered why she didn't buy flowers at a place nearer the bookstore. The man walking toward them wasn't carrying a potted palm tree tied with red ribbon, but Bask recognized the spitefulness. "Here comes Dale Carnegie," he said.

"The princess and her bodyguard," the man called in greeting. Strands of his long honey hair stuck to his neck. As he unlocked the shop door, his hands shook. He closed the door behind him and turned on the lights.

"No," she said when Bask started to follow her inside the shop.

She held out a green copy of his letter. A philodendron vine from a hanging basket groped her forehead.

"You like it?" he asked. "I wasn't too sure about some of the grammar, but that's nitpicking. Basically, I think it's brilliant."

The shop was cool. In a plastic bucket on the counter, a sheaf of gladioli, peach buds furled, aimed at the ceiling.

"I'm not coming back," she said.

"Do you like the sign? I did it myself." He'd trimmed his mustache.

"What's 'florality'?"

"I think of it as the morality of flowers." He poured water into a bucket of day lilies.

"We're split up. No more together. Ever."

"You're sweating, you know that?"

"I hope your store's a big success, I hope you get a great apartment, but you can stop writing letters because I'm not coming back and Howard Ritchie has nothing to do with it."

"Little one, don't do this so grownup and tough. You're full of shit, but I love you. Smile a little." His blue eye winked at her.

"That's good. The maudlin act."

He grinned. "Listen, baby—"

"Don't call me that."

"Listen. Cézanne used to take so long to paint that the apples he set up for a still life rotted. So he switched to paper flowers because they wouldn't rot. But he took so long to paint them that he said, 'They fade, the bitches.' Isn't that perfect?"

"Bye, Larry."

"Don't you want to kiss me goodbye?"

"No. Want a pretzel?"

"No. Want a rose?"

"No."

He was leaning against a brick wall, his chin up, when she came out. Sun kindled his red-gold hair. The empty pretzel bag stuck out of his shirt pocket.

"Let's get some juice or milk or something," he said.

"I have to work. And I have to go to the laundromat."

"Infinitely preferable to seeing me. How about after you do all that?"

She rolled her eyes and shook her head no, and he knew he was getting somewhere.

"It'll just be for a couple of hours. I'm leaving tomorrow."
He wrote his address at Jonathan's and his phone number on the
torn corner of a piece of green paper she gave him. "You like
Chinese food? It's great late at night. We can go to an arcade in
Chinatown and play Asteroids."

She put the scrap of paper in her jeans pocket and didn't
answer.

Maybe he would put off leaving for a few days. "Call me,"
he said.

She nodded, and he decided it might be better to leave that
night instead of in the morning.

She spent the afternoon in the coffee shop, rereading pages
of *Bandaged Moments*. She liked an argument between Father Boisvert and Lulu.

> "Sex is part of the Divine plan, not a plot. Carry a pack of
> Trojans in your pocket on Saturday night, but it doesn't make you
> a man."
> Lulu zipped up his jacket defiantly. "Yeah, but it helps keep
> me from being a husband."

She had a piece of Black Forest cake. She had two refills of
coffee. At the pay phone near the kitchen a chain yanked at the
phone book when she opened it. Heat and cries in Spanish came
from the kitchen. She checked under Lightman, Lietman, Leitman, Liteman, Lytman, Leytman, Lyetman, and Leyetman, but
there wasn't any Dina or D. She lived in the bookstore, just as
Vincent had said. There wasn't any Laurits Rabuchin, either.
Suzanne wondered if Rabuchin's wife—Howard's other lover,
according to the blue letter—knew about Dina Leitman. Did they
all go to bed together, trading literary insights? She could try
that. She'd read Tolstoy, even if she'd skipped the boring parts.
She found Newman Sykes listed, with an address on West Eleventh Street. Dina Leitman might be there. Suzanne had a vanilla
milk shake and French fries.

In late evening she walked to Eleventh Street. At the garden entry of a brownstone across the street from Newman Sykes's place, she crouched behind a stone planter on a pedestal and peeked through ivy. There was a spider web in the ivy, connecting threads from leaf to leaf. Inside the planter were balled-up gum wrappers and a twofer for an off-Broadway musical. She had to get a message to Dina Leitman. The ivy shivered in a breeze. It would be a message about the limits of selfishness. Something soft rubbed against her legs. She was too frightened to scream. It was a cat, gray or apricot. Only white on its paws showed clearly in the dark. Hugging the bag from the Karatasi bookstore, she stepped out in front of the ivy and stood openly on the sidewalk.

They were three pages into Chapter II, "The Pool of Tears." Matty'd had her bath and smelled of the designer soap he'd given Suzanne for Mother's Day. He'd already had four juice glasses of Grand Marnier, a Christmas gift from the print shop that turned out *Rosemary*. The bottle wouldn't have lasted so long— wouldn't have lasted past January, in fact—but for some reason it had been left in its red and green foil-wrapped carton on the floor of the hall closet. He discovered it when he came home that afternoon and dropped his laundry ticket while hanging up his cardigan. He wouldn't have discovered it at all if Suzanne had attended to the laundry the way she was supposed to. If his luck held, he would be around to get another bottle next Christmas; and he would send it, with his own greetings replacing the print-er's, to the university president. That hoarse tenor on the office phone a few hours earlier had promised, "I'm keeping an eye on you, Mr. Ritchie. Our reputation doesn't benefit from a deranged husband's bill of particulars darkening the sky over our campus. You may be completely innocent of any wrongdoing. You may not. I stood by Professor Diamond until the jury returned a verdict of guilty. It turned out he actually had been manufacturing speed in the chem lab. I believe in free enterprise, but I was disappointed. He was using school materials. In your case, Mr. Ritchie, I would advise you: when in doubt, keep your pants on."

He read aloud, pausing for sips from ineffably smooth glass number five. The book, a 1938 red leather-bound edition of *Alice's Adventures in Wonderland* with gilt-edged hand-sewn pages and four-color Tenniel pictures and an engraving of Lewis Carroll's signature in red on the title page, had cost fifty-five dollars at a cubbyhole bookstore flaunting its quaintness on Madison Avenue. "I'll give you forty-five," he told a robust old woman at the register. She chewed on a tiger's milk candy bar. "How about if we forget the tax?" he asked. He had to salvage something from this day of endangered writers and accusing letters and an insubordinate former mistress and a sullen, disappearing wife. Her mouth full, the old woman asked, "Cash?"

The cream-colored handmade paper hadn't yellowed; black Caslon Old Style type bit sharply into it. The slipcase, with a red leather spine and marbled paper covering, had faded spots and a blue inkstain. He could have bought a paperback edition with black and white drawings and a glopped glue binding for under three dollars, but he hoped luxury would impress Matty with the importance of the occasion. He was making amends for his negligence; somehow she had gotten far along in life without knowing this book. She wasn't going to hear a story, she was going to have an experience.

He sipped and mumbled,

"I'm sure I'm not Ada," she said, "for her hair goes in such long ringlets, and mine doesn't go in ringlets at all; and I'm sure I can't be Mabel, for I know all sorts of things, and she, oh, she knows such a very little! Besides, *she's* she, and *I'm* I, and—oh dear, how puzzling it all is! I'll try if I know all the things I used to know. Let me see: four times five is twelve, and four times six is thirteen, and . . ."

"You get the idea," he said. "Four times five isn't twelve."
"I know, Daddy," she said. "I know long division."
"You look bored. Are you bored?"

"I like it when you read to me. But I'm sorry Mommy missed dinner."

"I'm sure she's sorry too."

"When is she coming home?"

"When she does, she'll come in and kiss you while you're sleeping."

"Then how will I know?"

"You'll know."

"But how?"

Sitting at the foot of the bed, he leaned against the wall, to get more comfortable. From under the covers her toes pushed his thigh over the covers. "You have enough room?" he asked. He took another sip and lost his place. He ended up two pages ahead of himself, near the end of the chapter. After he read a paragraph, he said, "Something's not right." Matty didn't answer. She was sleeping.

It came back to him, not the way he'd imagined it would, not as a reward or praise, but it came back. He was standing naked at the window of the dark apartment, waiting to call Clare. He turned off the air conditioner—the night was cool enough—and opened the window. Down on the street a man backed an old convertible into a parking spot in front of the building. A woman on the sidewalk gave the man directions. "Keep going, keep going. I said keep going." The car's headlights didn't clear the rear fender of the car in front of it. The man shouted, "Forget it." The woman got in the car and they drove off.

That was when he saw the other woman, standing on the sidewalk across the street. She seemed to be looking up at his apartment. She clutched a package. In darkness and the shifting shadows of ginkgo leaves, she seemed to be looking up at him. She didn't move. He thought he knew her, or he wished he knew her. She might not have been real. Her face in shadows pledged forgiveness. He might have imagined her, so powerful was his desire for an angel against reason and tidiness. If she had held out her arms, he would have gone to her, naked as he was. The pressure of her fingers on his forehead would absolve him of thought. He wanted her to bless him, and his cock stood up.

The bathroom door opened behind him. A strip of light showed his nakedness to the street; he moved away from the window. "Please turn off the light."

The light went off. When he looked down at the street again, the angel was gone.

"Why don't you close the curtains?" Melanie asked, blond ponytail loosened. She was still undressed, all hipbone and cheerfulness. Hugging him, she discovered his erection. "Well, well," she said proudly. "I told you not to worry." She closed the curtains and turned on a light.

He squeezed his cock, stroked it. He admired its tension and its deepening color and the drop of clear liquid glistening at the head. He wanted to wave it out the window at passers-by. He wanted to call Clare and say, Guess what. He became afraid that it wouldn't get hard again unless he did whatever he had done to get it hard now.

"Come here," Melanie said.

On the way back to bed with her, he wondered what he was supposed to do next.

She thought of pumpkin bread. If Dina Leitman and Newman Sykes were in the house across the street, they were hiding. It was too early for pumpkins. A light went on. She saw a naked man at a window. He disappeared. It would have to be zucchini bread. Sift flour. Walking back to the bookstore, Suzanne tried to remember ingredients. The Karatasi shopping bag hit her knee. She didn't know if Dina Leitman would be there. It was closed. She had to return the keys anyway.

One fit the top lock, one the bottom. Her cleverness frightened her. She went inside the dark store. Through the front window stacked with books a street lamp lighted tables of books. Top-heavy bookcases leaned toward her. She passed through their shadows.

She put the keys back on the shelf under the cash register and left the shopping bag on the counter. She took copies of Laurits Rabuchin's letter and the store's pen from her purse and set them on the counter too.

The stairs curved up and away from her. The second step creaked. She tested the next step with a cautious foot. She'd met the Atlantic Ocean with the same foot fifteen years before. A band of seaweed wrapped her ankle. Climbing to the balcony, she heard a woman's voice. A door opened on a lighted room. She squinted into the crack along the hinged side of the door. Dina Leitman was sitting alone in a bed and reading aloud from a notebook. Everything around her was white.

It was terrible to be young and ignorant. It was worse to get old and still be ignorant. A scholarship named for Dina Leitman would be really nice.

" 'He turns her over and enters her from behind; in her new-found freedom she wails with excitement and fear. . . .' " Dina Leitman scribbled something, went on reading. " 'He turns her over and enters her from behind; in her new-found freedom she sees only her hands opening on the orange sheet, and she wails in pleasure and in fear.' "

It sounded like something Howard would approve of. If she could write, she would write like Dina Leitman. They might have been friends. The wood doorframe was cool at her cheek. They looked a little bit alike, she thought. The reading voice faded. The next-to-last step creaked again.

Downstairs, she emptied the shopping bag on the counter: the two books, the two cans of lighter fluid, and the matches. She sprinkled lighter fluid on the books. Dust with flour. She struck a match and dropped it on the books and leaped back. There was a flash, then flame. She waited for the flame to spread, but it went out, leaving blackened patches on the Italian poetry book. The cover of *Bandaged Moments* curled.

She ripped out a page of poetry, crumpled it into a ball, sprinkled it with lighter fluid, and added a lighted match. The page burned on the counter. As it burned, it opened and closed like a fist. She ripped out another page and fed it flat to the first one. It fluttered, it writhed. A cinder flew out. The fire died in ashes.

She moved a wicker trash basket from behind the counter and put it at the foot of the stairs. A rattan sliver punctured her forefinger, produced a bead of blood. She licked it off, testing the flavor. She tore the cellophane wrapping off *250 Years of Japanese Art*, by Neuer and Yoshida. The cellophane crackled as she pressed it between her hands. She added it, and the copies of Rabuchin's letter, to the paper already in the basket. She baptized the trash with lighter fluid, but didn't ignite it.

In the stacks where Dan had gone that afternoon, she found

more copies of *Bandaged Moments*. The pages she tore out of a copy blotted blood from her finger. She dropped them on the floor. Add lighter fluid. Stir gently.

Among a bin of prints were some wrapped in cellophane: old lithographs of beruffled men with captions in French, maps of the world depicting the four corners occupied by personified winds, their cheeks bulging with air. Fold in lighter fluid.

She dropped a lighted match on the prints, another on the pages from *Bandaged Moments*, and another in the wicker basket at the foot of the stairs. It was like lighting a birthday cake. Three flames burned steadily in the large room.

The familiar carved *R* caught her eye at a table of paperbacks: a Winter '74 issue of *Rosemary*. She spread it open until the spine cracked, and pulled it apart. She arranged the pages along the bottom of the stairs, leading up from the burning wicker basket, and poured the rest of the lighter fluid over them.

The darkened store had come alive. There was a pleasant hushed rustling in the stacks. The bin of prints flared. Burning cellophane oozed down to the floor, to the pages spread there. Near the stairs the basket glowed.

She took her library card from her wallet and tossed it in the basket. The heat at her hand surprised her. Something dropped. A print had bowed, burning, to the floor. Flames followed the arch. It was more beautiful burning than it had been as a print. She wished she could kiss the flames, they were so beautiful. The pressure on her bladder felt worse than it had when she was carrying Matty. She pulled down her pants and squatted on the floor and peed. She patted herself dry with the hem of her dress. Another print fell, and across the room the basket itself caught fire. It shimmered inside a suit of flame. Pages of *Rosemary* on the floor beside it lighted.

On the rare nights when company had visited with her parents, she'd felt cheated by her father's announcement, "Time for bed, sunshine." Now too she left regretfully, knowing she would miss the best part.

● ● ●

The prints burned. Paint on the wall changed to alligator skin. Pages of *Bandaged Moments* made a trail of fire on the floor. Flames spread up along the books in the stacks, feeding on up-standing loose pages, torn paperback covers, unfiled pamphlets of avant-garde poetry on recycled paper. The metal shelves heated; *The Flies of Western North America*, by Cole and Schlinger, warmed beside *The South Goes North*, by Robert Coles, which wasn't sup-posed to be in that section. On a bottom shelf an aisle over, the bound uncorrected proofs of a book about Van Eyck, *The Quest for Mrs. Arnolfini*, by Lee Vight, Ph.D., browned along with Vasari's *Lives of the Artists* and Vlaminck's *Dangerous Corner*. The basket and the pages from *Rosemary* joined in flames at the foot of the stairs, where the first riser and the first tread smoldered.

The paragraph was as good as it was going to get, no matter how many times she read it aloud. Her throat hurt. She checked her jeans pocket for the scrap of paper with Vincent Bask's num-ber. Going out with him would be something else to write about. It wasn't a date, it was material. Her face crowded her compact mirror.

At the open door of her room she hesitated, hearing noise downstairs. Burglars hoping for free best-sellers? Or was Dan working? Light flickered on the normally dim balcony. The shadow of the balcony railing wavered on the back wall. She stepped out into heat and light.

Below her, the store burned. Steel struts twisted and steel shelves relaxed. Books—it might have been the poetry section—tumbled to the floor. Shelving collapsed on top of them. The bin of prints on fire crashed. At the bottom of the stairs a black pattern of basket broke in the heart of flames. Three steps were on fire.

Screaming his name, she ran to Dan's apartment. She turned on the light and saw a room like hers, plain, with everything in it painted white, except that he had three black and white pho-tograph posters on a wall: Lenin, Lincoln, and Ray Charles. The light went out.

She ran to her room—the light was out there too—and in darkness relieved only by stars and a clouded fragment of moon through the skylight she collected her manuscript, much of it the only copy of new writing, and added the picture of her dead dog. By the time she ran back to the balcony with her pages in her arms, the fire had climbed more than halfway up the stairs. From down in the store came a loud popping. Flames reached as high as the top shelves of bookcases, eight feet and up. Another strut sighed and collapsed. Books flew into the flames. It was part of the used anthropology section. Smoke thickened over the fallen bookcase. Above her the ceiling groaned. Sprinklers spat water, a brief hissing in flames; the sprinklers stopped. A wall of heat pressed against her. The fire advanced up the stairs.

Again she ran to Dan's room, thinking to escape through the window. It had bars on it. Beyond them she saw a brick wall and the dark street behind the store. She took a white chair and, keeping her pages on the seat, carried it back to her room and shut the door.

The chair wobbled on the bed. Balanced precariously, she reached to the skylight. It was high above her. She climbed down cautiously: she would die by fire and not of a broken neck. "Help me!" she screamed. "Help!" The smell of smoke filled the room. She sat down on the white bed and cried.

The call to the 911 operator came from a woman. She sounded almost sleepy. She gave an address and added, as an afterthought, "There's a fire there. Really."

She tucked the white bedspread along the doorsill. At the sides and top of the door smoke drifted in. It stung her eyes and made her cough. Heat scratched her face. It wasn't happening to her. In California at that moment her mother and father were watching a movie on TV. She was trapped in the movie they were watching. She wanted her mother to hold her and say everything would be fine. She wanted to apologize to everybody she had ever met. Her life had been so short and pointless, she thought, that she had enough time for it to flash before her eyes twice. She wished she had been a grownup woman who'd written books and loved a man and had a baby, all in a hurry. She'd been worrying that she wasn't real; now she would learn how painfully real she was.

She flew above her terror to take notes—*she wishes she'd been kinder; fear makes her clutch the bedspread*—so that if she survived, she'd be able to write about it. "You're weird," she said aloud between coughs.

She heard sirens far away. Wood crackled outside the door. Or it was the door crackling. "I'm here!" she screamed. *Now she knows it's too late, now she knows she's going to die. She hopes she dies from smoke inhalation, not burning. She should have paid attention over the years to newspaper stories headlined "Tragic Fire in Brooklyn Kills Six." Always the same headline. Didn't the victims die of smoke inhalation? She doesn't want to be a victim in a newspaper story. She's somewhere else, laughing, with sun in her eyes. It's a field bordered by flowering trees. Central Park? A dog leaps up for a Frisbee. She shades her eyes with her hand.*

"Help!"

Something exploded, and she thought the building was collapsing. Fragments struck her where she huddled on the floor. They sparkled in the dimness. A second explosion sounded closer. The skylight shattered. She closed her eyes against glass raining on the bed, the floor, her shoulders. When she opened her eyes, the skylight's wire mesh had torn open and was giving birth to a fireman.

A black helmet dipped. A ladder touched down on the bed. Black rubber arms reached for her. She started to climb up but turned back for her manuscript.

"Forget it," the fireman shouted.

One-handed, she climbed to him. With her other hand she pressed the manuscript to her side. The picture of her dead dog slipped away.

"The man who owns the store?" she called.

"He's outside."

The fireman delivered her through the skylight. A wave of air struck her. She tucked the manuscript under her arm and shivered on the roof.

"You're crazy," he said. The helmet hid his eyes. His face was dirty. He pulled her after him over the side of the roof.

Another ladder took them a long cold way down toward red lights flashing. They were escaping from one fire to another. When she tried to steady herself, her hand grazed stubble on his cheek. A dark wall passed, and a red light picked up the dull gleam of a drainpipe following them down. He had her balanced against his rubber shoulder. "I think I'm going to fall," she said calmly.

"I never lost a crazy girl yet," he said, and his grip on her tightened.

It made her sad that the ground was getting closer. She wanted to keep traveling on his shoulder and never arrive. Other hands reached for her. "Will you marry me?" she whispered to him.

"I'm married," he whispered back. "But I got a brother Salvatore out on the Island."

The street danced under her. Someone put a blanket around her shoulders, as if she'd run a marathon.

"What's the name of the man who carried me down?" she asked.

"Stand back, sweetheart."

Dan was hugging her and her manuscript. He smelled like clean air. His beard kissed her. "I looked for you," she told him.

"Stretch the line," a voice shouted.

"Hey, Lieutenant," another voice shouted.

"I was coming home," he said.

"What the fuck was it?" a voice shouted.

Firemen hefting long hooks went into the burning store. Some of the men wore masks and had yellow tanks on their backs.

With their coats and boots, they might have been overdressed scuba divers.

"I don't think there's anything left in there," she said.

"I had a first English edition of *Godot* and a first edition of *Young Lonigan*. I'll miss them." Tears were running down his face. "Only thing to do is, start another bookstore."

"Can you?"

"Child, I've got friends. And as an American I've got something else." Crying, he grinned at her. "I've got insurance."

He sat up. The phone was ringing. The fifty-five-dollar *Alice* slipped from his chest to the sheet. Matty was sleeping, her face buried between the pillow and the sheet so that only her blond hair showed.

He answered the phone in the living room and checked his watch. His back hurt, his mouth was dry. Past eleven-thirty. He heard Suzanne. There were voices in the background, and a phone ringing. She might have been at a bar. She asked him softly if he would come and see her be arraigned in a courtroom downtown.

"Yes, I will," he said.

"Do you want to know what I did?"

"I'll find out soon enough."

He arranged for his neighbor, Mrs. 9-C, to stay with Matty, who was still sleeping. Portly in a snagged navy terrycloth kimono, the woman brought with her a copy of *TV Guide* and two teabags. "I'm allergic," she said. He thanked her and gave her the remote-control gun. She had questions about the zoom-in button.

Finding a lawyer was harder to do. The last one he'd dealt with had been Smiling Bob McGrath, Margery's champion. Michaels of Russian Studies wasn't home; the Thalia was running an eight-hour version of a twelve-hour Russian production of *War and Peace* with subtitles. Reinhardt the Joycean, awakened and feisty, said he had made it a guiding principle of his life never to do anything that needed a lawyer. "That downpouring letter about you today was agreeably excessive. Did you write it?" he asked. Reluctantly Howard called Bob Small, who was a lawyer. Anne answered the phone and, when she heard Howard's voice, hung up. A woman he'd had an affair with in February was a lawyer, but she'd moved to Taos to become a potter. By the end of their affair she wouldn't talk to him. He had no time to ponder his effect on women. Of the two writers he knew who weren't impoverished or undergoing detoxification, one lived without a phone but with a word processor in a palatial former barn appointed with old neon beer signs outside Macon, Georgia; and the other, who had a brownstone in the city, never answered his listed number and kept changing his unlisted one. "The number you have reached," the tape began.

He called up Newman, who knew of a lawyer, Wally Kaplan, who'd written a book called *The Law and How to Break It*. A woman in the critic's apartment laughed. "It wasn't a good book," Newman said. He sounded peculiarly exuberant.

He sat in the second row. The first row was empty, but a sign reserved it for attorneys and police officers. Behind him a woman with a straw drank something from her purse.

"Let's get this straight, Miss DaSilva," the judge said. "Your client says he doesn't know how two thousand stolen fur pelts got into his apartment?"

People with folders strolled past the bench. A court officer chewed gum. Except for a tall black man, nobody dressed well. It was more like an open classroom than a court. The court reporter rubbed his nose on his cuff.

"Mr. Rodriguez knows how they got there, Your Honor. He didn't know they were stolen." The lawyer, young, round-shouldered, with a grimy beige purse hanging over her arm, stood with her client, a brown Afro riding an upturned violet collar, at a table before the bench. A poster-size calendar and a large manila envelope with frayed edges were taped to the front of the bench.

The judge, in a black robe, his tie loosened, shook his head.

He was younger than Howard, and sleepier. "Looks like a guilt-to-the-hilt situation to me. I don't see bail here for under ten thousand dollars."

"Your Honor, Mr. Rodriguez's wife and his employer are both in the courtroom now. Mrs. Rodriguez had a baby last month. His employer stands behind him. Mr. Rodriguez isn't about to run away from his life here."

"How many pelts to a coat, counselor?" the judge asked.

A door to the right of the bench opened on gray-barred cells. Escorted by a court officer, two men and five women came out and sat on a banquette at the wall. One of the women applied two shades of orange lipstick. She had on pink capri pants. She rolled a forefinger across her front teeth. One woman nodded to sleep. One of the five women was Suzanne.

Tall Wally Kaplan with week-old hair-transplant plugs reddening his scalp conferred with her. She looked up shyly at Howard. He'd come to see her in a school play. The court officer chewing gum read out a docket number, and Wally Kaplan helped Suzanne over to the table in front of the bench.

The judge wanted to deny bail. "She admits she set the fire."

"But she called up to report it, Your Honor."

"That was nice of her, Mr., uh, Kaplan. Nevertheless, she set it. That's the fact."

"Your Honor, nobody was hurt. I think Mrs. Ritchie needs professional help."

"You're after a 730, Mr. Kaplan?"

"I'm a tax lawyer, Your Honor, not a criminal lawyer."

"We all have our problems, counselor. You're suggesting that your client may not be competent to stand trial? You're saying she may not understand what's happening now and may not be able to assist in her own defense?"

"Right. Yes, Your Honor."

"Then you request a 730 competency exam." The judge turned to Suzanne. "Mrs. Ritchie, do you understand why you're here?"

"I do."

She was getting married, Howard thought. She would toss her bouquet to him.

"Why are you here, Mrs. Ritchie?"

"Because they brought me here." She pointed at two policemen. "I can stay overnight if I have to." She took the black and white striped toothbrush from her purse.

"Do you know what the charges against you are?"

"Arson. But really it was attempted murder. And a billfold."

"Mr. Donato?" the judge said.

Mr. Donato, a suntanned young man in yellow seersucker, limped to the bench. He was wearing one loafer and one sneaker with the front cut out to accommodate gauze wrapping on his big toe. He must have been an assistant district attorney. It was hard to tell without a program.

The back of Suzanne's dress stuck to her legs. Something glistened at her ankle. A dark spot formed on the brown linoleum. "Hi," she said to Mr. Donato. She was peeing.

Mr. Donato said hi to her and asked the judge agreeably, "How about observation?"

It sounded like sightseeing. They sent her to Bellevue.

"Only for seventy-two hours," Wally Kaplan assured Howard. "I'm sure that's what it is. She said to tell you hi."

One reporter, a man in a sweatshirting vest and running shorts, peered past the policeman into the blackened doorway and estimated it would take the landlord fifteen minutes to announce a renovation plan for co-ops. "Gentrification proceeds apace," he said. A photographer asked a fire marshal where the bodies were.

"Say, Diane, how're you doing?" The photographer dropped his cigarette in a puddle. The camera strap crushed his collar. He had a brown beard but no mustache.

"The name's Dina," she said. She was sitting on the hood of a parked car, the manuscript on her lap.

"What do you think, Tina, were you lucky or what?" His

camera clicked and hummed as he spoke. "Where's the guy who rescued you? Maybe you'd like to give him a nice big thank-you kiss."

In front of what had been the store, Dan talked with two fire marshals. They held charred objects in plastic bags. The photographer went to snap them. One of the objects must have been a book: a college dictionary or *Gray's Anatomy* or the complete works of Shakespeare in fine print.

She rocked back and forth on the hood of the car. A few times she saw herself in the hot white room, crying. Each time it took longer for the skylight to blast open.

A wreck of a car rattled up beside her. It had a suitcase tied to the roof. The driver's door was a different color from the rest of the car. In the streetlights she couldn't tell what the colors were.

Bask said from the car, "You okay?"

She nodded.

"I waited for you to call," he said.

The last of the fire trucks drove away. The reporters and the photographer had already left. Bask parked his car near a dripping fire hydrant and got out. The wet street glistened around him. She followed his stare to the burned building.

Parts of walls were gone. The firemen's axes had made new windows. The fire had made new views. Beams had stopped holding. The building was black lace. She spread her hands to see them whole.

He took Dan and her to an all-night Greek coffee shop on University Place. Grilled cheese made her think of melted flesh. She didn't want a char-broiled hamburger. She didn't want toast. Facing away from the kitchen, she guarded a cup of coffee. Her manuscript lay on the table. She'd refused to leave it in the car. "I have to finish that," she said.

"Not tonight, I hope," Bask answered.

She had no clothes except what she was wearing. What she'd

left behind with Larry didn't exist for her. She had no money, not even to pay for her coffee. She didn't have a job. She didn't have a typewriter, blank paper, a pen. She had no place to sleep.

She had part of a book and the likelihood of money to finish it. The dedication would read: "To Salvatore's brother." She had no place to write.

She had parents who would buy clothes and a typewriter for her. They would buy twenty-four-pound one hundred percent cotton rag paper and a sterling Cross pen. If she preferred a gold-plated Parker pen, they would buy that. They would share their home with her. Hidden from the glare of the California sun, beneath a bulletproof, fireproof, floodproof plastic dome forming a germ-free environment, she would sit in an ironed turquoise designer writing outfit at a massive typewriter complete with automatic pilot and commiseration, and not write. She would be a professional daughter. She would have business cards engraved DINA LEITMAN, DAUGHTER and pass them out at parties on carpeted patios. A Spanish-style red roof tile diving three stories would intersect her path to the chip dip. She would die of a crushed skull inches away from the marble cake. The designer party outfit would be ruined. Somebody's Mexican housekeeper's daughter would end up with it, dye it black to cover the bloodstains, and wear it to see Diana Ross at the Hollywood Bowl.

"You can stay with me at my friend Bill's place," Dan said. "We'll work things out." He transferred a split radish from a mound of chicken salad to the side of the plate.

She leaned over and kissed him. "Thank you."

Bask said, "I have a great idea." His face reddened. He asked the waiter for more orange juice.

Dan said, "That's a *good* idea, not a great one."

Bask got very interested in his fork.

Because a suitcase and his typewriter took up most of the backseat, the three of them sat in the front, Dina in the middle. She smelled of smoke. He wanted to bathe her. He drove as slowly as he could, but soon they made a left off Greenwich

Street and onto Chambers Street. Across the river, in dark New Jersey, a lighted sign urged COLGATE.

"Right here," Dan said.

The car stopped in front of a bakery. "Bill's got a loft upstairs. In the morning all you can smell is bread." He got out, and Dina slid over to follow.

"Wait," Bask said. There was too much beach-towel seat-cover between them. Separation seemed worse than the fear of having her close. "I've got an idea."

Dan leaned into the open door. "A great idea?"

The horn startled Bask; he'd hit it by accident. His ears heated up. "I think you should come with me to Massachusetts," he told her. "For a while. No problems, no hassles, nothing you don't want. Just a lot of room in the country to finish your book in." He wondered if he should be on one knee.

"I don't know you," she said.

He needed more light to read her face. "You don't have to. It's common sense. I've got the room and I don't need to be alone up there."

"I don't have any money."

"I'll give you an advance on your advance. You'll pay your own way, don't worry."

"It's not your house, it's your friend's. Didn't you tell me that?"

"She won't mind and she won't be there."

"What if I don't like it?"

"I'll drive you to the train and lend you money for a ticket and a cab back to Dan."

"What if it turns out I don't get a contract and I don't get an advance?"

"Then I'll sell your body at a town meeting."

She turned to Dan for advice.

"You're welcome to stay with me and Bill," he said. "Or try it with Vince. If it doesn't work out, come back here." He stretched, as if he'd awakened from a nap, and smiled. "Vince's offer sounds good and communal."

She fell asleep sitting up before they got past White Plains. The safety strap ran neatly between her breasts. On the radio Willie sang "Blue Eyes Crying in the Rain." Headlights cruised past in time to the music. The car hit a pothole, but she kept sleeping. He slowed down. Her eyes were shut tight against the lights of the oncoming cars. Her hair blew against the headrest. He should have rolled up her window before they got on the turnpike. Bringing her with him was one step beyond dumb.

At a gas station outside New Haven she woke up and walked unsteadily to the bathroom. His hand was yellow in the station lights. She came back and asked for a quarter.

"I should've given you money before." He gave her two twenty-dollar bills and a ten. "How's that for now?"

"I still need a quarter," she said.

Past New Haven, she asked him to stop at a rest area.

"Hungry?" he asked, yawning in the almost empty parking lot.

"No."

The restaurant was closed for the night. She asked him for a dollar bill. He bought two cans of apple juice from a vending machine, and she bought four sanitary pads. An Oriental man in a soccer shirt mopped the restaurant floor.

She slept again till Springfield and woke up hungry. He gave her a can of apple juice. She was cold, and he told her there were shirts and sweaters in the suitcase in the backseat.

"Want to drive?" he asked.

"I don't have a license. It was in my purse at the store."

"Are you tired?"

"No."

"I'm tired. I vote you drive."

"I don't know where I'm going."

"Details, always details."

The car halted at the side of the highway. She rolled up the sleeves of a red and blue flannel shirt that covered her to the knees.

With the first light, she was the one driving past Holyoke on the way north.

They passed through a sleeping town, a village green with a high bare flagpole and a real cannon mounted on stone above a bronze plaque. The cannon was aimed at a white clapboard church needing paint. They passed a narrow cemetery with worn gravestones in tall grass. They passed a closed Friendly's. They passed a billboard selling antifreeze. They passed a windowless shopping mall sprawled in a field of unoccupied yellow-lined parking spaces. A dairy truck crossed yellow lines on its way to a supermarket at the end of the mall. They passed a stable and four cows. They passed signs for schools and deer crossings.

He slept, his thin lips together, his large body folded around the seat. He coughed once, sat up, and went back to sleep. A curl dropped on his cheek.

She drove through green country and saw barns and closed gas stations and stone fences and a dead skunk flattened on the road. A curdled red mass had spilled out of the skunk. White and black fur stirred in the wind. She saw brick houses with vegetable plots, a parade of sunflowers, a calf nursing. The cow had a yellow tag clipped to its ear.

When she saw a sign for a yarn outlet in the next town, she said, "Good morning."

He yawned.

"We passed the yarn sign."

"Turn left up ahead," he said. The road climbed. More cows, a sign for a garage sale. "Right." The road bumped. Trees pressed in on it, then thinned out again. There were no houses. A stream behind trees caught daylight. Another deer crossing. She knew where to stop because the road ended in front of a wooden house with part of a sun deck hugging it.

She turned off the ignition. She heard the far-off whoosh of cars on the highway. She heard a couple of birds talking.

"Are you going to let go of the steering wheel?" he asked.

•   •   •

292

She stood behind another man opening another door with another set of keys. She could lie down in the grass and cry. While he opened windows in the living room, she admired a fat brown sofa, a red afghan, a rush-seated rocking chair, blue-stenciled pottery, a polished lopsided table with a white porcelain drawer pull.

"Is the table yours?" she asked.

"Everything's Bonnie's. I installed this for her." A stained-glass panel of a monk was set into a window. "She bought it when they tore down a church. And I bought her that." It was a wooden candlestick carved in a braided pattern.

"So if I like this place, it's Bonnie I like, not you."

"Want to put that down?"

She held on to her manuscript. There was no place that was hers. She didn't belong anywhere. "I'd like to go to the train station." As she said it, she realized she was wearing his shirt.

"All right," he said slowly. "But it's a long drive again. I'd like to eat something first."

"Okay."

"I'm sure there's herb tea. Maybe there's something good in the freezer."

She put her manuscript on the polished table and went with him to the kitchen.

The room he'd shared with Bonnie was at the end of the upstairs hall. Next to it was Bonnie's study, with files he'd built in and an electric typewriter, and next to the study was the second bedroom. A window overlooked trees and glimpses of a stream.

He gave her flowered sheets, a pillowcase, and a striped blanket. "Regulation L. L. Bean," he said. He kept a set of flowered sheets, a pillowcase, and a plaid blanket for himself. "We can sleep till around three. There's a five o'clock train. The bathroom's over there."

She heard his bedroom door close. She closed hers. She made the bed, took off her shoes and her jeans. Dirty, she hid between clean sheets and slept.

She bought a notebook with Mickey Mouse on the cover because it was on sale and the plain notebooks weren't. She bought typing paper, three felt-tip pens, a gray sweatshirt, a sale package of six different color bikini underpants printed with ROCK LIVES, a blue tee shirt and a red one, two beige bras, a package of six pairs of white and navy tube socks, a pair of white sneakers, a natural canvas shoulder bag, a box of sanitary pads, allergy capsules, hand lotion, soap, shampoo, deodorant, three disposable razors, a comb, a hairbrush, a toothbrush, toothpaste, unwaxed dental floss, makeup base, blusher, gray-lavender eye shadow, gray eyeliner, black mascara, and a blue and brown nylon duffel bag to carry it all in. At the checkout counter the cashier, a girl with bitten bright red nails, rang up the shampoo twice and, hunching into her aqua smock, had to void the transaction and start over.

The mall stayed open till eight. At seven-thirty, as they were driving through the parking lot toward the market, she said, "I forgot to get a nightgown."

"I'll lend you something," he said. "We still have to get food." He glanced at her. "A tee shirt or something. Completely clean. Speaking of which, I know it's not your fault, but at close range you've got a charcoal kind of aroma."

She folded her arms across her chest. The rolled sleeves of his plaid shirt slid along her arms. "Then don't get too close," she said.

Sept. 14, 1980

Dear Mother & Dad,

I'm somewhere else, as you can see from the postmark. But it's not a permanent address where you can reach me. All the years I lived in New York, I wanted to stay in New England in the fall to watch the leaves change color. Guess I'm in the right place this year.

Love,
Dina

When he erased something, the table shook. The pepper mill shook. The mug of coffee became dangerous. She was writing the name Ned and got "Nel."

"Trouble with Paula?" she asked.

"I can't figure out what to call her husband. I don't want Harold and all I can think of is Glen and I don't want Glen."

"How about Howard?"

"No, I don't want that."

"You can name him after Howard Ritchie."

"*You* name a character after Howard."

"My characters already have names. How about Roger?"

"I'm going to type."

He left her alone in the kitchen. After she finished a sentence, she decided to do the dishes. Out the window above the sink a meadow invited walking. She put down the dish sponge and went back to the table. A paragraph and two crossed-out sentences later, she heard him at the top of the stairs.

"Okay, it's Roger. But don't expect any credit."

Oct. 10, 1980

Dear Mother & Dad,

A publishing house gave me a contract for a novel. And gave me money too. When it finally happened, I think you could have heard my screams all the way to California. From where I'm sitting, I can see a tree—an oak? an elm? I'm sure it's not a palm—that's got some genuinely scarlet leaves. Hope you're both okay.

Love,
Dina

She was brushing her teeth when he came in.

"Morning," he said. "It's beautiful out." In the bathroom mirror she saw the front of his secondhand varsity sweater. He touched her neck with cold fingers.

She spit toothpaste into the sink. "Don't do that."

"You look cute."

"I'm not cute." Her hair frizzed with static electricity. She had on one of his tee shirts for a nightgown and over it one of his flannel shirts for a robe. A pair of tube socks wrinkled at her ankles.

She shuffled to her room, socks flapping. He stood in the doorway, smiling.

"What is it?" she asked.

He bent down and kissed her mouth lightly. She said oh. She didn't move away, and he kissed her again. "I don't think we should do this," she said. When he kissed her again, she kissed back hard. "We shouldn't."

He put his hands at her waist. He was measuring her for a belt. He stroked her rib cage, her back, her breasts.

"Not fair." She reached up to his shoulders to push him away.

Another kiss, the flannel shirt being pulled over her head. She took off the tee shirt. They were his anyway. She kicked off her socks.

The clothes he was wearing went too, interrupted by kisses. He took off his blue briefs.

"Wait," she said.

"What?"

"That."

"I figure if a baby can fit getting out of you, I can fit getting inside."

"Maybe, but that's like saying you can pour stuff easily through the wrong end of a funnel." She sat on her bed, shivering.

"Scared?" he asked.

"Cold."

They got under the covers together. "I'll hold you," he said.

His tongue lashed a nipple. "Please," she might have said. She turned to water. He traveled down her under covers. Her legs rose on his shoulders, the covers fell away. "Please." He breakfasted on her, he fared, he gulped. He braced her thighs apart and drank her noisily. She shook with pleasure, called out, "No," then "Please," then "No." She tried to watch herself and couldn't. "Please please please."

He swallowed. "Please what?"

"Please fuck me." A moment later she murmured to his neck, "We could've been friends." Another moment and "Wait."

"What?"

"I don't have anything. Birth control."

"I won't come inside you."

"It's not the safest."

"Should we stop?"

"No. But don't."

Her bed dipped. The room he'd given her contracted. "Please" and "Yes," she said, and he said oh. The bed walked across the room. The bureau stopped it. The bed skipped in place, the sheets untucked, the morning sped. He said her name. Her high renunciation fell. "Vincent," she answered, she met him crashing, she held him far from home.

They kissed. Lying beneath him, covered by his skin, she bit his freckled shoulder.

"Don't do that," he said. "It hurts."

The skin wasn't red, didn't have teeth imprints. She kissed the shoulder, bit it again.

"Don't." He pulled his shoulder away.

A snapping turtle, she came after him. He pressed her down firmly on the bed. She wriggled loose and nipped his arm. He held her shoulders to the bed. She struggled to get free. When she was satisfied that she couldn't get free, she struggled harder.

"Promise you won't bite," he said.

She lay still. "I promise."

He let go of her, watching for any sudden moves. She stayed motionless. Her face showed a glimmer of remorse. When he relaxed above her, she bit his shoulder again.

"Stop it." He fastened her to a sheet. She launched herself and escaped from beneath him. She had the advantage of weakness; he wouldn't use his full strength against her. She trusted in that. They wrestled, kneeling on a striped blanket. She bit his hand.

He caught her and kept her away with long arms. Her hair

swung from side to side as she nipped near his wrists. "Stop," he said. She bit air, hoping to hurt it. Again and again she snapped her jaws. She ate air. With a quick move of one arm he dropped her to his thigh and pressed his cock against her neck, against her cheek. He was pushing his cock into her biting mouth. "Oh," she said. She became all mouth, no teeth. Her mouth had no room for crying. Head bent, her hands quiet at his thighs, she suckled.

Nov. 15, 1980

Dear Mother & Dad,

I didn't vote, so I'm not supposed to complain about the results, but I couldn't vote because I don't know where I live. Can you register by giving your address as "in transit"? I'm still here for a while. You both sounded great last week. I'll call again soon. I wish you wouldn't be so offended about not having my number.

Love,
Dina

Nov. 15, 1980

Dear Cal,

Glad you like the new pages. Sometimes I worry that Ned seems more selfish than necessary. There's a woman down the road I'm going to put in the book. She sells apple cider and claims it cures everything from impetigo to "real bad cavities." We're about the same age, but she's got three kids and knows secret things about dried chervil. She wants me to tell her about safe stops on the IRT.

Dina

The woman with the mink scarf held up her cigarette. Obediently he clicked his lighter. She had long gray hair and thick penciled black eyebrows. A rhinestone Santa pin winked from her scarf—at least he thought they were rhinestones. A man with part of a face passed. Howard pulled up the collar of his turtleneck and edged through the crowd at the bar for more wine.

He stationed himself in a corner of the gallery, next to two black and white blowups of a girl's profile. In the Before picture her nose had two steps leading up or down. She could have balanced a pearl between them. The nose in the After picture had been planed smooth. A sesame seed would have rolled down it. He missed the old nose. "That's my daughter," the black-browed woman said, smiling because she'd trapped him. He searched clumps of conversations around them until he saw the familiar faces of a man and a woman. Relieved, he shot his arm out toward them. "There," he said, "that's my wife."

Something about her seemed familiar. "We've never really met properly," she said. "That time you carried Howard home—I never got to thank you."

Newman found her shyness pretty. If she decided to burn down the gallery, he wouldn't mind. "One shouldn't be thanked for friendship," he said. Taking her arm, he guided her past two women and a man who each had the same remarkably perfect nose. He thought of writing an essay on the boredom of perfection. He held her arm loosely; any pressure might undo her. "Have you met my wife?"

Clare extended a large capable hand to Suzanne. "It's good to see you." He enjoyed Clare's new strength. It was a circumstance he could test himself against.

"I love the show. I love your pictures, really," Suzanne said. "I wish I could do something like this."

"Everybody can do something. The trick is to find out what it is." Clare's other, better husband, the slight Dr. Max Linker, intoned this and patted Clare's hand. His open navy jacket had cat hairs on it.

Newman wished he'd invited Steve, to back him up. "At the risk of sounding like an elitist, which I am, I must disagree with you."

"I'm speaking of art in the therapeutic sense," Dr. Linker said. He blinked his eyes twice.

"Do you know Dr. Frances Cohen? She talks about that." Suzanne slid a ruby heart along a gold chain at her neck. "That's right, isn't it?"

"I know of Dr. Cohen's work. She has a fine reputation," Dr. Linker reassured her.

"Dr. Cohen says art is anger made bountiful. Or beautiful. I think I said bountiful because of Thanksgiving. I think it's beautiful she says, not bountiful," Suzanne said.

"A perfectly natural confusion," Dr. Linker said.

"I love it, dear. I'm going to buy a Before and an After. Harry says I can." Sheila Dunne in fur touched Clare's cheek with hers and kissed the air. Perfume filtered through the group. "Now, tell me, which ones are yours?"

He would give Clare a copy of his list of women. He would describe each woman to her. He would demand that she imagine what his life was like. He would ask the other photographer of vanity and disease, that Bea in a tense jumpsuit across the room, to immortalize his cock. He would invite Clare to select her favorites from Bea's shots for a new exhibition. He would show the shots, fig-leaved, on TV as a preview of a new book.

"Matty here is going to be a film director," Howard told Newman. To Matty he said, "Mr. Sykes's wife took some of the pictures."

"A director. What made you decide on that?" Newman asked the girl.

She put her hands in the pockets of her corduroy pants.

"Mr. Sykes is talking to you," Howard said.

She looked up at Newman. "I don't want to be a director. I want to be a doctor."

"A respectable profession," Newman said.

"Like Mommy's doctor, Dr. Cohen."

"I'd feel very confident with you for my doctor. I hope you'll remember I'm a family friend and you won't charge me too much."

"Daddy says Dr. Cohen charges a lot of money."

"I'm sure she's helping your mother," Newman said.

"What happened to being a director or a sculptor?" Howard asked Matty.

The girl's gaze was his own. His own face, smaller and younger, was stubborn. "I can change my mind, can't I?"

"I don't want to embarrass you in front of Mr. Sykes, but your manners are—" He stopped because Matty had walked away.

Newman said, "She's delightful."

"She's rude."

Beneath enlarged black and white eye bags, Matty put her arms around Suzanne's skirt.

"You're lucky to have them both," Newman said.

"I'm so lucky that two insurance companies may sue me to recover payments for the Karatasi. I'm so lucky I'm supporting Dr. Cohen so five times a week Suzanne can tell her what a bastard I am. And now my daughter's going to be a shrink. I'm so lucky, I'm going crazy."

"Did that husband of Dina's ever bother you again?"

"No. Have you heard from her?"

"No."

"Me either. I wonder when her book's coming out."

"Ah yes, your debut."

"Yours too."

"Naked to the world."

"I hope not."

"Are you going to try and stop it?"

"Don't you know Dr. Cohen says art is burdensome?"

"I think it's 'Art is anger that's beautiful.' "

"Whatever. Who am I to stop that?"

"That's Leslie," Clare said. Near the punch bowl one of Newman's sons was talking to a girl with a repaired harelip. "And that's Will." The other son sat unhappily at the gallery reception desk and read a catalogue.

"They must be proud of you," Howard said.

"A little. I don't think Newman is, though."

The blond hair piled on her head crowned her with clouds. Her monumental body invited climbing, like Annapurna shrouded in mist.

"I'd be proud of Suzanne if she did something like this."

"Maybe she will."

He could try to persuade her to go with him to the gallery office and lock the door—if the gallery had an office. There would be a sofa or a deep-pile rug. And a heater. They would hear the others outside the door, muffled voices discussing Arbus and cropping. He would put out his cigarette in a hand-carved alabaster ashtray and wipe at the dried corners of his mouth. All that he desired was for her to remember him. Bowing, he would introduce himself: *I am a lover.* Curtsying, she would whisper in response: *And I am waiting to be loved.*

His eyes grew small. He gave her his beautiful smile and muttered, "Your pictures are flawless. Brilliant."

• • •

He stamped his boots to shake off the snow and hurried into the house before too much good warm air escaped. The hood of his down parka slipped over red curls and released a snow flurry through the living room. He put the bag of groceries on the kitchen table, careful not to get her notebook wet, and, bending to kiss her, placed two cold fingers at the back of her neck. She yelped and slammed shut a copy of *Bandaged Moments*.

"Lost my gloves," he said. He uncovered a pot of something tomato colored simmering on the stove. "What is it?"

"A couple of cans. With enough parmesan cheese it'll taste almost adequate." His secondhand varsity sweater surrounded her. She wouldn't wear any of Bonnie's clothes, which would have been big too.

"I see you're reading junk fiction."

"I started it this morning. Can't stop."

His ears grew warm. "Shouldn't you be writing?"

"Yesterday I wanted to kill everybody in my book. But I couldn't figure out how to get them all in the same Pinto. I'm on vacation till tomorrow."

He took the mail and a folded newspaper page from his pocket, unsnapped the parka, and settled its nylon bulk over a chair. "Lots of news. An invitation from Dan to the opening of his new bookstore, the Velocity, on Duane Street, in January. The emphasis for now is on cookbooks and books on antiques and guides to survival in the city."

Her delight made him proud, as if he'd caused the news instead of repeated it. He went on. "An eviction notice from Bonnie. The incoming administration has figured out she's not a closet conservative. She's coming back. We have to be out by the second week in January. Cheer up, it gets better. Word from Maris, addressed—notably—to both of us, as if we were a unit of some kind. She's saving on postage. Dan did the same thing. *She* says, among other things, she says, she says—"

"What?"

"There's this guy who called her to ask about the movie rights for *Bandaged Moments*. He wants to fly me out to meet him."

"You're going to Hollywood?"

"No, Munich. He's German."

"He wants to make a German movie about a boy growing up in New England?"

"He's offering a first-class ticket and a hotel room with its own bathroom." He held up the newspaper page. Three classified ads had blue ink circles around them. He pointed to them, one by one. "This is a house in Maine. For rent. This is a house—you know the road behind the mall? This is a couple of miles after that. I thought maybe you wouldn't like it because it's near here and maybe you wouldn't like being near where Bonnie is. And this one, this one is about an hour away, closer to Boston and a little more expensive, but it's month to month."

She shivered in his big sweater. She shook her head. He looked away and rubbed his nose.

"Vincent." Three grooves of sympathy, a Chinese character, appeared above her eyes.

He folded the newspaper page before he threw it in the garbage.

"We'll celebrate your movie." She turned off the low flame under the pot.

"It may not get to be a movie."

"I know what I'd like to do," she said.

In the living room he spread the afghan over the braided rug in front of the wood stove. "Minimizes frostbite," he said. She put down the blue plastic diaphragm case from the health clinic and a squashed tube of cream.

He thought he might be holding her for the last time. He released her from the folds of his varsity sweater, from his patched thermal undershirt, from his Celtics tee shirt. She took off her jeans and pink ROCK LIVES bikinis. She took off her overbleached socks. He kissed her mouth, chin, the back of her neck. He bent to her breast.

"Unfair." She tugged at his belt. She hurried him out of his clothes, kissing him, fighting his kisses, relenting, fighting again.

"What's unfair?" he asked, and kissed her before she answered.

Part of the stream behind the house had frozen: shallow patches of ice between rocks, ice on mud. Snow flew into her mouth. "It's a blizzard," she said.

"It's a regular day," he said.

She had on two of his sweaters and his down vest. She had on green knit gloves from Kids' Korner at the mall. She slapped her hands together.

"If you'd take my parka," he said.

Toby, a neighbor's dog, lumbered up, expecting a good time. One of his parents had been an Irish setter. Bask threw a stick high and far. A second dog, semi–German shepherd, raced Toby for it.

"Why are they out in this weather?" she asked.

"Same reason we are."

"A forced march?"

They followed the stream briefly until trees intervened and the meadow climbed away from the stream. Channels of frozen water cut the ground. Across the meadow whitening trees shielded the highway. She heard a car with chains rattling past. Her sneakers snared themselves in outreaching roots. She stumbled over one. "You *could* help," she said.

"It wouldn't be as much fun," he said.

Toby's blunt tawny head pushed at her thigh. She patted him and declared, "Good boy." Nearby, the other dog deposited an enormous foul-smelling turd in the snow. They walked on to sweeter pastures, past sentinel trees. The meadow widened under a low gray sky. Far behind them, the house was edged with white.

Snow soaked through her sneakers. "I bet the nails are blue," she said. She tossed two sticks for the dogs. They didn't have much of a run.

"Pretty feeble," he said. Snow settled on his red curls, wet his red-gold eyelashes. He sealed her gloved hand in his bare one.

"What does it mean if we get a house together?" she asked.

"It means we don't have to live outside." The sticks he threw sent the dogs chasing to the middle of the meadow.

"You pay your half and I pay mine?"

"Sure. It'll be the same as it's been up till now."

"No it won't. It'll be different. It'll be on purpose." Snow stung her face. She said sadly, "It'll be serious."

He grabbed her and lifted her up, higher and higher. The dogs barked. He was going to throw her instead of a stick. She breathed in snow. "Help!" She laughed above his wet curls. As he lowered her, she kept expecting the ground to arrive, but it didn't. It was a long way down. The waves had done that when she was little, before she stopped playing in the ocean. A wave would carry her up, her legs dangling in water above the ocean floor. She would ride, closer to the sun, with yellow-berried seaweed and browned palm fronds in a blue-green roar of water. The dying wave would drop her slowly. Her flat feet were ready for the ribbed sand bottom before it arrived. After the sweet terror of the uplift came what she'd thought of then as safety, shells tumbling at her heels, the sand running under her feet. Her wet sneakers touched ground.

She aimed for the middle of the meadow, but the stick fell a short distance from her, far from the target. The dogs dashed for it with indiscriminate happiness.

"I vote for the place closer to Boston," she said.

Snow fell on his boot tops. Her sneakers sank into snow. Wind shook snow from branches. The dogs danced for attention. Before he moved toward her, he seemed to be digging himself deeper in the snow.

"I'm scared," he said.

"Yes," she said. "That sounds right."

His most ambitious novel to date . . .

ANTHONY BURGESS

THE KINGDOM OF THE WICKED

This is an extraordinary account of the first years of Christianity,
recreated in vivid and meticulous detail.

"Burgess takes hold of an immense theme with magnificent mastery.
Detail and dialogue are incredibly vivid; one hardly knows which to
praise most".

LITERARY REVIEW

"All Burgess's skills are in evidence here: his ornate imagination, his
fascination with words, his sly wit, the prodigious energy . . ."

LONDON STANDARD

"His unassuageable energy can do nothing other than celebrate the
energy of life itself".

SUNDAY TIMES

"Both reader and author have marvellous fun".

SUNDAY TELEGRAPH

0 349 10439 5   **ABACUS FICTION**   **£3.95**

Also by Anthony Burgess in Abacus:
ENDERBY'S DARK LADY

THE GLAMOUR
CHRISTOPHER PRIEST

All Richard Grey wanted to do was recover, to return to normal. For four long, painful months he had been convalescing after the horrifying injuries that he sustained when a car bomb exploded near him.

He could remember the years he spent as a cameraman, covering stories all over the world, and he could remember taking a break from his career – but there was a profound blankness where his memory of the weeks before the explosion should have been. It was as if his life had been re-edited and part of it erased.

But then Susan Kewley came to visit him and she spoke of those weeks. And what Richard wanted most was a glimpse of what that time had held for the two of them. But the glimpses he was afforded took him into a strange and terrible twilight world – a world of apparent madness, the world of 'the glamour' . . .

Christopher Priest's rich and subtle narrative is mesmerising and deeply moving, as compelling and deceptive as a Hitchcock film.

'One of our most gifted writers.' *John Fowles*

'A bizarre and intriguing book.' *Guardian*

ABACUS FICTION   0 349 128103   £2.95

From the internationally acclaimed author of
ARARAT and THE WHITE HOTEL

SWALLOW
D.M. Thomas

Welcome to an extraordinary Olympiad, where the contestants are not athletes, but storytellers. An international panel of judges faces the task of selecting the winner of the coveted laurels. The judges argue violently, passions flare; unexpected controversies spring up and death stalks across the poetic landscape . . .

'A brilliant free-range skit.' GUARDIAN

'Richly enjoyable.' MAIL ON SUNDAY

'The point of SWALLOW is the artificiality of the boundaries between serious and funny, east and west, poetry and prose, and, more significantly, between people's individual consciousness . . . should be read.' SUNDAY TIMES

FICTION   0 349 13386 7   £2.95

Also available in ABACUS paperback:

FICTION

WAR CRIES OVER AVENUE C	Jerome Charyn	£4.95	☐
TOTAL CHESS	David Spanier	£3.95	☐
FOREIGN AFFAIRS	Alison Lurie	£3.50	☐
FIVE REHEARSALS	Susanna Johnston	£2.50	☐
A LATE DIVORCE	A. B. Yehoshua	£3.95	☐
SPLENDID LIVES	Penelope Gilliatt	£2.50	☐
THE GLAMOUR	Christopher Priest	£2.95	☐
PITCH DARK	Renata Adler	£2.95	☐

NON-FICTION

THE FIRST DANCE OF FREEDOM	Martin Meredith	£3.50	☐
BEYOND THE DRAGON'S MOUTH	Shiva Naipaul	£3.95	☐
T. S. ELIOT	Peter Ackroyd	£3.95	☐
THE MARCH OF FOLLY	Barbara W. Tuchman	£3.95	☐
STRANGER ON THE SQUARE	Arthur & Cynthia Koestler	£2.95	☐
PETER THE GREAT	Robert K. Massie	£5.95	☐
WEAPONS	Russell Warren Howe	£3.95	☐
IRELAND – A HISTORY	Robert Kee	£5.95	☐

All Abacus books are available at your local bookshop or newsagent, or can be ordered direct from the publisher. Just tick the titles you want and fill in the form below.

Name _____

Address _____

Write to Abacus Books, Cash Sales Department, P.O. Box 11, Falmouth, Cornwall TR10 9EN.

Please enclose cheque or postal order to the value of the cover price plus:

UK: 55p for the first book plus 22p for the second book and 14p for each additional book ordered to a maximum charge of £1.75.

OVERSEAS: £1.00 for the first book plus 25p per copy for each additional book.

BFPO & EIRE: 55p for the first book, 22p for the second book plus 14p per copy for the next 7 books, thereafter 8p per book.

Abacus Books reserve the right to show new retail prices on covers which may differ from those previously advertised in the text or elsewhere, and to increase postal rates in accordance with the PO.